Murder on Black Swan Lane

Center Point
Large Print

**This Large Print Book carries the
Seal of Approval of N.A.V.H.**

Murder on Black Swan Lane

A WREXFORD & SLOANE MYSTERY

Andrea Penrose

CENTER POINT LARGE PRINT
THORNDIKE, MAINE

This Center Point Large Print edition
is published in the year 2018 by arrangement with
Kensington Publishing Corp.

The text of this Large Print edition is unabridged.
In other aspects, this book may vary
from the original edition.
Printed in the United States of America
on permanent paper.
Set in 16-point Times New Roman type.

ISBN: 978-1-68324-778-4

Library of Congress Cataloging-in-Publication Data

Names: Penrose, Andrea, author.
Title: Murder on Black Swan Lane / Andrea Penrose.
Description: Center Point Large Print edition. | Thorndike, Maine :
    Center Point Large Print, 2018.
Identifiers: LCCN 2018005152 | ISBN 9781683247784
    (hardcover : alk. paper)
Subjects: LCSH: Clergy—Crimes against—Fiction. | Murder—
    Investigation—Fiction. | London (England—History—19th century—
    Fiction. | Large type books. | GSAFD: Mystery fiction. |
    Regency fiction. | LCGFT: Detective and mystery fiction. |
    Historical fiction.
Classification: LCC PS3566.I283 M87 2018 | DDC 813/.54—dc23
LC record available at https://lccn.loc.gov/2018005152

Murder on Black Swan Lane

To Saybrook College
"A company of scholars, a society of friends."

Thank you for inspiring a love of learning
and a lifetime of intellectual curiosity.

Lux et Veritas

ACKNOWLEDGMENTS

I'm profoundly grateful to all those who have helped me take the idea for Murder on Black Swan Lane and shape it into a finished book. First and foremost, thanks go to my agent, Gail Fortune, and my editor, Wendy McCurdy. No author could have more delightfully wonderful people with whom to work.

Special hugs also go to my fellow Word Wenches—Joanna Bourne, Nicola Cornick, Anne Gracie, Susanna Kearsley, Susan King, Mary Jo Putney and Patricia Rice—who are all fabulous writers and lovers of history. They helped unravel many a plot kink when I'd tied myself in knots . . . not to speak of always being there with cyber chocolate and chardonnay whenever I started whining to them in the dead of night.

As for the science in the book, to loosely paraphrase Sir Isaac Newton: If I have seen beyond my normal scope of knowledge it is by standing on the shoulders of giants. In my case, that "giant" is John R. Ettinger, whose masterful knowledge of chemistry, physics, and mathematics was instrumental in helping me comprehend the nuances of alchemy and the birth of modern science. (If there are any errors, the fault lies entirely with my feeble brain!)

And a big shout-out to my dear friends and writer pals who served as beta readers and so generously gave invaluable feedback as I poked and prodded the manuscript into its final form. Lauren Willig, Deanna Raybourn, Patrick Pinnell, Amanda McCabe . . . you guys are the best.

"History is the Devil's Scripture."

PROLOGUE

A flicker of weak light skittered over the stone floor, followed by the soft scrape of steps and the whispered *whoosh, whoosh* of mist-dampened wool. Quickening his pace, a lone man moved down the nave's aisle, the shoulder capes of his greatcoat fluttering darkly against the shroud of shadows.

At the transept, he paused and angled the iron lantern at a row of close-set granite pillars guarding the apse.

A figure slipped out from the slivered gloom. "You're bloody late."

"What I have to show you will be worth the wait. You asked me for proof—well, prepare yourself, my dear Golden One." In deference to the sepulchral silence of the deserted church, the man pitched his words to a low murmur. Which was, he mused, a pity, for his mellifluous voice could set the surrounding stone to resonating with a magnificent echo.

And if ever a pronouncement deserved a choir of angels . . .

"Yes, prepare yourself for a most wondrous revelation." A ghostly puff of vapor hung for an instant in the chill air as he withdrew a small leather-bound book from his coat pocket and held it out.

His companion hesitated. The slits in his black-as-Hades mask betrayed a flutter of movement as a wink of light gilded the downturned lashes.

Dear heavens, such silly histrionics, when here they stood on the brink of immortality.

Golden One eyed the frayed edges, age-blackened calfskin, and faint remains of the gilt-stamped title a moment longer before looking up. "You promised the manuscript—"

"This codex is the first key to unlocking the manuscript's secret. Call it a *petit goût*, if you will," explained the man smoothly. "A small taste to tease the appetite, to delight the mouth, as the French would say." He curled a small smile. "Though this is from the mountains of Bavaria. The Germans don't appreciate the art of living well, but they are awfully good at puzzling out conundrums."

With a muttered oath, Golden One shifted his stance and loosened the fastenings of his voluminous cloak.

It was, noted the man, of far finer quality and cut than the fellow's usual garments. Perhaps the prospect of coming riches—

"Save your little snippets of sophistication to impress your fancy friends," growled Golden One as he took the book and slowly cracked open the spine. "I know naught and care naught of France and the German principalities. My province is the natural world, which knows no borders, no boundaries."

Dust motes flew up, dancing like whirling dervishes through the narrow beam of lantern light. In contrast, the cavernous darkness looming all around was still as a crypt.

"Careful," chided the man, though he noted that for someone who toiled with his hands, the fellow had surprisingly smooth and well-tended fingers. "You are holding delicate parchment and pen strokes that will soon change the world."

"Assuming what you have read is . . . true."

"I have compelling reason to believe it is," replied the man. "Sir Isaac Newton's manuscript—"

"Newton was wrong. About a great many things."

"That is because he lacked the key documents that would have given him the knowledge he was missing. I have them, and the transformative secret is at our fingertips! It needs only a man of your unique talents to bring it to fruition."

Golden One turned through the pages, stopping occasionally to study the hand-drawn illustrations and scrutinize the spidery text.

"Satisfied?"

"No." The covers snapped shut. "This tells me nothing. I need to see Newton's manuscript and the other books before I fully commit to being part of your fanciful scheme."

The man felt a stab of anger at the unexpected

reply. "I've already paid you a great deal of money."

A shrug. "And I've already done a great deal of work. Whether I do more is up to you."

"How can you hesitate? This opportunity is a gift from God!"

"So you say. But I am a pragmatist, who takes a more earthly, empirical view of things. You promised proof of your claim, and I have yet to see it."

"The other books are too precious to carry around," he protested. "I have them hidden where they are safe."

"I'm not about to risk my present chances of advancement without more than your heavenly promises of fortune and fame," countered Golden One.

A strained silence stretched out for several heartbeats.

He would have preferred to win the fellow over with persuasion, but he wasn't averse to using force. It was, after all, for the Higher Good.

"Advancement?" repeated the man slowly. "Your chances of advancement would be virtually nil were I to inform certain people of your little secret."

Silence.

"You think I haven't learned your real identity?" A smile. "Surely you must sense by now that God has granted me special powers."

"Is that a threat?" asked Golden One softly.

"Simply a warning," he replied. "But come, let us not quarrel over theoretical conflicts. The truth is, you will soon be rich beyond your wildest dreams."

"What you ask is dangerous."

"Ah, but to reach out and grasp the immortal beauty of genius requires taking a leap of faith." A pause. "Just think of it—you will effect not just a worldly transformation but also a spiritual one as well." He couldn't keep his voice from rising a notch. *How could the fellow not appreciate the sublime wonder of what he was being offered?* "The risk is well worth the reward."

"I . . ." Golden One shot a nervous look at the far end of the transept. "Did you hear something?"

"No." The man cocked an ear.

Nothing.

"I assure you, there's no one else here at this hour. The watchman won't make his rounds for another hour."

"I tell you, I saw a flutter of movement."

He looked around, probing the darkness for several long moments before shaking his head. *The fellow was seeing specters. Such a volatile imagination would have to be carefully controlled.*

"There's nothing—"

As he turned back, a splash of liquid, burning

17

hot as the fires of hell, hit his face. "G-God Almighty!"

"Yes, say a prayer," said Golden One softly as he quickly pocketed the book and drew a carving knife from beneath his cloak.

"Heavenly Father, I beseech you . . ." Clawing at his blinded eyes, the man fell to his knees, the rest of his words spiraling into a piercing scream.

CHAPTER 1

A plume of steam rose from the bubbling crucible, the curl of silvery vapor floating ghost-like against the shadowed wood paneling before dissolving into the darkness. After consulting his pocket watch, the Earl of Wrexford scribbled a few more notations in his ledger, the scratch of his pen punctuated by the soft *pop, pop, pop* of colorless chemicals.

"The Devil's brew," he murmured, leaning back in his desk chair and staring at the brightly colored satirical print propped up against a stack of books. "Though I give the artist credit for coming up with a far more poetic phrase."

Satan's Syllabub. Pitchforks had been drawn in to replace the two *l*'s of the print's red-lettered title. As for the caricature of him . . .

A mirthless laugh slipped from his lips.

A pair of scarlet horns poked out from the tangle of long black hair. "I must remember to visit my barber this week," he murmured, brushing a strand of the shoulder-length locks from his collar. "And is my nose really that beaky? I have always thought it rather elegantly aquiline."

Shifting his gaze lower, he saw that the artist had drawn him without his trousers on and that

19

his bare hairy legs—a gross exaggeration—ended in cloven hooves. The fine print of the caption explained that he was in the habit of concocting his noxious brews right after enjoying an amorous interlude with his latest conquest.

"Lies," muttered Wrexford wryly, taking a moment to eye the clever caricature of a near-naked lady peeking out from the large copper crucible cradled between his knees. The deft pen strokes had captured Diana Fairfield's petulant pout with frightening accuracy.

Yes, the face was perfect, but the implied timing was all wrong.

"I never mix business with pleasure." For one thing, performing chemical experiments in the nude could have very painful consequences.

But then, he supposed the artist couldn't be blamed for taking poetic license. A. J. Quill had earned a reputation for creating London's most scathing satirical prints, and no doubt earned a pretty penny for his merciless skewering of those caught up in the latest Society scandal.

Be damned with truth. Ruthless images, cutting commentary—that was what the paying public wanted. Misery loved company, especially when the sufferer was one of the Privileged Few.

"Ah, I see you've found today's delivery from Fores's print shop." The door to the workroom closed quietly behind Tyler, the earl's valet and occasional laboratory assistant, as he carried a tray of chemicals to the small worktable by the spirit lamp.

"Yes. And this latest one is really quite upsetting." Wrexford glanced back at his timepiece and waited ten more seconds before turning off the flame. "Quill has made my legs look awfully spindly, and you know how vain I am about my shapely calves."

"It's gone beyond a jesting matter, milord."

A gentleman's gentleman would not ordinarily dare to rebuke his master. But Tyler was no ordinary valet, reflected the earl. To begin with, he didn't swoon over the task of removing foul-smelling stains and singe marks from a finely tailored evening coat. More importantly, his scientific education made him far more useful in other matters.

Tyler cleared his throat with a brusque cough—never a good sign. It meant a lecture was coming, a blunt one, delivered in a rough-cut Scottish brogue. "Perhaps you ought to consider ignoring Reverend Holworthy's attacks from now on. Engaging in a public war of words isn't doing your reputation any good."

Wrexford picked up the half-empty glass of brandy by his inkwell and drained it in one prolonged swallow.

He hadn't initiated the hostilities. The first salvo had been fired off several weeks ago when the Reverend Josiah Holworthy, a clergyman of rising oratorical note, had preached an emotional Sunday sermon decrying the corruptive influences of dissolute debauchery on a civilized society. Holworthy had used the earl as an example of Wickedness Personified, describing his recent behavior in lurid detail.

Wrexford knew restraint would have been the wiser course of action, and had the man's rhetoric been halfway clever, he would have let sleeping dogs lie. But the attack had been crude and so he couldn't resist sending a rebuttal to the editor of the *Morning Gazette.*

It had been published in the newspaper the following morning, and from there, the trading of insults had escalated, much to the glee of the rest of London.

A miscalculation. He wasn't as careful in his personal life as he was with his scientific experiments. Holding his empty glass up to the Argand lamp, Wrexford watched the shards of light refract off the cut crystal for several long moments before replying.

"Since when have you known me to care about my reputation?"

His valet carefully rearranged the chemical vials into two neat rows before fetching one of the decanters on the sideboard and crossing the carpet to pour out a fresh measure of brandy.

Or perhaps it was hemlock. Of late, his

mercurial moods had no doubt made him an awfully difficult fellow to deal with.

"It's just as well, I suppose," intoned Tyler. "For if that sanctimonious, self-anointed saint keeps attacking you as the Devil Incarnate, and you keep stirring the flames to a hotter burn with your outrageous comments on Society's narrow-minded morality, the only reputation you'll have will be black as sin."

"But it's so amusing to stick one of those clever French self-igniting matches up his pompous arse," muttered Wrexford, "and watch smoke come out his ears."

"Playing with fire is dangerous, milord."

He expelled a sigh. "He called me a witch."

"And you promptly corrected him," said Tyler, "pointing out that 'witch' refers to a female and he should properly refer to you as a warlock."

"I was right," retorted the earl. "The man is a bloody idiot."

"I believe what you called him in print was an illiterate widgeon, whose brain could fit twice over on the head of a pin."

"Ye god, can you blame me? All that blather about how my soul needs to be transmuted to a higher plane—"

Tyler cleared his throat to cover a snicker.

"Remind me again why I keep you in my employ," grumbled Wrexford. "Aside from your obsequious respect for my exalted person."

"I have concocted a polish for your boots that outshines Beau Brummel's secret recipe," replied Tyler.

"Dare I hope that you will tell me what's in it before I toss your insolent arse into the street?"

"Eye of newt, frog sweat—"

The earl let out a bark of laughter. The fact that Tyler didn't take his ill-tempered caustic comments to heart was also a mark in his favor.

"Pray tell, what is the point of all your chidings?" When his valet didn't answer right away, Wrexford pressed, "You think I should take steps to end this debate?"

Tyler shrugged. "It might be wise. Things appear to be on the verge of getting out of control."

"I shall consider it." Wrexford rose and stretched. Keeping precise control of the liquid's temperature and timing the addition of each ingredient had left him feeling fidgety. The conversation hadn't helped. Tyler was right— baiting a religious fanatic had been a bad decision.

Only one of many he had made in recent weeks.

But Wrexford pushed such musings aside for now. "There's no need for any further work here this evening. The liquid must cool completely, so we will wait until morning to continue with the experiment."

"You are going out again, sir?"

"Yes. I need a walk to clear my head." He reached for the print and folded it into a neat square before tucking it into his coat pocket. "And then I may stop at the new gaming hell on St. James's Street. Don't wait up. I shall likely be late."

"Good luck at the tables, sir. But then again, you usually do come away with your pockets stuffed with blunt."

"Luck is said to be a Lady, and you know that I have the devil's own way with women." The more accurate explanation probably lay in not giving a damn whether he won or lost. He gambled because watching the frenzy of brandy-fueled emotions—sweaty fear, giddy exultation, blank despair—play across the flushed faces was a diversion that kept boredom at bay.

"So we shall see how the cards fall."

"M'lady! m'lady!" The boy skidded to a breathless stop in the entrance hall and poked his head into the tiny parlor. "Bloody hell, ye've got te move yer pegs! The fancy church cove wots roasting His Nibs—"

Charlotte Sloane set down her pen and waved for silence. "Speak English, Raven."

"But I was!"

"The King's English. Pronounced clearly and like a gentleman," she chided. "And no swearing."

"Gentlemen swear," he shot back. "A lot."

Charlotte bit back a smile. "True. But under this roof, you must temper your tongue."

"I—"

"Hurry! Hurry!" Raven's younger brother peltered through the front door. "Wot's keeping ye?"

"Put a cork in it, Hawk. I'm trying te tell her." Drawing a deep breath, Raven turned back to her. "You must come quickly, milady," he said, this time enunciating his words like a proper little Etonian. "The churchman in your drawings has just been murdered. Skinny, the streetsweep who works the corner by St. Stephen's Church on Black Swan Lane, heard the watchman scream and run off to fetch the magistrate. If we move fast, you'll have time for a peek before they return."

Murder?

Charlotte flinched, nearly spilling the bottle of ink over her unfinished cartoon.

"Skinny said it's horrible," volunteered Hawk in an awed whisper. "The reverend's head is near cut off and there's enough blood pooled round the body to float a forty-gun frigate."

She hesitated. It wasn't that she was a ghoul, but a look at the scene would give her a great advantage over her competitors. In her business, knowledge was money.

And God knows, she needed money.

Having all the gruesome details at her fingertips . . .

Shooting up from her chair, Charlotte gestured at the stairs leading down to the tiny kitchen. "Fetch a lantern. I'll just be a moment changing into my breeches and boots."

A short while later, garbed as just another grubby urchin prowling the unlit streets, Charlotte squeezed through the back gate of the churchyard and followed the boys as they picked a path through the crumbling gravestones. Scudding clouds hid the crescent moon and the faint mizzle of starlight was lost in the thick malodorous mists drifting up from the river. Somewhere in the trees, a lone owl hooted.

Quickening her pace, she darted into the alcove between the buttresses and crouched down in front of the iron-banded side door. Raven was already at work on the lock, the thin shaft of his steel pick probing, probing . . .

Click.

The massive hinges swung open with a rusty groan.

"Keep watch out here," whispered Raven to his brother. "The usual signal—two sharp whistles— if we need te scamper quick-like."

Hawk nodded solemnly.

"I'll go first, m'lady." Raven drew a short cudgel from inside his jacket.

"No, stay behind me." Charlotte slipped past

27

him into the chill gloom. The air was damp and heavy with a cloying odor. *The smell of old bones and moldering sadness.* For those who lived outside the glittering opulence of Mayfair, life in London could grind even the brightest dreams into dust.

Shaking off such mordant thoughts, she waited to hear the door shut, then struck a flint to the lantern's wick and eased back the shutter.

The oily beam flickered over the thick granite columns, the age-blackened oak pews, the mortared stone tiles . . .

"Holy hell," hissed Raven through his teeth.

"Don't come any closer," Charlotte rasped as a spurt of bile, sharp and sour, shot up to burn the back of her throat. Swallowing hard, she crept closer to the body sprawled on the floor by the ornately carved lectern.

Dear God—so much blood.

Up close, the sight was more hideous than any demon-demented nightmare. The Right Reverend Josiah Holworthy—yes, she recognized him despite the disfigured face—was lying on his back, his arms outstretched as if in supplication to God for mercy.

If so, the plea had fallen on deaf ears.

His head . . .

Charlotte choked back a gag.

The slash of a blade had nearly severed the man's neck, and his head, attached to his body by only a few bits of tendon, bone, and flesh, had fallen awkwardly to one side. A dark, viscous pool was spreading out from beneath the crumpled coat collar, and rivulets of rusty red were snaking a serpentine trail over the grey stone.

Careful to avoid leaving any telltale scuff, Charlotte edged around for a different angle of view. *Steady, steady.* Her hand was trembling as she pulled a small notebook and pencil from her pocket.

"Cor, someone must have hated him awful bad," murmured Raven, who had snuck up behind her despite the order to the contrary.

"Hold this," she said, passing him the lantern to keep him occupied. It seemed pointless to argue with him. Having grown up in one of London's roughest slums, he was no stranger to violence.

But this . . .

Dark spots discolored the reverend's sightless eyes and his cheeks were badly burned by some sort of chemical. Faint streaks of a greenish-yellow substance had dribbled down to his chin and a white powder flecked the pitted flesh where the liquid had started to dry. Forcing her mind to concentrate on the tiny details helped control the violent churning in her stomach. She opened the book to a fresh page and hurriedly made some notes.

The powder, she noted, was also caked at the corners of his mouth and the protruding tongue had turned a mottled black. A strange smell . . .

She crouched down and sniffed, then jotted down a few more lines.

A low sound gurgled in Raven's throat.

"If you are going to cast up your accounts, kindly step outside," said Charlotte coolly, hoping the challenge would make him forget his nausea. "We mustn't leave any sign that someone has been in here."

"I ain't—I'm not—gonna shoot the cat," he vowed.

"Then move the light a little to your left."

"We gotta be going now." Raven shot a nervous look down the main aisle towards the front entrance.

"In a moment." Charlotte rose and slowly circled the corpse, making a few quick sketches. Stepping back, she noted a faint partial footprint in the dust of the side transept. Curious, she went to take a look. A boot—an oddly small one, with a distinctive mark cut into the heel.

Another quick crouch, another quick sketch.

"M'lady."

"Yes, yes." Charlotte stepped into the shadows to see where the footprints led, then changed her mind. The crime wasn't her concern, just the gristly details. She returned to the body and crouched down for a last look.

Raven let out another impatient hiss. As she turned slightly to chide him, she caught sight of something caught in the dead man's right-hand shirt cuff. *A scrap of paper?* After hesitating just a fraction, Charlotte reached out—

A sharp whistle, followed by another, shattered the silence.

"We gotta flee!" called Raven. He blew out the lamp.

"Now!"

Her fingers plucked the paper free, just as Raven grabbed her sleeve and yanked her to her feet.

Half stumbling, half running, Charlotte let herself be led. The boy was nimble as an alley cat and seemed to be able to see in the dark.

Thuds, shouts, and the clatter of boots echoed behind her. Up ahead, a sliver of starlight glimmered in the arched entryway.

"Hurry, hurry," urged Hawk in a frantic whisper as he pushed the door a touch wider.

Raven bolted through the opening, dragging Charlotte with him. She thought her lungs might burst, but somehow the boys hurried her to an even faster pace over the clotted earth and loose stones of the graveyard. Finally, after they were two streets away from the church, Raven allowed her to slow to a walk.

Pulse pounding in her ears, heart thumping hard enough to crack a rib, Charlotte bent over and braced her hands on her knees. "That," she gasped, "was close."

And then she began to laugh.

"You're mad, m'lady," wheezed Raven. "Mad as a Bedlamite."

"Yes, no doubt I am."

Wrexford took a seat at the gaming table to the chant of "Satan, Satan," from the other five men engaged in play.

While the others punctuated the words with a rhythmic pounding of their palms against the green felt, Fitzwilliam, a portly baron with a bald pate and ginger sidewhiskers, waggled a hand at one of the serving girls. "Bring us a bowl of syllabub!" he trilled. "Served hot as the devil's pitchfork."

"Stubble the attempt at humor, Fitz," growled the earl as the others laughed uproariously. "You have more hair than wit."

"Is it true that this morning's cartoon showed the Divine Diana as your latest paramour?" asked Pierpont, once the hilarity had died away.

"Aye, she was shown curled in a crucible under his chair—and wearing naught but a fancy sapphire necklace from Rundell and Bridge," piped up Sachem. "A price tag was attached to the clasp. If you looked closely with a quizzing glass you could make out the amount—fifteen hundred guineas." He looked at the earl. "True?"

"True," confirmed Wrexford.

"I didn't know you had seduced her away from

Radley," went Pierpont. "When did that happen?"

The earl shrugged off the question.

"I heard it was only three days ago," offered Fitzwilliam.

"How the devil does A. J. Quill know these intimate details?" queried Sachem sourly. "The information he had on Greeley's affair with the countess were of a very private nature."

A good question, thought Wrexford.

"Hell's teeth, the dratted scribbler must have spies everywhere. Perhaps Wellington should consider giving the fellow a general's commission and assigning him to combat Bonaparte," suggested Fitzwilliam. "The war would likely be over in a month."

"Speaking of war," said Pierpont, "things are getting awfully bellicose between you and Holworthy. If I were you, I would be tempted to march up to the pulpit and bloody his beak for mouthing such scurrilous slanders."

"There are other ways of silencing him," growled Wrexford. "But I'd rather not exert myself. What a pity A. J. Quill can't dig up some prurient scandal concerning the holier-than-thou reverend—"

"Well, I don't know about the scandals," interrupted a familiar voice. "But apparently Heaven has heard your prayer about silencing the pompous windbag."

Wrexford looked around. *Excellent—if anyone*

could tease him out of a sullen mood it was Kit.

Christopher Sheffield, the earl's closest friend since their Oxford days, sauntered up to the table and slouched against the back of Wrexford's chair, a sardonic smile on his unshaven face.

"Or perhaps I should rather say hell has caught wind of your incantation." Sheffield had a flair for theatrics. He picked at a thread dangling from his cuff, deliberately drawing out the moment of suspense.

"Cut wind, Sheffield," growled Pierpont as he gathered up the cards for a new hand. "If you've something to say, spit it out. We're in the midst of serious play here and are in no mood for interruption."

"Ah, but another far more interesting game is afoot," replied Sheffield, shifting his stance just enough to catch Wrexford's eye. "I've just come from White's, which is all abuzz with the news that the Reverend Josiah Holworthy has just been found dead in St. Stephen's Church on Black Swan Lane, his face burned by a noxious chemical, his throat cut from ear to ear."

The shuffling ceased.

"And wagers are already filling the betting book that you, my dear Wrex, are the odds-on favorite to be taken up for the murder."

CHAPTER 2

Her blood was still thumping against her temples as Charlotte slid into her chair and began to sharpen her quill.

Breathe, she reminded herself. Although her lungs were once again functioning normally, she couldn't seem to flush the ghastly metallic smell of death from her nostrils. That and the putrid stench of chemicals and scorched skin.

Like Raven, she had been a mere hairsbreadth away from puking at the horrible sight of Holworthy's ravaged face, though she had taken great pains to appear unmoved. Life in London's rougher areas was a hardscrabble existence. The boys needed a touchstone of steadiness and strength to set an example that poverty did not need to rob a person of hope or humanity.

So, too, had her late husband, reflected Charlotte, carefully working the penknife over the delicate tip of the goose feather. An uncharitable thought, perhaps. But no less true.

Anthony had often behaved more like a child than the two homeless urchins who had taken to sleeping in the entrance hall of her rented house. His resilience had slowly been worn away by the constant grind of survival, his optimism giving way to bitter complaints about the unfairness of life. While the young brothers showed a stoicism and resourcefulness beyond their tender years.

The oil lamp on her desk flickered weakly. Charlotte paused to turn up the wick, her gaze straying for an unwilling moment around the shadow-shrouded room. This was not how she had imagined her life either—mistress of naught but cramped quarters furnished with humble necessities. Squeezed cheek by jowl into a row of other similar structures, the razor-thin building was crumbling around her ears. The stove gave off a weak heat in winter, while the tiny windows did nothing to relieve the stifling heat of summer. In hindsight—

But looking back was a waste of time. All that mattered was the future and how she was going to create a more stable life for herself. Yes, her prints were becoming more and more popular, and earning more each week. Yes, she could afford better than this.

And yet Charlotte knew how fickle Fate could be. Just as she knew how poverty threatened to grind away one's hopes and dreams. After slowly paying off Anthony's debts, she had resolved to live frugally for the time being and save most of her earnings to build up a buffer against ever having to suffer through such hardships again. Perhaps there would come a time . . .

Be that as it may, for now she must focus on the present.

She shifted, and suddenly remembered the small scrap of paper she had plucked from the shirt cuff of Holworthy's lifeless hand. A whispery crackle stirred the air as she pulled it from her pocket and took a peek. It was nothing more than a scribble and for a brief moment she was tempted to get rid of the tangible proof that she had fiddled with the evidence.

What's done was done—she couldn't very well turn it into the authorities without risking her own neck.

But Charlotte hesitated. She had learned that having information no one else possessed, however insignificant it seemed, was a key to survival. *Life and death—one must fight tooth and claw* . . . Repressing a niggling sense of guilt, she quickly unlocked the hidden compartment in her desk, the place where she kept her most precious secrets, and hid it away.

Taking up the penknife, Charlotte finished making the last few cuts to the quill, then dipped her pen into the inkwell and set to work.

"Coffee, Thomas—and quickly." Wrexford squinted at the sunlight pouring in through the high arched windows of the breakfast room and shaded his eyes. "Do make sure it's strong and scalding hot."

"Yes, milord." The footman hurried off, taking extra care to move noiselessly over the Aubusson carpet.

The staff, observed the earl, had likely been warned that his temper was not to be trifled with this morning. They were a well-trained lot, working with oiled efficiency no matter his moods. He reminded himself to have Tyler send a bottle of brandy to the servants' table tonight.

As for himself . . . Wincing, Wrexford pressed his palms to his brow. In penance for the previous night, he ought to have naught but bread and water.

Thomas returned with the coffee, and then discreetly disappeared.

To hell with his sins. Wrexford poured a cup and closed his eyes, savoring the rich burn of the brew as he took a long swallow.

"You're up early." The door banged open, allowing Sheffield to saunter in uninvited.

"It's nearly noon," replied Wrexford. "Which begs the question of why you aren't sleeping off your revelries and allowing me to enjoy my breakfast in peace."

"Normally I would be dead to the world at this hour." Pulling out one of the Chippendale chairs, Sheffield sunk into a sinuous slouch and ran a hand through his unruly shock of wheat-gold hair. He was nearly as tall as the earl, but less broad in the shoulders, which accentuated the whippet-like grace of his movements. "However, I expect you'll have a visit from the magistrate this morning and I wouldn't miss such theatre for all the tea in China."

"Thank you for the moral support.

"Besides, I'm famished," added his friend. "And my pockets are temporarily empty. I lost heavily at the tables last night." He plucked a muffin from the basket of fresh pastries. "Luck really is a duplicitous bitch."

"You abuse her goodwill," pointed out Wrexford. Though that, he admitted, was rather like the pot calling the kettle black.

"True." Sheffield exhaled a penitent sigh. "I should reform, I know. But I haven't your mental discipline." He rose, just long enough to help himself to a heaping plate of shirred eggs and gammon from the chafing dishes on the sideboard.

Wrexford watched his friend wolf down a bite. "Remind me to inform Riche that you are to be barred entrance here until your table manners improve."

"Ha, ha, not a chance. He likes me more than he does you," retorted Sheffield. "I don't bite his head off half a dozen times a day."

The earl let out a grudging laugh.

"Now, will you kindly ring for more coffee."

As a footman entered with a fresh pot, the earl's butler followed behind him, frowning apologetically through the trailing plume of steam.

"Forgive me for interrupting your meal, sir. But a Runner—Mr. Griffin by name—is here from Bow Street demanding to speak with you."

"Right on cue," quipped Sheffield. He rubbed his hands together with an ill-concealed grin of glee. "This should be highly diverting."

"You have always found farces amusing," growled Wrexford.

"It's only natural, seeing as my own life veers to the absurd."

The earl made a pained face. "Show him in, Riche."

The butler reluctantly escorted in a tall, stocky fellow wearing a heavy overcoat and a fierce scowl. His red vest was garishly bright in contrast to the dull coloring of his other garments.

Wrexford winced. "Would you be so good as to step out of the sunlight. You are hurting my eyes."

If the Runner was intimidated by the ornate surroundings, he didn't show it. Ignoring the request, he pulled a notebook and pencil from his coat pocket and set to work. "Lord Wrexford, the magistrate at Bow Street has sent me here to ask you a few questions concerning the bad blood between you and the Reverend Josiah Holworthy. He was murdered last night."

"I have heard the news."

"I wish to enquire about—"

"About my whereabouts?"

"Precisely, milord." Griffin waited expectantly.

Wrexford took a bite of toast and chewed thoughtfully.

"Would you care for a cup of coffee, sirrah?" asked Sheffield. "It's black and scalding as the Devil's arse."

"I prefer not to accept His Lordship's hospitality," came the curt reply. "Especially when it concerns anything liquid."

Wrexford felt his lips twitch. At least the fellow possessed a sardonic sense of humor to balance his wretched taste in fashion. But then, a red waistcoat was required for the job, so perhaps it wasn't his fault.

"Now, as to your whereabouts, sir. Aside from a gaming hell on St. James's Street."

He put down his fork. The man, as befitting his sleuthhound job, had already begun sniffing around. "I was out walking."

"Alone?"

"Alone," confirmed the earl. "I find exercise stimulates the mind, and there were a number of things I wished to ponder."

The Runner didn't inquire as to what things. Instead he said, "You are said to have an interest in chemistry. Might I ask why?"

"Because I am curious. The workings of the natural world interest me. They have much to teach us."

"Curious," repeated Griffin with a sniff, as if he

had smelled something rotten. "You mean to say, your dabblings have no purpose except to satisfy your curiosity?"

Wrexford held his temper in check. "Knowledge is a purpose unto itself."

The Runner's eyes narrowed in suspicion. He turned a page in his notebook. "Getting back to last night, milord, did your walk take you anywhere near St. Stephens Church on Black Swan Lane?"

"I have no idea. As I told you, I am usually lost in thought."

More scribbling. The *scratch-scratch* sound made him grit his teeth.

Griffin finally looked up from his notebook. "Tell me, sir, what were your thoughts when you heard that the reverend had been murdered?"

"That the sanctimonious windbag deserved to have his throat cut," snapped Wrexford. "London's air is bad enough without having it further befouled with buffle-headed superstitions and ignorant lies."

Sheffield sat up a little straighter. "Careful, Wrex," he murmured. "Not everyone appreciates your peculiar sense of humor."

"And just how do you know the reverend had his throat cut?" the Runner quickly demanded.

The earl let out an impatient sigh. "Because the Honorable Mr. Sheffield here kindly informed me of that fact last night—"

"Along with the rest of the gentlemen present in the main gaming room of Lucifer's Lair," interjected his friend. "The gruesome news was all over Town. I heard the details at White's, where the talk was of nothing else."

"Hmmph." The Runner started to jot something more in his notebook.

"Bloody hell," muttered the earl.

But before he could go on, the breakfast room door opened yet again, admitting his valet. Tyler was cradling a thick roll of paper in his arms.

"I've just come from the print shop, and—" He stopped short on seeing the red-breasted Runner. "Forgive me, sir. I didn't realize you were entertaining company."

He waved off the apology. "Did Quill comment on the murder?"

"Indeed. Have a look for yourself."

Wrexford quickly cleared a place on the table. Tyler unrolled the print and anchored the four corners with the breakfast plates before stepping back.

Sheffield, all trace of ennui gone, joined the earl in studying the detailed drawing. After a slight hesitation, the Runner did the same. The room fell silent, save for the slight hiss of the oil burners beneath the chafing dishes.

A minute slid by, and then another, and another.

"Look at the coloring," murmured Wrexford, subjecting the half-severed head to closer scrutiny. "How in the name of Satan does Quill manage this?" He looked up sharply. "Is it accurate?" he asked of the Runner.

Griffin didn't reply, but the tightening of his jaw was an eloquent enough answer. He blew out his breath and countered with a question of his own. "Why don't *you* tell *me,* milord?"

Their gazes locked.

"You're wasting your time here. I didn't kill him."

"So you say, milord."

"As does the evidence," replied Wrexford. "For I am assuming if you had any tangible proof of my guilt, I would already be cooling my heels in a Newgate cell."

"The investigation is just beginning." The Runner snapped his book shut. "At the moment, I have nothing further to ask. But I daresay you will be hearing from me again."

Sheffield watched the man stalk out of the room. "What a tedious fellow."

"Tedious, but no fool," murmured Tyler. He looked to Wrexford, but the earl had already returned to examining the details of the print.

"It's uncanny—Quill must be a demon or a djinn," intoned Wrexford, "for the fellow certainly seems to possess unholy powers of perception. How else to explain his intimate acquaintance with every sordid secret in London?"

"A good question," replied Tyler. "But you're

44

right. I assume you're looking at the color and strange mottling on the reverend's skin."

"Yes. My guess is it was caused by oil of vitriol."

"Which is?" queried Sheffield.

"A very strong acid," answered Tyler, fixing Wrexford with a meaningful look. It's a common ingredient in chemical experiments."

"Ah. Well, assuming you didn't kill him, Wrex . . ." Sheffield raised an inquiring brow.

"I did not."

"Then it would appear that the murderer was intent on making it look like you did. And yet, having gone through all that trouble, why didn't he leave an incriminating clue?"

The same thought had occurred to Wrexford. "You heard Robin Red-Breast. The investigation is just beginning. There may very well be one and the authorities just haven't found it."

"Or they have, and are keeping the information tucked inside their scarlet waistcoats for the moment," pointed out his valet.

The earl frowned. "For what reason?"

"I have no idea, milord." Tyler rubbed pensively at his chin. "Perhaps it would be wise for me to return to Fores's print shop and ask a few questions about Quill and where he can be found. If anyone can tell us more about the murder scene, it is he. And that knowledge may prove useful to have."

"Indeed," mused Wrexford. "If for no other

reason than to learn how the fellow digs up his dirt. The next time I buy a ladybird a necklace, I prefer the price to remain private. The damn scribbler cost me five hundred pounds when La Belle Serena got wind of Diana Fairfield's gift and demanded an extra bauble not to kick up a dust over a certain embarrassing incident."

"Bracelets and baubles are not your primary worry, sir. The reverend had a great many followers here in London. The authorities will feel pressure to solve his murder quickly."

"And why, pray tell, should that concern me?" snapped the earl. "I didn't do it."

"What Tyler is tactfully trying to tell you is that whether you are guilty or innocent is irrelevant," said Sheffield. "It's all about appearances, and you have to admit, you are the most likely suspect."

Wrexford uttered a rude oath.

"Swear all you like," retorted his friend. "But you know I'm right."

Much as it galled him, he had to concede the point. "Very well, very well. Tyler, return to Fores's shop and find out Quill's address. I think it's time we had a little talk with the artist." He reached in his coat pocket and took out a purse. The muted clink of metal on metal sounded as it slid across the table. "Take this. Gold is an amazingly effective lubricant for even the most stubborn of tongues."

"Very good, milord. I shall report back later today."

"Seeing as things are well in hand, I shall toddle off to White's and spend the afternoon drinking other people's brandy and listening to the latest gossip," announced Sheffield sardonically. "Would you like me to place a wager in the betting book on whether you'll hang for the crime?"

"M'lady?"

Charlotte looked up from her sketch on the Prince Regent's latest peccadillo. Thank God Prinny was always a subject for satire when she was in need of subject matter for her next print. As of yet, she had not heard any juicy tidbits on how the murder investigation was progressing. But now that the boys had returned from the heart of Town that might be about to change.

"Do come in, Raven." Seeing the smaller shadow behind him, she quickly added. "And bring Hawk with you."

"I know ye don't like to be interrupted when you're working, but there was a fancy toff—"

"You mean a gentleman," she interrupted. Perhaps it was a lost cause, but she was doing her best to give the boys a modicum of education. They were both very bright, and under her tutelage they had learned to read simple texts. If only she could afford proper schooling—

"Aye, a gentleman," said Raven, cutting short her musing. "And he was arsking a lot of questions around the print shop."

Her fingers tightened on her pen. "What sort of questions?"

"He wanted te know where A. J. Quill lived," piped up Hawk. "But Mr. Fores told him nuffink."

Charlotte made herself relax. There was nothing to tell. One of the terms Anthony had negotiated with Fores was a promise never to betray his identity. And to make sure of that, he had given the print shop owner a false name—to protect his reputation, he had told Charlotte, for when his paintings became more famous than those of Rembrandt.

It didn't matter that those dreams had turned to dust and that Anthony was now no longer among the living. Fores didn't know that. Even if he somehow uncovered the truth, A. J. Quill's work was making bagfuls of blunt for the shop. He wasn't going to risk ruining a very profitable arrangement.

"Nor will he, Hawk," she assured him.

A look of unease still shadowed the younger boy's face, so she quickly added, "Truly, there is nothing to worry about. The people pictured in my prints sometimes have their lackeys visit Fores with either threats or bribes to avoid further ridicule. He always sends them away with a flea in their ear."

"Aye," agreed Raven. "No reason te get your guts in a twist."

"He wuz there to make trouble," insisted Hawk. "I wuz watching his peepers. They were sharper than Bloody Jack's razor."

Charlotte felt a clench in her chest. The boys shied away from any talk about their past, and she hadn't pressed them. But she was under no illusions about the brutal realties of life on the streets. Unspeakable horrors were rife in the twisting alleyways. She saw the wariness in their eyes, even around her. Trust made one vulnerable.

And predators pounced on those who betrayed any hint of vulnerability.

"Even with razor-sharp eyes, he won't find A. J. Quill." Taking up a rag, Charlotte carefully wiped the smudges of ink from her hands. "I'm famished. Will you join me in some bread and butter, and a cup of tea?"

Hawk shot his brother a pleading look. God only knew when was the last time they had eaten. They were nowhere to be found when she had come down from her tiny bedchamber this morning.

"Yeah, I suppose that would be all right," allowed Raven. The boy was thin as one of her artist's pencils, a fact made even more apparent by his having grown several inches over the last few months. But there was a whipcord toughness to his leanness, and a sense of coiled tension ready to snap at any moment.

He brushed back a tangle of hair from his cheek. At first glance it was black as his name implied, but as he moved through a shaft of sunlight, glints of mahogany softened the darkness. "That is, if you are fixing something for yourself."

"I am." She set the kettle on the hob and unwrapped a chunk of dark bread, wishing she had spared the extra expense for a fresh white loaf at the market.

Ah, but if wishes were horses then beggars would ride.

On that cheerful note, she set out three cups and cut off several slices. There wasn't much butter left, but she quickly fetched the jar of jam, which she used sparingly. She tried to feed the boys regularly, but they still were wary of accepting too much from her.

"Come sit."

They joined her at the little table close by the stove.

"Mr. Fores sent this. He says it's a small token of his appreciation." Raven fished out a purse and passed it over. "The print of the murder sold out in an hour."

Charlotte could see there was a promising bulge in it. An unexpected addition to her nest egg—any extra was most welcome.

"I heard talk in the shop that Bow Street sent a Runner to quiz the earl," volunteered Hawk. He was smaller and just as skinny as his older brother. But everything about him had less of an edge. Every angle and plane of his narrow face was softer, and his hair was several shades lighter. "Ye think he'll swing for it?"

"It's not for me to say," she replied absently, unknotting the strings and shaking the money into her palm. "Thank you for bringing it, Raven. Allow me to give you something for your efforts."

Charlotte slid a halfpenny across the scarred tabletop. The boy looked at it for a moment, then took a bite of his bread. "Naw, you keep it. I was comin' in this direction anyway."

"Don't speak with your mouth full," she chided. "It's very ungentlemanly."

Both brothers grinned.

"Aye, proper little gents we is," chortled Raven, setting Hawk to giggling.

"Well, you never know when you might be invited to take tea with the Prince Regent." It was a standing jest between them, but her efforts were having some effect. They no longer ate like wild little wolves.

Now, if only she could convince them to run a washrag over their grubby faces and hands more often . . .

"I've an idea," she went on. "How about I use your coin to purchase a bit of beef and I'll make stew for supper to celebrate our good fortune." She usually limited meat to a few nights a week, but the boys were looking painfully thin.

Hawk's eyes widened in delight. "Hooray!"

"I'll wager if the fancy toff swings fer the murder, your print of it might earn an even bigger token of appreciation," mused Raven. "Maybe even a bagful of guineas."

Hawk sucked in his breath. "*Guineas.*"

Guineas, thought Charlotte. Lud, wouldn't a bagful of them be a godsend. But a clench of guilt swiftly silenced the speculation. Yes, she made her living poking fun at the foibles and miseries of her betters. However, death was another matter entirely.

"Let us not speculate on profiting from the hangman's noose," she said softly. "We don't know if the authorities have any suspects for the crime."

Hawk sat up a little straighter. "While Raven was nabbering with Mr. Fores, a Runner came into the shop. He asked the clerk questions about yer print. Said he had just come from speaking with Lord What's His Name."

Charlotte snapped to attention, all thoughts of where to find the best bargain on beef gone in a flash. "What did this Runner look like, Hawk?" If the Earl of Wrexford was really a suspect, she could feast off the scandal for months, regardless of whether or not he hanged for the crime.

Both boys were very observant. Hawk was able to describe the man in great detail.

"That's very helpful." After jotting down a few lines in her notebook, she took a fresh sheet of paper from her desk drawer and dashed off a quick letter.

"Would you kindly deliver this right away?" She gave them the address. "You know the procedure." She tried not to pester her childhood friend too often. But given that he moved in the highest circles of Society, his information in this case could be enormously helpful.

"Shall we wait for an answer?" asked Hawk hopefully. Her friend's cook was apparently very generous with sweets.

"Yes, if there's a chance for one. Otherwise, you can return for it in the morning."

"I was just thinking, m'lady. Whiskers, the streetsweep who works the corner near Bow Street, might have heard some tittle-tattle about His Nibs. We could stop on our way back and have a jaw with him, if you'd like."

"That's an excellent idea." Charlotte had learned long ago that every bit of gossip was useful. Stitching together all the scraps of thread was how one embroidered the plain cloth of a scandal. A. J. Quill was the most popular satirist in Town because of the colorful details. "Thank you."

Raven tucked the folded missive inside his grubby shirt. "C'mon, Hawk, let's fly."

Wrexford paused in his pacing around the room to pull a book down from the shelf above his worktable. Something about the cursed print was niggling at the back of his mind, but he couldn't quite put a finger on it.

The colors depicted by A. J. Quill could be meaningless, a simple artistic artifice to convey the gruesome look of burned flesh.

But in his experience—which had become far too personal of late—Quill's pen was uncannily accurate in showing all the little details.

Once again he wondered how.

He resumed walking, this time his boots beating a steady tattoo back and forth in front of the blazing hearth as he thumbed through the pages.

The logs crackled, punctuated by the muffled *thump, thump* of leather on the polished parquet.

"Damnation." Wrexford had no sooner uttered the oath when his fingers stilled. He read over the section several times before turning to where he had tacked the print up on the wall.

He was still standing there, lost in thought, when his valet let himself into the workroom.

"Have you discovered something?" asked Tyler, noting the open book and gleam in the earl's eyes.

"Perhaps." Wrexford handed him the leather-bound volume. "Read that section."

Tyler skimmed over the pages. "Hmm, yes. I daresay that's possible."

"I'm going to the workroom. I want to experiment with a few things . . ." The earl's voice trailed off as he was already making mental note of some chemical combinations.

"We could try different percentages of the acids and test the effects." His valet quirked what might have been a smile. "That is, if you care to sacrifice your cheeks."

"It's more than acids," mused Wrexford. "As to empirical observation, let me remind you that I pay you very well for your services."

"Not well enough to be disfigured for life. But you—think of it this way, better your face than your neck."

"Your feeble attempt at humor falls far short of the mark." Wrexford crossed his arms. "I trust you did better with Mr. Fores."

"Alas, no. The man refused to divulge anything about the artist's identity or where he lives. Claimed he didn't know, and added that even if he did, A. J. Quill was worth more to him in the long run than your gold."

"Bloody hell! You, of all people, I expected to show more ingenuity—"

Tyler waved him to silence. "Do permit me to finish, milord."

The earl pressed his lips together, though the corners were quivering with ire.

"As I said, Fores was unhelpful, but when he left me to help another customer, I strolled to the side room and the clerk there was decidedly more friendly."

"Get to the point. My patience is wearing thin."

Tyler heaved a martyred sigh. "I purchased several copies of the infamous print, adding a generous tip. In return, I learned that A. J. Quill's drawings are delivered to the print shop by a ragged little guttersnipe—or sometimes two of them. They usually arrive in the late afternoon, which gives the engravers time to make the printing plate and run off an edition in time for the following morning. But in a sensational case, like Holworthy's murder, the timing can run closer to midnight."

"How—"

"If you were about to ask how many drawings Quill does every week, the answer is at least three, and sometimes four, especially when a scandal is on the tip of every tongue."

"Which means one may arrive tonight," mused Wrexford.

"Yes." The valet's expression turned somewhat smug. "And before you ring a peal over me for not being hidden in some damp, dirty, malodorous crevasse keeping the shop under surveillance, allow me to add that I took the liberty of hiring a Scottish compatriot to stand sentinel and follow the urchins back to their lair. Quiggs is very good—he can stalk a Highland deer through gorse and over sheer granite."

Wrexford exhaled a pent-up breath. "It appears that for once you've earned your weekly salary."

"I'll take that as a thank-you." Tyler turned to go. "Oh, just one more thing." He paused, his hand on the ornate door latch.

"I think I know where the chemicals that burned Holworthy's face came from."

CHAPTER 3

Charlotte sat back to study the nearly done drawing of the Bow Street Runner interrogating the Earl of Wrexford. She was pleased with the result. Exaggerating the bulk of the Runner to bull-like proportions had created a good visual drama to the composition . . .

Dipping her brush in the paint, she quickly darkened the red of his waistcoat just a shade, which made it even stronger. Granted, the snarling leer and the unshaven face were pure artistic license, but for most of the public, figures of authority were viewed with dislike and distrust. Poking fun at them was good for business.

As for the earl . . .

Charlotte regarded his pen-and-ink profile. She had seen him only once in the flesh, during one of her infrequent visits to the haute monde enclave of Mayfair. He had been walking down Bond Street, conversing with a friend, and their paths had crossed for merely a moment. And yet, the planes of his face had remained indelibly etched in her mind's eye. Or, rather, the air of haughty detachment that seems sculpted into every subtle curve and angle.

Most aristocrats wore their sense of privilege

and entitlement like a second skin, but Wrexford's attitude was different, though she was hard pressed to explain why.

Go to hell—that was the message that seemed to radiate from every pore.

She touched a finger to the long, wildly curling strands of coal-black hair she had drawn on the paper. Well, it seemed possible he would be meeting Satan sooner than he might wish.

It would take an act of the House of Lords for England to execute a peer of the realm. But given the sensational nature of Holworthy's murder, the public would be clamoring for blood. And the bluer, the better.

"If there is to be a trial, may it turn into a long one." Her livelihood demanded that she harden her heart—she couldn't afford a groat of sympathy, not with her own survival depending on her cutting commentary. Taking up her pen, Charlotte put the finishing touches on the drawing.

"If he is to suffer, I might as well profit from it."

"This way, milord." Tyler led the way down a long, dark corridor. The air was heavy with a fugue of sour smells.

"Humphry Davy's laboratory is located in a far more central part of the building," observed Wrexford, who was familiar with the rambling layout of the Royal Institution building. "But no doubt that has to do with the hordes of highborn ladies who flock to his public lectures and demand to see where their God of Enlightenment discovers the wonders of the universe."

Founded in 1799 by a group of the leading men of science in Great Britain, the Royal Institution was created to educate the public about the heady new advances in a variety of scientific disciplines. Its ornate new building on Albemarle Street housed laboratories and lecture halls, and the frequent presentations and demonstrations had become wildly popular within the highest circles of Society.

"Do I detect a note of jealousy over Davy's popularity with the opposite sex?" quipped his valet.

The earl made a rude sound. "I merely think he's a fool to mix business with pleasure. Davy possesses an excellent intellect and his methods are first rate."

Despite his diminutive stature, the charismatic Cornishman had become one of the darlings of London Society. His lectures on chemistry attracted overflow crowds, and talk of the wonders of science filled the drawing rooms of Mayfair.

"But," went on Wrexford, "he's an obsequious toadeater to the rich and famous, and that distracts him from his work."

"True." Tyler came to a halt in front of a closed door and knocked brusquely. "Be that as it may, this section of the Institution is, as you know, where the less exalted members do their research."

"Then why the Devil did you roust me from my work to come here?" he muttered. Second-rate minds bored him to perdition. Without a spark of originality—

A muffled call bade them to enter.

"Patience, milord," counseled his valet. "What Mr. Drummond has to say may be important."

The earl followed his valet into a dimly lit room. The fumes were even stronger here, and he quickly saw the reason why. On a table in the center of the space, a large metal crucible was suspended over a spirit lamp. The apparatus was turned up to full force, and red-gold tongues of fire were lapping against the dark metal, causing the contents to boil furiously.

Wrexford sniffed. Whatever the specific experiment, it wasn't going to yield very interesting results, he decided. The ingredients were too mundane.

A figure moved out from behind the table. The flickering play of flame and vapor gave him an otherworldly aura. An acolyte of Hephaestus, the ancient god of fire.

"Ah, it's you again, Mr. Tyler. As I told you earlier this afternoon, this meeting will have to be brief." Drummond's voice had a nasal quality, as if he had been breathing in too many noxious chemicals. "My experiment requires precise timing."

"We understand such things," said Wrexford, moving up to stand abreast of his valet.

Drummond's gaze flared for an instant in recognition, then turned guarded. "I didn't realize the figure of authority that Mr. Tyler mentioned would be *you,* sir. Dare I hope that means the Higher Powers have finally consented to give my protests the attention they deserve?"

Though the earl chose to conduct his research in his own private laboratory, he was a generous benefactor of the Institution. His recent large donation of funds to purchase a special collection of rare chemistry books from the late Lord Strathern's library had earned the governing board's gratitude, along with the title of Honorary Warden.

"That remains to be seen, Drummond," replied Wrexford. "As you are pressed for time, I shall dispense with the usual pleasantries and cut to the chase—"

"An unfortunate turn of phrase, given recent events," murmured Tyler. "But you take His Lordship's meaning."

Drummond looked at him blankly.

Ignoring the quip, the earl hurried on, though he was fairly certain that allowing his valet to bring him here had been a lapse in judgment. It already had the smell of a wild goose chase. "I understand you were heard complaining about a theft from your laboratory several days ago."

"Yes, and precious little good did it do me."
Drummond glowered. "The head watchman dismissed it as nothing more than a puerile prank among colleagues. But I know it had darker significance!"

"And why is that?"

"Jealousy," he replied hotly. "A man of your exalted position may not know such things, but it's a viper's nest of intrigue here in this section of the building, with everyone competing to catch the attention of Mr. Davy and his inner circle. I believe someone deliberately sabotaged my work by stealing some of my supplies."

"Can you tell us exactly what went missing?" asked Tyler.

Drummond rattled off a list of chemicals.

The earl frowned. They almost matched the ingredients of his own experiments as to what might have caused the burns on Holworthy's face. A coincidence, perhaps. But as the combinations were rather esoteric, Wrexford conceded that the odds likely favored a different explanation.

"Was that all?" he probed. The chemist struck him as a pompous ass, one whose delusion of specters lurking in every shadow provided a convenient excuse for his mediocre talent. But beneath the self-pitying complaints, there seemed an odd tension. Wrexford wondered why.

Drummond shifted his stance and brushed a lank shock of hair off his forehead. For an instant,

63

the dull straw color was gilded a bright gold by the gaseous flames. "I think I know the contents of my laboratory, sir!" He glanced at the clock on the work counter. "Now if that's all, I need to perform the next step in my experiment." A sniff. "In precisely thirty-four seconds."

"Do go ahead," said Tyler pleasantly. "We'll wait." He darted a glance at the earl. "Won't we, sir?"

Wrexford gave a curt nod. It seemed a waste of time, but he agreed because he sensed it would vex Drummond.

As the chemist turned and began to fiddle with an assortment of canisters, the earl moved to the opposite end of the room, where a pair of shelves flanked a narrow counter on which was set an elaborate brass scale. The titles stamped on the book spines revealed nothing out of the ordinary. In the background, Tyler continued with his routine questioning, but Wrexford was fast losing interest. Coincidences did happen, and Drummond seemed far too unimaginative to be involved in a ghoulish murder.

The scale, at least, offered a diversion. It was precision crafted, with the weights and balances designed for measuring miniscule amounts . . .

In shifting for a better look, he noticed a small, shallow metal storage cabinet on the back of the counter, half hidden in the shadow of the scale. It looked to be heavy and the door boasted several intricate levers. Out of idle curiosity, he pressed the main latch to see if it would open.

Click.

Inside were four horizontal shelves, each filled with a neat row of glass-stoppered vials and containers.

Save for a spot on the bottom one, where a gap appeared.

Wrexford looked more closely and saw three circles visible in the faint powdering of dust, which seemed to indicate that the items had only recently been removed. Also catching his eye was a small pocket notebook lodged beneath the bottom shelf.

A glance across the room showed Drummond was still at work. Turning back to the cabinet, the earl opened the book and began to thumb through the pages.

The clatter of the canisters soon quieted. A momentary *whoosh* of the flame reigniting filled the air, followed by Drummond's querulous voice. "I really don't know what more I can tell you, Mr. Tyler. Now, I really must turn all my attention to—"

"Perhaps you can clarify what happened to the three bottles that appear to have gone missing from this cabinet?" called Wrexford.

Drummond dropped his stirring spoon and rushed over.

"According to your very detailed notes, the

missing substances are rhodium, palladium, and mercury." *Which also matched the ingredients of his own experiments.* Wrexford held up the notebook. "You list the position of each container and the date it is used up. There is no entry for those three, so I assume they, too, were stolen."

The chemist blinked. A sheen of sweat coated his forehead. Whether it was from the heat of the crucible or some other cause was impossible to discern. "That cabinet should have been locked!"

"It wasn't," said Wrexford. "Rhodium is quite expensive. And the amount of mercury listed is rather large. Did you have them for a reason?"

"I . . . I wished to try out an idea I had in mind, once the current phase of my experiment is finished," answered Drummond stiffly. "I would rather not elaborate on the details, milord. I believe it to be a very original idea."

"I have no intention of stealing a march on you," said Wrexford dryly. "Tell me, do you keep the main door to your laboratory under lock and key?"

"Yes, of course. And as I told Mr. Tyler, there was no sign of forced entry," replied Drummond. "Perhaps now the Institution will take my complaints seriously. It's plain as a pikestaff that this was no random prank. Someone who is familiar with the laboratories here wants to discredit my reputation with Davy and ruin my career!"

The chemist's mouth pinched to a pout. "I had

"Very," replied Charlotte, exaggerating only a little. She was inordinately fortunate that her friend was willing to pass on information that she could access nowhere else. But she knew she was dancing along a razor's edge with her questions. Their friendship had been formed in childhood, when his circumstances had been far more humble than they were now. They had formed a strong bond of trust, and had shared secrets. But life had changed for him, and she didn't want to force him to decide where his true loyalties lay.

"These letters are important, and I don't know how I would manage them without you."

"S'all right," mumbled Raven through a mouthful of stew. To his brother he added, "Oiy, mind your manners. No slurping."

Charlotte bit back a smile.

"We can go whenever you need te send one," continued Raven.

"Or any other errand," chirped in Hawk.

"Thank you." She passed them both an extra hunk of bread.

"I almost forgot, we heard more from Skinny about the Runner," said Hawk, once he had chewed and swallowed his food. "His Nibs—"

"Lord Wrexford," corrected Charlotte.

"Yeah, him—when the Runner was questioning him, there was another cove in the room. His name was Field . . . Field . . ."

"*Shef*-field," finished Raven. "The Runner told Skinny he was a friend of Lord Wrexford."

Sheffield. Charlotte made a mental note to ask Jeremy about the earl's circle of friends. "Did the Runner describe him?"

Raven repeated what he had heard. *Tall, fair-haired*—It wasn't a lot to go on, but Charlotte saw a way to add a new element to her drawing before sending it to the engraver.

"Oh, and Skinny said one of His Lordship's servants delivered your print—the one wiv all the blood—while His Nibs was being raked over the coals," added Hawk.

That would make a nice touch, she thought wryly. There was just enough room to work it into the drawing before sending it off.

"And Skinny heard that Lord Wrexford was oogling the 'orrible burns on the reverend's face."

"Ha! The devil admiring his handiwork," said Raven after spooning up the last mouthful of his stew.

"We don't know that he committed the crime," she pointed out, though the concept of truth likely meant little to the boys. In their world, guilt or innocence was about how fast one could run or how much money one had for bribes.

The truth was, all signs pointed to Wrexford being the culprit. But pedigree and prestige were dauntingly powerful, as she well knew.

The authorities would have to be awfully sure of themselves to arrest him.

"Cor, you should have seen the body, with all that scorched flesh and putrid color, Hawk." Raven made a face. "It was disgusting."

Intent on changing the subject before it turned too gruesome, Charlotte gathered up the empty bowls and set them down by the wash pail. "If you're not too tired, would you be willing to take my drawing to the engraver later this evening instead of tomorrow afternoon?"

She was loath to ask the boys to go out at night. But they often went off on their own, and from what they had told her, the authorities looked to be intensifying their scrutiny of the earl. Come morning, a new print in the shop's display window would fan the public's prurient interest. It would sell well, and it was wise to take advantage of such a juicy scandal.

"Yeah, all right," agreed Raven with a shrug. "S'no trouble. We were already planning te head that way."

She didn't ask why. Though a part of her yearned to play the mother hen, she knew they wouldn't thank her for it. The laws of life here were a world away from those of her own childhood, but she had learned to accept them. The choice to cross the boundaries and venture into unknown territory had been a voluntary one.

There was no going back.

"Thank you. Just give me a little time to add the extra details."

Raven sprawled out on the rag rug by the stove and began toying with a handful of skittles he had pulled from his pocket. Hawk was quick to join him. "Aye, m'lady. We'll be right here when you need us."

"Are you saying you saw the Right Reverend Josiah Holworthy here inside the Royal Institution?" demanded Wrexford.

"Yes," insisted Drummond. "More than once."

The earl thought about the corridor and the fact that the wall sconces were few and far between. "Are you sure? At night the shadows must be nearly black as Hades."

The jut of Drummond's chin rose another notch. "I know what I saw." A pause. "And heard."

All of Wrexford's senses had now come alert. The reverend had a deep, sonorous voice. It was very recognizable. If what the chemist claimed was true—

Drummond seemed to read the earl's thoughts and a self-righteous smile slowly spread over his face. "I've heard the reverend preach several times. His oratorical style is unique."

"Indeed." And yet something didn't ring quite true. "However, if he was here at night, and—as you point out—had no business being here, I doubt he was rattling the walls with his preaching voice."

A sharp *crack* rose from the bubbling crucible, along with a ghostly plume of steam. Drummond flinched.

"Which means you must have been rather close to him to identify his voice."

"I—" The chemist wet his lips. The smile had quickly faded to a petulant pout. "I had every right to investigate when I heard people in the corridor at odd hours. As you see, the theft shows I had every right to fear mischief was afoot."

"More than you might think," murmured Tyler. "You are aware, aren't you, that the reverend was murdered last night."

Drummond gasped, the blood draining from his face.

Unless the man was a consummate actor, thought Wrexford, the shock was real.

"Who was with the reverend?" he pressed, hoping to take advantage of the chemist's rattled nerves.

Silence hung heavy, the weight of it dampening the soft bubbling of the liquid and the whispery hiss of the spirit lamp.

"Mr. Drummond?" urged Tyler.

"As you said, it was dark, and the other man's voice was muffled," replied the chemist evasively.

Wrexford could easily visualize the scenario— the reverend and one of the members of the Institution entering the corridor, Drummond hearing the voices and sneaking out to spy on what was going on . . .

Speaking of reptiles and cold-blooded creatures that slithered through the shadows.

Unwilling to let the chemist wiggle out of his accusations, he pressured the man for an answer. "Yet you must have noticed what laboratory they entered."

Drummond hesitated, drawing out the moment with a long exhale before replying, "Mind you, I can't be entirely certain. But from what I could make out, it was the one belonging to Lord Robert Canaday."

Tyler frowned slightly, though Wrexford wasn't sure why.

Shifting uncomfortably, Drummond ran a hand through his hair. "That's all I can tell you. And now, I really must attend to my liquid. The experiment has already been ruined once."

The earl decided that they had gotten all they could from the chemist. At least for now. "Thank you for your time. We will leave you to your work." He turned for the door.

"You'll be sure to tell Davy about the seriousness of the theft, and how sinister forces are conspiring to ruin my experiments?" came the whiney question.

Wrexford responded with a vague wave, his thoughts already preoccupied with what he had just heard.

Double, double toil and trouble; Fire burn, and caldron bubble. The words from Shakespeare's *Macbeth* suddenly popped into his head. The revelations—if true—were interesting. Though whether they would shed any light on the murder was far from clear. There were any number of mundane explanations for why the reverend might have accompanied a friend to the Institution.

So far, nothing about the murder was making any sense. And as a man of science, that irritated him. "For a charm of powerful trouble, Like a hell-broth boil and bubble," he muttered aloud, adding more lines from the scene.

What malevolent witchcraft was brewing here in London?

"Eye of newt, and toe of frog, Wool of bat, and tongue of dog," responded Tyler, his brows tweaking up in amusement. "You have to agree this has all the ingredients for a corking good play involving mystery, murder, and mayhem."

Wrexford grunted. He hadn't realized that his valet's skills included an expertise in English literature.

"So, how do you intend to follow up on this new information?" continued Tyler.

"I see no reason why I should do anything at all," snapped Wrexford. "It's not *my* responsibility to find Holworthy's murderer. Let the Runner do his job." He blew out his breath.

"Though judging by his interest in me, he's likely to make a hash of it."

They reached the street and walked on for several minutes in silence. "Why the devil did you bring me here in the first place?" he demanded of his valet. "I'm not sure why you are so afire to have me investigate this murder."

"Given your very public quarrel with Holworthy, it's clear the magistrates at Bow Street have felt compelled to dispatch a Runner to conduct an official investigation of your possible involvement. So it may prove useful to have evidence that corroborates your innocence should things take an unpleasant turn," pointed out Tyler. "But more to the point, you have been bored of late. And you behave badly when you are bored. An intellectual conundrum always helps you keep your demons at bay."

He paused. "Solving this one has the added incentive of avoiding a trial for murder."

It was, reflected Wrexford, a confounded nuisance to employ a servant who was so infuriatingly astute.

"Bah." He made a face, but had to admit that the meeting had stirred a whole new set of questions. He wasn't sure he trusted Drummond. But if what he said about Canaday was true . . .

He hadn't realized that Canaday's interest in science was advanced enough to merit a laboratory at the Institution. And given the reverend's fiery orations against the pursuit of Godless Knowledge, a friendship between him and the baron seemed an odd match.

Against his better judgment he found himself curious as to what thread tied them together.

"Shall I flag down a hackney to take us home, milord?" inquired Tyler.

"You go on," he replied. "I think I shall first pay a visit to my club." It might be a waste of time, but he had an idea on where to start.

As his valet said, the hunt for answers might keep boredom at bay.

The reading room of White's exuded an aura of masculine comfort. The scent of well-worn leather, aged brandy, and printer's ink wafted through the fire-warmed air, punctuated by soft snoring and the occasional crackle of newsprint. Sheffield was ensconced in an armchair set near the blazing hearth, sipping a glass of ruby-red port while perusing the latest news from the Peninsula.

"Who was generous enough to indulge your taste for fine wine?" asked Wrexford as he approached. The bottle on the side table was an expensive vintage.

"You," replied his friend without looking up. "I told Jenkins to put it on your tab."

Wrexford signaled to the steward to bring another glass. "Dare I hope there's any left for me?"

"Naught but the dregs. You had better order another one."

He took a seat next to Sheffield and crossed his legs. "What do you know of Lord Robert Canaday?"

"Other than that he's a dab hand at cricket and a bit of a toadeater around those of higher rank?" Sheffield pursed his lips. "Hmmm, let me think."

"An exhausting task, I know."

"Do you wish to hear what else I know?" inquired Sheffield. "Or would you rather vent your ire by insulting me?"

Wrexford signaled the steward to uncork the fresh bottle of port. The wine was exceedingly good as well as exceedingly expensive. "Beggars can't be choosy."

Sheffield chuckled. "Point taken." He refilled his glass. "Canaday fancies himself an aesthete. He writes poetry—badly, I'm told—and belongs to an exclusive club whose members consider themselves artists and intellectuals."

"Do you know which one?" The description fit any number of smaller societies in Town. The interests were diverse—ranging from music and rare books to history and aeronautics—but what they all had in common was a pretentious preciousness about their own level of taste and discernment.

He preferred the simple snobbism of White's and Brooks. It was at least honest.

Sheffield tapped his fingertips together as he contemplated the earl's question. "Hmm. It's something like . . . The Artists." *Tap, tap.* "No, wait—The Ancients. It's called The Ancients."

Wrexford had never heard of it. "Any idea who else belongs to it?" he asked.

"Not a clue," answered Sheffield. He made a pained grimace. "I'd offer to stop by the Wolf's Lair this evening and make some inquiries. But I haven't a feather to fly with, and I can't very well strike up useful conversations if I'm confined to watching from the shadows."

Wrexford knew that despite his friend's outward nonchalance, it hurt his pride deeply to be kept on such short financial leash by his family. "Tyler tells me I should take the threat of a trial seriously, so you would be doing me a great favor if you would play at the tables tonight and see what you can learn." Exaggerating a sigh, he passed over a handful of bank notes. "Just remember that, unlike you, I expect a return on my investment."

CHAPTER 4

"Forgive me for interrupting your breakfast." Closing the door behind him, Tyler approached the head of the table. "But I thought you might wish to see this without delay."

Wrexford eyed the roll of paper and set down his cup. "I take it A. J. Quill's pen has not been idle."

"No." The oily bite of fresh ink cut through the aroma of coffee as the valet spread out the print.

"How the devil . . ." muttered Wrexford.

"How indeed," responded Tyler. "It would seem that the artist is as all-present as Satan."

"For him to know that Sheffield was present when the Runner was interrogating me, and that we were looking at Quill's print of the murder . . ." The earl pursed his lips. It would seem there were only two possible explanations. Neither of which were pleasant to contemplate. "The artist must be bribing the Runner." He looked up. "Or he is bribing you."

Tyler met his gaze without twitching a lash. "I shall forget you said that," he replied. "You never think very clearly before you have your eggs and gammon."

Wrexford chuffed a grudging laugh. "Not precisely true. I can on occasion exert myself. But point taken."

"By the by, if I needed money," added his valet, "I'd simply abscond with the family jewel collection that you keep in the safe of your study."

"It has an exceedingly complicated German lock."

A sniff. "Oh, please."

The earl let out another chuckle. "It's lucky for you that your arsenal of unusual skills proves useful at times."

"And for you, milord."

"True." A pause. "I'm quite aware that no one else would tolerate my peculiar sense of humor."

"I shall take that as both an apology and an expression of heartfelt thanks for enduring your irascible moods."

"Don't press your luck." Wrexford refilled his cup and took a sip. "It must be the cursed Runner who's selling his secrets."

"I think that unlikely," replied Tyler. "From what I've heard, Griffin is the best of the Bow Street lot. He has a reputation for scrupulous honesty. And dogged determination."

"Well, in this case, he is barking down the wrong vermin hole." Leaning back in his chair, he contemplated the ornate painted detailing on the Adam ceiling. *Twists and twines.* "I really do think it's about time I paid a visit to A. J. Quill. Any news from your Scottish tracker?"

Tyler curled a faint smile. "As a matter of fact, sir, he is waiting downstairs in the kitchen."

• • •

Rain pelted against the narrow mullioned window, as if the gods were taking perverse pleasure in echoing the faint *thump-thump* of foreboding inside her head. No doubt, mused Charlotte, the thought of primitive, pagan forces controlling the universe would be considered blasphemous in civilized London.

"Civilized—ha!" she whispered. A leading churchman savagely slaughtered, orphans and widows left to fend for themselves in the hardscrabble streets, the ravages of war draining the country's coffers. "The concepts of charity and kindness to all seem to have gone to hell in a handbasket."

Charlotte put down her pen and stared glumly at the drawing she was trying to finish. Prinny's accusing eyes stared back at her, half hidden in the corpulent folds of flesh she had made for his face. Normally she felt no compunction about skewering the Royals, but a dark mood had taken hold of her this morning, brought on perhaps by seeing the boys head out into the gloom. Raven had said that he wanted to search for more gossip on the Earl of Wrexford and the ongoing murder investigation.

She hated that they felt compelled to dig up dirt for her.

But dirt sold her satirical prints. And money put food in their mouths.

Ergo unum oportet esse pragmaticam.

"I must be pragmatic," she repeated aloud, hoping the spoken words might help chase away her malaise.

A gust of wet wind rattled the glass.

So much for incantations and talismans. They were fiddle-faddle for the foolish. Railing at Fate was a waste of breath. If one hoped to shape destiny, one had to do so with one's own hands.

After sharpening her quill, she resumed her work.

An hour passed, though as she glanced out the window Charlotte realized it might have been two. She often lost track of time when she was working. It was the growling in her stomach that had broken her concentration.

Or perhaps it was the faint rasp of metal on metal.

She froze and cocked an ear.

The sound came again.

The outer entryway had nothing to steal within the bare-bones space. But she always kept the main door locked, and aside from her only Raven had a key.

Snick. Snick. The latch slowly lifted.

Swallowing a spurt of panic, Charlotte grabbed her penknife. A meager weapon, to be sure, but if push came to shove, she'd learned a few nasty tricks over the years to fend off attack.

Steady, steady. She slipped off her chair.

The wall lamp shivered as the door creaked open. A figure stomped through the opening, his skirling overcoat sending a spray of raindrops spattering over the floor. Great gobs of viscous mud clung to his black boots.

They were exquisitely made, noted Charlotte in spite of her fear, the leather buffed to a soft sheen.

A gentleman, not a ruffian from the stews.

She jerked her gaze upward.

Well-tailored wool, burnished ebony buttons. Shoulder capes that accentuated the breadth of his shoulders.

She took an involuntary step back.

He pulled off his hat and slapped it against his thigh, sending more drops of water flying through the air. Wind-whipped hair, dark as coal, tangled around his face. At first, all Charlotte could make out was a prominent nose, long and with an arrogant flare to its tip. But as he took another stride closer, the rest of his features snapped into sharper focus. A sensuous mouth, high cheekbones, green eyes, darkened with an undertone of gunmetal grey.

Ye god, surely it couldn't be . . .

"Forgive me if I have frightened you, madam." He didn't look the least contrite. Indeed, there seemed to be a momentary flash of amusement as he flicked an emerald-sharp glance at the knife in her hand. "I am looking for A. J. Quill."

"You have come to the wrong place," replied Charlotte, dismayed to hear her voice had come out as a mouse-like squeak.

"I think not." He came closer. "The two little imps who deliver Quill's drawings were followed back to this house."

"Stay where you are!" she warned, trying to regain some semblance of control. "Another step and I'll scream."

"By all means go ahead and shriek to the high heavens. Though I imagine it will be a prodigious waste of breath." He placed a fist on his hip. "I doubt there are many Good Samaritans in this part of Town."

She thinned her lips, unwilling to give him the satisfaction of being right. "How dare you invade my home! Whoever you are, I demand you leave at once."

"How ungentlemanly of me. You're right—I neglected to introduce myself." A mocking bow. "I am Wrexford. I daresay you're familiar with my name."

Charlotte maintained a stony face. "No, I'm not. Now please leave, or . . . or . . ."

"Or you'll cut out my liver with that dainty little penknife?" He made a *tsk-tsk* sound. "Yes, well, A. J. Quill is quite skilled in skewering my person. Let him fight his own battles." Wrexford looked around the room. "Where is he?"

"I tell you, sir, you are mistaken—"

For a big man, he moved with feral quickness. A blur of wolf black, leaving the sensation of predatory muscle and primitive power pricking against her skin.

"Stop!" she began, the protest dying quickly as Wrexford leaned over her desk. And began to laugh.

"Your husband has captured Prinny's self-indulgent squint to perfection." He looked up. "That is, I assume he is your husband."

Charlotte didn't answer. Like a helpless mouse, she seemed frozen by her fate, waiting for the paw to flash out and deliver the inevitable coup de grace.

"Or perhaps it is a more casual arrangement?" His lidded gaze lingered for a moment on her face.

Think! Think! But all that came to mind was the overwhelming urge to stick the knife into one of his eyes.

"Ah, I see you're in no mood for pleasantries." Wrexford hooked one of the stools with his boot and pulled it over. "No matter. I'll wait."

Panic seized her. Charlotte felt as if its unseen hands were crushing her ribs, squeezing the breath out of her.

"You cannot!" she rasped. The knife slipped from her grasp and fell to the floor. Her hard-won existence shattering into a thousand tiny shards . . .

Suddenly fury crested over fear. She flew at

him, fists flailing. Be damned with the consequences. Her life was already over.

Wrexford caught her wrists, not before she
landed a nasty blow to his cheek. "Tut, tut, there
is no need for violence, madam. Your husband
and I can—" He stopped abruptly, those infernal
eyes now focused on the fingers of her right hand.
One by one, he pried them open.

She tried to pull away.

"Bloody hell," he breathed, studying the
smudges of ink. "Let me guess—it's not your
husband. It's *you* who are A. J. Quill."

Before his captive could answer, Wrexford heard
a primal cry and a pelter of footsteps. A ripping
sound, and in the same instant pain lancing
through his leg.

Whipping a knife from his boot, he spun around
and snagged the writhing little beastie before
it could stab the flashing blade into his flesh a
second time.

"Let him go!" screamed Mistress Quill. She
had her knife in hand again, and a fear-crazed
look on her face that said she would use it.

He drew the boy—he assumed it was a boy and
not a wild animal only because he had glimpsed
a hand rather than a hairy paw—close to his
chest, holding hard to control the wild thrashing.
Curses were falling like rain. A bottle, thrown
from somewhere to his rear, glanced off his skull.

And the infernal Mistress Quill had grabbed a cleaver from the stovetop—

"Silence!" he bellowed, brandished his weapon. "Not another word, not another movement or there will be hell to pay."

Everyone froze. Utter stillness descended upon the room.

A finger of chill air tickled through the rent in the finespun melton wool. Wrexford felt blood snaking down his skin. "Damnation," he muttered. "These were a pair of new trousers."

His words broke the fragile peace. The boy in his arms tried to break free. "Did he harm you, m'lady? If he did, I swear, I'll kill him."

"I'm quite fine, Raven," she assured him. "Please do as he says." Her gaze darted to the doorway. "And you, too, Hawk."

Pivoting, Wrexford spotted the second boy moving stealthily out of the shadows. Bloody hell, they were like rats spewing out of the moldings.

"Ye big bastard, are ye going to slit our throats with that shiv like ye did to the reverend?" rasped the boy in his arms.

"No one is going to be murdered," answered Wrexford. Whether that would prove true was by no means certain. "Perhaps if we all agree to cease hostilities and discuss the matter in a civilized fashion . . ." He looked back to Mistress Quill, tossing the gauntlet at her feet.

She hesitated, tucking an errant curl of unremarkable brown hair behind her ear. Her gown was an even drabber shade of the same color. He noted a discreetly mended tear at the cuff. All that dullness made the sapphirine glitter of her blue eyes appear even more arresting.

Their gazes locked for an instant, and as she gave a curt nod, he was suddenly aware of her height—she was tall for a woman, and though slender as a willow sapling, her form radiated a steely strength.

"No more attacks, lads." To Wrexford, she snapped, "Now put him down, and sheath your knife. You should be ashamed of yourself, frightening children with that monstrous weapon."

He couldn't hold back a snort. "Children, you say? My first guess was weasels."

The smaller boy crept a little closer. "Cor, that's a bloody big blade. Can I hold it?"

"Absolutely not. Your friend here did enough damage with his pinstick."

The earl gingerly set down his captive, who responded with a string of obscenities.

"Raven," chided Mistress Quill. "Mind your manners."

To his surprise, the boy mumbled an apology as he crouched down to retrieve his weapon. It was, noted Wrexford, a simple scrap of steel, sharpened on one side and tapered to a lethal point. Crude but effective.

"Aye, it may be a pinstick," added Raven belligerently. "But lay another hand on m'lady and you'll find it shoved straight through your guts."

What the wretched little imp lacked in size and bulk, he made up for in courage. Wrexford acknowledged the warning with a solemn nod. "Fair enough, lad."

As the boy put away his blade, the earl did the same, using the moment to take another look around the room. There was no evidence of a male presence, only the telltale signs of a household living on the edge of respectability. The table held only the simple necessities, and the lamps were burning cheap tallow candles— save for a fancy Argent lamp on a large work desk. As for food, he saw only the remains of a rye loaf on the sideboard.

He straightened, aware that the two boys were watching him, the flickering flames setting off sparks of gold in their fierce little eyes. Their avian monikers were appropriate. They reminded him of baby raptors. All gristle and bone. Wary. Wild. Primed to explode into savage violence.

Wrexford reached into his pocket and slowly pulled out his purse. "I have always found that negotiations go more smoothly over a meal." He shook two guineas into his palm and held them out to the one called Raven. "Why don't you and your companion run out and buy us some meat pasties . . . and whatever else you wish."

The glittering coins had a mesmerizing effect. Their eyes widened but they didn't move a muscle.

"Come, take them," he murmured. "You have my word of honor your m'lady will be safe with me. I simply wish to talk."

Longing lit in the scrawny face of the one called Hawk. He let out a tiny sigh.

Mistress Quill flicked a subtle signal, a mere tweak of her finger.

Raven's reaction was swift. He snatched the money and flew for the door, his smaller shadow right behind him.

"Now, as I was saying before we were so rudely interrupted," intoned Wrexford, once they were gone, "I came here looking for A. J. Quill, and it appears that I have found my quarry." He indicated one of the stools. "Do have a seat, m'lady. We have a great many things to discuss."

CHAPTER 5

"Actually, I have nothing to say to you, sir," said Charlotte.

"I beg to differ." Wrexford spoke softly, but his tone was all too familiar. The aristocratic assumption that his Word was God.

She hated him already.

"You are clearly privy to all sorts of secrets here in Town. I wish to know how you obtain them."

Charlotte responded with a harsh laugh. "If wishes were unicorns, we could all fly to the moon."

His dark brows pinched together. She had angered him. Whether that was wise or not remained to be seen.

Auribus teneo lupum. There was an old Latin adage about having a wolf by its ears.

In the shifting shapes cast by the candle flames, the earl had a decidedly lupine look. Dark hair tangled around a long face, sharp chin—

"A whimsical image," growled Wrexford. "But allow me to remind you this is not a whimsical moment. There's been a grisly murder, and your artwork is provoking the public to believe that I am the culprit."

Charlotte inhaled sharply. The earl was accusing

her of inflammatory behavior? "I am not to blame for your sordid reputation," she retorted. "I simply observe and listen to what goes on around me, then depict facts that I have gathered. How people choose to interpret them is not my concern."

His gaze turned lidded, the black scrim of lashes hiding his eyes. "An interesting explanation. I'll not argue that my actions attract a certain notoriety." He shifted as a gust of air blew in through the cracks in the window casement, setting the shoulder capes of his dark coat to flapping like the wings of a bat.

She looked away, swallowing a spurt of fear. This man could destroy her with a snap of his well-tended fingers. She must temper her outrage and try to survive.

"What I do care about," continued the earl, "is how you gather your facts. They are . . . frighteningly accurate."

Strangely enough, he sounded faintly amused.

Perhaps there was hope.

"And as it would seem that you don't come by your information through bribery or influence, I can't help but ask—how the devil do you learn all these things?"

The edge of wry humor was now unmistakable. Charlotte decided there was little harm in giving him a halfway truthful answer.

"It's not nearly as nefarious as you might think. The notion that a secret can remain sacred is, for the most part, a delusion. We may think we hide them away in the deepest, darkest private places, where they will remain safe." She curled a rueful grimace. "But secrets have a way of slipping out. I merely pay attention to their whispers."

His expression remained inscrutable. "How?"

A smile crept to her lips. "I see no reason to divulge that secret so easily to you. If you wish to discover the answer, you are welcome to try."

He gingerly shifted his stance, and Charlotte suddenly remembered the nasty ripping sound of expensive fabric. That quality of wool would likely cost her a fortnight's earnings.

"Do you require a bandage for your wound, sir?"

"No. It's just a scratch. I'll survive." He took a moment to examine the gash. "Alas, the same cannot be said for my trousers."

"My apologies," she said stiffly. "Raven and Hawk have no nest of their own. I suppose the fact that I allow them to shelter here whenever they wish and feed them when I can makes them feel protective of me."

Wrexford seemed surprised. "They aren't yours?"

"No."

He waited, as if expecting her to add a further explanation. When she didn't, he shrugged. "Loyalty is an admirable trait, m'lady. But given the lad's current size and strength, he needs to be more careful. Not everyone will be as tolerant as I am."

"I have endeavored to explain that to him."

"Try again." Lapsing into silence, he moved to her desk and regarded the drawing of the Prince Regent for an uncomfortably long interlude before settling himself on one of the stools. "Why do the lads call you 'm'lady'?" he asked abruptly.

The question wasn't entirely unexpected. Charlotte had long ago come up with a facile explanation. "My late husband called me that as . . . as a silly endearment. The boys simply mimicked him."

His gaze darted back to her desk. She wasn't sure why.

"Was your loss recent?"

Charlotte hesitated, wondering why he was probing.

"Perhaps eight months ago?" he added.

The room suddenly began to sway. She sat, praying the light-headedness would quickly pass. It was imperative to keep all her wits about her. The earl struck her as a man who would give no quarter. And she still did not know why he was here.

"W-Why do you ask?" she countered.

Another glance at her desk. She felt a trickle of sweat slide down her spine. Had she left some telltale clue exposed?

"Because," Wrexford finally said, "now that I think of it, A. J. Quill's style changed right around then. The drawing became surer, the satire sharper."

The earl was far more perceptive than she imagined. Which made him exceedingly dangerous.

"My guess is, your late husband was the original artist, and you continued his business when he stuck his spoon in the wall."

Deciding it was pointless to deny it, Charlotte gave a confirming nod. "It seemed the pragmatic thing to do. It earns more than scrubbing floors for the likes of you and your privileged peers."

Wrexford steepled his fingers. "Oh, I think it's more than pragmatism. Art is passion, not a practicality, Missus . . ."

"You know nothing about me," she replied coldly.

"Not even your name," he quipped.

Charlotte was tiring of the cat-and-mouse games. "Let us cut to the chase, sir. Why are you here?"

As the question hung in the unsettled air, Wrexford was acutely aware of a number of sensations. The sting of his lacerated flesh, the hardness of the stool, the chill of the room, the scrutiny of m'lady, whose stare was like a myriad of needles prickling against his eyeballs.

This meeting was not at all what he had expected. It had seemed a simple undertaking. His rank and influence would intimidate A. J. Quill into spilling his secrets. But the earl sensed there was nothing simple about m'lady. Bullying wouldn't work. She had already shown herself to have a spine of steel, along with a quickness of wit in their thrust-and-parry battle of wills.

And here she was, unblinking.

"As I said," he answered slowly, "I'm looking for information."

"Look elsewhere," she snapped. "Sharing isn't good for business. I make my living knowing things that others don't."

"It's not entirely out of idle curiosity, though I confess that how you do it intrigues me," said the earl. Her eyes seemed to possess an unfathomable depth. Shadows spiraled beneath the surface, plunging down through shades of cerulean to indigo black. "My valet is urging me to gather the facts about the murder, as it may prove helpful in avoiding a hangman's noose." He stretched out his legs and crossed his booted feet at the ankles. "In case it matters to you, I'm innocent."

"It doesn't," she said. "Matter, that is." As she turned her head slightly, the lamplight caught the subtle Mars-red highlights in her hair. Cinnabar and auburn shades were woven through the mouse brown. Yet another reminder that nothing about her was as if first seemed.

97

"As I've told you, it's simply a business, milord," she went on. "I do what I have to do in order to survive."

"Don't we all?" he muttered.

Her face tightened in the uncertain candlelight. Slanted cheekbones, full mouth, both a bit too strong for her to be considered a conventional beauty. No doubt she frightened many men.

"Somehow I doubt that the fight for survival is an experience you confront every day," she replied.

"As we only die once, the number of threats seems irrelevant."

Perhaps it was merely a quirk of the flames, but it seemed that a smile flitted across her lips.

"You seem a shrewd woman. Surely we can come to some sort of bargain."

She looked down, and several long moments passed as she considered his words.

Deciding on what sum she dared to demand? It would be a hefty one. She was no fool.

"Sorry, but I'm not interested in making a deal."

"Is there a particular reason?"

"Whether you believed me or not, I *am* pragmatic. And you are worth a great deal to me as a murder suspect. Bow Street hounding you . . . a trial in the House of Lords . . . the gibbet going up at Tyburn. Why, the scandal could go on for months and months."

Wrexford blew out a mournful sigh. "I had hoped to appeal to your better nature, m'lady—"

"Do stop calling me that," she interrupted. "It's a moniker reserved for my friends."

"You've given me no other name," he pointed out.

"Mrs. Sloane," she said tersely.

"Very well." A small bit of information about her. As were the row of leather-bound books at the back of her desk, whose titles included classic works of history and modern poetry. Mrs. Sloane was a far more educated woman than her present circumstances indicated. Whether that would prove useful remained to be seen.

"As I was saying," he went on, "I would prefer not to resort to threats, but it seems you give me no choice."

Charlotte waited, the *thump-thump* of her heart against her rib cage making it hard for her to breathe.

"Your career as a satirist depends on anonymity. Were I to expose your identity, I doubt Fores would wish to keep you employed. A woman poking fun at the great men in Society?" He shook his head. "It wouldn't fadge."

Bile rose in her throat, hot as acid. "You would strip me of my livelihood?" She pitched her voice low, yet it was shaking with rage "Force me—and the lads—to become paupers to fend for ourselves on the streets? All because I am a woman who dares exercise her talents to survive?"

The earl's face might well have been carved of granite. Not a muscle twitched. Shadows danced, dark on dark, through his long, curling hair. He appeared implacable, impervious to any appeal for mercy.

Charlotte knew she should have been repelled, but something about the hard-edged planes and sculpted contours of his features held her in thrall. There was a cold beauty to him, and she felt her fingers itch to take up her paintbrush and capture that chilling aura of a man in supreme command of his emotions.

"I'm merely asking for any information you hear that relates to Holworthy's murder, nothing more. And I am not asking you to aid me from the goodness of your heart." Wrexford added slowly, his growl rough with sarcasm, "I shall pay you very well. Far more, in fact, than you earn from your tawdry scribbles."

Stung by his scorn, Charlotte retorted, "Call them what you will, but my art makes quite a lot of blunt."

"And as I said, I'll pay you more." He then named a sum that made her blink.

"H-How do I know you'll keep your bargain on that?" she demanded.

"Because you have my word on it." Wrexford

shifted on the stool, the slight movement causing the candle flames to sputter. "As a gentleman."

"Ha. You may have a high and mighty title, milord, but from all I know of your life, you are no gentleman."

That brought the first flicker of emotion to his face. "You are welcome to ridicule my less than admirable exploits, Mrs. Sloane. But question my honor and—"

"And what? You will challenge me to a duel?" she cut in. "Be advised, I, too, have a very large knife and know how to use it."

The room went unnaturally still. Charlotte tensed. The earl was notorious for having an explosive temper. And she had just tossed a handful of sparks into the powder keg.

He leaned forward—and let out a peal of laughter.

"Carve me to shreds on paper, Mrs. Sloane. But I have a feeling that in person we will rub together quite enough.

"W-What makes you think that?"

"Because I take care never to underestimate the absurdity of mankind."

"You have a very cynical view of human nature, milord."

"Which is something we have in common," he replied.

The statement took Charlotte aback. "There is a fundamental difference between us, milord. I observe the nuances of how people behave and record what I see in order to earn a living. But, unlike you, I take no glee in the foibles of others."

"And yet you expose those unfortunate to draw your eye to public ridicule and profit from it. So do you really think you have the right to stand on higher moral ground?"

Charlotte looked away, feeling a little shaken. Was he right? A part of her did take satisfaction in skewering greed, arrogance, and hypocrisy. Did that make her a hypocrite too?

"I make no claim to be a saint, Lord Wrexford," she said softly.

He laughed again. "All the more reason we will deal well together." He cocked his head. "We *do* have a deal, don't we?"

"Given the alternative, you seem the lesser of two evils," answered Charlotte. "However, I do have one other demand before the bargain is sealed."

"The sum I offered is a handsome one—"

"I'm not asking for more money, sir."

His brows rose in question.

"What I want from you is time. Not a great deal of it, as I imagine you are a busy man."

"Might I ask for what reason?"

In for a penny, in for a pound. "You have an interesting face. I'd like you to sit for a sketch."

"You've already drawn me," he said dryly. "Numerous times."

"Not a caricature, sir. A watercolor portrait," explained Charlotte. "Simply for art's sake. It won't be displayed in public."

"The request seems harmless enough," he murmured. "Very well, I agree to your terms."

"Then yes, we have a deal, sir."

"Excellent." The earl looked pleased. Or perhaps a better word was *satisfied*. He took out another purse from his coat pocket and carefully pushed it across the table. It was considerably larger than the one he had shown to the boys. "Consider this an advance on my promise, Mrs. Sloane. A token that you may trust me."

Trust. He could purchase a great many things from her, but trust was not one of them.

Charlotte reached out and took the purse. The chamois was tantalizingly soft against her work-callused fingers, the sonorous kiss of gold against gold a sound she hadn't heard since . . .

Since a long time ago.

Was she making a pact with the Devil? Shaking off a frisson of unease, she tucked it deep within the folds of her gown. It was simply business. There was no reason to feel as if a jolt of unseen electricity had singed her skin.

"I assume you want a token in return," she said, meeting his gaze. It was unwavering, and yet she sensed he, too, was not unmoved by the moment. "You came here for information—where shall we start?"

The earl didn't hesitate. "I'd like to have an idea of how you hear all the whispered secrets that you say are floated so freely around Town."

"As I said, it's not nearly as nefarious as you think," answered Charlotte. "I hear things through a great many different sources. To begin with, servants offer a wealth of information. Take, for example, my neighbor's daughter, who works as a tweeny in one of the mansions of Mayfair. The things employers allow their hired help to see and hear would make your hair stand on end. And of course they gossip among themselves, so the secrets spread like wildfire through the underbelly of your gilded world."

Wrexford nodded thoughtfully. "Go on."

"I'm patient and willing to piece together all the little bits of color that paint the larger picture. The boys also know a great many of the ordinary eyes and ears in London—the people you think of as invisible. Chimney sweeps, costermongers, flower sellers, shopkeepers." She paused. "The urchins who clean the muck from the street crossings so you don't befoul your expensive boots."

He gazed down at the muddy tips. "I have noticed you seem inordinately interested in my boots. You keep staring at them."

She shrugged, not ready to reveal her reason quite yet.

Wrexford didn't press her. His attention was

already elsewhere. "Your overview has been most enlightening, but I have a few specific questions I'd like answered." He sat up a little straighter, the intensity of his eyes sharpening. "Were your depictions of the burns on Holworthy's face accurate?"

"Yes," said Charlotte.

"How?" he demanded.

Ah, secrets must now be sacrificed for shillings. She must be very careful in deciding what was—and was not—for sale.

This detail, however, seemed safe enough to hand over. "Because I viewed the body before the night watchman returned with the authorities."

He looked about to speak, but Charlotte quickly added, "Raven and Hawk heard the watchman screaming about a murder, and rushed to fetch me. And before you ask, I am very observant. I get the little details right."

He made a face. "You are a singular woman, Mrs. Sloane. Most females would have swooned at the grisly sight."

"I am not like most women, Lord Wrexford."

"So I am learning." He rubbed at his chin. "Hell's bells, I would have liked to see the body for myself. Observant as you are, you're not an expert in chemistry. It might prove very helpful to know exactly what substances were used."

Charlotte saw a way to earn a bit more of the small fortune he had just paid to her. "I happen to know the body was taken to Basil Henning, a medical man in Seven Dials, whose surgery was closest to the church."

"Henning?" repeated Wrexford. "A gruff, gravel-voiced Scot?"

She nodded. "You know him?"

"Our paths crossed briefly just before the debacle at Corunna."

Wrexford was in the Peninsula during General Moore's ill-fated retreat from the French army? That took Charlotte by surprise. "I didn't realize you had been in the military, Lord Wrexford."

"Ah, so not all my secrets are grist for your scandal mill?" His voice held no edge. "In fact, I had no official rank. I was only there for a short time gathering facts for a friend in the Foreign Office."

Charlotte suspected there was far more to the story, but the earl's past was none of her concern. She said nothing, waiting for him to go on.

"Can you give me his direction?"

She described the surgery's location.

"Thank you, Mrs. Sloane. You've already proved that my investment in you was a wise one." Wrexford stretched out his legs. There had been no man in her house since Anthony's death, and the earl's presence seemed to dominate the room, crowding out all else.

Charlotte tried to draw in a deep breath. But even the air felt squeezed from the space.

"I wish to pay Henning a visit, so I shall leave you and your two fledglings to your feast." He rose with a lazy grace. "Just one last thing before I go. Though you claim to be ruled by pragmatism, I doubt you would have agreed to partner with me if you thought I was guilty of Holworthy's murder."

"Money persuades most people to forget their tender scruples."

"But, as you pointed out, you are not like most people," he answered.

She shifted, uncomfortably aware of the purse's weight in her pocket.

He was watching her intently. "What are you holding back?"

"Nothing," lied Charlotte.

The earl stood very still, an ominous black silhouette against the grey-misted panes of the window. "Very well, we will leave it at that." Turning, he put on his hat and angled the brim to hide his face. "For now."

CHAPTER 6

A fugue of festering smells assaulted his nose as he crossed the narrow swath of yard between the surgery and the small outbuilding that served as the mortuary.

Death was never pretty, reflected Wrexford, save in the grandiose heroic paintings of war and sacrifice made by artists who had never experienced the stench of blood or screams of the dying.

He rapped on the door, and after a long moment a muffled voice bade him to enter.

"I'm busy." The guttering lamplight illuminated a man hunched over a stone slab. He had not yet bothered to turn around. "Whatever you want, be quick about it."

"I doubt the fellow you are tending gives a rat's arse whether there's a slight delay in wrapping him in his shroud." The earl could just make out a pair of bare legs and yellowing toes behind the surgeon.

Henning—Wrexford recognized the man's profile as he looked around—squinted uncertainly. "Your voice is familiar. Who are you?"

"Wrexford," replied the earl. "We met during Moore's campaign."

"Bloody idiot."

He wasn't sure whether Henning was referring to him or the late general.

"A senseless slaughter of our soldiers," muttered the surgeon. "A brave man, but bacon brained when it came to organizing the retreat."

Ah, the general.

"So," went on Henning, "have you come to ask me to prepare your corpse for the Hereafter, after the Crown's executioner has finished with you?" The surgeon was known for his sardonic sense of humor. "It appears your recklessness has finally caught up with you. A pity. You have a decent mind when you choose to use it."

"I'm not dead yet, and I intend to keep it that way for a little while longer. Speaking of which, how is Saybrook?" Wrexford knew the surgeon was a good friend of the Earl of Saybrook, an acquaintance of Wrexford's from his Oxford days.

"His wounds are slowly healing. But the laudanum is taking a toll."

Yet another casualty of the interminable war with France. The brutal conflict had cut down more friends than he cared to count. Lord Saybrook had nearly lost a leg in the fighting. "I've stopped by his town house on several occasions, but was told he turns away all visitors."

"Aye. For now, he prefers to battle his demons alone," said Henning, wiping his none too pristine hands on his bloody apron. "So, what battle brings you here, laddie? For I am assuming you did not stop to take tea and cakes in my drawing room."

"Correct." Wrexford moved closer and eyed the half-stitched incision in the cadaver's chest. "I have a few questions about Reverend Holworthy's corpse. I was told by an acquaintance of yours that his body had been brought here after its discovery."

"It was," confirmed Henning. "Do you mean to say it wasn't you who doused his phiz with chemicals and sliced his throat open from ear to ear?" He began rearranging the set of scalpels on the slab. "I heard rumors on the Peninsula that you were a dab hand with a blade."

"Knives and chemicals? Oh, come—I may be reckless but I'm not stupid, Henning. I might as well have left a calling card with the corpse." He spotted several canvas-covered shapes deep in the shadows. "I don't suppose you still have the remains here?"

"The Church of England was quick to remove his carcass from my unholy ground." A grim smile. "I would have assured them I'm not a Presbyterian, but I doubt they have any higher regard for atheism."

"I see," murmured Wrexford. "Dare I hope you took a close look at his face before they carted him away?"

"Interested in the chemical burns, eh?"

He nodded.

"Lucky for you I have an interest in science and not simply sawing bones." Henning set aside his surgical tools. "Come let us step outside where the air is a trifle less noxious."

Wrexford repressed a smile as they made their way to the far end of the yard. Henning resembled a walking gorse bush—his salt-and-pepper hair stuck out in spikey points, his jaw bristled with a two-day stubble, his pockets bulged with all sorts of sharp implements.

Turning, the surgeon pulled a pipe and a pouch of tobacco from inside his coat. A strike of flint against steel produced a plume of pungent blue smoke.

"What, exactly, do you want to know?"

"Based on your friend's satirical print—which, by the by, she claims is quite accurate—I have a suspicion of what chemicals were used," answered the earl. "I'm hoping you might be able confirm it."

"Ah, so you've met Mrs. Sloane. An interesting woman. And yes, I've found her to have a very observant eye," murmured Henning. "Luckily for you, I have some knowledge of chemistry. A friend at the University in St. Andrews is a leading expert in the field." He then rattled off a list.

Wrexford nodded thoughtfully. His experiments were right. But that didn't quite explain . . .

Henning interrupted his musings. "One thing that did strike me as unusual. The discoloration

111

of the flesh had a strange hue around its edges. It looked to me like a rather large quantity of mercury had been part of the mix."

"Mercury is an odd element to add to a caustic liquid. It doesn't make any sense."

"Nor does nearly severing a man's head from his neck," remarked Henning dryly. "However, I long ago ceased to be shocked by the atrocities man will inflict on his fellow man."

"Anything else I should be aware of?"

Henning drew in a mouthful of smoke and slowly let it out. "Nothing that comes to mind."

Wrexford wasn't sure if the surgeon's information would be of any use, but nonetheless he thanked him for sparing the time.

"No matter. I was anxious to blow a cloud—though a dram of whisky would be even more welcome. The fellow inside is getting rather ripe, which makes stitching him up deucedly difficult." Henning took another few puffs. "Why the interest in Holworthy's body? As far as I've heard, there is no tangible evidence to tie you to the murder. And the House of Lords isn't going to hang one of their own based on gossip, no matter how lurid."

"Let's just say I'm curious," answered the earl.

"Auch, just remember, laddie—it's said that curiosity kills the cat."

"It's also said that cats have nine lives."

"The question," shot back Henning, "is how

many of them have you already used up?"

Wrexford shrugged. "I'm not very good at mathematics." Which was a lie. In any case, simple addition showed that the ledger added up in favor of the Grim Reaper.

A laugh, short and rough, rumbled in Henning's throat before giving way to a cough. "I, too, find I'm curious about something. How did you learn that Mrs. Sloane is A. J. Quill? She takes great care to keep her identity a secret."

"To toss out yet another old adage, what's good for the goose is good for the gander," quipped Wrexford. "I merely employed the same tactics of careful observation that she uses."

"Don't make trouble for her," said the surgeon, a note of warning shading the casual comment. "She doesn't deserve it."

Henning was hard as Highland granite. That he appeared to have a soft spot for the widow piqued his interest. "How is it that you know her?"

"Her late husband was a patient. His health was fragile—weak lungs, a condition exacerbated by their return to London from the warmer, drier climes of Italy."

"What made them return?"

"Anthony Sloane was a brilliant artist. He craved recognition for his talents." Henning tapped his pipe against his boot, sending a shower of burnt ashes over the muddy ground. "But I've seen his wife's paintings. She possesses an even greater talent. I can't help but wonder if that drove him mad."

"Mad?" The earl raised his brows. "That sounds rather gothic. Like something out of *The Castle of Otranto*, what with its clanking chains, supernatural curses, and tortured villains."

"Aye, well, Sloane's behavior turned awfully erratic in the weeks before his death. He was always a sensitive soul. Perhaps too sensitive. He started having inexplicable mood swings, uncontrollable tremors, and terrible headaches." The surgeon's expression hardened. "I had the feeling that his wife was forced to take on all the responsibilities of running the household and finances as well as to minister to Sloane's increasingly irrational behavior."

It wasn't an uncommon story within the less prosperous parts of London. Hardship seemed to suck the life out of men, while the women found the strength and resilience to survive.

"At the end, he was muttering to me about guilt and shame—about what he wouldn't say," went on Henning. "Delusions, no doubt. Indeed, I suspect that he might have deliberately taken too great a dose of laudanum to silence the devils in his head. But I did not say so to Mrs. Sloane."

Wrexford suspected that if that were true, she would know it without being told. Nor would the damning knowledge crush her.

"She seems a very resourceful woman," he said

aloud. "It was clever of her to think of taking over her husband's trade."

"Aye, Mrs. Sloane is sharper than a scalpel. But a hard life hasn't dulled her elemental kindness. Despite her own straitened circumstances, she comes regularly to my clinic, where she teaches women from the rookeries to read."

Yet another facet to the widow. Which only made her more of an enigma.

"I wouldn't have taken her for one of the selfless women who dedicate themselves to doing good works."

Henning let out a low snort. "She claims it's not out of simple Christian charity. She believes knowledge is power, and reading is a skill that helps her fellow females fight back against those who would take advantage of them. It's also a way to find a decent job, rather than be forced to toss up their skirts in order to survive."

"Educated women?" The earl gave a mock grimace. "It makes a man shudder to think about it."

"Auch, laddie, they couldn't do worse than us at running the world." The surgeon tucked his pipe into his pocket. "I better get back to work. I have to run a clinic for wounded war veterans later this afternoon, and I need to have that slab o' meat inside ready for the mortuary wagon before then."

Making a mental note to send a generous

donation to the surgery, Wrexford cocked a quick salute and turned for the gate leading out to the alleyway.

"Wait!"

He looked around.

"I just remembered an odd bit of news I heard from my local apothecary last week," called Henning. "Apparently there have been a rash of robberies at apothecary shops over the last fortnight. The only thing taken was mercury. Quite a lot by the sound of how many shops were struck."

Mercury was a prime ingredient in a number of common medicines, but Wrexford didn't see how that would make it a valuable commodity for a thief.

"Any idea as to why?" he asked.

"Not a bloody clue," answered the surgeon cheerfully. "You're the curious cat looking to sniff out answers."

"Owwff." Hawk rolled onto his back and looked longingly at what remained of the buttery chunk of cheese in his hand. "It's so good, but I can't eat another bite."

"That doesn't surprise me," said Charlotte. "You and Raven already finished off two kidney pies and an eel pasty."

"And a wedge of apple tart," volunteered Raven. He, too, was lying on the rag rug by the stove, peeling an orange.

Oh, the tart, thick with creamy custard, had been gloriously good. Charlotte couldn't remember the last time she had indulged in such a luxury. "We can save the cheese, along with the rest of the food, for tomorrow." She rose and gently pried it from Hawk's sticky fingers. He was already half asleep, and though his face was liberally caked with crumbs, she didn't have the heart to wake him and insist that he wash himself.

Stepping over Raven's outstretched legs, she watched him pop several slices of the fruit into his mouth. "I vow, we've enough food left over te feed a regiment."

He grinned. "His Lordship was daft enough to give me that much blunt for vittles, so I figgered there was no harm in spending it." He fished out some coins from his jacket. "We tried, but we couldn't gobble it all up." A sigh. "Do we have to give it back?"

"I don't think Lord Wrexford expects it. You keep it, so that you and Hawk may purchase pasties when you are hungry."

"Naw, you keep it. Mebbe next week we can have another feast."

"An excellent suggestion." Charlotte carefully selected two shillings from the remaining coins and handed them back. "Still, I would rest easier knowing you have these in your pocket."

The boy didn't argue. After inching closer to the

warmth of the stove, he laced his hands behind his head. "Is His Lordship going te make trouble fer you, m'lady?"

"No." She hoped that was the truth.

"What did he want? A fancy toff like him don't come to this part of Town fer no reason."

Damnation—Raven was too sharp by half. She had hoped he wouldn't ask. Deciding it was best to tell him about the arrangement she had made with the earl—or a simplified version of it—Charlotte answered, "He wanted information about the reverend's murder. We came to an agreement about sharing what I know."

A frown pinched at his narrow face. "How did he cobble that you're A. J. Quill? You've always told us that it be very dangerous for anyone te know."

"It doesn't matter," she said quickly. "Lord Wrexford has agreed to keep my secret safe in return for my cooperation. And I believe he'll keep his end of the bargain."

As long as I keep mine.

Thankfully Raven seemed satisfied with the explanation. He let out a yawn and rolled onto his side. In another moment, his soft, snuffing breathing indicated he was, like his brother, fast asleep.

Her belly full, Charlotte was feeling pleasantly drowsy, too. And yet a niggling sense of foreboding kept her awake. Had she made a grave mistake? The first steps on the road to perdition were always taken with the best of intentions.

Choices, choices.

"Aye, but I chose my path long ago," she whispered, "and now I must follow it, come what may."

The earl's money would allow her to splurge and purchase some much-needed clothing on Petticoat Lane for the boys. And perhaps weekly lessons from the young curate of the parish church. *A new oil lamp for the dining table, extra blankets, caulking to fix the loose windowpanes . . .* Compiling a list of long-delayed necessities helped ease her misgivings.

If she had made a deal with the devil, at least he was a wealthy one.

Charlotte ignored the pricking of her conscience as she recalled the small scrap of paper tucked in a safe hiding place, along with the earl's bulging purse. Yes, she had held it back. But life in this part of London had taught that a bargaining chip was always a valuable commodity.

Thoughts of money slowly stirred her to pick up her pen. Lord Wrexford's payments wouldn't last forever. Survival hinged on keeping her own skills razor sharp.

Ex nihilo nihil fit. From nothing comes nothing. Time to get back to work.

She pulled a fresh sheet of drawing paper from her desk drawer and started to sketch.

・・・

Mercury. In Roman mythology, Mercury was the god of financial gain, mused Wrexford. He was also the god of trickery and thieves.

The irony was not lost on him.

Some perverse power seemed at play here. The more he learned, the less all the facts fit together into any coherent pattern. And as a man who respected scientific principles, that annoyed him.

Most everything had a logical explanation. One just had to see it—

"Ah, there you are!" drawled Sheffield as Wrexford entered his study. "I was wondering when the devil you would return. I've been waiting here for hours."

"It does not look as though you have been enduring any great suffering in my absence."

A bottle of prime Madeira was open on the side table, and a plate of sliced roast beef, bread, and pickle was resting in his friend's lap.

"Riche thought I looked a little peaked. So he offered refreshments," replied Sheffield. "Alas, he refused to hand over the humidor containing your special spiced Indian cheroots."

"He knows I would have had *his* head as well as yours on a platter," growled the earl.

"Tut, tut, let us not speak of severed necks. It rather ruins a fellow's appetite."

Wrexford poured himself a glass of wine and sat down in the facing armchair. He was tired and out of sorts. "Be so good as to swallow your witticisms along with your food and then be on your way. I need some peace and quiet in which to think."

"About what?" inquired Sheffield.

"About how to keep *my* neck from being stretched several more inches," he snapped back.

"Pffft." His friend waved off the comment. "Unless Griffin has found new evidence at the church, there isn't a snowball's chance in hell that you will swing for the murder." He took a large bite of bread topped with beef and chewed thoughtfully. "He hasn't, has he?"

"Not to my knowledge." Wrexford sunk deeper into the leather cushions. Suspect or not, the crime was now like a thorn rubbing against raw skin. "But I thank you for your overwhelming concern."

"No need to be sarcastic," responded Sheffield. "I haven't been frittering away the hours in idle pleasure." Setting aside his plate, he rose and sauntered to the sideboard to refill his glass. "It turns out you were right to be curious about Lord Robert Canaday."

CHAPTER 7

Wrexford sat up a little straighter. "Now you have my attention."

"I thought I might." Sheffield took a swallow of wine.

"Ye god, you should have pursued a career on the stage," he groused. "You bloody well play a dramatic moment to the hilt."

"While often overacting the role of court jester," conceded his friend. "Now, about Canaday— word around the gambling salon last night was that Canaday and Holworthy did indeed know each other. Holworthy was also a member of The Ancients, and they shared an interest in religious poetry."

"Interesting," murmured Wrexford.

"Yes, but even more interesting is the fact that they apparently had a recent falling-out. One of the gamesters heard that there was quite a shouting match between them, and it ended with Canaday threatening the reverend with violence."

"Over what?"

"No one seemed to know."

"Well done, Kit." Finally, a lead that felt as if he wasn't just chasing after shadows. "I think I shall have to pay Canaday a visit."

"I thought you might say that." Sheffield looked

very pleased with himself. "I've learned that he engaged to dine at White's with Yarmouth tonight. After their meal, they will be playing whist with Fielding and Barbury in the card room."

Wrexford angled a look at the mantel clock. He had a few hours to spare, and he found that the solitude of his laboratory and the precise focus needed to perform an experiment often stimulated sudden moments of clarity concerning other problems.

The mind, he had discovered, worked in strange ways.

"Excellent. I shall plan on meeting him there."

"Would you care for company?" asked Sheffield casually.

"By which you mean you want me to pay for your supper."

"A man can't live on thanks alone."

That provoked a laugh. "You look to be living quite well on the largesse of my wine cellar and kitchens."

"You can afford it."

"Leave me in peace for a few hours and I shall consider it. I have a few things to attend to in my laboratory."

Sheffield drained his glass. "Then I shall return anon."

"A moment, Canaday." Wrexford caught up with the baron as he and his friend turned down the corridor to the card room. "Might I have a word with you?"

"I'm engaged for a game of whist right now," answered Canaday. "Perhaps tomorrow—"

"It won't take long," interrupted Wrexford. He indicated one of the side rooms. "And I'd rather not wait until tomorrow."

The baron frowned, but after a slight hesitation, he signaled for his friend to go on without him. "Very well. I can spare a moment. But no more."

Wrexford closed the door behind them. On spotting Sheffield standing by the mullioned window, Canaday's tone turned even sharper. "I say, what's this all about?"

"Your close friendship with the late Reverend Holworthy. I understand the two of you were members of a club called The Ancients."

"Yes, we were both members, but I would hardly call us friends."

"And yet you were overheard having a very heated argument. One that you ended by threatening the reverend with violence," countered the earl. "Would you care to explain that?"

The baron bristled. "No, sirrah, I would not! Indeed, I don't intend to answer any of your damnably insolent questions. Now kindly step away from the door."

"I shall do so, but first allow me to point out that either you may answer my questions here in private, gentleman to gentleman, or you may answer a Bow Street Runner's questions in whatever venue he chooses for the confrontation." Wrexford paused. "And I daresay his will be a good deal more insolent than mine."

Canaday's fleshy face tightened and turned a mottled red, but after releasing an angry huff, he retreated a step. Some vestiges of athletic quickness remained, but his large body was turning flabby. "As I said, I was not friends with Holworthy. We shared an interest in poetry and occasionally discussed Wordsworth and some classical Latin works, but that was the extent of our acquaintance. In fact, if you must know the reason of the quarrel, it concerned poetry books."

"You threatened to come to blows over books?" Wrexford raised a brow. "Forgive me if I find that hard to believe."

"Nonetheless, it's true," insisted Canaday. "My estate library in Kent is known for its collection of rarified books. Holworthy sent me an urgent request several weeks ago asking if he could borrow some volumes of Elizabethan poetry. Said he needed them for a sermon."

The baron grimaced. "Thinking him a gentleman, as well as a man of God, I agreed. He came down the following day and spent a number of hours perusing the shelves. In the end, he took away three books. And then, to my shock, the scoundrel refused to return them! So yes, I threatened to box his ears. They were *very* valuable books."

Wrexford darted a glance at Sheffield, who appeared equally nonplussed. The claim was plausible, he decided. But whoever killed the reverend had shown himself to be cold-bloodedly cunning. Canaday still had a great deal of explaining to do.

"So you say," he replied gruffly. "But what about the nocturnal visits you and Holworthy made to your laboratory at the Royal Institution over the last few weeks?"

"What utter fustian, Wrexford!" said Canaday hotly. "I never invited Holworthy to my lab, sir. Why would I? He had no interest in science. Granted, he tried to ask me some bizarre questions about medieval alchemy, but I told him that while I have no expertise in chemistry, I have enough scientific knowledge to know alchemy is naught but hocus-pocus nonsense."

"Mr. Drummond says he saw you and the reverend visit your laboratory," he pressed. "Several times."

"Then he is spouting bald-faced lies," snarled Canaday. "Drummond's a smarmy, spying little weasel, always sneaking around the corridors, trying to sniff out what others are working on. I once found him skulking around inside my laboratory. He claimed he had found the door half open and was merely trying to ascertain whether I needed assistance—"

"Did you keep it locked?" demanded Wrexford.

"Yes, of course I did. I simply figured I had been careless and not turned the key properly. You can be sure I was far more careful after that." The baron scowled at the memory. "I rang a peal over his head that is likely still ringing in his ears."

Wrexford felt the interrogation slipping away from him. "According to Drummond—"

"You're more of a fool than I thought if you believe a word he says," cut in Canaday. "Ask anyone who works in that section of the building. Drummond is considered an odious piece of shite. The only reason he has a position at the Institution is because he's some sort of distant cousin of Davy's wife. Otherwise he wouldn't be tolerated." A snort punctuated the assertion. "He has naught but an inferior intellect—and certainly no discernable skills in chemistry."

Making one last effort to put the baron on the defensive, Wrexford countered, "Drummond was quite specific about his claim to have seen you and Holworthy. He claims he saw you there last Thursday evening, somewhere around nine o'clock."

Canaday let out a rude sound. "That's impossible. Last Thursday evening I was at a meeting of the Royal Geological Society."

"I assume the Society will confirm that," said Wrexford. He was beginning to have more sympathy for a Bow Street Runner. It wasn't very edifying to be made to look like a donkey's arse.

"By Jove, of course they will," retorted Canaday. "I was one of the featured speakers of the evening, and my lecture on the history of tin mines in Cornwall began at exactly the hour you just mentioned."

Wrexford thought hard but couldn't come up with any other questions to ask.

"Now, unless you have any other absurd accusations to make, my friends are waiting."

Maintaining a grim silence, the earl stepped aside, allowing Canaday to brush by.

Sheffield made a wry face as the door slammed shut. "Well, that did not go according to the script."

Wrexford shot him a daggered look.

"Er, quite right—it may not be the right moment for frivolous humor," murmured his friend, assuming an air of contrition. "All jesting aside, it strikes me that he is telling the truth."

"The lecture is certainly easy enough check, and I will do so. But yes, my sense is it's not Canaday who is telling the lies," he replied grimly. "Which means I will be paying another visit to Mr. Drummond in the morning. He has a great deal of explaining to do."

Charlotte set down her packages on the table and hung her cloak on the wall peg. The rain was growing heavier, the chill drops taking on an extra sting in the gusting wind. A gunpowder greyness shrouded the streets, muddling with the mists blowing in from the river.

The boys had not returned to the house the previous evening after taking her finished drawing to the print shop. That wasn't unusual, but she found herself feeling more and more unsettled at the idea of them roaming the stews on their own. *Were they dry? . . . Were they hungry? . . . Were they safe? . . .*

She forced herself to stop fretting. Worry would only beget worry, and she wasn't yet sure what she wanted.

Love was a two-edged sword. A force of light and dark. Of joy and pain. For now, she was taking care to stay just beyond reach of its flashing blade.

Turning to her work desk, Charlotte began to straighten up the jars of powdered pigments and check that her brushes were properly cleaned and pointed. No new gossip on Holworthy's murder had come in from her regular sources. She would need to come up with yet another jab at the king's profligate sons. The public never tired of seeing the Royals skewered by her pen.

The Duke of Cumberland would make an easy target. He was said to have—

"Oiy! M'lady!" Raven's shout rose above the patter of running steps.

"Slow down," she chided, as the boys skidded through the doorway. "Wipe your feet and make a proper greeting."

Raven chuffed in frustration but knew arguing was a waste of breath. House rules were one of the few things Charlotte could control in her world. Short of Gideon's trumpet sounding the call to Judgment, they were inviolate.

"Good day, m'lady," went on Raven in a rush as he bobbed a quick bow. Hawk nearly tripped over his own feet imitating his brother.

"*Now* can I spill the beans," he demanded.

"Now you *may*," she answered.

"George—y'know George, the ostler at the King's Crown?"

Charlotte nodded. With all its comings and goings, the coaching inn and its taproom were an excellent font of information.

"Well, last night he was guzzling a tankard of ale with his brother, the one what works at that fancy gentleman's club on St. James's Street." Raven hitched in a breath. "White's—that was the name."

The most exclusive establishment in Mayfair. Raven now had her full attention.

"And the brother said one of the porters caught wind of an argument in one of the private rooms." The boy's voice rose in excitement. "Between Lord Wrexford and some other toff—"

"Did he perchance know this other toff's name?" asked Charlotte quickly.

"Aye, it was Canaday," replied Raven.

The name provoked a sudden tingling sensation at the back of her neck.

"And His Lordship was badgering him wiv questions about the dead reverend, which made Canaday cross as crabs."

"Said he didn't know nuffink," piped up Hawk.

"*Nothing,* not nuffink," corrected Charlotte without thinking. Her mind was still tangling with the name of Canaday.

Why is it striking a chord? Some memory from the past seemed to stir, but as yet it was too deep in shadow to discern.

"George's brother said the porter didn't hear the rest of the quarrel," continued Raven, drawing her attention back to his story. "Other than that His Nibs said a man named Drummond had fingered Canaday fer bringing the reverend to the . . ."

"The Royal Institution," piped up Hawk.

"Right—and that Canaday said it was a bald-faced lie."

Charlotte frowned in thought.

"It sounded important, so Hawk and me—that is, I—rushed back here te tell you," added Raven.

"Thank you, I am very glad to know all this," she assured the two boys.

"Are ye gonna do a drawing of Lord Wrexford breathing fire and smoke?" asked Hawk.

A good question. Charlotte realized that she and the earl had not discussed the subject of her future drawings. Perhaps he had simply made the lordly assumption that he was no longer fair game for her pen.

Droit de seigneur. For men like Wrexford, a sense of entitlement was woven into the very fabric of their being.

She thought about the purse, and whether or not she had sold her soul.

"Did George mention any other details?" asked Charlotte. "Was anyone else present in the room?

Raven looked uncertain. It was Hawk who spoke up. "Didn't he say Lord Wrexford's friend Sheff . . . Sheffield was there?"

"Yeah, he did," agreed his brother with a rueful grimace. "There are times when having you glued te my bum is useful."

Hawk sniggered. "Don't say 'bum.' It ain't gentlemanly."

"You both did very well," interjected Charlotte. She dug a coin out of her pocket. "Why don't we celebrate with meat pasties and an apple tart for our supper. That is, if you don't mind braving the rain again."

Raven crowed in delight. "No matter—we're already wet as eels."

She was hoping they would say as much. Her call of "Take a piece of oilcloth to cover the food!" was lost in the noisy clatter of footsteps and slamming doors.

As soon as they were gone, Charlotte quickly

moved to her desk and drew out a slim leather-bound volume from the row of books lined up against the back wall. Opening the back cover, she slid a fingernail under the loosened end-paper and jiggled. A small brass key fell to the blotter.

Drawing in a ragged breath, she opened the lower desk drawer. Beneath the sheaf of cheap writing paper was a secure compartment disguised as a false bottom. The key released the lock with a soft *snick*. She removed a packet of letters tied in brown twine, along with a scrap of paper bearing a few markings in black and red ink, and, repressing a twinge of trepidation, turned up the wick of her lamp.

The niggling feeling about the name Canaday had been growing stronger with each passing moment. The answer, she thought, lay in these old letters. So, too, did sleeping demons.

For an instant she was tempted not to wake them.

But if she was right, the truth could not be ignored.

Another deep breath. Paper crackled. Her fingers, she noted, were trembling. Odd—she prided herself on her steady nerves. Knowing the boys would soon return, Charlotte forced herself to hurry. One by one, she opened the travel-stained letters and skimmed over the neat copperplate script. In places, the ink was blurred.

By rain or by tears? At this point it didn't really matter. As she read, she summoned a sense of detachment. The words became just words. They couldn't hurt her.

It was there, in one of the long letters she had received in Rome. Her mind had not been playing tricks on her. Smoothing out the sheet, Charlotte stared at the sketch of a symbol and the accompanying text.

> The house is quite grand, and Edward's friend Canaday is a gracious host. There is riding and shooting each day for the gentlemen, but I occasionally demur and choose to spend the day in the baron's magnificent library. His grandfather was a noted collector, and there are all sorts of arcane treasures tucked away in the endless nooks and crannies of the cavernous space. You would be delighted by the clever design of the bookmark— an ornate "T" flanked by two tiny wolf-hounds.

Here her correspondent had penned a detailed sketch.

> The design is printed on a small strip of paper, which is placed inside the front cover of every book. Numerals and letters

are handwritten below it, indicating its exact place on the shelves. It's an ingenious system . . .

Dear God in Heaven. Charlotte looked up and pinched at the bridge of her nose, suddenly seeing the connection. Drawing a shaky breath, she carefully unfolded the scrap of paper she had plucked from the murdered reverend's shirt cuff.

There could be no doubt. Jeremy was an excellent artist. The two drawings matched.

"Damnation," whispered Charlotte, wishing it were not so. She stared a moment longer before returning all the papers to their hiding place and relocking the compartment.

Cry "Havoc" and let slip the dogs of war? She was now caught in the jaws of a moral dilemma. Should she keep a leash on her tongue and guard her own peace? Telling Wrexford about what she knew could put her own secrets in jeopardy. The earl, for all his faults, struck her as a man who could fight his own battles.

"Damn, damn, damn." Closing her eyes, Charlotte pressed her palms to her brow. Perhaps come morning, the answer would be clearer.

Tyler followed Wrexford up the steps to the Royal Institution. "Remind me again of why it was necessary to roust me from my bed at the crack of dawn."

"Stubble the whining," retorted the earl. He wasn't any happier than his valet at the ungodly hour. His mood was never at its best before a pot of coffee. "You pick a lock faster than I do. I want to have a look around Drummond's laboratory while he is not there."

"*I'm* expected to break the law? How jolly."

Wrexford didn't answer. Quickening his steps, he marched past the watchman, who didn't dare issue a challenge, and headed up to the top floor of the building. Rank had its privilege. Even if Drummond walked in on them, he didn't think the chemist would dare to accuse him of foul play.

The corridor was quiet as a crypt. The tattoo of their boot heels as they started down its shadowed length echoed loud as gunfire off the dark wood wainscoting.

"It seems the Institution's acolytes of science keep gentlemen's hours," quipped Tyler. The aristocracy rarely rose until after noon.

"Unfortunately not all. Mr. Drummond appears hard at work, despite the early hour." Wrexford spotted a pool of oily light up ahead. It was leaking out from beneath the door of the chemist's laboratory.

So, too, was a tendril of smoke.

At the sound of glass exploding he broke into a run.

The door was ajar. The flames licking up from a large crucible had set the wall shelf on fire, and the burning wood ignited another loud bang as several more jars of chemicals exploded.

Hunching down, Wrexford covered his nose with the tails of his cravat and darted toward the long workbench, looking for something with which to smother the flames. There looked to be a second blaze rising at the far end of the room. Heat swirled through the air, punctuated by an ominous hissing and crackling. He could just make out books and papers were piled in a pyramid . . .

What the devil is going on?

A cloud of smoke, dark and gritty, was fouling the room, making it hard to see. Tyler, he noted, had found an overcoat, and had set to work extinguishing the crucible. Choking back a cough, he spun around and started for the other fire, only to trip over a fallen chair.

Cursing, Wrexford put out a hand to break his fall . . . only to hit hard up against an outstretched boot.

Drummond was lying faceup, a peaceful expression on his face, as if he were sleeping. When a hard shake didn't rouse him, Wrexford abandoned the effort and hurried to deal with the bonfire erupting out of the books.

"Here, take this!" Having put out the fire at his end of the laboratory, Tyler tossed Wrexford the singed coat. "I'll go warn the watchman and have him fetch help."

"Tell him to send for a doctor as well!" shouted

the earl. Whether Drummond had been overcome by fumes from an experiment or had come to the laboratory befuddled with narcotics, he was going to need medical attention.

Opium seemed the only logical explanation, thought Wrexford grimly, as he fought to bat down the fire and keep it from spreading to the cabinet of chemicals. Why else would Drummond have wreaked such havoc on his own work if not in the grip of drug-induced delusions. A glance around showed several drawers had been upended and the contents doused with what looked to be lamp oil.

The sparks finally sputtered out, and after gingerly rubbing the soot from his raw palms, Wrexford was about to turn his attention to the unconscious chemist when a fluttering of fire-curled paper atop the smoldering books caught his eye. There looked to be several pages of notes, though much of the contents had been reduced to ashes. He recognized Drummond's handwriting from having thumbed through the man's ledger of chemicals on his previous visit.

Observations from his experiments? Perhaps another failure had pushed the chemist over the brink.

Curious, he leaned closer. The paper had toasted to a nut brown color, and the letters had a nervous squiggle to their slant, making the words difficult to decipher.

Hearing footsteps in the corridor, Wrexford looked up. Tyler must be returning, though by the sound of it he was alone. Seeing a magnifying glass by the cabinet, he grasped the still-hot handle and focused the lens on the writing, sure that he must be mistaken.

But no, winking larger than life in the polished glass was the same strange phrase—*The Golden One is the Devil and must be stopped from destroying* . . . A charred patch, and then, *Dangerous! The Philo. Stne.*

The rest of the message was burned to a crisp.

"The watchman is organizing the porters to bring up buckets of sand," called a breathless Tyler as he hurried back into the laboratory. Water was known to be dangerous around chemicals.

Wrexford turned, and set down the glass. "The fire is out here, so I think things are safe enough for the moment. It's only by the grace of God that no sparks fell into the spilled oil. The place would have turned into a raging inferno."

The acrid smell of smoke and singed sulfur hung heavy in the air.

"Let us see if we can revive Drummond," he went on, "and learn what happened here."

His valet was already kneeling down by the chemist. "He doesn't look to be injured, and yet I can't detect any sign of breathing."

"Perhaps if we shift him . . ." Wrexford dropped to a crouch and slid a hand under the chemist's shoulders. Feeling something sticky, he pulled back, and found his fingers were covered with blood.

Tyler exhaled sharply.

"Help me lift him," commanded the earl.

There was a tiny rent in Drummond's coat, just below the left shoulder blade.

"Some sort of blade, I would guess," he muttered. "Shoved in with enough force to penetrate straight to the heart."

"From what we've heard, the man had his fair share of enemies," said Tyler.

"Yes," mused Wrexford. "We know he was an odious little sneak. But for someone to murder him and seek to destroy his books and papers seems to indicate a far more serious transgression than simply annoying his fellow members." He rose and looked around at the disarray for a long moment. "The murder weapon . . . the murder weapon . . ."

Tyler shook his head. "There won't be a trace of it—"

"Aye, I'm sure there won't be," interrupted a loud and unpleasantly familiar voice from just outside the doorway.

The pot of strong coffee and a leisurely breakfast was now looking even more appealing, thought Wrexford with an inward oath.

The Runner appeared, a dark-on-dark shape framed by the fluted white molding. "Your

140

lackey may have disposed of the evidence, but no matter." Eyes narrowing to the sharpness of a razor's edge, Griffin allowed a ghost of a smile to flit over his lips. "It seems this time you've been caught red-handed, Lord Wrexford."

CHAPTER 8

"Don't be daft, Griffin," snapped Wrexford. "Your cockloft can't be that empty. If I had murdered the man, I would hardly be so stupid as to send for help and then linger to fight the fire."

"So it would seem at first blush," replied the Runner. "And yet, it might also be interpreted as the diabolically clever actions of a cunning killer." A pause. "Especially when a suspect just happens to be looming over the corpse with the victim's blood dripping from his hands."

Tyler wordlessly handed Wrexford a small towel from one of the overturned drawers.

His temper flared, but the earl quickly tamped down the spark. A shouting match would serve no good purpose save to spew more smoke and vitriol into the room.

"A closer look at the empirical evidence will show that I can't be guilty of the crime. The watchman will testify that no more than eight or nine minutes passed between our entering the building and my valet's rushing to raise the alarm." Wrexford gestured at the ransacked room. "Look at the mayhem and the advanced state of the fires—not to speak of the dead man. I may be the Devil Incarnate, but even Lucifer himself could not have created all this in such a short space of time."

"As for the murder weapon, I did not exit the building, so it's either in here or somewhere in the corridor," pointed out Tyler.

"Hmmph." Griffin entered the laboratory and made a slow circle through the work space, stopping every few steps to examine the damage.

"As you see," murmured Wrexford once the Runner had returned to the doorway, "there is no weapon. Which proves I didn't kill him."

"What's to say you—or your lackey—don't have it on your person?" countered the Runner.

The earl stripped off his coat and tossed it on the counter. Tyler quickly followed suit. "You are welcome to search us."

Griffin cracked his meaty knuckles. "Which I shall do, milord."

And the fellow made quite a thorough—and rough-handed—job of it, thought the earl, though he managed to remain impassive throughout the process. In the cat-and-mouse game of nerves, he was not going to be the one to flinch.

"Now that you are done," he said with deliberate politeness after the Runner had finished pawing over Tyler, "I assume we are free to have a closer look around." He made a show of dusting his coat before putting it back on. "Just in case we see something you miss."

"Nay," replied the Runner. "I'll not have the

two of you mucking things up before I have a chance to study the scene."

"But—"

"Lord Wrexford, the only reason I'm not arresting you is because there's no weapon. But you can be sure I'll be looking *very* closely at the rest of the evidence."

"Do," said Wrexford calmly, though he couldn't help adding, "However, what you've seen so far does not inspire me to have much confidence in your ability to find the real culprit."

"Get out," snarled Griffin. "Milord."

A tactical mistake, conceded the earl. He had wanted to make a more thorough examination of the half-burned papers. A clatter in the corridor announced that the watchman and his bucket brigade were about to arrive, and once they set to work, the details were likely to be destroyed.

"Just one last thing," murmured Wrexford. "Might I inquire how you happened to arrive here so quickly?"

"As it happens, I was coming to speak with Drummond about your argument with Lord Canaday."

Wrexford must have betrayed a spasm of surprise for the Runner curled a slow smirk. "Have you not seen A. J. Quill's latest print?"

Tugging her shawl a little tighter around her shoulders, Charlotte edged forward on the bench and darted a nervous glance up and down the graveled walkway. The modest park in Red Lion Square was far enough away from the opulent environs of Mayfair to pose no threat of discovery. Still, a meeting with Jeremy always made her insides twist in knots.

It was why she avoided arranging them unless absolutely necessary.

And much as she had tried to convince herself she was overreacting, she couldn't deny the moral obligation.

A conscience was a cursedly inconvenient encumbrance.

Charlotte shifted again, feeling chilled despite the sunlight and the cheerful chatter of the rustling leaves.

"Good morning, Charley."

She jumped, so lost in brooding that she had missed her friend's approach.

Jeremy sat down beside her, a pinch of concern shadowing his smile. "It's a lovely morning for a picnic. I brought some pastries from Gunter's Tea Shop."

Her stomach lurched. "How thoughtful."

"But you are in no mood for spun-sugar treats."

A reluctant laugh slipped from her lips. "Alas, you know me too well."

"Well enough to know you wouldn't ask for a meeting unless it was important," he replied softly.

"It *is* important," she confessed. Jeremy was one of the very few people who knew about her secret identity. Their bond of friendship, and their sharing of secrets, went back a long way—to childhood, before a twist of fate had made him heir to a barony. The change in his life hadn't altered their closeness. And though she knew he questioned her choices at times, he had always been willing to answer her questions about the beau monde, no matter how odd.

She hoped this time would be no exception.

"How can I help?" he whispered.

Charlotte checked that no one was nearby before asking, "I believe you are acquainted with Lord Robert Canaday?"

He nodded.

"Is he a religious man?"

Jeremy made a wry face. "No more than most gentlemen of the *ton.*"

Which was to say, he worshipped his own pleasures more than the Word of God. A sardonic thought, admitted Charlotte, but no less true for being so.

"Then he had not struck up a friendship with the late Reverend Holworthy in the last few years?"

Her friend frowned in thought. In profile, his fine-boned features and tousled honey-gold hair made him look like a brooding Renaissance prince in a Botticelli painting. "It's possible," he conceded. "I hadn't thought about it, but now that you mention it, I believe I had heard mention that they belonged to the same club."

"What sort of club?" pressed Charlotte.

"A small and rather exclusive one, so I don't know much about it, save for the fact that its members have an interest in literature and the arts."

"Given the late reverend's sermons castigating worldly indulgences, that seems strange." She clasped her hands together to keep them from shaking. "D-do you perchance know the name of this club?"

"I believe it's called The Ancients," answered Jeremy.

All at once Charlotte felt the acid burn of bile rise up in her throat. She swallowed hard, willing her voice to remain normal. "Which I suppose means their focus centers on classical Greece and Rome?"

"I'm afraid I don't know much about them," he apologized. "They tend to be rather secretive."

She wished that she were blessed with the same ignorance. But now, there was no more pretending that she could remain silent about certain things.

"Thank you. This has been a great help." The trill of children's laughter floated up from the far end of the little park. Closer by, hidden in leaves of a linden tree, a lark was twittering, each note like the chime of a tiny golden bell.

Birdsong? How could this moment be filled with sweetness and light? The sound ought to be the snarly rasp of a black-as-Hades bat . . . Did bats rasp? Or was that simply a figment of her own febrile imagination?

"Just one more question," said Charlotte. "Is Lord Canaday prone to violence?"

Jeremy fixed her with a searching stare. "Ye god, Charley, why on earth would you ask that?"

She drew in a breath, and then simply let it leak out of her lungs.

"Surely you don't think . . ."

"Please don't ask me to explain," she said quickly. "I'm simply trying to get a sense of the man. You know that in my line of work it's important to understand the strengths and weaknesses of the people I draw."

"What's Canaday done to draw your attention?"

"Apparently he had quite a quarrel with Lord Wrexford at White's last night."

Jeremy let out a low whistle. "How do you—" A rueful grimace. "Right, right, how silly of me to ask."

"It is better that you don't," she agreed.

He looked upset—Lord, she hated doing this to him.

"Come, let me help you leave the past behind and start afresh," he urged. "A new life, an easier life. Enough time has passed. Mistakes can be forgiven."

She shook her head. "Most people aren't nearly as generous spirited as you are, Jem. We both know it's best that some secrets remain hidden."

"True." He blinked, the tiny muscles of his jaw tightening. "But darkness begets darkness. You deal in misery and scandal, and I worry that it's slowly eating away at your soul."

Charlotte looked away.

"You don't need to do this anymore, Charley."

Oh, but I do.

Jeremy waited. The lark fell silent. "But I see that I'm not going to get you to change your mind."

"I'm sorry." How to explain when she couldn't make any sense of it herself.

"So am I."

Hoping to dispel the tension, Charlotte quickly switched to a less provocative topic. "I do have one more question, if you're willing. It's not one that asks you to betray any private peccadilloes."

He nodded, though a flicker of unhappiness lingered in his eyes.

She hated to disappoint him. But that did not stop her from asking, "Might you tell me a little about Mr. Christopher Sheffield? I understand from my sources that he and Lord Wrexford are close friends, but I don't recall having heard his name before."

"That surprises me." Jeremy made a rueful face. "For Kit always seems to be treading on the razor's edge of scandal."

"A dissolute rake?" she asked. Gifted at birth with a pedigree of privilege, and no sense of morality to go with it. Like so many of the young blades who called themselves gentlemen.

"No, I wouldn't say that," he replied after a moment of thought. "There's little debauchery in Sheffield, merely an aimlessness. He's considered charming, but his caustic wit and meager allowance—he's a younger son of the Earl of Marquand, who's known to be a nipcheese—frighten the matchmaking mamas of the *ton*. It's clear he'll need to marry a girl with a very plump dowry to ensure a comfortable life. However, without the title and influence that his eldest brother carries, he's not considered a very good catch."

Jeremy quirked a humorless smile. "A wealthy father expects more from his investment."

Partnering money and power. A dance that had involved a dizzying array of steps and spins.

"In every strata of Society, there is a price to pay for admission to its highest circle." Charlotte shrugged. "So, how is it that Sheffield and Wrexford are friends? Sheffield seems a fribble, and my sense is, the earl is not."

"I believe they formed a bond during their years at Oxford." Jeremy paused again to give her question careful thought. "My impression of Sheffield is that he has a sharp mind, but he has no way to put his intellect to practical use. And boredom often begets cynicism."

God forbid that a gentleman sully his lily-white hands in business or a profession other than the military, the government, or the church. Charlotte didn't envy the aristocracy. The cage might be gilded, and filled with sumptuous pleasures and glittering amusements.

But it was still a cage.

"You've been incredibly helpful. I . . ." She couldn't think of any words that might lessen the hurt of their earlier exchange. Choices, choices. Hers had been made a long time ago.

"I ought to be going," finished Charlotte softly. "I've a drawing to finish by this evening."

Jeremy rose, and knowing better than to offer her an escort home, he held out the unopened box of pastries. "Please take this. The lads are fond of apple tarts."

She accepted it with a nod of thanks.

"I may not like your decision, Charley." The knuckles of his gloved hand brushed against her cheek. "But that doesn't change our friendship, or our current arrangement. I am here for you whenever you need my help."

"I'm grateful—truly grateful, Jem." Charlotte wished she could banish the demons lurking deep within the recesses of her being. But they had always been there. In that the two of them were kindred spirits. But Jeremy had always been by far the wiser in how to deal with his inner devils.

"If it makes you uncomfortable," she went on,

"I will not ask again for information about the foibles of your peers."

He forced a smile. "And miss the point of your quill puncturing the pompous, puffed-up arrogance of Polite Society?" His expression turned serious. "You keep them honest, Charley. I applaud your courage, even though it terrifies me."

It terrifies me as well.

Touching the brim of his hat in salute, Jeremy turned without further words and crossed to the open iron gate.

Charlotte stared down at the tips of her half boots, unwilling to watch him disappear into the shadows of the side street. She sat for several more minutes, curling the fringe of her shawl around her fingers so tightly that the pain brought tears to her eyes.

Pain is good. It reminds us that we are alive.

She opened the box and took a small bite of a tart, savoring the thick grains of crystallized sugar flecked with spicy cinnamon. So, too, did the small moments of sweetness.

She was strong. She would not let the darkness consume her.

Wrexford paused in the corridor to consider his options.

Which were virtually nil. Although he was a member of the Royal Institution, he had no

152

official authority to ignore the Runner's orders, and given the circumstances, it would not be wise to test just how far he could push the man.

"Bloody bad timing," he muttered.

"I take it you saw something you wished to examine more closely," murmured Tyler.

"Yes. But Griffin's ham-fisted handling of things will likely destroy it."

"Perhaps I can help." His valet darted a look at the group of porters emerging from the stairwell with their buckets and brooms. "I can switch coats and hats with one of these fellows, and Griffin may not notice me in the commotion."

"It may work," said the earl. "There are several half-burned papers atop the charred books. Try to find a way to smuggle them out. It won't be easy—they are damnably fragile and it's key not to have them—"

"Lord Wrexford!" A slender man of medium height shouldered his way past the porters. "I didn't realize you were here in the building." He heaved an out-of-breath sigh as he hurried to join them. "Good Lord, what a hideous business."

"Indeed it is, Lowell," agreed the earl. Lord Declan Lowell, younger son of the Marquess of Carnsworth, served as superintendent of the building. A skilled administrator, as well as a man interested in science—Wrexford couldn't recall his specific field of focus—he had been asked by the Royal Institution's head to handle the logistics of the public lectures and research laboratories.

At the present moment he didn't envy him the job.

"As it happens, I came to have a word with Mr. Drummond. But it seems someone else arrived here first."

Lowell blanched, his well-shaped features pinching to a mask of harried concern. "I came in quite early, in order to sort through the paperwork for the upcoming chemistry lectures. In a sense, it's a blessing in disguise, as I'm able to deal with the terrible news and have some control as to how it becomes public knowledge."

He ran a hand through his neatly trimmed auburn hair. "I hope you don't think me callous. Of course I am devastated about Drummond—a terrible loss of a respected member. But, to be honest, I am concerned about the Institution as well."

His lips thinned in a momentary grimace. "There are many people who don't like what we do here—the forward thinking, the modern ideas, the willingness to change the way things are traditionally done frightens them. I fear they will use this as some sort of sign from heaven that our experiments are against the natural order of the world."

Wrexford gave a curt nod of sympathy. "I don't doubt that you are right." Lowell had always struck him as a smart, shrewd, and pragmatic fellow. He moved in a circle of up-and-coming young and influential intellectuals—Babbage, Herschel, Peacock—and like them was a voice for reforming old rules. Perhaps he could use those qualities to his own advantage. "We men of learning understand each other—you may count on me to do all I can to keep the details from leaking out."

Lowell chuffed a sigh of relief.

Lowering his voice, he went on, "Like you, I have an interest in seeing this solved quickly and quietly." He shot a meaningful look at the porters, who were huddled a respectful distance away, waiting for a signal from the superintendent on how to proceed. "I'd like a look at the laboratory before your men fling around their sand and cart away the debris."

Lowell instantly came alert. "Anything in particular?" he asked softly.

"I simply want to get a better impression of the scene," lied Wrexford. It wasn't that he didn't trust the man, but there were too many strange pieces to the puzzle scattered around. Until he could begin to make sense of them he was wary about revealing anything.

"However, the Runner has taken an unreasonable dislike to me." A sardonic smile. "And so has tossed me out on my ear."

Lowell nodded in understanding. Drawing a large ring of keys from his coat pocket, he moved quickly to the other side of the corridor and unlocked a storage room. "Wait in here. I will handle the matter."

Wrexford and Tyler slipped into the cramped space. The door closed quietly, leaving them in darkness.

A few minutes later, the agitated *clop-clop* of boots beat a hobnailed tattoo on the corridor floor. The sound receded fast.

Silence. Wrexford smiled to himself.

Lowell returned and eased the door open. "I told him I needed to clear the dangerous chemicals from the room and couldn't permit him to stay. However, he'll be returning in a half hour. That was all the time I dared demand."

"It's quite enough. Thank you," replied the earl, grateful for the superintendent's coolheaded and decisive handling of the situation. "As for you and your men . . . in order to work quickly and efficiently, it would be better if my assistant and I could have the room to ourselves."

"Yes, yes, of course." Lowell looked around. "Haversham is out of Town. I'll take my men into his laboratory, which is identical to Drummond's layout, and go over the procedures for dealing with the damage."

"Much obliged," said Wrexford, signaling Tyler to proceed. "I shall come let you know when we are finished."

He wasted no time in following his valet into

the laboratory, and took the precaution of locking the door from the inside.

The reek of smoke hung heavy in the still air, pungent with a harsh chemical tang that burned the throat with every breath. The main Argent lamp had given up the ghost, and the two surviving oil lamps were burning low, their weak flames casting ghoulish shadows over the jumbled furniture and equipment.

Drummond's body lay half turned on its side, the dark pool of blood spreading slowly through a spill of powdered sulfur. Wrexford repressed a twinge of pity as he stepped over the chemist's lifeless legs. Would anyone care about his passing?

However odious, no man should die unmourned.

Dismissing such momentary musings, the earl turned his attention to the here and now. "Move the lights closer," he said to Tyler, indicating the far end of the work counter. A quick search of the drawers revealed one filled with scientific instruments. Wrexford found several pairs of long, needle-nosed tweezers, along with a thin copper spatula, and carried them over to the pile of charred books.

"Let us salvage as much of the note paper as possible," he said.

Tyler leaned in to assess the damage. "It will be tricky. I suggest we find an undamaged book and place the fragments between the pages. That way, we can always cut through the binding and move

157

them under your microscope for examination."

"Having a valet who knows more than the fine points of starching a shirt is a distinct advantage in certain situations," murmured Wrexford.

"I shall remind you of that, said Tyler, after scavaging an unsinged volume from the side closet. "Especially as these 'certain situations' appear to be escalating with increasing frequency." A pause. "Alas, the same cannot be said for my wages."

"I pay you very well." The earl handed him one of the tweezers.

"Not well enough to risk a stay in Newgate Prison."

Wrexford grunted and shifted to allow a better angle at the papers in question. "Hold up the cover of Levoisier's *Treatise on Chemistry* so I can better reach the fragments." What an irony that the famed French chemist was known for his experiments on the role of oxygen in combustion. "And be ready to slide in the spatula to stabilize the paper."

Holding himself very still, the earl carefully maneuvered his tweezers into the remains of the notes. It required extreme delicacy. The paper was fragile, a mere breath away from crumbling to dust. One errant move . . .

Tyler gave an involuntary wince as a large fleck of ash broke off.

Damnation. Steadying his hand, Wrexford

slowly extracted the top fragment and placed it in the undamaged book. His valet ever so gently covered it with several pristine pages.

They repeated the process until all of the fragments had been retrieved. Whether it would yield enough to reveal the dead chemist's full message remained to be seen.

"Anything else, milord?" inquired Tyler.

Wrexford took a few cursory glances inside the half-burned books. "Nothing of interest here. And we haven't much time." He handed his valet the fruits of their labor. "Hide this under your coat and wait in the corridor. I'd rather no one see what we're removing. I'll make a quick circuit of the work space and see if I spot any other useful evidence."

Tyler took the extra precaution of wrapping an old rag around the book. "Very good, sir."

Wanting to avoid another clash with the Runner, Wrexford hurriedly checked through the instrument cases on the center table and the fallen drawers, hoping to find Drummond's laboratory journals with the records of his experiments. But they were either burned or buried under the debris. He paused over the chemist's corpse looking for . . .

He wasn't sure what. Something was bothering him, but he couldn't quite put a finger on what.

"Milord, are you finished in there?" Lowell entered gingerly, taking care to keep his well-polished boots clear of the muddled ash and liquids. "Mr. Griffin will be . . ." His voice trailed off in a sharp exhale as he halted abruptly. "Good Lord, what a gruesome sight."

The earl straightened. As murders went, it was actually quite civilized. However, he kept that thought to himself.

"Hopkins!" Lowell called to one of the unseen workmen. "Send for someone to remove the, er, remains of Mr. Drummond—discreetly, and as soon as possible, mind you."

"Where will the body be taken?" asked Wrexford.

The question made Lowell grimace. "Good Heavens, what difference does it make? I just want it out of here."

Wrexford nodded, and left the agitated supervisor to begin the process of clearing the damage. Spotting Tyler near the doorway to one of the side stairs, he joined him and led the way down to the main floor, where they exited the building through the lecture hall.

"Wait here," he said in a low voice as they turned down Albemarle Street. "I want you to intercept whatever mortuary wagon is called, and have the body taken to Henning's surgery."

"Given my charm and your money, that should present no problem, milord," replied his valet. His tone then turned serious. "Did you spot something irregular?"

"I'm not sure. But Henning has an eye for reading the details of foul play."

"Very good, sir." He shifted his hold on the wrapped book.

"In the meantime, I have several visits to make."

"I shall have the parcel unpacked, and your microscope and magnifying lenses set up by the time you return home," responded Tyler.

"That may not be for a while," said Wrexford, thinking about the Runner's unexpected mention of A. J. Quill's latest satirical print.

"Aye, well, just remember to keep your temper—and your cutthroat blade—in check," said Tyler dryly.

His valet might not be speaking so glibly if he knew the truth about Quill.

"After all, they say the pen is mightier than the sword."

CHAPTER 9

The pen, fumed Wrexford, jamming his hands into his pockets as he walked away from the print shop window, was in this case mightier than a battalion of cavalry sabers. It certainly sliced with far more deadly precision, each stroke a perfectly designed cut.

With an inward wince, he admitted that the satire was perhaps deserved. Neither he nor Canaday had showed to advantage. Though how Charlotte had learned the embarrassing details was a matter for further exploration. A man's club was supposed to be sacrosanct, a haven where a strict code of honor ruled within its walls, a refuge where one was safe from ridicule.

But apparently those pillared, patrician walls had ears.

And Charlotte would likely retort by asking why should women play by the rules when they were all written by high-and-mighty men.

A fair point, he conceded, albeit a sharp one that was now sticking rather painfully in his arse. His pique was quick to dissipate as he conceded she had warned him that her livelihood depended on feeding juicy tidbits of gossip to the public.

As he climbed into a hackney and ordered

it to head east, his thoughts turned back to the morning's murder and how it was connected to the death of the Right Reverend Josiah Holworthy. For he refused to believe it was naught but coincidence. The universe, despite its apparent chaos, worked according to fundamental laws of Nature that could, as Newton had so ably proved, be explained by reason and logic.

One simply had to employ careful observation.

What am I not seeing? Leaning back against the squabs, Wrexford brooded on the question until the vehicle made its way past St. Martin-in-the-Fields. Rapping on the trap, he ordered the driver to halt, then paid the fare, choosing to walk the rest of the way.

The streets narrowed, their crooked turns quickly becoming crisscrossed by alleyways. The area was clinging to genteel poverty, but stews and their rough-edged violence were clawing closer.

He turned up the collar of his coat and let his shoulders slouch. Next time, he must take care to dress in a less lordly fashion. Mrs. Sloane would not thank him for drawing unwonted attention to her. Hugging close to the shadows, he made his way to her lane and approached the front door of her house.

The knock went unanswered.

He tried again.

Damnation. He hadn't stopped to consider that she might not be at home.

A surreptitious jiggle of the latch showed it was locked. And aside from the moral question of invading her privacy, he hadn't brought a set of picks.

"Oiy!" A voice, trying to sound deeper than it was, rose up from his rear. "Wot's ye doing there? Better bugger off quick-like, 'less you want a shiv stuck in your pegs."

Wrexford turned. "If you stab a blade into my leg again, brat, I will birch your bum until you can't sit down for a week."

Two dirty faces fixed him with matching scowls.

"Just try it," challenged the older boy.

"I would rather behave in a more civilized manner." He rattled the latch again. "I assume you can open this?"

"Yeah." Raven—or was it Crow?—held up a key. "But I don't see why should I let the likes of you in."

"Then allow me to give you a good one. I need to have a word with Mrs. Sloane, so I won't be going anywhere until she returns." He gave a pointed look at the adjoining house, where already the window draperies were twitching. "And I daresay she would rather not have the neighborhood gossiping about strange men loitering outside her door."

The younger boy whispered something in his brother's ear. The scowl grew fiercer, but after a small hesitation, Raven stalked past him and

164

opened the lock. "I suppose you can come in. But we've got our eyes on you."

"I expect no less," he murmured, following the boys through the small entrance foyer into the jack-of-all-trades room that served for cooking, dining, and working.

Drawing out a stool from the table, the earl sat and crossed his legs.

The two boys did the same.

Repressing a smile, he took a leisurely look around. Despite the shabby furnishings, it had a comfortable coziness to it, a sense of life that belied the nicks and dents.

"Have you any idea when Mrs. Sloane will return?" he inquired.

"Naw," muttered Raven.

Wrexford recalled his earlier visit. "I doubt she would approve of slurred gutter language in front of guests."

Raven narrowed his eyes, but both boys sat up a little straighter.

"Milady went out te meet a friend," volunteered Raven's brother, carefully enunciating his words. "She didn't say when she would be back."

"Hawk," chided Raven in a sharp whisper.

The younger boy looked confused. "I wuz just trying te be polite. M'lady says a gentleman is always polite te guests."

"He ain't—he *isn't*—a guest," said Raven. "He's nothing but trouble."

Was he? Wrexford considered the statement carefully. His own concerns had dominated his thoughts, and his actions. He hadn't paid any attention to how his demands had affected her life.

Granted, she was making money off his scandal, but it likely wasn't that simple. Nothing was.

As he looked up, his glance caught a pile of books on the table. An elementary Latin textbook, a history of Great Britain, a primer on penmanship—with a start he recognized them as the same schoolbooks he had had as a boy.

"Lessons?" he murmured.

"Aye," answered Hawk. "M'lady is sending us te a tutor once a week. We're learning all about knights in armor." He fixed him with a shy look. "D-D'you have a suit of armor, m'lord?"

This time his brother didn't try to shush him.

"There are several at my country estate," he answered. "As a lad I did attempt to try one on. It weighed more than a sack of stones and reeked of rust." The memory provoked a wry grimace. "As I recall, I fell over when I tried to take a step and my brother had to fish me out of the dratted thing."

Hawk giggled. Raven tried to hide a smile.

"Do you have swords?" pressed the younger boy.

"A whole wall of them," answered the earl.

166

The boy's eyes widened. "Great big ones with jewels on the handle, just like the one in the picture of Richard the Lionhearted?"

"Even bigger. There's a Viking broadside nearly as tall as I am."

Assuming a look of boredom, Raven had slipped back into a slouch. But talk of blades tested his resolve. "You're bamming us. Nobody could lift a sword *that* big."

"It has a double handle, made for two hands." Wrexford went on to describe it in great detail.

"Cor," Hawk exhaled an admiring sigh. "Mebbe some day I'll get te see a sword like that."

"Yeah, and mebbe someday we'll take tea with the Prince Regent," muttered Raven. But a wink at his brother took any sting out of the sarcasm.

Undeterred, Hawk asked. "Wot other weapons have ye got?"

Maces, battleaxes, pikes—what ruthless little savages! He had forgotten how bloodthirsty boys were at that age. Hawk peppered him with questions about the arsenal, and when talk turned to daggers and rapiers, Raven couldn't resist joining in.

Blades, thought the earl wryly, appeared to have a particular appeal to him.

"And then there are the crossbows," said Wrexford. "My brother and I were birched 'til our bums were scarlet for stealing one from the wall and taking it out to the fields to test its aim." He paused, recalling the long-ago incident. "It was likely a good thing we were caught by one of the servants. Trying to shoot an apple off Tommy's head probably wasn't the wisest idea."

"I'll bet ye wacked swords wid each other when nobody was looking," said Hawk.

Memories, memories. He had not thought about the bonds of brotherhood in a long while.

"Many a time," he replied. "Though not with real ones."

"Who won?" asked Hawk.

"I was older, so I had the advantage when we were boys."

The boy darted a glance at Raven, then a hopeful look at the earl. "And now?"

"And now . . ." A pause. "And now Tommy is dead." Strange how the pain was still like sharpened steel lancing through flesh and bone. He had thought that locking it away would have dulled its edge. "So all that larking about through the forests and fields with sticks as our sabers is long in the past."

"Aye, well, people cock up their toes all the time. Even toffs," said Raven, trying to sound tougher than his years. "Nothing much you can do about it."

A glimmer of fear lit for an instant in Hawk's eye, but he nodded gamely. "Aye."

As silence settled over them, Wrexford

regretted his words. Death seemed to have him on the defensive this morning.

"Wot's it like in the country?" asked Raven abruptly.

The earl thought for a long moment. How to explain to these boys the wonders of exploring the fields and woods, the magic of catching polliwogs or spying a badger's sett? Of climbing trees, of wrestling matches in new-mown hay. Of biting into a fresh-picked apple and letting the sweet juice dribble down one's chin.

"There's no smoke in the air," he answered slowly. "It's quiet, and you can walk for miles without seeing any people."

Their faces scrunched in thought, as if they were trying to imagine such a foreign world.

The click of the door latch lifting forestalled any further talk. He turned as Charlotte entered the room, a pasteboard box carefully cradled in her arms. She looked pensive, preoccupied— until her eyes met his.

Then her expression turned to wariness.

Trouble, he reminded himself. To her, he was naught but Trouble.

"He was waiting outside," explained Raven quickly, "and said it was important. I figgered it was best to let him in."

"Yes, you did the right thing," assured Charlotte with a forced smile. She took a moment to set the box down on the table. "You lads have your lessons with Mr. Keating soon. Gather your books and be off. It would not do to be late."

"But we've plenty of—" began Hawk, only to be silenced by a nudge from his brother.

"Aye, we best be going," said Raven, rising quickly. "Come on."

Charlotte waited until they were out of the house before speaking again. When she did it was simply to issue a curt challenge. "Well?"

"I think you know why I'm here."

She turned and busied herself with adding a few chunks of coal to the stove.

"You are angry." A statement, not a question.

"I am curious."

More thumps, and the metallic rasp of raking the embers to life. The door clanked shut.

Charlotte swung around and placed a fist on her hip. "I daresay you can be both."

Wrexford acknowledged the statement with a gruff laugh. She, of all people, understood the complexities and contradictions of human emotion. "I daresay you are right. But anger seems a waste of time. While curiosity may yield some useful information. I had not realized that your tentacles reached into the inner sanctums of the aristocracy."

"I warned you, no secrets are safe in London."

"So you did." He paused. "I simply assumed—"

"Assumed what, sir?" she cut in. "That you had purchased my silence?"

Strangely enough, the thought had never occurred to him. "Could I have done so?" he asked, half amused at his own lack of guile.

"Don't toy with me, sir. This is no jesting matter."

"I am well aware of that, Mrs. Sloane." He had stood up when she entered the room. As she moved back toward the table, his shadow fell across her face, hiding her expression. "There has been another murder this morning."

Charlotte sat down heavily, her face leaching of all color. "Who?"

"A man named Drummond. An acquaintance of Lord Canaday," answered Wrexford. "And of mine, in case that was your next question."

She sat still as a stone. He wasn't sure she had heard him.

"Mrs. Sloane?"

"I mentioned him in my print. And now he is dead."

"Given the timing, I think the killer had already decided to eliminate the fellow." Wrexford was not at all sure of that. But beneath the cloak of cynicism, he sensed Charlotte still had a tender conscience. He didn't wish for her to be plagued by guilt.

A current of air stirred the draperies over the kitchen window. The faded chintz whispered against the wooden moldings.

Releasing a pent-up breath, she said, "Sit

down. We need to talk. I haven't been completely forthcoming with you, Lord Wrexford."

"You have my full attention."

The earl sounded utterly calm. Bored, even. While Charlotte felt every tiny nerve in her body twitching with dread.

"Do go on." The lordly drawl might well have been ordering a servant to pour tea.

Somehow that helped dispel her fear. "Shall I put on a kettle to boil?" she shot back. "And serve a plate of ginger biscuits?"

"I prefer almond." The earl sat with a careless grace. Despite the stool—it was, she knew, hideously uncomfortable—he looked completely at ease. "Dare I hope that is what's in the box? I recognize the markings as those of Gunter's Tea Shop in Berkeley Square. Their pastries are the best in all of London."

"Impossible man," said Charlotte through gritted teeth, and yet she couldn't keep the corners of her mouth from tweaking up. "Do you take nothing seriously?"

Wrexford flicked a mote of dust from his cuff. "The world begs to be seen as absurd. And don't try to deny it—that simple truth is your bread and butter."

"There is nothing simple about the truth," she replied. "As Lord Byron said, it is but a lie in masquerade."

"Actually, he said it the other way around." He smiled. "But I like your version better. The punch is aimed more squarely at one's vitals."

Once again, Charlotte was reminded of how dangerous he was. In ways she couldn't begin to define.

"You have something to tell me, Mrs. Sloane," Wrexford murmured after several moments of uneasy silence had rippled between them. "Shall we call a truce and refrain from further verbal sparring? I am not the enemy."

Would that she could believe that. But trust was also a weapon, all the more lethal for how swiftly and silently it struck.

"A truce," agreed Charlotte, wishing she didn't find his face so interesting. There was arrogance plainly writ in every pore, and yet indefinable nuances that hinted at hidden facets. "We are both pragmatic, sir, and it seems we are in a position to help each other."

He waited.

She wouldn't have guessed patience was one of the earl's virtues, given that he was known for possessing a hair-trigger temper. But once again he was surprising her.

"It's difficult to know where to begin," she went on. "Perhaps it's best to start with the murder of Holworthy. As I told you at our first meeting, I saw the body right after the crime was committed. I depicted the wounds and the burns to his skin with great accuracy in my drawing." A pause. "What I didn't include were two other details."

Wrexford recrossed his legs.

"The first was a faint footprint I had spotted in the transept. It was fresh, and I suspect it was made by the killer."

"What makes you say that?" he interrupted.

"Two reasons. The church is very old and riddled with drafts. An imprint in dust would not lie undisturbed for very long," replied Charlotte. "And there was a side door there that was slightly ajar."

He nodded thoughtfully.

"Did not the Runner mention that as evidence?" She had been stewing over the question.

"No. According to him there was no evidence left at the scene to point to a culprit."

"I may be the unwitting cause of that," she admitted. "In our haste to leave before the authorities arrived, Raven and I must have scuffed it out."

"Or Griffin is not as observant as you are."

"His reputation is one of a man who is good at what he does." Having committed to a certain degree of honesty, Charlotte made herself go on. "So I owe you an apology, sir. Had he seen it, he would have had good reason to dismiss you as a suspect."

Again, he waited calmly, betraying no signs of impatience.

"The size of the print," she explained. "It was made by a small foot—smaller than yours."

"Could it have been made by a woman?"

She shut her eyes for a moment, recalling the memory. "My impression is no. The tread of the heel and the width of the foot all indicated it was a man's boot."

"Interesting." Wrexford tapped his fingertips together. "Though at the moment we have no way of knowing if it will prove useful. I daresay there are a great many small-footed men in London."

"Yes. But there was a distinctive mark on the heel—a star with the letter *B* centered in it was imprinted in the leather."

He thought about the information for a moment. "That sounds like the bootmaker's mark of Burdock. He's one of the second-tier craftsmen. Good, but catering to a clientele who can't quite afford Hoby." Pursing his lips, he added, "It's interesting, but I'm not sure it's of any real use. That the killer is a member of the beau monde is not really a surprise. The fact that he's small-footed doesn't help narrow the possible suspects—after all, small is a relative term."

Charlotte flushed, realizing how silly the detail must have sounded. "That's not all. Far more important than the footprint, I found a scrap of paper stuck in Holworthy's shirt cuff. I didn't intend to take it—but we had to flee when the authorities arrived and somehow I did."

At that, the earl straightened, his gaze sharpening in interest. "What was written on it?"

"A symbol, and below it, a string of numbers." *Alea iacta est*, she thought to herself—the die is cast. Now was the moment when she must decide whether to throw caution to the wind. There would be no going back.

Without hesitation, Wrexford went right to the heart of the question. "Do you know what they mean?"

"I had no idea at the time," answered Charlotte. "But in my work, I've learned to seize small things that may matter." She met his gaze with a spark of defiance. "You may think it wrong, but survival tends to blur the fine lines of morality. For that I make no apology."

She paused for breath. "But I am sorry that my impulse may have resulted in the Runner seizing on you as a suspect, rather than someone else. However, after I thought more clearly about the implications of taking evidence from a murder scene, I saw no way to turn it over to Bow Street without it being dismissed as a hoax, or risking being implicated in the crime."

"As you have taken pains to point out, I have no right to be holier than thou."

Their eyes remained locked. A test of wills? Charlotte had stood firm in the face of far more threatening men. She didn't flinch.

Wrexford seemed amused by the moment.

He deliberately shifted, and took a peek in the pastry box. "Gunter's makes an excellent apple tart. Alas, I assume you are saving these for the imps." He cocked his head. "Or is the one with the missing bite fair game?"

Charlotte rose and wordlessly fetched a plate.

"Bring a knife as well," he murmured. "It seems only fair that we split it."

In her experience, gentlemen rarely did what was fair regarding their dealings with women, she reflected. But the earl scrupulously divided the pastry into two equal portions.

"Forgive me if I eat like a savage," he said, picking up one of the pieces with his fingers. "I'm famished."

"I'm used to savages," she quipped, and did the same. "There is bread and cheese if you wish additional sustenance."

"Thank you, but I shall survive." He popped the remaining pastry into his mouth. Unlike the boys, he waited until he had swallowed before speaking again. "I take it from your earlier statement that you now know the meaning of the paper you took from Holworthy."

"I know what it is," corrected Charlotte. "As to its meaning, I have no clue." It wasn't that she meant to be melodramatic, but she found herself needing to draw a deep breath before she went on.

"It's a book marking, one that indicated where a

volume belongs in a private library. The numbers indicate a place on the shelf. And the symbol is the mark of the owner . . ."

Wrexford had gone very still. Yet the air seemed to thrum with an unseen force. Powerful muscle and wolf-sleek strength, coiled to strike.

"And that gentleman is Lord Robert Canaday."

"You are sure it's a mark from Lord Canaday's library?"

"Quite," answered Charlotte firmly.

"I trust you will understand," said Wrexford softly, "that I feel compelled to ask you to explain how."

"And I trust you will understand," she countered, "that I feel compelled to refuse to reveal the exact reasons. You will have to take my word that I am telling the truth."

"The truth as you know it." He expelled an audible breath, the first sign that whatever hold he had on his volatile temper was beginning to slip.

"Something sinister is afoot here. Two men lie dead, each foully murdered. So before I step deeper into this serpent's nest of twisted intrigue and vague innuendos, I would prefer to be sure that I am not chasing after the wrong clues. A mistake, as you can see, might prove lethal."

Charlotte swallowed hard. It was a reasonable request, one she would make in his position. Yet she would not—*could not*—reveal the source of her certainty for it would put her own hard-won life at risk.

There was, perhaps, a compromise.

"Lord Wrexford, I am willing to show you the paper. You will see the crest on it, and I'm sure you have ways of confirming that it is indeed the marking of the Canaday estate library."

He turned in profile, the lamplight catching the purse of his chiseled lips. He wanted more, but he could not have it.

"That is all I can offer," said Charlotte. To do otherwise would make her too vulnerable.

"You drive a hard bargain."

"I told you, sir, I do what I have to in order to survive."

"Get it," he growled.

Damnation. She hesitated, now caught between a stone and a wedge of granite.

CHAPTER 10

"Ah, I see." Wrexford watched the war of conflicting emotion play across her face. "You don't wish to reveal the place where you keep your most secret possessions hidden."

Serving as part of a special military intelligence-gathering mission in Portugal, he had gained some rudimentary training in searching for hidden information. And a quick look around her quarters made him certain that it would take him less than half an hour to discover all the places where she might be keeping private treasures.

People were predictable. More so than they wished to believe. However, he decided to keep mum about it. Life had left her with precious few illusions. He would allow her to keep this one.

"I shall be happy to step outside while you retrieve it."

Still she hesitated.

Charlotte did not frighten easily. What sort of secret could elicit such a look of apprehension? A dark one, he decided. Let her keep that as well. He had enough of his own demons to wrestle with.

"You may feel free to lock the door to make sure I do not interrupt you," he added.

The offer spurred Charlotte to action. Rising, she took down the iron key from the peg by the entrance and led the way to the outer door. "I shall fetch you shortly."

The lock, noted Wrexford, was not very sturdy. He must look into having a better one installed. Edging back into the shadows of the eaves, he considered how the events of the morning had given a new and alarming twist to things.

He had drawn Charlotte into something more dangerous than he had imagined. The victims of her pen might curse her, but they had not sought to kill her.

That, however, might change.

Which was cause for further concern. Tyler's tracker was good, but there would be plenty of other men lurking in the underbelly of London who could be hired, and for a pittance, to learn where A. J. Quill resided. The boys, though quick and clever, were not yet a match for the ruthless cunning of a hardened criminal.

She was not stupid—she knew the life she had chosen entailed risks. But he couldn't help feeling a twinge of guilt.

A conscience was a cursedly inconvenient encumbrance.

Perhaps Henning, with his razored array of scalpels, could surgically remove it.

"You may return now." Charlotte's voice drew him back from such mordant musings.

Wrexford stepped through the half open door and shut it behind him. "I assume you keep it locked at all times?"

"As a lone woman, I'm aware of the need to take precautions," replied Charlotte.

"Then I shall not shilly-shally around my meaning, Mrs. Sloane," he said. "This second murder has, shall we say, painted a whole new picture of things. Until I've discovered how and why they are tied together, you had best be on guard."

"We," she said coolly. "Until *we* have discovered how and why they are tied together."

It took him an instant to absorb her meaning. "This isn't your fight," he said softly. "My neck may be in peril, but yours is not. Turn your quill on another subject, so you're not drawn into further danger."

The weak flicker of the lamplight caught the tightening of her jaw.

"And you need not fret. I will continue to honor our original bargain," he took care to add. "You will be well compensated for the loss of income suffered by looking at some other scandal."

Her smile only accentuated the ice in her eyes. "Gentlemanly honor demands that you protect the fairer sex?"

Her sarcasm was like a pinprick—shallow but painful, all the more so for being unexpected.

"You surprise me, Lord Wrexford," she went

on. "I took you for a man ruled by pragmatism, not sentiment."

"Don't take it personally," he replied. "As of yet, I have no blood on my hands. I'd like to keep it that way." He perched a hip on the edge of the table. "Too messy otherwise, and my valet abhors it when I get troublesome stains on my linen."

"God forbid we upset your valet."

"He's a very useful fellow."

Charlotte sighed, which seemed to trigger a retraction of her prickly hedgehog spines. "You need not try to shield me from unpleasantness. I know how to take care of myself."

"I have the utmost respect for your survival skills, so don't take it amiss when I point out that you've never faced a cutthroat killer who may decide you're sticking your nose in places where it doesn't belong."

Her reaction was cleverly evasive. "I thought you were all afire to see the scrap of paper."

"I am." Wrexford held out his hand. "Consider me a slave to fusty old notions of manly traditions, but I would also like to ensure that you aren't burned to a crisp."

Charlotte placed the Canaday library marking on his palm. "I may also have another useful bit of information for you," she said. "I shall explain once you are satisfied with my judgment about this clue."

"A day of revelations. What has prompted it?" he asked.

"One thing at a time, sir."

His mouth crooked, the left corner dropping a touch lower than the right. She was beginning to recognize his subtle quirks of expression—he was used to being in command and didn't like having his questions ignored.

Deal with it, she thought, holding back a smile. Disappointment chiseled away the weak parts of one's character. *Tap-tap.* Steel against stone, it shaped resolve.

Ignoring her silence, the earl was studying the symbol and numbers inked on the paper. His irritation was gone, replaced by a more pensive look. Charlotte tugged nervously at her skirts, though why she cared whether he believed her or not was a question she didn't care to contemplate too closely. Instead she made herself study the planes of his profile, and found her fingers itching to pick up a pencil and sketchbook.

Light and shadow, hard and soft. His face was infinitely intriguing. *A contradiction.* Which made it a conundrum.

He was right—there were too many puzzles, too many missing pieces. The unknown was dangerous.

The brusque sound of Wrexford clearing his throat drew her back to the problem at hand.

"The letter *C* could stand for a great many

names. I'm not familiar with Canaday's family crest, so I don't know—"

"The Canaday family crest shows two wolf-hounds rampant serving as supporters of the escutcheon," she interrupted. "The library symbol is clearly a variation, twining the canines with the *C*. Consult your copy of *Debrett's Peerage and Baronetage* and you will see I am right."

He fixed her with a searching stare. "How is it that you are familiar with *Debrett's*?"

"I don't live in the wilds of Siberia, though it may seem so to you, milord," replied Charlotte. "Ye god, the book is no havey-cavey secret! It's the bible of the beau monde, and is mentioned nearly every day in the drawing rooms of Mayfair. Of course I'm familiar with it."

For an instant he looked a little nonplussed, but quickly seized the offensive. "That may be, but"—his gaze shot to her desk and back—"I see no copy of it among your books, so unless you have magical powers of memory, how is it you know the exact details of Canaday's crest?"

"I consulted with a friend." It was not precisely a lie. Though that would depend on to what degree one was permitted to parse the English language.

Wrexford, however, accepted her answer without further fuss. "Very well, let's assume you are right about the library marking." He lapsed into thought. "Canaday admitted to lending

185

Holworthy three rare books on poetry, which the reverend refused to return. But I can't see him being murdered over a collection of verses, however valuable."

"I agree. There seems no rhyme or reason for it," she said dryly.

He gave no sign that he had heard her. She watched as his dark brows drew together.

"Unless . . ."

"Unless," murmured Charlotte, "Canaday was not forthcoming about any other books Holworthy borrowed."

"True. Though what I was about to add was that it might depend on how valuable the rare books were. You see, I've learned that both Canaday and Holworthy belonged to an exclusive club that caters to gentlemen with a love of literature and art. Collectors can be passionate about possessing certain works. Perhaps enough so to commit murder."

"Ah, yes. The Ancients," replied Charlotte.

Light sparked on his lashes as he started at her mention of the name. His eyes narrowed.

"As to that other bit of information I mentioned earlier," she went on quickly, "it concerns The Ancients."

Revelation. It was, thought Wrexford, a rather apt word to have pop to mind, considering the Reverend Holworthy and his grand biblical orations on Good versus Evil. Charlotte was, by her own admission, loath to share information. She hoarded each sordid nugget like a precious gemstone, selling them only when the price was right.

They were certainly not given away for free.

So that begged the question, What did she want in return?

Whatever it was, she was on edge about it. He had been surreptitiously watching her face, her gestures—as she had been doing of him. Oh yes, he had been aware of her scrutiny. The low light and shifting shadows obscured much, but he had been aware of her scrutiny. Her gaze was like the flicker of a candle flame, a soft, yet unmistakable whisper of heat.

The stool scraped over the floor as he shifted to face her head-on.

Charlotte jumped at the sound and seemed to withdraw into herself.

He waited. If she had something momentous to say, she would do it on her own terms.

"I am telling you this because through my own sources, I have learned that Holworthy was involved in The Ancients, which may in turn mean the club is somehow connected to the murder," Charlotte finally said. "And as you seem intent on discovering who is responsible for the crime—"

"Two crimes," he corrected. "And yes, I would

prefer to protect my own neck. So my intent can be termed purely pragmatic."

"As is mine. There is something very corrupt about The Ancients. A darkness that swirls beneath the polished manners, the self-proclaimed appreciation of art. I think they are responsible for . . . for evil acts, and I would like to see them destroyed."

"Would you care to elaborate?"

Her features pinched. "I can't give you specific facts, sir, if that is what you mean. I am basing the statement on . . . feelings. Or rather, suspicions." Her chin rose a notch, a wordless challenge. "I am aware that men think those of my sex are flighty creatures, incapable of rational thought and objective observation. But they are wrong."

"Mrs. Sloane, you strike me as the least hysterical person I know. Whatever the reasons are that have made you suspicious of The Ancients, I should very much like to hear them."

She let out a shuddering sigh. "I first met Lord Percival Stoughton a little over two years ago. My husband and I were living in Rome, where Anthony was pursuing his painting and studying classical art. To earn additional money, he served as a guide to wealthy Englishmen doing the traditional Grand Tour, showing them the antiquities and serving as a purchasing agent with the local art dealers."

The Grand Tour was an English rite of passage

that developed during the early eighteenth century. Young men of good breeding and wealth embarked on a journey through Paris, the south of France, and on to Rome, usually accompanied by a private tutor. It was expected that they returned home as polished, educated gentlemen of the world— bringing with them a collection of classical art for their country homes, with which to impress their neighbors.

Stoughton. Wrexford thought hard to place the man. "Viscount Stoughton, heir to the Earl of Northfield?"

She nodded. "You know him?"

"Merely by name," he answered.

Her shoulders relaxed ever so slightly.

"Do go on," he added gently, sensing her great reluctance to divulge any details of her personal life.

"Stoughton seemed eager to strike up a friendship with my husband," continued Charlotte. "Anthony was flattered by the attention. Like most struggling artists, he craved recognition of his talents, and Stoughton was effusive in his praise. I . . . I was happy for him at first, but something soon began to make me feel uncomfortable about it."

"In what way?" asked the earl when her pause for breath stretched out for several long moments.

"The flatteries felt overdone." Charlotte swallowed hard. Wrexford had never seen her appear so unsure of herself. "Please don't misunderstand me," she said haltingly. "My husband had great talent. He was a gifted painter. But he came from a modest background, and Stoughton from the highest circle of Society. It seemed odd to me that such a man would bestow such enthusiastic support on . . . on a nobody."

The earl nodded in understanding. It was important for one's own prestige to play patron to rising star, someone who would become an influential member of the art world. An unknown with no family connections was not a good choice to champion, no matter how skilled he was.

"Still," he mused, "while Stoughton may have displayed poor judgment, his behavior does not appear to merit the word *corrupt*. That is, unless there is more."

"There is," she replied, her voice growing firmer. "Along with the flatteries—and the purchase of two small canvases, which eased our financial worries—Stoughton began to encourage Anthony to return to London. He promised to put in a good word with friends and help secure admission to the Royal Academy. Anthony was, to put it bluntly, seduced. It had always been his greatest dream to gain admission to the Academy, to show his work there, to be acknowledged as an equal . . ."

Her voice trailed off as she took a moment to pour a cup of water from the jug on the table and take a sip.

"So, with his head filled with dreams of making a name for himself in London, and enough money to purchase our passage, he insisted we return to England, despite warnings from his physician that the climate was not good for his health." Another sip. "My husband had a very delicate constitution. One of the reasons we chose to live in southern Italy was because of its sun and mild weather."

"As soon as we found lodgings in Town, Anthony contacted Stoughton. To his delight, he was immediately invited to join a gentleman's club."

"The Ancients." Wrexford said it as a statement, not a question.

"Yes. And a few small commissions came in from several of the members, enough for us to scrape by. But the promised introduction to the Royal Academy and its members seemed to stall. There were always explanations for the delay. After a while, Anthony grew dispirited."

Charlotte reached for the fringed shawl draped over the back of her work chair and wound it around her shoulders, not before he saw a spasm shiver down her spine.

"More than that, he grew disturbed, prone to odd mood swings. He took to spending more time at the club, often not coming home until late at night. I pressed him to tell me what the allure was, for it seemed . . . unlikely that the wealthy well-born aristocrats had accepted him as an equal."

She had phrased her reservation carefully, but she was savvy and sensible enough to know the stark truth. There wasn't a snowball's chance in hell that the gentlemen who belonged to The Ancients were hobnobbing with a nobody out of the goodness of their hearts.

"You're right. It seems very unlikely," he agreed. "What was your husband's answer?"

Her expression remained stoic, but the shadows seemed to deepen beneath her eyes. "Evasive mutterings," she answered tightly. "And unhappy ramblings about how his talents were misunderstood, misplaced. I thought for a time that he meant the satirical cartoons, which he had begun shortly after our arrival in London. He had a knack for caricature, and keeping company with The Ancients allowed him to hear Society gossip. I arranged all the logistics for delivering them, and getting the payments."

Wrexford suspected she managed all the details of keeping the family afloat. Her husband struck him as rather weak, an ethereal, self-absorbed man-child lost in his own dreams.

"Thank God, Anthony was wise enough never to tell Stoughton about *that* artistic endeavor," murmured Charlotte, brushing away a lock of hair that had escaped its pins and curled over her cheek. "But as I said, though I first thought that was the reason for his mental agitation, I came to suspect it was something worse." A fraction of a pause. "Much worse."

The earl repressed the urge to ask what. It was, he saw, a struggle to confide the painful story to a near-stranger.

She met his eyes for a moment. "I can't tell you what it was. Anthony's health went into a rapid decline. At times he seemed drugged, disoriented. His ramblings became incoherent—at times, all he would mutter was the word *alchemy* over and over again."

"Alchemy?" Wrexford looked up sharply. "Your husband mentioned alchemy?"

"Y-Yes." Charlotte looked unsettled by the sudden question. "Why do you ask?"

"There was a fragment of half-burned paper in the laboratory that bore a strange reference to alchemy." He thought for a moment. "But then, much of the early experiments in chemistry had their roots in medieval alchemy, so I suppose it wouldn't be unusual for Drummond to have books on the subject." He decided to leave it at that. Given her agitated emotional state, he didn't wish to stir unwarranted alarm before he had a chance to study the evidence. "I expect it won't mean anything."

Her expression remained tense. "I don't see how it could. Anthony cared nothing about science. His passion lay in art."

Wrexford refrained from saying that in London

it had become quite fashionable for artists and men of science to think of themselves as kindred souls, creative spirits exploring the mysteries and wonders of Life.

"I know this is hard for you, Mrs. Sloane," he said quietly. "But please do go on."

Charlotte composed herself with a deeply drawn breath. "My husband's lungs then began to give out and he couldn't rise from his bed. I'm not quite sure how, but Stoughton learned of our address, and he and a friend came to visit several times. They claimed a grave concern for Anthony's well-being, and offered to pay for a physician. But I have learned to read people, milord. There was a far darker reason.

"They were angry over Anthony's illness—they needed him for something. I never learned what. Henning was kind enough to pay a visit when he heard of our troubles, but there was nothing he could do to halt the ravages of whatever was ailing him. All that was left was to make Anthony's last hours more comfortable, and for that he gave me a bottle of laudanum. Anthony passed away the day following Stoughton's visit."

Her gaze turned shuttered, and in that instant he was sure she suspected her husband of ending his own life.

It was, mused Wrexford, no secret that opium brought blessed oblivion from earthly suffering.

Charlotte stiffened her spine, as if steeling herself for his skepticism. "I did not tell you all this to elicit your pity, sir. And perhaps you think I am seeing demons when the real culprit was my husband's hopeless naïveté. Nonetheless, I wanted you to know that I believe The Ancients are the nest of vipers for whom you are searching. And I want you to cut off their heads before they sink their fangs into other people and poison more lives."

"Be assured, I take your beliefs very seriously, Mrs. Sloane."

The tightly wound tension in her body loosened a notch, and a ghost of a smile touched her lips. "Thank you. For not considering me a delusional peagoose."

"I wouldn't dare. Your pen is too sharp." His eyes strayed to the counter by the sink. "As is your chopping knife."

"If I'm tempted to cut anyone's throat, it won't be yours."

He let out a gruff laugh. "The hangman will be relieved to hear that. He has first claim on it."

Amusement momentarily chased the look of troubled uncertainty from her eyes.

"Be that as it may, I'm as anxious as you are to uncover what evil may be lurking within The Ancients," he went on. "Think hard, Mrs. Sloane. Can you recall any other details that could help indicate what your husband was involved in?"

"Trust me, sir, I have wracked my brain trying to think of what it might have been." In a fleeting gesture that was nearly lost in the flutter of shadows, Charlotte pressed her palms to her brow, a here-and-gone moment that left her looking very vulnerable.

It was the first real slip of her mask. And Wrexford guessed she would not thank him for seeing it. Quickly dropping his gaze, he carefully smoothed a crease from his shirt cuff. She deserved privacy for her pain.

"You mentioned your suspicions before. Were there any specific things that sparked them?" he pressed.

Charlotte slumped back in her chair. "Yes, there were two small things that struck me as odd," she said slowly. "Though you may think me mad, or merely a victim of an overfebrile imagination."

"We should not dismiss any evidence, no matter how odd it may seem. You are a very astute observer, Mrs. Sloane. I doubt you are prone to fits of melodramatic fantasy."

"I am beginning to wonder . . . Recent events feel like they have stepped off the pages of a horrid novel."

"No dungeons, clanking chains, or moaning ghosts have made an appearance," he quipped. "Yet."

Charlotte made a face. "If you are trying to be reassuring, you are making a hash of it."

However, the moment of humor seemed to dispel some of the tautness in her features.

"I'm simply stating the facts." Wrexford let the words sink in. "As should you."

"Very well, since you insist," she said, after stilling the twitch of her lips. "The first thing was, Anthony often came home with paint smudges on his hands. He was very fastidious about his appearance when going to the club—he wished to fit in with the gentlemen—and I am quite sure he never left our lodgings in a less than pristine state."

"Odd, but not inexplicable," he mused. "Your description of your spouse has painted the picture of a man passionate about his art. I've known artists who carried a small box of pigments and a sketchbook in their pockets for when inspiration struck."

"Lord Wrexford, I know the difference between watercolors and oil paints," answered Charlotte.

He nodded. "Point taken."

She tugged again at her shawl, knotting the fringes round and round her fingers. "At the end, there was something even more disturbing about his hands. I . . . I had thought it was another symptom of his nervous disorder, as his physical condition was fast deteriorating." The deepening shadows beneath her eyes were now dark as bruises. "But now that you've pressed me to look at things through the lens of Reverend

Holworthy's murder, I think it may have a more menacing explanation."

A shrill whistle from outside pierced the stillness of the room. Someone shouted a curse as a heavily laden cart clattered over the rutted lane.

The muscles of her throat contracted as she swallowed hard. "When he returned from his last visit to The Ancients, there were small burn-like discolorations on his fingers. And the pattern resembled splashes of liquid."

CHAPTER 11

The ensuing silence seemed to amplify all the tiny sounds in the room. The scrabbling of mouse feet behind the walls, the faint creaking of the rafters, the ragged hitch of her breathing . . .

He thinks me mad, thought Charlotte. *And perhaps he's right.* Her usual dispassionate sense of detachment had been knocked to flinders on hearing Jeremy mention The Ancients.

Such a tastefully civilized name, and yet the very whisper of it had sent a chill coursing through her veins.

"I make no pretense of being objective, milord," she announced, her voice sounding brittle as broken glass to her ears. "My reaction is very personal—some might call it primitive, based as it is on visceral emotion. I don't like or trust them, and so I am primed to see evil lurking behind their actions."

Wrexford crossed his legs. His boots, she noted, had a heavy spattering of straw-flecked mud marring the highly polished leather—strange how the mind seized on insignificant details as a distraction from difficult situations.

The seconds continued to slide by as if mired in molasses. His expression was a conundrum—a smile appeared to be waging a tug of war with a frown. Charlotte didn't trust herself to decipher its meaning.

At last, his gaze turned from some distant point in the gloom. "Death," he said, "is not a cerebral subject that one contemplates from afar." Though his voice held an edge of mockery, there was an undertone of raw emotion she hadn't heard in him before. "One's reaction to it does tend to be personal."

"Which does not make it right or rational."

"True," agreed the earl. "But I have great respect for your powers of perception, Mrs. Sloane. If you think something is dreadfully wrong, then it likely is."

Charlotte was surprised at how relieved she felt by the fact that he didn't find her crazy. "So, how do we go about proving it?" she said in a low voice.

Wrexford considered her question for a long moment. "Let us order the facts we have now. Your husband was lured back to London and invited to join The Ancients by Stoughton—for what reasons we don't yet know. He began to earn a little money, but you began to notice unsettling things about him, including unexplained paint on his hands, and an alarming change in his behavior. And then signs of acid burns and death."

She nodded.

"And then there is Holworthy's murder, which also involves acid and a connection to The

Ancients through Canaday and the bookmark you found."

"Yes," she said softly. "We have a great many pieces of a puzzle. The question remains, how do we begin fitting them together?"

"Slowly and methodically, as in a scientific experiment," he answered. "First of all, I need to visit Henning and see whether he's found anything unusual about Mr. Drummond's corpse."

"How do you know the body was brought to Mr. Henning?"

"My valet is useful for more than merely ensuring that my cravats have the perfect amount of starch," answered the earl. He held up the library marking. "Might I keep this? The next step will be to pay a visit to Lord Canaday's estate in Kent."

Charlotte nodded. It made sense for him to have the piece of paper.

"I will also take a closer look at the fragments I found in Drummond's laboratory."

"I thought you considered them a mere coincidence."

He hesitated. "They probably are nothing."

"Why is it that I'm beginning to sense you don't believe that?"

The earl evaded her question by ignoring it. "And then I want to learn a little more about what goes on at the Royal Institution. I pay little attention to its connection with the social swirl of London, but as science and its new wonders have become the darlings of Society, it's worth a closer look. Power and knowledge can be a potent combination."

The world of lords and ladies was closed to her, and yet she chafed a little at finding herself left standing outside the gilded gates, with no way to help in the hunt for the truth. Unlike the earl, she had no prestige, no influence, no favors to call in. She had naught but her pen.

"A moment, milord," she said quickly as he rose and reached for his hat. "About the murder this morning—describe the scene for me."

A scowl scudded across his face, clouding the austere angles of his face.

"Look, not only would it seem strange if A. J. Quill did not comment on the latest death, but it also serves our purpose to keep attention focused on the crimes," she explained before he had a chance to protest. "Serpents prefer to slither in the dark, so to shine a relentless light on their doings may provoke them into making a mistake."

Charlotte paused for thought. "I'll spend the next few days whipping up a lurid interest in this latest murder, and I shall start a series that focuses on The Ancients."

"You mean to poke a stick in the nest of the vipers?" he asked in a flat tone.

"Your valet has his particular skills and I have mine, sir. Satire can be a powerful weapon. We know its members use their prestige to keep their activities shielded in secrecy. They won't like public scrutiny. It may force them to try to cover up their tracks," she replied. "And cause them to make an errant move."

"Or cause them to coil and strike at their tormentor."

"It's a risk I am willing to take."

"You have courage," conceded Wrexford. He blew out his cheeks. "Too damnably much of it for your own good. A woman is supposed to—"

"Supposed to be seen and not heard?" interrupted Charlotte. "Like you, milord, I have little interest in conforming to the rigid expectations of my station in life."

The barb seemed to prick just enough to silence further warnings.

"And just remember, I've been forthcoming in helping you. I expect you to do the same."

"I am paying you a good deal of blunt," he reminded her.

"And I," responded Charlotte coolly, "am affording you the means by which to save your neck. So I'd call the exchange an even one."

His expression remained unreadable, but there seemed to be a momentary rippling beneath the flat opaqueness of his eyes. He hid his feelings well, but she had honed her skills at seeing the subtle signs that most people missed. Her survival depended on it.

The earl was wavering. She had but a moment to sway him to her side.

"You came to me because you were convinced that with my help you could discover the real culprit. That hasn't changed. Together, we can smoke him out, but only if you trust me with what you know."

"It's not a matter of trust. It's a matter of . . ." The skin tightened over his sharp cheekbones. His mouth thinned.

"Honor," he finally finished, the word barely louder than the whisper of the breeze stealing in through the cracked casement. "I don't want your blood on my hands."

"Be damned with honor," said Charlotte. "It's a bloody hollow notion you high-born gentlemen trot out only when it suits you." She tilted her head back, forcing him to meet her gaze. "I want justice."

An oath slipped through his clenched teeth.

She waited, keeping still and silent.

A moment passed, and then another. His stubbornness, she realized, was as iron-willed as her own. *Meum est propositum in contumax—my resolve is unyielding.* No wonder things were a constant struggle between them.

Finally, he relented, releasing a pent-up breath, along with another curse.

"Very well. But you seek it at your own peril."

Charlotte didn't bat an eye. "Describe the

laboratory and the position of Drummond's body," she said calmly, reaching for a notebook and pencil.

He grudgingly did so.

"You are an astute observer, milord. Not many people are." The pages snapped shut. "We shall make a formidable team."

Wrexford set his hat on his head and tugged down the brim to a jaunty angle. Perhaps it was just a quirk of the shading, but it appeared he was trying to disguise a smile.

"And don't forget, I expect to be supplied with the details on your future encounters, enough to craft a titillating drawing," she went on. "I can, of course, find them out on my own, but it would save me time and bother if you would do so."

"You drive a hard bargain, Mrs. Sloane."

"Not as hard as the king's hangman."

He cocked a silent salute and sauntered off without further comment.

The room seemed to lose a little of its warmth as the front door opened and shut. A draft, she decided. The air outside had taken on a chill bite.

Charlotte watched the momentary swirl of tangling shadows, then roused herself to rise and reset the lock. Despite her show of nonchalance to the earl, she was careful to take precautions.

Lord Stoughton had paid her no attention once she had made clear during their first encounters that his carnal glances were not welcome. For men like him, women had no God-given talents save to serve a very primitive physical purpose. There was no reason to think he would ever connect Anthony or her to A. J. Quill. But it would be naive to underestimate the depths of his depravity. He might not have murdered her husband outright, but she was sure that the metaphorical knife bore his bloody handprints.

Caught up in such melancholy memories, she retreated to her desk and began to draw.

Lost in laying in lines, crosshatchings, and color, Charlotte didn't look up until the scrape of the bolt sliding back broke her concentration. Rolling the stiffness from her shoulders, she forced a smile, unwilling to let the boys see how reliving Anthony's ghastly last days had left her feeling utterly expended.

"How did your lessons go?"

"I read a whole page on King 'Enry the Eighth aloud without making a mistake!" chirped Hawk. "And Mr. Keating showed us a globe, and what a werry tiny place England is!"

"*Very,*" corrected Charlotte gently. "What a *very* interesting report." To Raven she asked, "And you? How did you find it?"

"Could have been worse, I s'ppose," allowed the older boy. He was always far more wary about showing enthusiasm than his brother. Perhaps because he had several more years of experience in seeing how quickly and cruelly the world could crush hope and happiness. One learned early that it was best not to put a hex on the things one cared about.

"High praise, indeed," she said dryly. "Though it seems I shall have to ask Mr. Keating to spend more time on proper pronunciation of the English language."

That drew a grin from Raven. "Oiy ken natter the King's English wivout sounding like me mouff is full o' marbles iffen Oiy want to."

"Then pull your stool up to the table and prove it to me and your brother while we have some tea." She moved to put the kettle on the hob. "And apple tarts."

"Hooray!" cried Hawk, as he hurriedly climbed to a perch on his seat and set his elbows on the table.

Charlotte decided to overlook the less than lordly table manners. "I managed to save them from the jaws of Lord Wrexford, which was no small feat. He was very hungry, but I insisted two brothers deserved two tarts."

It was said lightly, but the words dispelled the boyish gleam in Hawk's eyes. His gaze grew troubled as he slowly traced a finger over one of the many scars in the old wood. "Lord Wrexford had a bruvver," he said in a small voice. "But he's dead."

Dear Lord. Her grip tightened on the kettle

handle. She couldn't imagine what had provoked the earl to mention such a thing.

"He—he sounded sad. But I s'ppose even a high-and-mighty lord can't stop the Reaper." Hawk looked up through his lashes in mute appeal for her to tell him he was wrong.

"No. That's beyond the power of any man, be he prince or pauper," said Charlotte, knowing it would do more harm than good to tell him false fairie stories. The boys needed to trust that she would always be truthful with them, no matter how much it hurt. "None of us knows when the Reaper's blade will strike. That doesn't mean we should hide in the shadows of despair. It's even more reason to live our lives with hope and optimism."

She saw Raven watching her intently and added, "We mustn't fear loving someone. Yes, there may be pain, but it's far overshadowed by joy."

Raven wiped his nose on his sleeve, using the gesture to dart a sidelong look at his younger brother. "His Nibs didn't look very joyful."

"Lord Wrexford may be sad," countered Charlotte quickly. "But I am sure he wouldn't give up the happy memories for all the tea in China."

"China," mused Hawk, "is a werry big place on the globe—much bigger than England. It must have an awful lot of tea."

"It must, indeed!" She let out an inward sigh of

relief. A hardscrabble life in the stews had at least taught the boys resilience. A cloud of fragrant steam rose up as she quickly filled the teapot from the whistling kettle and carried it to the table. "Now, tell me more about your lessons."

His boots crunching over the rubble of loose stones and broken bricks, Wrexford entered Henning's outbuilding. Flies were buzzing around the lantern that hung above the stone slab, leaving a trail of black blurs in the beam of oily light. Metal scraped against metal, though he couldn't make out the source of the sound.

"Have you found anything of interest?" he asked without preamble.

The surgeon dropped his scalpel into a metal bowl. "The human body, whether dead or alive, is always interesting, laddie. But I doubt you meant it as an abstract philosophical question."

"Correct." Wrexford moved closer. "I was hoping for something more practical, like what weapon might have caused the fellow's death."

"It was very neatly done, a clean stroke angled perfectly to pierce the heart cleanly through the left ventricle." Henning looked up, his habitual scowl looking even more pronounced in the yawing shadows. "Would you care to have a look?"

The earl noted an amorphous fist-sized shape sitting in the belly of a brass scale. Its dark surface had a liquid sheen in the wavering light.

"Thank you, but I saw enough butchered body parts in Portugal. I trust your professional eye to have caught the important details."

A laugh scratched at Henning's throat. "Aye, my peepers are still sharp as a saber."

"Dare I hope that means you can tell me what weapon killed Drummond?"

Henning rubbed a hand over his unshaven chin. "A carpenter's awl, an ice pick—you may take your choice between any number of everyday tools. All I can tell you is it was done with a needle-like length of metal, not a blade. And whoever wielded it knew what he was doing."

Wrexford considered the information. With a waggish lift of his brow, he couldn't resist challenging the surgeon. "Not a she?"

"Not unless she was tall as an Amazon and as muscled as that mythical Warrior Queen to whom you and your countrymen bow and scrape." Fiercely Scottish, Henning had no love for the English.

"Boudicca," murmured Wrexford. "Actually you should find her a kindred soul. She was fighting to keep her people from being oppressed by an invading force."

A grunt, impossible to interpret.

"So, you are of the opinion the killer possessed physical strength, and a familiarity with the art of murder," he said. "A soldier, perhaps?"

Henning blinked several times, the lamplight

210

setting off a winking of sparks on the tips of his lashes. "Or a student of medicine."

"Which unfortunately doesn't help to cut down the list of possible suspects," responded the earl. "The Royal Institution is the center of the scientific community in London. Many of its members have training in medicine."

A shrug. "Tracking down the criminal is up to you, laddie. I can only pass on what Mr. Drummond's recently abandoned mortal coil tells me."

"And I take it," said Wrexford dryly, "the mortal coil has nothing more to say?"

"Ah, a good question." Henning hunched over and appeared to be examining the dead man's hands. "The answer would be yes . . ." More movement, light flickering softly off the dexterous play of the surgeon's fingers.

"If not for the strange symbol penciled on his left palm."

After rinsing her brushes and putting away her paints, Charlotte carefully set to work with her pen-knife to put a fresh point on her quill. *Snip, snip.* It was a ritual that served to calm both mind and spirit after the intensity of creating a new satire.

However, her thoughts refused to quiet. *Snip, snip.* Each small cut seemed to add a new question to the unsettling ones already colliding inside her head. Had the earl been right? Should she have closed her eyes to the new evidence connecting The Ancients to the present murders?

There were, after all, plenty of other scandals at which to poke her pen. She could have left it to him.

"Honor." Charlotte whispered the word, feeling a chill skate down her spine as her breath tickled over her lips. She had thought cynicism had rubbed away all vestiges of such pompous platitudes. But maybe some things simply remained ingrained in one's being.

Whatever Anthony's weaknesses—and she hadn't been blind to the frailties of his character—he didn't deserve to have his life and his death dishonored by the foul manipulations of Stoughton and his fellow club members.

Snip, snip. The quill's point was now razor sharp. A test to her fingertip drew a tiny bead of blood.

Setting aside the pen and the knife, she stared down at her bare desk. Twilight was falling, the muddled shades of purple and pewter filtering in through the window warning that a squall was scudding in to cloud the night sky. The boys had taken her latest drawing to the engraver, and whether they returned before the rain began to fall would depend on Raven's mood.

He seemed unsettled of late, and she hadn't wanted to press for the reasons. No one else could fight his battles. He must wrestle with his personal demons, no matter that the match was an unfair one.

Her gaze strayed to the row of books lined up against the wall. The gilt titles stamped on the leather spines glowed with a mellow warmth, and Charlotte ran her hand along the bindings, hoping the familiar textures would help lift her spirits.

She hated feeling so helpless. Wrexford moved freely within aristocratic circles, allowing him to follow the clues. While she was shut out.

Charlotte inhaled deeply and let the air out in a *whoosh* of frustration.

Or was she?

The bookish scent of mingled paper, ink, and leather stirred an idea. *Alchemy.* However tenuous, there was a connection between the alchemy and the death of both her husband and Drummond. Learning more about the subject might allow her to discover something useful.

Charlotte quirked a wry grimace. But for that she would need a different selection of books. Her collection of history, poetry, and Latin classics would cast little light on the arcane mysteries of volatile chemicals and bubbling crucibles. And she didn't dare walk into the fancy bookstores or lending libraries of Mayfair.

There was, however, one person who might possess the books she needed to borrow.

CHAPTER 12

Henning shifted, carefully uncurling the dead man's fingers to display the pale palm. "See for yourself."

Crouching down, Wrexford strained to make out the faint marks penciled on the lifeless flesh. "What the devil is it?"

"Haven't a clue, laddie."

The surgeon's irascible demeanor was proving even more abrasive than usual. "Any other pearls of wisdom to offer?" he asked sarcastically.

A rusty chuckle. "Only that you might wish to make a copy of it, to study at your leisure. I daresay they will be coming to cart off the corpse for burial sooner than later." He tore off a non-too-pristine blank page from his dissection notebook and placed it on the stone slab, along with a heavily chewed pencil.

Wrexford looked at the offerings and heaved a martyred sigh.

"Bothered by a little blood and saliva? Good God, what a fastidious fellow you have become. The lordly life is making you soft as a sow's underbelly."

"Stubble your infernal nattering and angle the hand a little higher." The earl leaned in closer. Ignoring the unpleasant odors wafting up from the corpse, he quickly copied the strange symbol onto the paper.

Henning let the hand flop back onto the slab. "It may be a pebble, not a pearl, but considering that our recently departed friend here was a chemist, it could be that scribble is from one of the early books of secrets."

"That's the first useful thing you've said," muttered Wrexford as he folded the sketch and tucked it into his pocket. A medieval manuscript on chemical compounds and medicinal formulas was often referred to as a "book of secrets" because of the arcane language used to describe the experiments. Out of curiosity, he had looked at a few of them during his time at Oxford. But he had dismissed them as incomprehensible fiddle-faddle. His own interests lay in more practical work based on modern methods.

However, he had a sinking suspicion that was going to change.

For what the term *book of secrets* really referred to was the art of alchemy.

"That very thought had occurred to me," continued the earl. "I don't suppose you know anything on the subject."

Henning pursed his lips. "Not really. Much of it is based on wild superstitions rather than empirical knowledge, and teeters on the edge of witchcraft. But from what I understand, there is also much sound science in the early experiments."

Wrexford nodded. "So I have been told." He thought for a moment. "I wonder why he would make the mark on his palm? He was in his laboratory, with plenty of paper at hand."

"The body stinks of smoke and there was soot on his clothing," said Henning. "And the driver of the mortuary wagon said the laboratory was a half-burned shambles. Given that he was murdered, he might have sensed that he was in trouble, and feared that whatever the symbol means it was too dangerous to put down on paper."

"That makes sense." The earl blew out a harried sigh. "And yet it doesn't. By all accounts, Drummond was a mediocre chemist. He spent most of his time at the Royal Institution . . ."

Skulking around and spying on his fellow chemists.

Henning was watching him closely and slowly curled a smile. "Knowledge can be a dangerous thing, eh?"

"So it seems." Wrexford rose, feeling perplexed. "My thanks for your help."

"I have a feeling you may soon reconsider that," said the surgeon dryly. "Watch your step, laddie. I'd like for the next autopsy I do not to be on your carcass."

Tyler turned up the wick of the tall Argand lamp, brightening the illumination falling on the workbench holding the microscope. "I've pressed the fragments between glass, milord, and made sure the lenses are in proper alignment. The first one is ready for your inspection."

Wrexford shrugged out of his coat and dropped it on the chair by the door. "A pox on secrets and shadows," he growled. "Science is supposed to be about reason and logic."

"I take it your day has not brought you any closer to solving either murder."

The earl shook his head in disgust. "The path is only taking more twists and turns. Indeed, the mystery has deepened—it feels as if I've tumbled into a black hole." A netherworld of suspicions, lies, and innuendos, slithering through a noxious mist.

"You are not usually so fanciful," murmured his valet.

"I am usually not so frustrated." Wrexford took a seat at the workbench and began fiddling with a few of the brass dials on the microscope. "What do you know about alchemy?" he asked abruptly.

"I'm no expert on the subject, but I did a fair amount of study on it while a student at St. Andrews," answered Tyler.

"And here I've always credited your university with being a leader in modern scientific thought."

"Many of the early practitioners were quacks and charlatans. But many were serious students of proper scientific method," replied his valet.

"Much of Sir Isaac Newton's work involved explorations into alchemy."

"I would have thought he had more sense," muttered Wrexford.

"Don't rush to judgment, milord. Some of their ideas might surprise you," counseled his valet.

"I am heartily sick of surprises." The earl leaned up against the eyepiece and brought the charred paper fragment into focus. He studied the words for a few moments, though the razor-sharp magnification of the precision lenses did nothing to make their meaning clearer.

"Any ideas?" he asked tersely. "I'm assuming you took a careful look at it before I arrived."

"Yes and yes," replied Tyler. "As for ideas, I do have a few to begin with. Alchemists tended to be a secretive lot. Their writings were often encoded with all sorts of obscure references, often mythological, to make them incomprehensible to a layman. For example, Golden One could refer to the mineral sulfur, or some arcane chemical compound." He made a wry face. "I've seen recipes that call for one part fiery dragon, four parts dove of Diana, and seven eagles of Mercury. It may sound absurd to us, but other alchemists would understand the hidden meaning."

"So you think it may refer to a chemical and not an actual person."

"Possibly."

Wrexford let out a frustrated oath.

"But as for the second term on the fragment, I can be more specific, milord. In writings on alchemy, it's a common abbreviation for the philosopher's stone."

Wrexford vaguely recalled the term, but had long since forgotten its meaning. "Which is?"

"The holy grail of alchemy—by the by, alchemy was known as chymistry until the late sixteen hundreds, when Newton and his contemporaries began to call their scientific work chemistry, to differentiate it from the undisciplined efforts of the past."

"A fascinating history lesson," muttered the earl, "but might we return to the philosopher's stone?"

"Very well." Tyler sounded a little disappointed at having his explanations nipped in the bud. "It's said to be a substance with unique powers to change one element into another. Add a drop of the philosopher's stone to a common metal like lead, and it will be transmuted into gold," he explained. "Naturally, the idea that such a powerful concoction could be formulated inspired an obsession among many to make the ultimate discovery."

"Which would give the fortunate fellow unimagined riches as well as unimagined power." Wrexford huffed a snort. "Little has changed since Adam gobbled down the Apple—men simply cannot resist the Serpent of Temptation, with its seductive promises of God-like powers."

"True," agreed Tyler. "Indeed, there were those who believe that the philosopher's stone would not only turn lead into gold, but would also transmute the soul to eternal life."

"Eternal life? Ha, if you ask me, that could be more of a hell than a heaven."

"With all due respect, milord, you do tend to have an eccentric view of the world."

"I prefer to call it realistic." Wrexford turned his attention back to the fragment. "So, let us apply reason and logic to assess what we have here. Drummond believes something—or someone—is the Devil and is going to destroy . . . we don't know what."

"Presumably something of a grand nature—like Society, England, or the world," suggested his valet.

"A reasonable assumption," said the earl. "And presumably the philosopher's stone is dangerous because it's the instrument of this destruction."

"My thinking exactly, milord."

"So, we have Drummond's message." The earl rose and fetched the sketch he had made at Henning's surgery. "And we have this." He passed it over before resuming his seat. "Drummond had this symbol penciled on the palm of his hand. Do you have any idea what it means?"

Tyler took his time in studying the paper. "No,

I don't recognize it. But it looks very much like the type of pictograms used in alchemy."

"Which simply leaves us spinning in circles trying to connect them." Sarcasm shaded his voice. "We have deciphered Drummond's dire warning. We see a clear link with ancient alchemy." Wrexford gave another quick glance at the fragment, and then looked up. "And it all adds up to damnably nothing."

"Not yet."

Tyler, ever unflappable, was a cursed nuisance at times. "Kindly refrain from being so reasonable," he growled. "I would prefer to work myself into a truly foul temper and smash a few beakers against the wall."

"I am aware of that, milord. But we are running short of specialty glassware, and the order from Lutz and Münch in Zurich won't arrive for another fortnight."

Wrexford felt his scowl twitch upward. "Oh, very well. I shall put aside thoughts of smashing glass, no matter how soothing the sounds would be, and concentrate on a more practical expenditure of energy." He leaned back from the microscope, his fit of temper giving way to the challenge of solving the conundrum. "Let's examine the other scraps, in case there is any other information to be gleaned. But I have been thinking, and trying to apply logic to the facts we have in hand . . ."

Tyler perched a hip on the edge of the workbench. "Go on."

"We know Drummond was a sneak, and spied on his fellow chemists. My guess is he either overheard something, or stole some papers from a colleague's laboratory that put him in grave danger. And he didn't realize just how lethal the threat was until it was too late."

"So you believe he was in his laboratory the morning of his death trying to remove the incriminating evidence?" asked his valet.

"It seems a reasonable assumption," he answered. "Once I discovered the unlocked chemical cabinet, and Drummond understood that his laboratory had been broken into, he might have been spooked and realized keeping the papers there could be dangerous. He intended to hide them somewhere, however, the villain beat him to it."

"And so the villain kills Drummond, and as it's too dangerous to spend time searching for the evidence, he simply decides to reduce the laboratory to ashes," mused Tyler. "I see no flaw in your thinking."

The earl rose and began to pace around the room. "Then it stands to reason that the villain is a fellow member of the Royal Institution. I must learn more about the chemists working there, and what experiments are going on."

"Modern men of science tend to be just as

secretive as the ancient alchemists. They may not literally be trying to make gold, but certain chemical innovations would be worth a great deal of money," pointed out his valet. "They won't respond well to direct questioning."

Tyler was right, mused Wrexford. A host of new technologies—steam-powered engines, cloth manufacturing, the mass production of common implements like nails and cutlery—were revolutionizing everyday life, and all branches of science were fueling the changes.

"Then I must be discreet in how I gather information."

Tyler strangled a laugh with a brusque cough. "Discreet. An excellent strategy, milord."

The earl conceded the humor of his statement. But Tyler was not aware that he had a powerful ally in the fine art of uncovering secrets.

He halted by the hearth, the smile fading from his lips as he stared at the banked coals. Though in all honesty he was still conflicted about allowing Charlotte to put herself in mortal peril. The murderer had proved ruthless.

And remorseless. He would give no quarter.

"There are also The Ancients to consider," he murmured. "I mean to learn more about their private little circle."

"How?" inquired his valet.

"By exerting a bit more pressure on Lord

Canaday. I sense he's hiding something that he doesn't wish to come to light. I—"

"Hidden scandals?" Sheffield threw open the closed door without knocking and strolled into the workroom. "Excellent. The day has been deucedly boring. I knew I could count on some excitement stirring here."

Wrexford regarded his friend for a long moment. "You are acquainted with Lord Stoughton, are you not?"

"Yes." Sheffield adjusted his cuff. "A nasty little prick, if you ask me. More than a few people at the Wolf's Lair suspect he cheats at cards, though no one has yet caught how he does it."

"Honor among thieves? How quaint," quipped Wrexford. And yet the truth was, there was no greater insult to a gentleman's reputation— innuendos that he had strangled his grandmother would be far less damaging.

"Ha, ha, ha," chuffed his friend. "Unfortunately, you have the right of it. Lady Luck has shamelessly picked my pocket of late."

"You make it excruciatingly easy for her. If you would bother to apply mathematics to the game of vingt-et-un, the results would be different. Pascal's essay on chance proves—"

Sheffield silenced him with an offhand wave. "I'm not nearly so erudite as you are, Wrex."

"And not nearly so frivolous as you would have everyone think." He placed a chunk of coal on the embers and paused to watch a flame lick to life. "I wonder why that is?"

His friend's jaw tightened, and though his smile remained in place, it did not come close to reaching his eyes. The placid blue momentarily froze to a silvery shade of ice. "Do you really wish to engage in a discussion of our respective behaviors—both in private and in public?"

There were far more pressing battles to fight, and this one could be bloody. His advice to Sheffield on changing reckless behavior—admittedly rather like the pot calling the kettle black—might be well meaning, but his friend was clearly in no mood for their usual verbal thrusts and parries.

"I see I am hoist on my own petard." Shifting from the center of the fire, Wrexford leaned an arm on the marble mantel. "Let us put our blades away and cry pax."

Sheffield walked over to the set of decanters by the window and poured himself a brandy. "Pax."

The earl waited for him to take several swallows before asking, "If you're willing, I could use your help."

"It's hard to say no when you serve such a fine vintage."

"Find out as much as you can about Stoughton. I have reason to suspect he's involved in some very dirty dealings."

"Including murder?" asked Sheffield quietly.

The earl considered the question carefully before answering. "I'm not sure. But be discreet, Kit."

"*Moi*?" Sheffield contrived to look injured. "I am the very soul of discretion."

Tyler lifted his gaze to the ceiling, making his expression impossible to read.

"When I so choose," added his friend.

"I'm deadly serious. Confine your risk taking to the gaming tables. Our unknown adversary is dangerous." The earl suddenly realized that Sheffield had likely not heard of Drummond's demise. "There was another murder this morning, and likely connected to Holworthy, though I cannot yet connect how or why. But I intend to do so."

Tyler cleared his throat. "As to that, milord, I have just recalled that there is an important lecture taking place at the Royal Institution tomorrow. Davy is delivering further thoughts on his Bakerian Lecture, which drew such accolades. All of the members will likely be in attendance, along with most of the beau monde."

"A good place to begin," mused the earl

"I'll come along," volunteered his friend. "Two pairs of eyes and ears may prove useful. I will, of course, need to know what we are looking for."

Wrexford hesitated. "I—"

His reply was cut off by a soft knock on the door. "Forgive the interruption, milord," intoned his butler, the dark oak making the man's murmur even more muted. "But the man from Bow Street is here. And he is demanding to speak with you."

Wrexford went to the decanter and filled a glass with a dark amber malt from Scotland. "*Sláinte*," he muttered to his friend, raising a sarcastic toast. "To yet more chaos and confusion raising hell with my peaceful existence."

"He is being very insistent, milord," pressed the butler.

"Lucky you," murmured Sheffield.

"Show him to the Blue Salon." The earl tossed back a swallow. "I shall be there in a moment."

Charlotte put away the bread remaining from breakfast and poured herself a cup of tea. The boys had scampered off after the simple meal, leaving the house quiet. A fresh sheet of drawing paper lay ready on her desk, ready for the idea that had come to mind in the midnight hours. And yet, after the first few desultory lines had been sketched in, she set down her pencil, too distracted to focus on the task at hand.

Anthony. Alchemy.

When she had laid her husband's body in the grave, she had tried to bury the memories of that terrible ordeal—and her terrifying suspicions—along with him, God rest his soul.

But recent events had brought them back to life. Ghostly whispers begging for justice to be done. A part of her was afraid to listen. She had

227

managed to scrape out a niche for herself here in London, one that kept food on the table and a roof over her head. Dare she risk destroying all she had worked for by challenging gentlemen of power and influence? Gentlemen who could, with the flick of a finger, quash her like a bug.

"And yet, dare I risk living with my conscience if I choose prudence over principle?" whispered Charlotte. Wrexford had counseled caution, and she knew he was right.

But her head had rarely listened to her heart. Passions had always been the ruling force of her life, that fierce force of emotion that bubbled like liquid fire through her blood, that burned through reason and restraint like a flame through dry tinder.

Ironic, really, that she understood all too well the power of alchemy. Mix together the right combination of volatile elements and its sorcery cast a potent spell.

Huffing a sigh of surrender—a tiger was a tiger and could not change its stripes—Charlotte pushed aside her paper and rose to fetch her cloak.

Despite the spitting rain and swirling fog of the storm-tossed morning, the twenty-minute walk through the puddled streets did nothing to dampen her ardor. Casting caution to the wind was no more a choice than breathing. Arriving at a shabby brick building backing onto a back alleyway, she entered through the unlocked door and hurried down the ill-lit corridor to the back office.

A rumpled Henning looked up from his untidy desk, a look of grim resignation winking behind the lenses of his spectacles. "I feared you might be paying me a visit, lassie. I don't suppose I can convince you to let the past lie buried."

"No," replied Charlotte. "Not with demons alive and sauntering streets, their evil hidden beneath a thin veneer of well-tailored and smooth-as-silk lies."

"Pay no heed to the rumors and gossip. Wrexford is a clever fellow, and tenacious as a bulldog when he has a bone between his teeth. I know him from the Peninsula. He'll not shy away from bringing the truth to light, whatever it may be."

"He's an aristocrat," she said softly. "Bonded by the blue blood of his class."

Henning shook his head. "Nay, lassie. The earl possesses rather heretical views on the absurdity of inherited privilege." The surgeon paused to flick a bit of ash off his sleeve. "And a great many other subjects. As I said, don't underestimate him. He tends to surprise people."

A challenge. She was used to that.

Charlotte met his flinty stare with a show of steel. "As do I, Mr. Henning." A faint whiff of sparks and sulfur seemed to crackle in the air. "Whether or not you're right about His Lordship, I've learned over the years to rely on no one but myself."

He shuffled slowly through his papers. "It's a pity you've had to learn so hard a lesson."

"I have little patience with pity," she replied a little sharply. "The strong survive. It's as simple as that."

Her answer appeared to amuse him. A twinkle flashed in his shrewd eyes. "You have grit, I grant you that."

A signal of approval, Charlotte hoped. It was something the surgeon gave grudgingly.

"Will you help me?" she asked flatly.

"What is it you need?"

"Any books you might have on alchemy."

Frowning, he scratched at his chin. "Not my cup of tea, Mrs. Sloane. I'm a pragmatist, not a dreamer. I care about lessening the misery of everyday ills, not chasing after imaginary miracles." He pulled a face. "Though the secret of turning lead into gold would be a damnably practical one to possess."

"Lead into gold? Wasn't that just an obscure medieval fantasy?" said Charlotte. "Surely it's been dead for centuries, along with the mad monks who had created it."

"Greed is timeless," answered Henning dryly. "And while the idea might seem mad, a number of serious men of science devoted their efforts to alchemy, believing it possible."

She felt a shiver skate down her spine.

"As to books, I may have a few from student

days at St. Andrews." The surgeon levered to his feet and ambled over to the overflowing bookcases crammed around the perimeter of the room. "I warn you, though, a few of them are in Latin."

After a moment's hesitation, she replied, "That doesn't present a problem."

His brows winged up slightly, but he merely turned and began to search the shelves.

Stepping a little closer to the hearth, Charlotte sought to warm her hands over the barely glowing coals. Papers rustled, punctuated by a grumbled curse and the loud thump of something heavy falling to the floor. She remained tactfully silent.

"Auch, so that's where you benighted buggers have been hiding," he finally muttered.

He returned to his desk and set down an armload of books, along with several manuscripts, each one tied together in rough brown twine. "Here ye go, lassie: *The Aurora of the Philosophers*, a classic work by Paracelsus, the famous Swiss alchemist; *The Triumphal Chariot of Antimony* by Basil Valentine; a medieval translation from Arabic of Jabir ibn Hayyan's work; and a handful of other titles, though Lord only knows what you hope to glean from them."

Henning stacked the books in a haphazard pile. "And several copies of Newton's notes on alchemy, along with a recipe called *Preparation of Mercury for the Stone*, written by Eirenaeus Philalethes."

"The poor man," murmured Charlotte. "His name sounds as if one is choking on a piece of rotten fish."

"Alchemists were very secretive about their writing—and with good reason," explained the surgeon. "It's been illegal for centuries to practice alchemy, both here in England and on the Continent, and the penalties were quite severe, including death—transgressors were to be hung from a gilded scaffold."

"That seems rather extreme," responded Charlotte. "Was it for religious reasons?"

"Only partly," he replied. "Governments—being made up of pragmatic souls like me—were aware that if individuals could make gold at will, it would devalue the country's finances and destroy the economy." A smirk. "That certainly put the fear of God into them."

"Interesting."

"So a number of men who practiced alchemy wrote under secret pen names. In the case of Eirenaeus Philalethes, his real name was George Starkey. He was an upstart American who studied at Harvard College in Boston, where he became enthralled with alchemy. After earning fame practicing medicine in his country, he came to England in 1650 and established himself as a leading physician," went on Henning. "But he also became a leader in the occult arts, greatly influencing his contemporaries, including such notable men of science as Robert Boyle and the great Sir Isaac Newton himself."

Henning ran a hand over the knotted twine wrapped around the manuscripts. "Newton was extremely careful to keep his interest in alchemy very quiet. He never published any of his writings on the subject, but his private papers show he spent a great deal of his time trying to formulate the philosopher's stone—though he often disguised the chemical ingredients he was using by giving them fanciful names like 'dove of Diana'."

Chariot of Antimony, dove of Diana, the philosopher's stone. Charlotte felt her head was beginning to spin with all the arcane terms.

Henning, a careful observer of others despite his own disheveled appearance, must have read something of her thought in her face. "So tell me, Mrs. Sloane, what exactly do you hope to find in all this?"

"I'm not sure," she answered slowly. "Granted, unlike Lord Wrexford, I have no formal knowledge of chemistry or science. But sometimes bringing a different perspective to a problem can help in seeing the solution." She hoped she sounded more confidant than she felt. "The untutored eye is not influenced by expectations of what it is supposed to see. It can respond to intuition, to . . . imagination."

Henning's mouth quirked in what may or may not have been a smile. "The art of perception?"

A faint flush rose to her cheeks. "It may sound silly to you—"

"Nay, not at all. These days, there are many very prominent intellectuals who believe that science and art have much in common." After rummaging through one of his drawers, he found a large piece of oilskin cloth and set to wrapping the books and manuscripts against the inclement weather. "I don't envy you the task, but I wish you well."

"Thank you." Charlotte took the package and started for the door.

"Two last things, lassie. My door is always open to you. Despite my snaps and growls, I'll not bite your head off if you come to me needing help."

The weight in her arms seemed to lighten ever so slightly. "I'm grateful for that, Mr. Henning." Knowing it would nettle him—prickle for prickle seemed only fair—she added, "You've a soft heart under that crusty hide."

He chuckled, but the sound quickly gave way to a harsh exhale. "Watch your step, Mrs. Sloane. As I warned Wrexford, I've already had two people connected to strange chemicals and strange writing end up as corpses on my slab. I'd like not to have a third."

CHAPTER 13

Wrexford squeezed into the crowded lecture hall, followed by Sheffield, who reluctantly left off flirting with a young lady of his acquaintance to keep company with the earl. Few seats were left, though there was still a quarter hour to go before the talk was to begin. Finding a pair at the upper railing that afforded a good view of the stage, Wrexford quickly claimed one and turned his attention to the audience.

The buzz of conversation and trill of muted laughter filled the cavernous room, along with the swish of silks and satins as the ladies and gentlemen settled into their places. It seemed to his eye that in addition to the serious scholars of science, most of the beau monde was present.

"Humphry Davy has drawn quite a crowd," he observed.

"Including his usual legion of adoring ladies," quipped Sheffield, tugging at his carelessly tied cravat. His hair was uncombed as well, but the aura of raffish insouciance fit him like a glove. Wrexford had noted on their arrival that Davy wasn't the only one attracting interested glances from the opposite sex. "It's said they bring their notebooks and pencils not to record any intellectual thoughts but rather to write him billets-doux, which they pay the porters to deliver to his private office."

"How edifying to hear that men of science have become London's leading celebrities," said the earl, not lifting his gaze from the crowd below his vantage point.

"What—have you not received a bundle of love notes? Perhaps you should pay more attention to amatory pleasures, seeing as the Runner seems to be striding closer and closer to having you arrested for murder."

The earl ignored the barb. It was true—the meeting with Griffin had not gone well. The Runner had come to ask a number of pressing questions about what had brought the earl to Drummond's laboratory, and had clearly been unsatisfied with the answers. So far, he had not dared arrest a peer of the realm, but the circumstantial evidence was building enough of a case to give him just cause.

All the more reason to uncover the truth.

"Might you pull your mind from the boudoir and focus on the reason you are here, Kit?" he retorted. Sheffield had made the rounds of the gaming haunts in St. Giles the previous evening, and though his inept play at cards had cost Wrexford a small fortune, he had come away with some very useful information. "See if you spot any members of The Ancients."

Heaving a martyred sigh, his friend began

a closer study of the hall. "Well, well, there's Stoughton," he murmured a few moments later.

Wrexford felt himself stiffen. "Where?"

"There, in the third row back from the stage, sitting next to Sharpley."

"Sharpley isn't on your list," he said softly.

"No, but he recently inherited a tidy sum from a bachelor uncle, and Stoughton is drawn to money."

Which made his interest in Mrs. Sloane's late husband even more of a conundrum.

Wrexford took a moment to study the man. An elaborate cravat of perfectly starched white linen, anchored by a large ruby stickpin, immediately drew the eye to Stoughton's face. His features were handsome—a straight nose, sculpted cheekbones, a well-shaped mouth with an easy smile. A crown of glossy chestnut curls accentuated the air of aristocratic confidence. *Interesting,* thought the earl. Stoughton was only of average height and build but he understood the subtle art of manipulation enough to accentuate his strength rather than his weakness.

"By the by, what led you to suspect Stoughton of evildoings?" asked Sheffield.

"The information was given to me in confidence." Wrexford hadn't told his friend about Charlotte's story. It wasn't his to share.

Humphry Davy's arrival on the stage cut short any further speculation. Despite his diminutive stature, the charismatic chemist exerted a powerful magnetism on the crowd. An expectant hush fell over the hall as he stepped up to the lectern. Taking out his notes from a red leather document case, he graced the audience with a smile and began to speak.

Leaning back, Wrexford settled in to listen—the subject matter was of great interest—though he continued to observe his surroundings.

In the opposite gallery, he spotted Declan Lowell seated half in shadow, an expression of satisfaction on his face. He had a right to look pleased, thought the earl. It was an impressive turnout, and quite a feather in the Royal Institution's cap that it had become so popular with high society.

Lowell, he knew, was a big part of its success. His charm and social standing allowed him to curry favor with arbiters of style, while his discipline and work ethic ensured that things ran smoothly behind the scenes. Did he perhaps have hopes of being named the next head of the Institution, as it was rumored that Davy would soon be stepping down from the position?

Lowell caught the earl's gaze and acknowledged it with a polite nod and smile.

Sheffield noted the exchange and murmured, "Lowell plays the perfect aristocrat."

"He seems a pleasant enough fellow. Are you implying you don't like him?"

"Not really. It's just that beneath the choirboy

looks, he's not an angel." Sheffield pinched a wry grimace. "But then, neither am I."

"Lowell has vices?" Wrexford didn't much care about the fellow's personal proclivities, but as the murders were proving so diabolically difficult to make sense of, he was trying not to overlook any detail, no matter how irrelevant it might seem.

Grasping at shadows. Or so it felt. Perhaps by luck he would pull a clue from out of the dark.

Sheffield shrugged. "No more than most of us. At least, not that I know of. He's been known to rack up large gambling debts, and be late in settling them. But I, of all people, understand the travails of being a younger son—it's hellish hard trying to live the life of a buck of the *ton* on a pitifully small quarterly allowance."

"I see," said the earl neutrally, sensing that his friend might be exaggerating the amount of the debts. Most every gentleman gambled. It wasn't likely that Davy and the board of governors of the Royal Institution would entrust the job of superintendent to anyone whose reputation might be in question.

"Forget I mentioned it," grumbled Sheffield, as if reading his thoughts. "I'm simply in a foul temper over my own execrable performance at the tables last night. And misery loves company."

"Learn to count," advised the earl.

"Ha, easy for you to say." Sheffield slouched

lower in his seat. "I am not blessed with intellect."

"Like any muscle, the brain needs exercise to toughen it up."

That drew a reluctant grin. "Touché." As Sheffield shifted, his eyes suddenly narrowed. "Lowell may be a perfectly fine fellow, but the man sitting to his left—see there, deep in the shadows—is St. Aubin. A thoroughly dirty dish."

"So you implied." Wrexford inched forward in his seat for a better look at the man. "That surprises me. I've heard no hint of dark rumors about him."

"You don't circulate in the same dens of iniquity as I do on occasion," replied Sheffield, dropping his voice to a whisper. His expression, normally one of cheerful cynicism, hardened to one of grim-edged anger. "He may look like an angel, but word is, he's not welcome at some of the discerning brothels. The madams hate turning away money, but it's apparently not worth the damage to their girls."

He darted another glance at St. Aubin's smoothly handsome face. Who would guess it to look at him? His gaze lingered, noting that the man's carefully combed hair, cut in the latest a la Brutus fashion, was a light enough honey hue to be considered golden.

"It's also said that he was encouraged to resign from his regiment," added Sheffield. "There were rumors about cheating at cards, and though no formal accusations were made, his fellow officers didn't trust him."

Lordly privilege could cover a multitude of sins, reflected Wrexford. Some highly respected families boasted naught but a centuries-long line of scoundrels and wastrels. Glitter and glamor cast a bright enough sheen to disguise the rot beneath the surface.

"And yet he's welcome within the highest circles of Society, and considered a catch on the marriage mart."

"Yes. In fact, he's courting the Marquess of Greenfield's daughter." His friend's eyes had now darkened to the same gunmetal grey shade as a thundercloud. "I've known Harriet since we were children. She deserves better—much better. And now she will have a chance to find a more suitable husband." A harsh exhale squeezed from his lungs. "It may be an unspoken rule among gentlemen that we don't tell tales on each other's foibles. But in this case it would have been dishonorable to remain silent."

"You spoke to Greenfield?" asked Wrexford. He suddenly thought of Charlotte, and how many women were at the mercy of men like St. Aubin. They could, quite literally, get away with murder.

"Of course I did," said Sheffield. "Ye god, how could I have lived with myself if I hadn't done my best to protect a friend."

A smile touched Wrexford's lips. "Perhaps we

241

are both not quite the devil-may-care rogues that most people assume we are."

"Hell's bells," Sheffield gave a mock shiver. "Don't let *that* cat out of the bag."

Wrexford darted another glance to the far gallery. "Any idea of the connection between St. Aubin and Lowell?" It seemed an unlikely friendship, given what he had just heard.

His friend thought for a moment. "I believe they know each other from Eton."

Ah, the innocence of youth. Schoolboy bonds could be lasting, no matter how much a fellow might change.

"I wonder what brings St. Aubin here?" he mused. "To my knowledge he has no connection to the Institution. And somehow I doubt he has an intellectual interest in science."

"Perhaps he's stalking a new victim," muttered Sheffield. "As you see, most of the leading ladies of the *ton* are attending."

"Do me a favor, Kit, and see what more you can learn about St. Aubin's activities from your sources. Let's see if he does indeed have any connection to Holworthy."

"With pleasure." Sheffield shifted in his seat. "Though I'll need another infusion of funds. I was bled dry last night."

"God Almighty. No wonder your father longs to disown you."

Before Wrexford could add any more barbs,

the lecture ended to a loud and lengthy applause.

Davy exited the stage, and as the audience began to rise and make their way out of the lecture hall, Lowell reclaimed the earl's attention. The superintendent had moved smoothly to the archway of the gallery in order to greet the spectators who were filing out. He watched him exchange words with the dowager Duchess of Ayrthorpe and her granddaughter. The ladies laughed at something he said, and allowed themselves to be led to a private salon off the lecture hall, where refreshments were being served to a select group of important guests.

Gracefully done, thought the earl. Lowell had the well-mannered ease of someone born into a world where style and charm counted for more than substance. And unlike most gentlemen of the aristocracy, he had found a way to use his talents to do something useful.

The vast majority of them were bored to flinders.

And boredom could be dangerous.

"Come, let us go join the private party," suggested Wrexford. "And see what gossip bubbles up."

"You go on," replied Sheffield. "I think I shall stroll over to White's and start seeing what more I can learn about St. Aubin. Grenfall is usually there at this hour, and he was in the same Guards regiment."

"Discretion, Kit," reminded the earl.

His friend cocked a mock salute and headed off.

Charlottte set Henning's package on her desk, then removed her damp cloak and stirred the embers in the stove to life. Thankfully, her finances now allowed her to add some extra chunks of coal. Though the clouds had started to clear, the watery sun was too weak to chase the chill from her bones.

And an unwilling glance at the dark oilskin wrapping did nothing to dispel the feeling.

Strange how the minds of men could be capable of creating both poetic beauty and coldhearted terror. How was it that some individuals believed they had the right to transcend their mortal powers to play God with the universe?

She blinked as the lamplight sputtered, the just-lit wick needing another instant to steady its flame. No possible answer came to mind, save for that the temptation of Evil had been an elemental part of the human condition since the Garden of Eden.

Settling into the comfortable contours of her work chair, Charlotte felt a frisson of surprise at how loath she was to cut the cording around the books. Since Anthony's death, she had kept her fears and suspicions—and yes, her guilt—locked away, telling herself the past was the past. That nothing would bring him back had seemed a compelling reason for focusing on the future.

And now?

Somehow, she knew in her heart that with the flick of her penknife, she would be taking an irrevocable step.

A crossing of the Rubicon. There would be no going back.

Once she committed to an active investigation, not simply confiding her secrets to Wrexford and allowing him to act, she would have to face her doubts, and the demons whose taunting whispers implied that she should have been strong enough to save Anthony.

Perhaps even more unsettling, she would have to face her own niggling resentment at feeling guilty. The roles should have been reversed, but Anthony had always been ethereal, incapable of shouldering the responsibilities of everyday survival. He had retreated into his art and his dreams, leaving her to manage the realities of life.

Leaving his death—along with all the conflicting emotions shrouding it—buried might be for the best.

The truth would, of course, also remain entombed, moldering for eternity in the same deep, dark crypt . . .

Footsteps peltered across the foyer. The inner lock yielded to a key and the door flung open with a *thump*.

"Look, look, m'lady!" A breathless Hawk skidded to a halt, followed by Raven, who was moving at a slightly more sedate pace. "I found a ha'penny in the mud at Covent Garden market and I bought these for you!"

As Charlotte looked up through the flitting shadows, the small clutch of pale pink roses was like a blaze of sweet sunlight brightening the gloom.

Her throat tightened. "Oh, how lovely," she said in a small voice.

"You like 'em?" Hawk came a step closer, suddenly looking a little uncertain. "There wuz other colors, but Raven thought ye'd like pink best."

"On account of your fancy shawl," explained his brother.

The boy had sharp eyes. These days, Charlotte wore sturdy, serviceable garments fashioned in muted shades of grey and brown. But tucked away in her armoire was a Kashmir paisley shawl from long ago, woven in soft shades of pink and rose madder. She had put it on once, in celebration of Anthony's birthday.

"They're perfect." She rose and gave Hawk a swift hug before taking the bouquet and placing it in an earthenware jug. "See how they make the room look so cheerful." The leaves fluttered as she set it on the table, as if casting a spell to banish the grim ghosts from the place.

"Silly, if you ask me, te make a fuss over bits of greenery," said Raven, but his mouth curled up at the corners as he took in his younger brother's beaming face.

"Beauty lifts the spirits," she told him. "As do art and poetry and music."

"But they'll just be dead in a few days," he replied.

"All the more reason to appreciate this moment, and hold it close to brighten a darker day."

Raven shrugged, and yet beneath the fringe of his dark lashes, Charlotte could see his gaze had turned pensive.

"And now it is my turn to give a gift." She took a shilling from the purse in her desk drawer, along with two pencils and several sheets of sketch paper, and handed them to Hawk. "There is still plenty of daylight left. Treat yourselves to a visit to the Tower Menagerie. I would like for you to draw me some pictures of the lions."

"Huzzah! Lions!" cried Hawk. He made a fearsome face and let out a throaty roar.

"Aye and you're just the right-sized morsel for their afternoon tea," teased Raven. "Have a care, runt. You're puny enough to tumble through the bars and end up as pudding fer the beasts."

"I'm growing," protested Hawk. "Soon I'll be nearly as big as you!"

His brother answered with a very rude sound.

"Run along and enjoy yourselves," said Charlotte, finding their youthful exuberance had given her the courage to smile.

As they ran off, playfully pushing and shoving to see who could get out to the street first, she carefully relocked the door and returned to her desk.

The gloom shivered, sending dark-on-dark ripples through the shadows as it came back to life and started to creep out from the corners of the room.

Drawing a shuddering breath, Charlotte looked down at the bundle of books. She picked up her penknife. Though feather light, its weight pressed heavily against her palm.

Choices, choices.

Snick, snick. The blade severed the cords.

"*Alea iacta est*," she whispered, tugging the twisted hemp free of the covering. *The die has been cast.*

Lowell was surrounded by a circle of prominent Institution patrons by the time Wrexford made his way to the salon. There was, he noted, no dearth of other luminaries crowded into the room. Davy's good friend the famed poet Samuel Coleridge was present and chatting with Joseph Banks, the éminence grise of scientific London, while the dashing Count Rumford, one of the principal founders of the Institution, was regaling the novelist Maria Edgeworth with stories of his adventures on the Continent. And, of course, the ladies of the *ton* were flocking round them, like so many brilliant butterflies in their gossamer silks and jewel-tone colors.

After accepting a glass of champagne punch, Wrexford strolled over to join a group of fellow members, curious to hear what was being said about Drummond's demise.

"Though it may not be kind to speak ill of the dead, he was an unpleasant fellow," responded Lord Thirkell to the earl's casual question. "His attention was focused more on snooping around what the rest of us were doing, as if looking for a way to steal the march on our discoveries."

Several nods confirmed the sentiment.

"You don't think he was engaged in his own research?" probed Wrexford. "I thought I heard somewhere that he had become interested in old writings on the philosopher's stone?"

A chorus of guffaws greeted the question.

"The stone?" Farnum made a pained face. "What utter fustian. Though I suppose it doesn't surprise me that Drummond would be drawn to such fiddle-faddle."

"Aye. The man didn't have a sensible—not to speak of original—idea in his cockloft," agreed Lord Greeley. "We shall have to be more careful as to who is elected to take his place."

As the men began to debate the merits of several potential candidates, Wrexford drifted away, pausing to exchange inconsequential conversation with a few other acquaintances before spotting Lowell break away from the Scottish visitors and take refuge in the lee of a massive floral arrange-ment set atop a marble plinth.

"An impressive turnout," he murmured, lifting his glass in salute as he joined the superintendent.

Lowell gave a wry smile. "Murder may have added to the allure of the event. People have a ghoulish fascination with scandal."

"Yes, I'm well aware of that," he answered dryly.

A chuffed laugh. "Sorry if I have touched a sore spot, Wrexford."

"I assure you, I've long since ceased to feel any sort of discomfort from what is said about me."

"You truly don't give a fig for what others think?"

"Not particularly."

"An admirable sangfroid." Lowell sighed as his gaze glided over the crowd. "Alas, my position requires I make compromises. As in somehow finding polite platitudes to deflect the dowager's suggestion that I court her granddaughter."

"There could, I suppose, be worse fates," said the earl.

"Not many." Lowell gave a mock shiver. "I'd rather be boiled in nitric acid. The girl can't string two coherent words together."

Wrexford chuckled, but the quip made him curious about how the man had come to be working for the Institution. "Speaking of acid, have you an interest in chemistry? Is that what drew you to serving as superintendent here?"

"No interest, and no knowledge," confessed Lowell. "I'm afraid I couldn't distinguish sulfur from saltpeter or sugar. However, I've a need to earn my own keep, and as I seem to have a knack for administrative details, my father used his influence with Rumford to help me secure the position."

"You must find all the talk of science a bit boring."

"On the contrary. I have an interest in *Lepidoptera*—butterflies in particular—so I understand the curiosity to observe and understand the world around us." A wry smile. "Though some might call it an obsession."

Wrexford nodded. "Clearly you understand the workings of the scientific mind."

"I dabble, that is all, and my interest is likely frivolous, for I'm simply drawn to the beauty of form and color," replied Lowell. "Despite my lack of seriousness, the board has kindly allowed me to have a small study space in the basement for my specimens. But, of course, my main focus is on the work of running the Institution, which requires most of my time."

"You do it well," replied the earl. "Not everyone has the gift of dealing smoothly with difficult people."

Lowell took a small sip of his wine. "I have

had a great deal of experience—my family is notable for its collection of irascible eccentrics and curmudgeons." A note of humor crept into his voice. "I seem to be the only levelheaded, even-tempered one of the lot."

"Drummond's murder must certainly have tested those qualities." Wrexford decided not to waste the opportunity to learn what he could about the Runner's investigation. "Is Mr. Griffin making any progress in identifying a suspect?"

"Other than you?"

Wrexford grinned at the gallows humor and found himself liking the fellow more and more. "It would be far more comfortable if he would fasten his jaws on the real culprit. It's a cursed nuisance to have the man constantly nipping at my heels."

"I take it you found nothing in the laboratory that might help direct his attention elsewhere?"

"There was nothing of interest," he lied.

Lowell's expression remained politely neutral. Whatever he was thinking, he masked it well. "How unfortunate."

A comment that could hold a number of different meanings.

"Nor," added Wrexford, "did I abscond with any incriminating evidence. I didn't kill Drummond."

"Actually, I didn't think you did. Else I wouldn't have allowed you to go back inside the room," said the superintendent. "I simply meant it was unfortunate that there is nothing to help Griffin catch the murderer. After the first flurry of prurient interest, the beau monde will begin to find the scandal distasteful, and that may affect our attendance. So naturally I would prefer to have the crime solved as soon as possible. To that point—"

A hail from across the room interrupted the exchange. "Alas, duty calls," said Lowell. "Lord Boscobel is demanding my presence. If you would excuse me."

"But of course," replied Wrexford.

The superintendent set down his drink on the plinth. "As I was about to say, do let me know if there is anything else I can do to help."

"I shall." Though at the moment the earl couldn't think of anything that might prove useful. He still felt damnably in the dark. Though he had a number of tantalizing clues in hand, as of yet he could make no logical connections between them.

Logic. Charlotte would no doubt chide him to trust more in intuition. Though that sense seemed to be failing him as well.

After a few more desultory conversations with the other guests, Wrexford left the party and headed down to the street. On reaching the corner of Piccadilly Street, he hesitated on which way to turn. His club was just a short walk down

St. James's Street, and at this hour, Canaday was likely to be in the reading room, enjoying a cigar and a glass of port. Instead, he crossed the street to flag down a hackney and ordered it to head east.

CHAPTER 14

Charlotte slowly unwrapped the oilskin and set the twine-tied bundle of manuscripts aside for later. After examining the books, she decided to begin with the one filled with exotic imagery. Setting her notebook and a pencil close at hand, she returned to the beginning and started to read.

> All things are concealed in all. One of them all is the concealer of the rest— their corporeal vessel, external, visible, and moveable. All liquefactions are manifested in that vessel. For the vessel is a living and corporeal spirit . . .

The pictures ranged from simple geometric shapes and complex symbols to elaborately detailed engravings, and the deeper she delved into the pages, the more mystified she became. Many of them appeared based on ancient mythological or biblical references, while other weirdly fantastical images had no point of reference in her scope of knowledge.

In some ways, the sheer scope of imagination was extraordinary. But Charlotte found she could not admire them. Some, in fact, were deeply disturbing. Their essence was all about seeking control and power.

Even if it meant making a Faustian pact with the Devil.

As she read, she stopped occasionally to make a rough copy of an image in her notebook and add a few notes on its meaning. With each new chapter, it felt as if another portal was opening, drawing her deeper and deeper into a strange and mystical world.

It took several loud raps on the front door to jar Charlotte into reality. Her nerves already unsettled by the images, she slipped a small pocket pistol out of her desk drawer before rising and moving quietly into the foyer.

"Bloody hell." The oath, edged with exasperation, rumbled through the thick oak.

She slid back the bolt. "To what do I owe the honor of yet another visit? Is someone else dead?"

"Not that I know of," answered Wrexford. "I wanted to ask you a question about . . ." He paused, his words pinched off by a quizzical frown.

"Yes?" she encouraged. "About what?"

"Might I come in?"

"That would be best." Charlotte quickly stepped aside. "If you are going to make a habit of paying a visit, you might try to be a trifle less conspicuous." She eyed his exquisitely tailored clothing and tasseled Hessian boots. "I live quietly and simply, milord, and do nothing that might draw attention to my home. I'd prefer to keep it that way."

"My apologies. I will be more careful in the future," he murmured. Her movement must have set off a glint of metal, for his gaze had dropped to her right hand. "I am glad to see that you heeded my earlier warning to take precautions for your safety."

"I'm always careful, Lord Wrexford." The hammer uncocked with a tiny *snick*. Loath to appear rag mannered, she added, "Alas, I can't offer you pastries from Gunter's Tea Shop, but would you care for a cup of tea?"

Wrexford followed her into the main room. "Thank you, but no need to trouble yourself. I've just come from imbibing ample refreshments." He took a seat at the table, and crossed his legs. An odd sort of mood seemed to have hold of him.

But then, Charlotte reminded herself, she was hardly in a position to judge the nuances of his moods. Despite their recent conversations, most of what she knew about him was based on rumor and innuendo. And she knew all too well how those prisms could distort reality.

"A surfeit of champagne and lobster patties, no doubt," she murmured as she returned to her desk.

"You appear to know a great deal about the extravagances of the beau monde parties."

"Of course I do," she replied. "Have you forgotten that I make my living by knowing all the gory details of how Polite Society amuses itself?"

"That would be rather difficult to forget." A sardonic smile flashed for an instant. "By the by, this morning's print of Drummond's demise was particularly striking. The scene was rendered quite well, save for the details of the body. You made it appear terribly gruesome. I did mention there was very little blood from the wound, didn't I?"

"Artistic license, milord. The public is not looking for subtlety."

Another smile. "Is that why you insist on exaggerating the beakiness of my nose? Were I a sensitive soul, your pen would cut to the heart of my vanity."

Charlotte couldn't hold back a low laugh. "Word is, you don't have a heart."

He gave a mournful sigh. "True. Cut me and likely I would bleed claret, not blood. But it would be from an excellent vintage."

"I shall keep that in mind for a cartoon on a day when scandal is quiet. I'm sure all of London would lap it up." As she shifted, the open book on her blotter caught her eye, a reminder that she should be concentrating on more serious endeavors than trading clever quips with the earl.

"Now that we're done with social pleasantries,

sir, you said you had a question for me. What is it?"

Rather than reply right away, he turned away and let his gaze wander around the room.

You are wasting your time, Lord Wrexford. If the answers to life's mysteries were hidden in the woodwork, I would have found them by now.

Charlotte, however, decided to let him speak first.

"Likely I've come on a fool's errand," he finally said. "I wanted to show you a sketch and see if it meant anything to you. Not that I expect it will." His eyes shifted back to meet hers. "I suppose I simply wanted an excuse to discuss the investigation. Each clue along the way has been a Pandora's box—lifting its lid for a closer look has released a whole new slew of conundrums instead of answers." His dark brows pinched together. "There seems to be no rhyme or reason as to how they are all connected."

On impulse, Charlotte reached for her sketchpad and a stick of charcoal. "And that troubles you?"

"It troubles me greatly," he confirmed, though she would not have guessed it from the Sphinx-like smoothness of his face. "As a man of science, I am skeptical about the notion of random coincidences. In my experience, most things can be explained by logic."

"Your experience," said Charlotte softly as she

began to draw, "has been different than mine."

His expression altered, and yet remained a cipher. She had never met a man so hard to read.

"Sometimes random patterns can be just that, like the way the pigment spatters from a brush onto drawing paper when one makes an errant flick of the wrist."

"Newton's laws of motion," he murmured.

"You are being too literal, sir. Sometimes one must apply artistic sensibilities to a problem in order to see it clearly."

"I shall take your word for it, Mrs. Sloane." The lamplight flickered over the contours of his face, accentuating the shadow of doubt pooled in the hollows beneath his eyes. He looked tired, and tense. Charlotte guessed it wasn't often that he second-guessed himself.

She could assure him that it wasn't a feeling that grew more comfortable over time.

"What are you doing?" Wrexford asked, suddenly taking note of the movement of her hands.

"Making a drawing of your face," Charlotte replied. "Remember, it was part of our agreement."

Uncertainty shaded his face. She guessed he wished to protest, but something was holding him back.

"I'll be done in a moment. I just wanted to capture the way the light is playing over your features." In truth, it was the conflicting look of hardness and vulnerability that had caught her eye. "Keep talking. You truly think everything can be explained by strict rules of logic?"

He didn't answer right away. The light from the lamp showed the crinkling of his eyes as they narrowed in thought. That pensiveness was something she had noticed from their very first meeting.

"There is an underlying order to the way things work," he finally replied. "One only has to look at the natural world to see that. So yes, I do believe there are universal rules. For eons, the change in seasons was thought to be ruled by divine whim. But Kepler, through careful observation and the application of mathematics, formulated his laws of planetary motion, which rationally explain them. Many complex forces may be beyond our power to comprehend right now, but that does not mean they can't eventually be figured out."

"A very intriguing philosophy, sir." Charlotte added a few quick strokes, hoping to catch the look in his eyes. "You like pushing the boundaries."

"That is the essence of science." He turned to face her full on. "Just as it is the essence of art."

"If the two have anything in common, it is imagination. It's what inspires discovery."

Wrexford's gaze was suddenly unnerving. As if he were able to see through her skin.

She set her pad aside, the drawing done. "Where is the sketch you wanted to show me?"

He pulled a folded piece of paper from his pocket and wordlessly passed it over.

"Is that blood?" she asked as she gingerly set it on her desk and smoothed it open.

"I imagine so. And given that it came from Henning's mortuary notebook, blood is likely the least offensive substance gracing its surface."

The image quickly dispelled all such distractions. Leaning closer, Charlotte carefully studied the penciled lines and felt her flesh begin to prickle. "Where did this come from?"

"Drummond had drawn it on his palm," answered Wrexford. "God only knows for what reason."

God—or the devil, thought Charlotte. "Is it an accurate rendering of the original? I am trying to make out this tangle of squiggles at the bottom . . ." She looked up in question.

The earl gave an apologetic shrug. "I have no pretensions to being an artist. My rendering is likely crude. But Drummond used a pencil and appeared to have been in a rush." He rose and joined her at the desk. "What a hodgepodge. I don't suppose we'll ever know—"

His voice cut off abruptly as he spotted the open books she had pushed aside. "Hell's teeth, what are those?" he demanded.

"Books on alchemy," she replied. "I borrowed them from Mr. Henning."

Wrexford slowly turned a page, and then another.

"I cannot move within the highest circles of Society in pursuit of clues, so I decided to delve into the one realm that is easily open to me," Charlotte continued. "Granted, I know nothing of science, but there is a chance that my talents may be of use." She pointed to the top of the sketch. "Already that part of the drawing looks familiar. From what I've read so far, it's the symbol of divine geometry, which is an elemental image in alchemy."

Perching a hip on the edge of her desk, the earl continued to page through the book. "And it means what?"

"Ye god, I'm no seer or soothsayer!" She expelled a harried breath. "But even if I were, I sense there is no simple answer to that."

"Light and darkness . . . resurrection . . . ladder . . . serpent." He looked up from reading the headings interspersed among the images. "This is not science, it's fantasy."

"There are different planes of perception, milord." Charlotte watched the sway of the lamp's flame. "How we interpret them may lead to surprising discoveries."

"I am not sure whether you are a genius or a Bedlamite, Mrs. Sloane," he muttered.

Charlotte made a face. "Neither am I."

They sat in silence for a long moment. In the stillness, the sounds drifting in through the window seemed unnaturally loud—a dog howled, a costermonger cried out the price of his cabbages. Ordinary life. Which seemed a world away from the swirl of shadows and secrets that held them in thrall.

"But whether I am mad or not, it can do no harm for me to keep studying these books. Perhaps I'll stumble on something that will help answer some of our questions."

"Hope springs eternal," said Wrexford sarcastically. "Unlike us mortal creatures, no matter how much we might rail against a finite existence."

"Oh, ye of little faith," murmured Charlotte.

That drew a grudging smile. "True. As I said, I prefer to base my beliefs on empirical knowledge."

"Then leave the more nebulous artistic and spiritual matters to me. If it's merely a wild goose chase, you've lost nothing in the bargain."

"I am happy—nay, grateful—to do so, Mrs. Sloane. Though I'm not very sanguine about your chances." He stood, and she was once again reminded of what a large and imposing figure he cut.

Shifting out of his shadow, she looked up and asked abruptly, "Is there a reason you told the boys you had a brother—and that he's dead?"

"Should I not have done so?" His expression was back to its usual granite-like hardness. "They seem to have a healthy awareness of life's realities. Death is a part of that."

"Yes, I am aware of that, but for heaven's sake, sir, they are brothers. And Hawk was . . ." She bit her lip, realizing how foolish she must sound. "Oh, why bother trying to explain. You wouldn't understand."

"Quite right. The Devil Incarnate has no use for children—save to eat them for breakfast."

Beneath the sarcasm, there was a hint of some other emotion. Uncertain of what it was, she pretended not to notice. "Actually, I imagine you would much prefer a plump beefsteak to skin and bones."

A smile softened the stone. "Correct. So you see, the fledglings are safe from my jaws."

Loath to part on that strange note, Charlotte quickly changed the subject.

"Have you any more promising leads to follow?"

"I've yet to talk to Canaday about the library mark you found. If we could discover what book Holworthy had with him when he was murdered, that might be helpful," answered Wrexford. "And my valet is taking a closer look at the charred scraps of paper from Drummond's laboratory, in case there is some other clue hidden there."

"And the Runner, sir? Has he not found any new evidence that might lead him to the real killer?"

"Mr. Griffin does not appear to be looking beyond his nose. And said nose is locked firmly on my scent. He came by my town house for yet another interview last night. And though he's not yet dared to arrest me, I suspect that may change sooner than later."

"Then we must do his job for him," said Charlotte, "and identify the guilty party before he can act."

The earl reached for his hat. "*Carpe diem quam minimum credula postero*," he murmured.

Seize the day, trusting as little as possible in the future. She nodded. "Yes, indeed we must."

He paused, and fixed her with an odd stare.

Damnation, a foolish slip of the tongue. "That is," she quickly added, "I'm assuming anything that sounds so impressive must be a call to arms—like all those fancy mottos under the lordly crests in *Debrett's*."

"Yes, well, I find that Latin adds a certain gravitas to any words," replied Wrexford slowly. "No matter if those around you have no idea what you are actually saying." With a quick touch to his brim, he turned and was swallowed by the shadows.

"Damnation," whispered Charlotte as the door fell closed. She must be more careful. Paper crackled as she shifted the sketch to make room for the alchemy books.

The chase was on. Though just who was stalking whom was far from clear.

Lost in strange thoughts—he couldn't shake the images of mythological beasts dancing over shields emblazoned with Latin aphorisms—Wrexford entered his town house and passed by his butler without hearing a word the fellow said.

To his consternation, when he turned down the corridor to his workroom, he found Tyler blocking the way. "I think you had better go to the Blue Salon first, milord. Griffin is back, and is in a roaring fit of pique."

In no mood for another pointless confrontation with the Runner, he grimaced and snapped, "Have one of the footmen throw him out. Preferably so he lands on his arse."

"I don't think that would be wise. He's learned that we entered Drummond's laboratory after we had been ordered to leave."

"How—" began the earl.

"Read this," said Tyler, thrusting a letter at him.

Wrexford took it and immediately noted that the wax seal had been cracked.

"It arrived just before Griffin, and as the messenger said it was urgent, I took the liberty of opening it," explained his valet quickly. "Lowell sent a warning that the Runner would be coming, along with his apologies for having to admit our transgression to the authorities. He had no choice—two of the workmen saw us enter and revealed it when Griffin questioned them about the morning's activities."

"So, the fellow is more competent than I thought," he observed.

"So it would seem," replied Tyler. "As Lowell points out, had he tried to lie it would have painted us in an even blacker light." A pause. "And what he didn't add was that it would have put him in danger of losing his position at the Institution."

The earl skimmed the contents for himself and uttered an oath. "Bad luck we were spotted," he muttered. "But you're right. I don't expect the fellow to put his neck in the noose for me."

"Now it remains to be seen whether we can extract yours from a precarious position," said his valet dryly.

He thought for a moment. "Griffin didn't enter the workroom, did he?"

Tyler made a pained face. "Do you think me an utter lackwit?" Lowering his voice, he added, "Speaking of the workroom, I was able to salvage several more scraps. I have the microscope all prepared. There's something you should see."

"I'll be there shortly."

His valet headed off to the rear of the house, leaving Wrexford to retrace his steps and enter the salon.

"This is getting rather tiresome, Griffin," he announced, letting the double doors slam shut behind him. "Have you any new evidence?"

"I might have found just what I needed to confirm the identity of the murderer had you and your lackey not stolen it away from under my nose," countered the Runner.

"A serious charge," said the earl softly. "I assume you have proof of that."

Griffin's face darkened in anger. "I may not need it. There is more than one way to skin a cat—and you are fast using up your nine lives."

"Did you come simply to spout aphorisms, or is there a reason for your visit."

"Given Mr. Lowell's admission, I've a few more questions about your activities on the morning of Mr. Drummond's murder." Griffin made a show of pulling out his notebook and touching the tip of his pencil to his tongue. "Now, sir, let's begin with what time you left your residence . . ."

Wrexford held his ire in check as the Runner repeated the same set of questions he had asked during his previous interrogation.

"As you see," he said, after the brusque exchange was finished, "I have not changed my story. Nor will I, so you may spare us both another visit here."

The notebook snapped shut. "Privilege protects you now, but it can stretch only so far, Lord Wrexford. The next time I appear here, it will be to arrest you for the cutthroat killer you are."

The earl flicked a mote of dust from his sleeve. "As you are familiar with my residence, I assume you can see your own way out."

As the Runner stalked off, Wrexford moved to the sideboard and poured himself a measure of brandy. But the fiery liquid felt like acid, leaving a raw trickle of unease burned at the back of his throat. Candlelight darted through the cut-crystal facets of his glass, casting shuddering fragments of amber over the pristine white plaster of the far wall.

Hubris was, he conceded, an elemental flaw of his character. Dangerous to others as well as himself.

A painfully obvious truth, and yet by its very nature, it refused to let him learn from past mistakes.

He stood very still, gripping the glass so tightly that its intricate etching nearly drew blood. His gaze was drawn unwillingly to a gilt-framed painting hung in the shadows of a recessed alcove. Death seemed to take a perverse pleasure in haunting him. This time, however, it was time to break the pattern. It was time to slay its ghost.

Setting down the drink, Wrexford quietly let himself out of the salon and went to join his valet.

Intent on the charred paper beneath the lens, Tyler did not look up from the microscope when he entered the room. "Griffin did not clap you in irons?"

"Not yet. But his fingers are twitching." He approached the worktable and angled a look at the scrap pressed between the two thin sheets of glass. "What have you discovered?"

"Stuck between the heavier notepaper was a sheet of stationery. It looks like Drummond was writing a letter to the governing board of the Institution warning them that something . . ." Tyler slid out of his chair. "Here, look for yourself."

Wrexford took charge of the microscope and turned the brass dial to adjust the focus. The fire had darkened what was left of the paper, and heat had altered the ink, making it hard to read. Drummond's spidery script added to the challenge. Squinting, he shifted the polished metal reflectors ever so slightly to catch the lamplight.

The scrap brightened, accentuating the charred holes that had eaten away most of the message. As the earl slowly moved the glass plates in order to view the entire contents, he saw there were only a few fragments of disconnected writing:

> Golden One must be stopped . . . I appeal to the board of governors . . . discover his identity and stop his . . . dangerous discovery . . . threatens

"What do you make of it?" asked Tyler when finally he looked up from the eyepiece.

"It appears Drummond was writing a letter to Davy and the board of the Institution accusing someone of creating something dangerous."

"So it would seem," agreed the valet.

"Let us think," mused Wrexford. "Combined

with the other fragment we found, what more can we piece together?"

Tyler pursed his lips. "Given the reference to the philosopher's stone and the word *discovery,* I'd say it's reasonable to assume Drummond was talking about some sort of chemical compound."

"Agreed." The earl propped his elbows on the worktable and steepled his fingers. "Furthermore, based on the first scrap, you pointed out that 'Golden One' could be an alchemy term for a chemical substance. But based on this new evidence, I think it's clear Drummond is referring to a person."

"My thoughts exactly, sir. It also seems safe to say that 'Golden One' is a member of the Institution."

"Drummond certainly believed he was," amended the earl. "We know he had a penchant for eavesdropping and snooping around in the private spaces of other members. And the fact that he was murdered and his papers set afire is proof that his suspicions were all too real."

"So we've learned a great deal."

Rising from his chair, Wrexford began to pace. What were they missing? In science, it was a cardinal mistake to allow assumption, not observation, to shape a conclusion.

Water boils at 212 degrees on the scale devised by Daniel Gabriel Fahrenheit—a fact based on empirical evidence.

Right now, they were making too many leaps of logic. That bothered him.

"We've conjectured a great deal," he muttered. "We may be right, but we need to prove it."

"Unless there's some alchemy that transmutes ash back into a pristine piece of paper, we will need to keep looking," quipped Tyler.

Another turn of the room and still he felt as if he was spinning in circles. *Logic,* he chided to himself. When in doubt return to the basics and start again.

"Golden One." He came to a sudden stop. "Can you think of any member of the Institution who has blond hair?"

"Sykes and Fairmont come to mind—and I'm sure there are others," replied Tyler. "Shall I look into it?"

"Yes, compile a list," said Wrexford. "Lowell would know, and he's just as anxious as we are to have the killer caught." He hesitated. "But let us first compile the list and look it over before bringing anyone else into the investigation. If the killer is indeed a member, we must be very careful not to warn him of our suspicions."

"With a list we could then match the men with their area of expertise in chemistry. That would help eliminate some of the names," suggested the valet.

But before they could muse any further on the subject, Sheffield burst into the room.

"Bloody hell, pour me a brandy. I've run hell for leather across half of London," he wheezed, his breath coming in ragged gulps. "I did what you asked and dug around for more information about St. Aubin—and discovered that he, too, is a member of The Ancients. But for now, he's not of primary concern—I think I've discovered who the murderer is."

CHAPTER 15

Tyler moved to the pearwood console at the far end of the room, where a silver tray of elegant decanters sat centered between the two tall storage shelves filled with jars of chemicals.

"Make that Highland malt," called Sheffield as he sank into a chair with a theatrical wince. "I need some fire in my belly to revive me."

Wrexford crossed his arms and waited.

"There were no hackneys to be had in St. Giles," continued his friend. "I've ruined a perfectly good pair of boots mucking through those stinking alleyways." He flexed his hands. "Not to speak of bruising my knuckles fighting off a footpad."

"I concede a round of applause for your valiant heroics," said the earl. "And your flair for melodrama." He waited for his friend to toss back a long swallow of his whisky. "Now kindly stubble the playacting, Kit, and tell us what you've learned."

Sheffield straightened and assumed an air of injured dignity. "I'll have you know I've put myself at considerable risk to pull your cod out of the fire. The least you could do is show some appreciation."

"Kit," warned the earl.

"It's Canaday," announced his friend without

further ado. "He's been lying through his teeth about his connection with Holworthy."

"Which is?" queried the earl.

"They are cousins!" A note of triumph shaded Sheffield's voice. "Granted, second or third cousins through Canaday's mother. But according to Grantley, who grew up on the neighboring estate, the two of them have known each other since childhood. In fact, Holworthy spent several summers living with the baron's family."

"Cousins," mused the earl. "And yet he took great pains to hide that fact."

"Precisely! And the question is why," said Sheffield eagerly.

Why, indeed. But this was no time to go off half cocked. Knowing his friend's penchant for exaggerating, he moved to the bank of mullioned windows and stared out at the night shadows, carefully reviewing all that he knew about the baron.

The facts—look at the facts. As he considered the empirical evidence, this latest bit of information about Canaday made all the disparate pieces suddenly fit together.

"The question is why," repeated Sheffield.

"That," said Wrexford slowly, "is something I intend to ask him first thing in the morning. And this time, I shall rattle the truth out of him, if I have to break all two hundred and five bones in his body."

"Two hundred and six," murmured Tyler.

"To do that, you will have to journey to his estate in Kent," said Sheffield. "On top of all else, I've learned he left London yesterday to spend a week at his estate in Kent."

"Even better," he replied. "I was already planning on having a look at his library. This will give me a chance to kill two birds with one stone."

Charlotte let out a laugh as she thumbed through the drawings of the Tower lions. The childlike exuberance was endearing. There was an unfettered freedom to the lines and squiggles, an innocent enthusiasm that replaced the all-too-present street-wise wariness.

However, the humor quickly left her lips. She worried about the boys, especially Raven. He seemed more withdrawn of late, as if the weight of worldly responsibilities was pushing him inward. Charlotte knew he considered himself his brother's protector. And she sensed that he had also taken her under his fledgling wing.

No boy that young should bear those burdens.

Raven had no idea of his age. To her eye he looked to be no more than eleven, and yet the recent spurt of growth might indicate he was a year older. She found it hard to think of him as more than a child. But in the stews, the age of twelve would be considered on the cusp of manhood. Why, boys of fourteen or fifteen routinely marched off to the hell-cursed war raging on the Continent.

A chilling thought.

She blinked back the sting of tears. Wrexford's money would at least allow her to take better care of their basic needs. More nourishing food, a modicum of education, warm clothing . . . She made a mental note to make another visit to Petticoat Lane and buy less tattered garments for both of them.

It wasn't nearly enough. They should know the joy of carefree play, of youthful laughter, of sweet, fresh air and streets free of pestilence and predators. Ah, but Life was often stingy with its favors. She had learned to be a pragmatist and take what was given.

The musing was a sharp reminder to turn her attention back to the books on alchemy. The boys had eaten their supper and hared off to deliver her latest drawings to the engraver, leaving her with several quiet hours in which to continue her study of the strange images.

As art, they were fascinating, and yet repelling. She couldn't help but feel there was a darkness to their spirit, some malevolent force lurking behind the marvelous technical skill of the detailed engravings. Power run amok. Or maybe it was just her imagination. She had always disliked any force that tried to bend others to its will.

Picking up her pen, she began to jot down notes as she read the descriptions. *Green Lion, Neptune's Trident, Scepter of Jove*—Good Heavens, what bizarre names the alchemists chose to hide the real ingredients of their chemical potions. It would seem laughably absurd if men were not being murdered over these arcane writings.

After another hour of cross-checking texts, Charlotte finally found a reference that indicated *Diana* was a code word for silver. Now, if she could just figure out the meaning of *dragon,* which was appearing more and more often in the various formulas. Exhaling a sigh, she took a moment to flex the stiffness from her hunched shoulders and then set back to work.

Wrexford guided his curricle through the last, sweeping turn of the drive and slowed his horses to an easy trot. Up ahead, the manor house sat at the top of the hill, surrounded by broad lawns, a small formal garden, and a grove of birch and elms that would wind down toward the stables. Constructed of limestone, its classical columns and pediments lit with a honey-gold light as the sun broke through the scudding clouds.

It was a handsome building from afar, with tasteful lines and pleasing symmetry. And yet, as Wrexford came closer, he noted the small signs of neglect—a few missing roof tiles, the unpruned hedges rising up within the garden. Either Canaday was a careless steward of his family home, or he was not as plump in the pocket as he would have people believe.

After drawing to a halt in front of the entrance portico, he jumped down from his perch and tossed the reins to a waiting groom, along with a shilling. "Rub them down well and give them a measure of grain."

Without waiting for a reply, Wrexford took the stairs two at a time and rapped the brass knocker. He had left at dawn, driving hard and making good time along the toll road that wound down from London through Tunbridge Wells. The baron would likely be just sitting down to his noonday meal. The thought of rousting him from the pleasures of a well-cooked joint of beef was immensely cheering. His own breadbox was empty, and the dust from the rutted country roads had parched his throat.

"Yes?" The butler, a cadaverous figure whose shabby black clothing accentuated his colorless face, fixed him with what was meant to be a quelling look. "The master of the house is not expecting any company."

"Tell him Lord Wrexford is here to see him," he replied. "And advise him that it's not a request."

The man looked frozen by indecision.

Wrexford stripped off his driving gloves and

slapped them softly against his palm. "Or would you rather I tell him myself?"

The butler opened his mouth, revealing a set of bad teeth, and then appeared to think twice about a show of bravado. He silently retreated into the gloom of the unlit entrance hall.

"I'll wait in the drawing room." Wrexford stepped over the threshold. "Have a footman bring me a tankard of ale and a collation of ham and bread. And do it quickly. I'm famished."

The refreshments arrived before Canaday. Wrexford stood by the bank of arched windows and kept an eye on the graveled path leading to the stables as he ate, half expecting the baron to try to evade the meeting. But at last the door opened and Canaday entered.

"What's the meaning of this, sirrah!" His face was flushed, as if he had sought courage in a bottle of brandy. "How dare you invade my house, and give orders to my staff."

"Be grateful that I give you the courtesy of coming to speak with you myself, instead of dispatching the Bow Street Runner who is handling the investigation of Holworthy's murder."

"Have him come!" blustered Canaday, brushing back the strands of receding hair from his brow. "I told you, I know nothing about the crime."

"So you did, and that turns out to be a bald-faced lie."

"Y-You question my honor as a gentleman?"

Wrexford answered with a mocking laugh. "Clearly you're no gentleman, Canaday. Though I haven't quite decided whether you are a snake or just a miserable worm."

Canaday's hands were shaking. Clenching them into fists, he sputtered, "I'll not stand to be insulted in my own—"

"You're wasting your breath," he interrupted. "I suggest you save it for telling me about your cousin, and what you were really arguing over."

The air leached from the baron's lungs in a whispery hiss. Beads of sweat broke out on his forehead.

"Did you think you could keep your relationship with Reverend Holworthy a secret?"

Canaday leaned heavily against the back of an armchair for support. "You truly are the Devil Incarnate."

"Perhaps. But given that you have a choice between the Runner and the Devil, I am the lesser of two evils." Wrexford let his words sink in for a moment before adding, "I may be able to help you, while Griffin simply wishes to slip a noose around someone's neck, be damned with whether he's guilty or not. And with this new bit of evidence coming to light, you've just taken my place as the prime suspect."

Panic bubbled up in the other man's voice. "I swear, I had nothing to do with his death!"

"Why were you quarreling with Holworthy?" he pressed, giving the man no quarter.

And yet, more evasiveness. The baron's gaze slid away. "It was a private family matter."

"Suit yourself." Wrexford reached for his driving coat, which he had slung over a tea table. "If I recall correctly, a mere baron cannot claim the right to be tried by his peers in the House of Lords. What a pity. The Old Bailey's judges tend to be quite severe for the crime of murder, especially when they get their hands on a minor noble."

"Wait." The word came out as a whisper.

Wrexford paused, hat hovering just above his head.

All the fight drained out of Canaday. Slumping into the chair, he closed his eyes for an instant, and drew a ragged breath. "Several investments have gone bad, leaving me a . . . a little dipped for funds." He blotted his brow with his sleeve. "Good God, you know how it is—it takes a hellish amount of blunt to keep up an estate and London residence."

"I'm not interested in gentleman-to-gentleman palavering, Canaday. As a man of science, I care only about the facts."

The baron shot him a hateful look. But it quickly sagged into surrender. "Josiah learned about my financial troubles, and offered to buy some of the rare books and manuscripts in my library," he admitted. "Said he had an acquaintance, an avid collector of arcane books on the occult, who would pay a fortune for them. As it was just musty old medieval nonsense, I readily agreed."

"How did he know about them?" asked Wrexford, curious as to whether the baron would answer truthfully.

"He spent a number of summers here, and was always more interested in ancient books than I was. I assume he had come across them during the countless hours he spent poking around in there."

So far, so good. "Go on."

"My cousin made a down payment, but then he kept putting me off about the rest. That wasn't part of the deal." Canaday wet his lips. "So yes, I was angry. But for God's sake, I-I certainly didn't kill him."

Then why was it that the baron had gone white as a ghost?

"What else aren't you telling me?" he asked softly.

"Nothing! I swear it!"

Wrexford could smell the fear oozing out of Canaday. Along with yet more lies. No question the baron was holding back secrets. But for the moment, he decided to put that aside and pursue the matter of the library.

Moving to the decanters set on the sideboard, he poured a measure of brandy into a glass and handed it to Canaday. "What books did Holworthy buy from you?"

The baron gratefully gulped down a swallow before answering. "I-I really don't remember."

"Your collection is said to be quite large. Surely you have a ledger cataloguing it." Most estate libraries had records of their contents. Like land, livestock, and jewelry, books were valuable commodities.

"Yes. Though I've not used it much." Canaday took another swallow of brandy. "You are welcome to look through it if you wish."

No doubt thinking there wasn't a snowball's chance in hell of spotting what was missing. It would take days, or perhaps weeks, to cross-check every entry against the endless rows of books.

"Thank you." Wrexford smiled. Using the library mark Charlotte had found, a search for the book's title within the ledger should yield a result, and finding its position on the shelves would make guessing what other books had gone missing an easier task. "I shall take you up on the offer."

Canaday appeared surprised, but he couldn't very well refuse. Draining the last of his drink, he set aside the glass and levered to his feet.

"Follow me."

CHAPTER 16

Smoothing the creases from her walking dress, Charlotte did a slow turn in front of the cheval glass. She had lost weight since last wearing the patterned silk and it now hung too loosely from her hips to be fashionable. Not that a four-year-old gown could ever hope to be a la mode here in London. Still, it brightened her spirits to feel it against her skin. *Memories, memories.* The fine-spun fabric and delicate flowers reminded her of Italian sunshine and the smell of country air washed clean with summer rain.

Her reflection stared at her in mute reproach.

"Yes, I know. It does no good to think of the past." Charlotte reset a few of her hairpins before putting on a plain chipstraw bonnet and tying the ribbons in a neat bow. Her hair, she noted, had long since lost any of the golden highlights from her time abroad. Mouse brown, which perhaps was fitting as her present life was all about creeping through the shadows and avoiding notice.

A dark merino cloak, more iron grey than blue, completed her outfit. One that wouldn't draw a second glance from the beau monde.

Thank God for that.

A fool's errand, perhaps. In return for the latest

favor she had asked of him, Jeremy had demanded one of his own—being allowed to take her to Gunter's Tea Shop for a treat of their special ice cream confections after they finished their serious business. She should have insisted on a different forfeit. After all, classical mythology was rife with warnings on the dangers of crossing back and forth between two worlds.

With a turn of the key, she carefully locked the front door behind her.

But of late, Charlotte reflected, she seemed to be testing the goodwill of the gods.

"You look tired," said Jeremy as she joined him on the bench in Green Park an hour later. "You shouldn't have walked here."

"Beggars can't be choosy," she replied, then instantly regretted it on seeing his face tighten. "It's just a common saying, Jem."

"But no less true for being so. If you would let me—"

"No." Charlotte summoned a show of steel.

He sighed. "I won't give up, you know."

"And I won't give in." There, the game had played out, as it had in the past and would again in the future. They both understood the rules.

That made him laugh. Even as a boy, Jeremy could never stay angry for long. Leaning back against the slats, he looked up and watched the clouds scud by, wisps of white against the sun-washed blue sky.

Charlotte used the silence to observe her surroundings. Lush green grass, tidy walkways, two well-dressed children at play, their governess hovering close by.

"Thank you for finding the book, Jem." Knowing a lone woman asking for arcane writings would raise too many unwanted questions, she had asked her friend to look around in the scholarly bookstores on Sackville Street for a certain work by Eirenaeus Philalethes, the American whose alchemical ideas had greatly influenced Newton, Boyle, and the other scientific titans of the late seventeenth century.

"It led me on a merry dance, I'll tell you that. *A Breviary of Alchemy, or, A Commentary upon Sir George Ripley's Recapitulation: Being a Paraphrastical Epitome of His Twelve Gates*—I assure you, I received some odd looks on asking for *that* title." He grinned. "I likely now have the reputation of being a half-mad eccentric."

"My apologies—" began Charlotte.

"Oh, no need for them," he interrupted. "It was actually quite exciting to feel like a clandestine agent, helping to ferret out hidden secrets." He lowered his voice. "Holworthy was burned with chemicals, so I'm assuming this has something to do with the recent murders."

"I'm not sure." It wasn't precisely a lie, she told herself, simply an evasion. "I've heard some strange things and am trying to learn a little about the secretive world of alchemy in Newton's day."

"Secretive, indeed, and with good reason. The penalty could be death for trying to turn lead into gold." Jeremy handed over the small, neatly wrapped package he had been holding in his lap.

"I owe you a great debt of thanks for this," said Charlotte, as she tucked the book into her reticule.

"Which I shall collect very shortly," he reminded her.

The idea of having to venture into the heart of Mayfair sent a shiver of trepidation down her spine. But a pledge was a pledge. She would not renege on her word.

"You know, I had a friend at Cambridge," mused Jeremy, "a member of Trinity—Newton's old college—who was fascinated by the subject of alchemy. I remember him regaling me with the fanciful names the practitioners used to disguise their basic chemicals." A chuckle. "Like green lion, liver of sulfur, and dragon."

"Dragon?" Charlotte covered her rising excitement with an amused laugh. "Did your friend ever discover what the terms meant?"

"Not all of them." His brow furrowed in thought. "Though I seem to remember that 'dragon' referred to mercury."

A sudden roaring seemed to fill her ears. She

had seen many images of dragons within the books lent to her by Henning. And now, with this vital clue sparking a new way of looking at the scribbled lines, the sketch found on Drummond's palm became clear.

That was it—the dead man had taken pains to draw the symbol of mercury on his flesh.

She plucked at a fold of her gown, trying to hide her excitement. One mystery was solved. As to the greater conundrum of what it meant . . .

That would be up to Wrexford.

"Come," said Jeremy, interrupting her thoughts. "Enough of secrets and science. It's time for more frivolous pursuits." Rising, he offered his hand. "I highly recommend the strawberry ice cream. It's their most popular flavor. Though you may prefer to try a more exotic one, like bergamot, white coffee, or parmesan."

Quelling her impatience to rush home and dash off a note to the earl, Charlotte forced a show of good grace and followed her friend's lead. He deserved no less.

Still, she felt her chest tighten as they crossed Piccadilly Street.

"Relax," he murmured.

"I am," she answered.

"Liar." Jeremy turned their steps up Bolton Street. "You forget that I know you too well—the right corner of your mouth twitches whenever you are telling a bouncer."

Was she really so easy to read?

Charlotte smiled in reply, but inwardly chided herself to learn from Wrexford how to keep her emotions better masked.

That proved even more of a challenge once Jeremy had escorted her inside the elegant tea parlor and had the waiter seat them at a table looking out through the large windows onto Berkeley Square. A parade of fancy carriages rolled by, the wheels clicking smoothly over the smooth cobblestones. Ladies frothed in silk and satins strolled along the neatly raked gravel paths of the central garden, accompanied by gentlemen dressed in the first stare of fashion.

"A sunny day always draws even more business," explained Jeremy. He, too, was stylishly attired. He had always had exquisite taste, and now with the unexpected inheritance of a title, he had the money to afford fine clothing. His subtle choices of fabrics and colors created an understated elegance that complemented his fine-boned features.

He was, mused Charlotte, a very attractive man—and by the sidelong looks he was drawing from the other ladies in the shop, it hadn't gone unnoticed here in Mayfair.

She shifted in her chair.

Agile waiters darted around horses and curricles, carrying confections from the shop to the groups of laughing couples who were loitering under the stately maples, enjoying their treats alfresco.

All the glitter of the brass buttons, silver-threaded trim, and bejeweled rings was making her eyes ache.

Nodding absently to Jeremy's suggestion of strawberry ice cream, she turned her gaze to the mansions on the opposite side of the square. The columned entryways, the high mullioned windows, the carved limestone facades glowing like burnished gold in the afternoon sun—this was the heart of aristocratic London, a charmed rectangle of power and privilege.

It was ironic, thought Charlotte with an inward smile, watching the tea shop's famous gilded pineapple sign gently swaying in the breeze. Pineapples were a symbol of hospitality, yet only the wealthy were welcome here.

She was an intruder.

Jeremy noticed her faraway look. "Shall we eat our ice cream outdoors?" he inquired as the waiter delivered their treats. The garden had a number of benches beneath the shade of the trees.

She nodded gratefully, happy to escape the cloying sugar and spice scents of the shop.

They found a quiet spot between two tall ornamental shrubs and made light conversation in between spoonfuls of the creamy confection.

Which was, Charlotte admitted, sinfully good.

She was sitting still, savoring the delicious sensation of cold melting into sweetness on her tongue, when the sound of footsteps on the other side of the shrubbery caught her ear.

They came to a halt.

"Are you sure?" The voice was pitched low but couldn't quite disguise the Scottish accent.

"I've just come from White's. Featherton is a good friend—and he's also the brother-in-law of one of the justices in the Bow Street magistry." The second voice spoke with a perfectly polished London accent. "So he confided that he just heard new evidence has been discovered concerning Drummond's murder. And it's not good for Wrexford."

A muttered oath.

"Have you any idea when he'll be returning to Kent?"

Every muscle in Charlotte's body tensed.

"He didn't say, Mr. Sheffield, but my guess is tomorrow," replied the Scottish voice. "He was in no mood to linger there."

"An arrest warrant has not yet been issued. However, the chances are it soon will be. Is there any way to warn him?"

"No, and I doubt it would do any good even if we could," came the wry response. "You know the earl—he won't shy away from confronting the authorities."

"We need to convince him that discretion is the better part of valor."

"I wish you good luck with that."

"My luck is due to turn—let's hope it's now," replied Sheffield. "Send word to me as soon as he arrives home."

The crunch of retreating steps quickly faded, leaving Charlotte struggling to draw a breath.

Jeremy shifted and let out a low whistle. "It appears you will have plenty of material for your future drawings." She had told him nothing about her partnership with the earl. "It appears Lord Wrexford is guilty after all."

She didn't believe it for an instant. But for all their efforts, they still seemed no closer to proving who was the real culprit.

Setting aside her dish, Charlotte looked up at her friend. "I'm so sorry to cast a cloud over this lovely interlude. But I fear I'm more fatigued than I thought. If you don't mind, I think it best that I return home."

"Of course." He was on his feet in a flash, and guiding her out to the street. "But this time I'll brook no argument from you. I'm taking you as far as Red Lion Square in a hackney."

For once, she didn't object. She needed to think—and to strategize. If the murderer was Canaday, or one of the other members of The Ancients, he was a powerful figure in London.

But so was she.

Her pen exposed dirty secrets, it influenced public opinion . . . it could draw scrutiny away from Wrexford and focus it elsewhere.

As Jeremy flagged down a hackney and helped her climb inside, Charlotte was already envisioning the design for tomorrow's satirical print.

Shadows hung heavy in the high vaulted ceiling, casting a pall over the deserted library. It wasn't just the cavernous silence or pervasive chill that gave the massive room a crypt-like feel. The books, decided Wrexford, had lifelessness to them, an aura of disinterested neglect. They sat slumbering on their shelves, the bindings cracking, the leather shriveling, the pages turning brittle with age, waiting to be awakened.

The only signs of stirring were the silvery clouds of dust motes kicked up when he moved from alcove to alcove.

The library ledgers, a set of three thick volumes penned in a number of different handwritings, were difficult to decipher. The index number given to each book in the collection seemed to be based on a bizarre system of logic only the first cataloguer could explain, and figuring out how they fit into the accompanying map of the room was a challenge. But finally, after several hours of poring over the faded pages, and exploring the alcoves formed by the jutting shelves, he began to make some sense of things.

A short while later, his diligence paid off. There, near the bottom of a page he matched the scrap found by Charlotte to an entry.

Artephius his secret Book. Manuscript 103.4—penned by Isaac Newton.

"Eureka," he murmured, chafing some warmth back into his crabbed hands. He wished he had thought to bring the bottle of brandy with him. Setting the ledger aside, he took up the map. The next task was to track down its spot on the shelves and see what other volumes were grouped with it.

As he passed the central work cabinet, where all the ledgers and receipts were kept locked, Wrexford noted a magnificent gilt-framed oil painting hanging on the far wall. The daylight was weak in this section of the room, but something about it caught his eye.

He moved closer and studied it for a long moment. Though no expert in art, he had a modicum of knowledge on the subject and could recognize certain styles. This looked to be a Rembrandt—and a fine one at that. His own family seat had two similar works, but not nearly as grand.

A previous baron had possessed extremely good taste, he reflected. Or damnably good luck. It must be worth a fortune.

Which begged the question of why Canaday didn't simply sell the painting if he were desperate for blunt. Discreetly, of course. No one liked to admit to stripping family treasures from future generations.

And there was always the possibility that the entail on the estate forbid the sale of such assets, he reminded himself. Like land, valuable items could be included in the patrimony that must be handed down through the ages. In many ways, a titled lord was merely a steward for his successor, though a goodly number of them squandered the family money, leaving their heirs with huge expenses and little recourse save to marry an heiress.

Wrexford gave it one last admiring look before turning back to the shelves. Whatever Canaday's woes, they were not his concern.

Working methodically through the section indicated on the map, he found the manuscript's assigned position. A quick search showed that according to the cataloguing system four, not three, other volumes were missing. He jotted down the numbers and headed back to the ledgers, his work almost done.

Another half hour passed before he stood and carefully tucked his notes into his pocket. At least he now had more than mere guesses as to why Holworthy had been murdered.

Not that the evidence made any sense. At least, not yet.

He found Canaday back in the main drawing room, his chair drawn close to a blazing fire, an empty bottle tipped over by his feet, its last dregs pooled darkly on the patterned carpet. He looked like death warmed over.

"I'm finished here," he announced.

The baron raised his head. His throat muscles twitched, but he couldn't seem to manage a word.

"What I found may be helpful in keeping both our necks out of the noose," continued Wrexford. "Assuming what you have told me about not killing your cousin is true."

A nervous nod and a croaked whisper. "As God is my judge, I'm not guilty of murder."

"Your appeal ought to be directed to a more earthly power," said Wrexford dryly. He retrieved his coat and hat. "By the by, if you're so badly dipped, why not consider selling that striking Rembrandt painting hanging in the library? It's worth far more than the books you dealt to Holworthy."

Canaday looked as if he was going to be ill. "N-Never that! It's of great sentimental value to the family. And besides, it's part of the entail—couldn't sell it if I wanted to."

"Bad luck for you," murmured Wrexford. "I'm familiar enough with the Old Masters to know it would solve your money worries in one fell swoop."

With a few quick flicks of her pen, Charlotte drew in some shadowing around the faces, then leaned back to assess her handiwork.

It was, she decided, suitably provocative.

Anthony had described the main room of The

Ancients's clubhouse in great detail many times. As for the members, she knew all too well what Stoughton looked liked. His crony—St. Alban? St. Aubin?—she had seen only once, but she had a good memory for faces. And Wrexford's description of Canaday was still fresh in her mind.

She was sure it was accurate, and once she added highlights of garish color to accentuate the grotesquely exaggerated portraits, it would be sensational enough to grab the public's attention.

Especially when she penned in a titillating title and subtext.

Propping up the paper, she stared at the three men and the shadowy silhouettes she had sketched in behind them. Was one of The Ancients a murderer? Both Wrexford's evidence and her intuition said yes.

If so, perhaps shining a glaring light on the club's dark doings would spook the guilty man into giving himself away.

Charlotte took up a pencil and began to play with possibilities for the wording for the headline. It had to be titillating—and outrageous enough to provoke gossip.

Why was Reverend Holworthy REALLY murdered?

Yes, that should throw oil on the fires of speculation. She tested a few phrases to write in under it, but crossed them out as too tame.

"Think, think," she murmured, looking at the details of her drawing. The pile of old books, the large open volume on the ornate table, with the men cackling over the strange symbols on the yellowed pages.

Ah, inspiration struck.

Does the answer lie in an ANCIENT secret?

It was perfect—the thinly veiled references would soon have all of London abuzz with speculation.

CHAPTER 17

"Dratted woman," muttered Wrexford. He kicked a clump of rotting cabbage out of his path, and took savage satisfaction in hearing it explode against the grimy brick of the narrow alleyway. The day had already taken an unpleasant turn. At breakfast, his exasperation over the Runner's misguided investigation had quickly given way to a more visceral emotion on having Charlotte's newly published satirical print delivered along with his eggs and muffins.

A grim-faced Tyler had come home from his daily trip to Fores's shop and wordlessly unrolled the offending art on the dining table.

Dropping his plans to march over to Bow Street and confront Griffin, Wrexford had instead grabbed his coat and set off at a brisk pace for another part of Town.

He had to admit, she had a reckless courage. He would have applauded it—had he not instead wanted to wrap his hands around her bloody neck and shake some sense into her.

"Willful . . . Stubborn . . . Unreasonable." The ricochet of a stone punctuated each growl. He would have moved on to epithets had he not grudgingly admitted that there was a degree of ironic humor in the proverbial pot calling the kettle black.

No wonder his friends—what few he had—found him so aggravating to deal with.

A sardonic smile touched his lips, but quickly tightened to a frown. However brave, Charlotte had put herself at grave risk by poking a stick into this particular nest of vipers. He was fairly certain that at least one of them was a murderer, one who already had shown no compunction about eliminating anyone who might be a threat to exposing his identity.

Multiply the danger by at least two other unscrupulous dastards, or maybe three . . . He didn't peg Canaday for the murderer—the man lacked the nerve. Was it Stoughton or St. Aubin? Or someone who as yet had been too clever to show his colors?

Whatever the number, only rudimentary math skills were needed to calculate that she was dancing on a razor's edge.

The earl was several streets away from Charlotte's house when he spotted Raven and Hawk in the entrance to an alleyway, taking turns pitching rocks at a half-broken bottle.

"You there—weasels!" he called. "Come here."

The younger boy laughed and trotted over to him. Raven was slower to respond, and crossed the muddy lane with deliberately slow steps. "Whatcha wont?" he demanded, lifting his chin to a pugnacious tilt.

The earl fixed him with his most imperious stare. "Let's try again, shall we? I'm sure Mrs.

Sloane would prefer something more along the lines of 'Good morning, Lord Wrexford. Did you wish to speak with me?' "

The boy's eyes narrowed, but after a heartbeat of hesitation, he reluctantly repeated the greeting—in perfectly enunciated King's English.

"That's better," he murmured. "And yes, I do wish to speak with you weasels." The narrow lane looked to be deserted, but in this part of Town, there was always someone watching. "Come, step over here."

The doorway to the brick warehouse was tucked within the shadows of a sagging overhang. He motioned the boys to step under it and crouched down to put himself at eye level with them.

Scowling, Raven shifted from foot to foot.

Wrexford pulled two pocketknives from inside his coat. The handles were made of dark textured stag horn, trimmed in nickel silver. He held one up and pressed a hidden lever, which, with a whisper-soft *snick,* released a wicked-looking blade.

"Cor!" Hawk's eyes were suddenly wide as tea saucers.

"If you two are intent on protecting Mrs. Sloane," he said, "I'd prefer you do it with a proper weapon, rather than some primitive shank of half-sharpened steel."

Raven's gaze moved slowly over the shiny lethal curves to the razored point.

The earl held the knife still a moment longer,

then snapped the blade shut and held it out to the boy.

For an instant, their hands touched as Raven carefully closed his fingers around the horn handle.

"Keep these hidden away. They are not toys. They are only to be used in an emergency," counseled Wrexham as he passed the second one to Hawk. "It's for your own safety. There are men in the stews who would hurt you to take possession of them. Do you understand?"

Hawk nodded solemnly, looking too over-whelmed for words. Raven quickly slipped the weapon into his boot, and helped his younger brother do the same.

A low "Aye" was all he said. But Wrexford was satisfied.

"May we tell m'lady?" asked Hawk.

"I think it best we keep them a secret—a secret between us men." He held out his palm faceup. "Give me your pledge."

Raven laid Hawk's hand on the earl's, then covered it with his own.

"Remember," said Wrexford, "be discreet."

"Wot's discreet?" whispered Hawk.

"Very, very careful," he answered.

A ghost of a grin flitted over Raven's narrow face. "Yes, milord," he said in the plummy tones of a London aristocrat. "Weasels know how te be discreet. It's how they stay alive."

"Discreet," repeated Hawk, testing the word on his tongue. "Ye have my word on it, sir."

"Excellent." Wrexford ruffled the boy's hair and then stood up. "I am counting on you two to keep a close watch on the neighborhood. Any suspicious people loitering around, you send word to me immediately." He gave them his address on Berkeley Square.

"Aye, we know where you live. We keep our peepers open." Raven met his gaze with an unblinking stare. "You expect trouble, m'lord?"

"Yes," he answered frankly. "And when it comes, let us try to be ready for it."

Like the restless alleyway shadows, the boys flitted away into the gloom. They would be sharp-eyed sentinels, but the earl was under no illusions as to the cunning of their adversary.

He was gratified to find Charlotte's front door securely locked, and that she was careful to challenge his knock before sliding back the bolts.

"You're a damnable fool," he uttered, after making sure the door was secured.

"And good morning to you, too, sir," she replied. "I would offer you coffee if I had any, for clearly my inferior brand of tea isn't strong enough to awaken a more cheerful mood."

"This is no jesting matter, Mrs. Sloane."

"I assure you, I have never been more deadly serious."

"How fitting," he retorted. "Because you have

certainly put yourself in deadly peril with that devil-cursed print."

"I am aware of that."

"Perhaps you didn't look closely enough at Holworthy's mutilated corpse." Wrexford was deliberately harsh. "It was not a pretty ending."

Charlotte didn't blanche. "You forget, sir, that I watched my husband suffer through days of physical agony and half-mad delusions. So spare me the lectures on not understanding what I am up against. Not only is it patronizing, but it's also insulting. Whatever you think of me, I am not a fool."

Damnation. In his righteous anger, he had forgotten about that. "You're right, it was," he admitted. "I'm sorry."

She shrugged off the apology. "We've more important things to talk about. I've made a very important discovery—"

"So have I," he interjected. "However, as a gentleman, I shall allow ladies to go first."

"I'm not a lady, which, as you well know, is a distinction reserved for members of your upper class. I'm merely an ordinary woman."

"Artistic license. Surely I may be granted the same bending of the rules as you are," he replied. "Besides, the boys call you m'lady, so I am simply following precedent."

"Let us not waste time in idle chatter," chided Charlotte. She looked more agitated than the momentary banter merited. But then, he reminded himself, there was good reason for her nerves to be on edge.

He took a seat. "I'm listening."

"I think I've figured out what the sketch on Drummond's hand means." Charlotte moved to her desk and scooped up several books, which she carried back to the table. "I spent hours looking at the various engravings and reading the explanations of the iconography, and slowly began to understand the meaning of the visual representations."

She paused to open up one of the books and spin it around to face him. "See this one here?"

"The dragon?" asked Wrexford.

"Yes." Charlotte had bookmarks in the other volumes and flipped to the pages. "Now look at these illustrations. What do you notice?"

He studied them carefully. "There are certain similarities in detail despite the different drawing styles. The tail is always curled in the same design, the wings slant at the same angle, the tongue has three points . . ."

"Precisely!" Paper cracked as she smoothed out the page from Henning's mortuary notebook. "Now, look again at the mark you copied from Drummond's palm."

It took some imagination, but Wrexford saw why she sounded excited. "By Jove, you have a falcon's eye." He lifted his eyes to meet hers. "Now, if only we knew what it meant."

A smile curled on her lips. "In alchemy, dragon is a code word for mercury."

The impact of the revelation took a moment to sink in. "Well done, Mrs. Sloane. A brilliant bit of sleuthing," he murmured. "It would seem that art can indeed be a powerful tool in science."

Was that a faint blush stealing to her cheeks? Or merely a reflection of light off the cover of the oxblood-colored leather binding.

"Now it's your turn, milord," she said, closing the books and arranging them into a neat stack. "What discovery have you made?"

Charlotte watched Wrexford recross his legs, a habit she had noted meant he was about to say something he considered important.

"Actually, I've made a number of them. I'll start with books, too. My trip to Canaday's estate in Kent proved useful in several regards. I obtained access to the library and learned what book matched the catalogue number you found in Holworthy's hand." He went on to explain about his search, the Newton manuscript, and the revelation of the three other missing books.

"Alchemy." Charlotte said the word very softly and yet its echo seemed to transmute itself into a booming sound that filled the room. She waited a moment, and then added, "It's clear it's at the heart of the murders. But how and why still isn't—"

"Patience, Mrs. Sloane." Wrexford held up a hand. "I haven't finished."

She sat back.

"Yet another revelation—uncovered by a friend of mine—is that Canaday and Holworthy are cousins, and that the baron was lying about what books the reverend had borrowed from him. In truth, knowing that Canaday was in desperate need of money, Holworthy had purchased the four alchemy books for a large sum of money, but reneged on making the last payment."

"So you think Canaday murdered him? And that somehow Drummond discovered the fact and was killed to keep him from revealing it?"

Wrexford shook his head. "No, actually I'm convinced Canaday is not involved in the murders. He hasn't the nerve for it. Holworthy is at the center of whatever evil is afoot. He took advantage of the fact that the baron was in financial trouble."

The earl paused. "By the by, Canaday possesses a magnificent painting by Rembrandt. As an artist, you would have appreciated the exquisite nuances of detail. I'm no expert, but he used lights and darks to create a very powerful portrait of a Dutch burgher in all his glory."

Charlotte felt a sudden tightening in her chest. Her heart began to thump against her ribs. "Could you describe it to me?"

His brows arched in bemusement. "I understand

you are passionate about the subject, but given the other pressing concerns, perhaps we should defer a discussion on art until later."

"Please. It could be important."

Though still looking faintly puzzled, he did as she asked.

Charlotte quickly fetched a small portfolio from the tiny back room and spread out some pastel sketches on the table. "Was it like this one?"

She heard a sharp intake of breath.

"Yes, that's it exactly."

"Good Lord. I think I may know . . ." Charlotte had an idea but it seemed too awful to put into words. And yet, its very smarminess was exactly the reason why it might be right.

"Know what?" pressed Wrexford.

"What attracted Stoughton and his friend—I've remembered that his name was St. Alban or something like that—to Anthony."

Wrexford went very still and his gaze turned shuttered. In the silence, she could almost hear the gears whirring inside his head.

"Copying masterworks is an exercise many painters do in order to keep their technical skills sharp. It's a little like a musician playing scales, though the added benefit is that by seeing a subject through the eyes of a great artist one gains a new perspective on creativity." She studied the sketches, feeling a surge of both sadness and anger well up inside her. "I assumed Anthony

310

was simply copying a painting on display at the Royal Academy. But in this light, it seems like it had a more sinister purpose."

"You think he was recruited to forge the painting?"

"It makes sense of all the things that seemed inexplicable until now." Charlotte thought back over the hellish last months of her husband's life. "His long absences, his mental anguish." She bit her lip. "His guilt. Anthony loved the idealism of art. He would have hated himself for perverting that."

"But you said he repeatedly mentioned the word *alchemy* in his final days," pointed out Wrexford. "And that he had strange burns on his hands. How do you explain that?"

"I can't." Her hands balled into fists as she thought about the drawing she had made the previous night. "However, I am positive that we've discovered part of the answer, and I would bet my life that the other part also lies within the group of miscreants who call themselves The Ancients."

He rose and began to pace, the *thump-thump* of his boots on the rough-planked floor beating an agitated tattoo.

"Old Masters paintings are worth a great deal of money," she went on. "A ring who could create superb forgeries of the originals and then sell them to wealthy collectors could have a very profitable business."

"I've a friend who is acquainted with St. Aubin and says he's a veritable son of Satan," he muttered. "So I can well believe he's mixed up in some havey-cavey business."

Wrexford pivoted and retraced his steps. He was a very large man in a very small space—he must feel like one of the caged lions on display at the Tower.

"Facts." The earl was frowning. "We need to find the facts that tie alchemy and art together."

"And just how do you intend to do that?" It came out a little more sarcastically than she intended. "From what I hear, Bow Street is within a hairsbreadth of arresting you for both murders."

"I shall solve this blasted conundrum by taking care that the distance between Mr. Griffin's grasping hands and my humble self does not get any narrower," he answered.

Confident words, bordering on arrogance. Charlotte wondered what it would be like to feel that aura of invincibility. In her experience, the gods did not look kindly on such hubris.

Still, she found her spirits buoyed by his attitude. "You harp on facts—very well, let us compile a list of them."

Paper and pencil was close at hand. Charlotte slid over a sheet of foolscap and wrote two headings at the top, then drew a dividing line down the middle to make two columns. "It seems we have two different conundrums going on. One that concerns art and one that concerns alchemy. Let's start with art, which seems the simpler one to assess."

Together they created a numbered list, based purely on the knowledge they had in hand, not conjecture. Then they moved on to start filling out the second column.

"There are still some facts about alchemy that I've not yet had a chance to mention." Wrexford turned abruptly and came over to perch a hip on a corner of the table. "My valet and I were able to salvage some charred papers from Drummond's laboratory and remove them to my town house before Griffin was allowed to examine the room. They caught my eye because a small fragment held a very strange message."

He shifted slightly. "It said, 'the Golden One is the Devil and must be stopped from destroying . . .' There was a hole, and then the word *dangerous,* followed by an abbreviation that we interpreted to mean the philosopher's stone."

"From my readings, I know that the philosopher's stone lies at the heart of alchemy," said Charlotte. "It's the elemental substance that has the power to transmute one material into another, like lead into gold."

"Yes," agreed the earl. "And its exact composition has been the Holy Grail of alchemy for centuries."

"But," she said slowly, "most practitioners agree

that mercury has to be one of the key ingredients."

Their eyes met and for a moment the air seemed to thrum with an unseen energy.

Wrexford looked away first. "At first we thought that 'Golden One' was a code word for a chemical—possibly sulfur. But on closer inspection of the other scraps, which were magnified under the lens of my microscope, we found the partial remains of what looked to be a letter. This second mention made it clear that Golden One referred to a person." He made a face. "And before you ask, I've set my friend—"

"Mr. Sheffield?" she interrupted, her curiosity roused by what she had overheard in Berkeley Square.

"Yes. He's trustworthy, and in any case, I've told him nothing about A. J. Quill's involvement in my investigation."

"And what have you set him to doing?"

Wrexford made a wry face. "Compiling a list of all members of the Royal Institution who have fair hair."

"I suppose that makes perfect sense to think 'Golden One' refers to appearance."

And yet . . . A niggling thought stirred somewhere in the back of her head, but for the moment it remained naught but a vague shadow within shadows.

She shook it off. "So on one hand, all the evidence points to an evil chemist who is concocting an unknown substance, most likely containing mercury, in order to destroy an unknown target."

"Which is a great deal more than we knew a half hour ago," quipped the earl.

"It still leaves us nowhere."

He took up the list.

"And then we have what looks to be a ring of art forgers," mused Charlotte. "What the devil ties them together?"

"Holworthy has to be the key," said Wrexford decisively. He reached for a pencil and some paper. "I need to sit down and think."

Hide-and-seek sunlight tangled in his dark hair as he set to work constructing a diagram of connections. Leaving him to the faint scratch of his scribblings, she turned away, suddenly feeling terribly unsettled.

A part of it had to do with the new revelations about her late husband. Sorrow warred with exasperation, a conflict she had yet to sort out in her own mind. Anthony had been such a perplexing mix of idealism and weakness. That his craving for recognition had allowed him to be seduced into betraying all that art stood for was disappointing.

But, at heart, she could not say she was completely surprised. His character had been too malleable. He was easily led.

Was that disloyal to admit?

Charlotte found she had wandered into the tiny back room that held his easel, his paint box, and the array of powdered pigments and linseed oil used to mix his gorgeous colors. Spiderwebs covered the small mullioned window, the angle of the sun causing the finespun filaments to cast exaggerated shadows over the supplies.

Art, she reflected, was all about perspective, and the infinite number of ways one could view a subject. Even here, in this cramped space, everything was constantly changing. Color and shading shifted. The air rippled, sending flickers of light undulating over the walls.

But principles should be unyielding. Integrity had but one form.

"I forgive you, Anthony," she whispered.

To honor his memory—or perhaps to redeem his memory—she would not rest until this particular evil was stamped out.

A loud banging on the front door jolted her out of her brooding. Spinning around, she shot out of the room—

And hit up against Wrexford.

"Shhhh," he commanded in a low whisper, hooking an arm around her waist and thrusting her none too gently against the side of her desk. He had a pistol in his other hand and was already looking to the shadowed entryway. "Go back where you came from, and bolt the door."

A grim calmness had hold of his features.

Without waiting for answer, he moved in a blur of quick panther-like strides.

Be damned with retreating, thought Charlotte, fumbling in her desk drawer for her own little weapon. Steadying her hands with a gulp of air, she cocked the hammer and took up position at the inner doorway.

The hammering came again.

Her heartbeat kicked up another notch. Wrexford remained silent as stone.

"Mrs. Sloane?" The gruff hail had a distinct Scottish burr to it. "It's Henning. Forgive me for stopping by unannounced, but I've found something that might interest you."

CHAPTER 18

Wrexford slung the bolt back, admitting the surgeon, then relocked the door.

"I'm pleased to see you're taking the threat of trouble seriously, lassie," said Henning, eying her pocket pistol. "But for now, you may put your weapon aside."

Stepping back a pace, Charlotte eased the hammer down.

"You, too, laddie," quipped the surgeon. "I'd prefer not to have to dig a bullet out of my bum."

"I doubt a ball of lead could penetrate your ornery hide," replied the earl, his tone a little testy. The sudden interruption had reinforced just how alone and vulnerable Charlotte was.

Ignoring the comment, Henning took off his hat and combed his fingers through his untidy hair. "The coffeehouse on Red Lion Square is all abuzz with speculation about your latest print," he said without preamble to Charlotte. "To hint that there's such rot beneath the polished veneer of the aristocracy is a very provocative charge."

"It was meant to be," she answered.

"Well, I do hope you know what you're doing. And given his presence here, it would seem His Lordship has the same concerns." The surgeon raised a brow at the earl. "I don't suppose you can convince her to dull her quill?"

"No," he answered curtly. "Mrs. Sloane has an iron will. One that refuses to bend to reason."

"Reason, like beauty, is in the eye of the beholder," she shot back.

"Hmmph."

Wrexford wasn't sure whether Henning's snort signaled disapproval or amusement at her stubbornness.

"Yes, well, unfortunately death leaves no room for interpretation, Mrs. Sloane," replied the earl. "Crossing your pen with a murderer's blade was a reckless move." Seeing a protest form on her lips, he quickly added, "And spare me the platitude about the pen being mightier than the sword. Let the idiot who said such drivel try walking through the stews of London at night."

"I can't match the miscreants in physical strength or lordly influence, so I fight with the weapons I have."

"As I have taken pains to point out, there is a third option," said Wrexford. "You may leave the fight to me."

Charlotte turned her back, an answer more eloquent than words. "Would you care for a cup of tea?" she asked of Henning. An offer that had not been made to him, noted the earl.

"Nay, I'll not be troubling you for social

niceties." The surgeon set a slim book on the table. "I simply stopped by to drop off a book."

Wrexford had a feeling that despite Henning's prickly demeanor, he felt protective of the young widow.

"I remembered it last night, and thought it may be of use to you," continued the surgeon. "It's the text of a lecture given at the University of St. Andrews by Edward Charles Howard a number of years ago. In it he discusses the work of the early chemists, like Newton and Boyle, and the transition from alchemy to a more disciplined approach to science."

"Howard—the Duke of Norfolk's younger brother?" asked Wrexford. "He was an early member of the Royal Society, wasn't he?"

"Aye. Along with Banks and Rumford, he helped to pioneer a respect for science in this country. He's a brilliant chemist in his own right. If I recall correctly, he won the Copley Medal at the turn of the century for his work with mercury."

Wrexford straightened from his slouch against the doorway. He had forgotten that. His gaze shifted to Charlotte and their eyes locked for an instant before he moved to the table. "Indeed? Might I have a look?"

Henning picked up the book and tossed it over. "I've only a rudimentary knowledge of chemistry, so he loses me in his later ramblings. However, the first part on the ancient practitioners and their interest in mercury might interest Mrs. Sloane. There are several engravings showing the arcane symbols."

"Mrs. Sloane has already made momentous progress in deciphering the art of alchemy. In fact, she's identified the drawing on Drummond's hand. It's a dragon—which is the symbol of mercury."

The surgeon let out a low whistle.

"His Lordship has made some interesting discoveries as well," offered Charlotte. "He discovered papers in Drummond's laboratory that warn of evil brewing within the Royal Institution."

Wrexford quickly explained about the charred fragments of writing and his interpretation of their meaning.

"You think Drummond's accusations are credible?" asked Henning.

"The man was murdered," he pointed out. "And we've also uncovered a connection between Reverend Holworthy, Canaday, and a batch of rare books on alchemy."

"Well, that certainly tosses a few more ingredients into the bubbling crucible," observed the surgeon. "Tell me more."

Charlotte, who had been drawing random images on her sketchpad, looked up, a troubled expression clouding her eyes.

Wrexford felt a pinch of guilt. At this moment,

she must be feeling as if her carefully constructed world was in danger of crumbling into dust.

His own life was, he supposed, hanging in the balance, but he hadn't spent any time worrying over the vagaries of Chance. A certain sense of fatality, perhaps. Or, more likely, a casual confidence that Lady Luck, who had always been sweet on him, wouldn't withdraw her favors quite yet.

He watched the subtle play of emotions on Charlotte's features as she stared into the shadows. Then again, the heart of it was that he didn't really care enough about anything to feel as deeply as she did. Sheffield, in a moment of alcohol-induced honesty, had accused him of using detachment as a defense.

You hide behind a facade of devil-may-care indifference, Wrex.

Was it true? Wrexford quickly dismissed the thought. Let Byron and his fellow poets plumb the depths of regret and despair. He wasn't much interested in introspection.

And while he admired Mrs. Sloane's passionate belief that truth and justice mattered, he wondered whether she had fully realized until now that passions always come with a price.

Or whether she was truly willing to pay it.

Death had a way of bringing out secrets. The revelation of A. J. Quill's true identity would end her life as she knew it.

Henning cleared his throat with a cough, drawing Wrexford out of his musing.

"Mrs. Sloane found evidence that Holworthy had a book on alchemy with him when he was murdered," he answered, and then went on to give a summary of what they had pieced together so far.

Listening to his own words only amplified his frustrations with the investigation. For an instant, he was bedeviled by the sensation that in spite of all the discoveries, the shadows still had no substance. *Poof*—like vapor, they simply dissolved into nothing as his fingers closed around them.

Logic, logic, Wrexford reminded himself. Scientific method called for an orderly sequence of steps in order to discover the correct answer.

"At this point, the next reasonable step seems to concentrate on identifying any of the Institution members who are fair-haired. It may be a wild goose chase, I know, and yet it's the only solid clue so far." He paused, feeling another clench of frustration. "It would be enormously helpful if I could ask Lowell, but given his position at the Royal Institution he might feel compelled to inform the Runner."

"Lowell?" repeated Henning. "Slender fellow, of average height with auburn hair?"

"Yes."

"I hadn't heard that he'd been appointed as a

lecturer," mused Henning. "But it doesn't surprise me. Davy has a knack for spotting the best minds in the scientific world, and Lowell is a brilliant chemist."

Wrexford shook his head. "You're mistaken," he replied. "The fellow has no interest in chemistry. His only scientific focus is butterflies, and that's merely a hobby. As for his position at the Institution, it's merely administrative."

"Nay, it's you who's got it argle-bargled, laddie," insisted the surgeon. "Lowell spent a year in Scotland studying under a good friend of mine. McLachlan's an odd duck—got himself dismissed from the faculty at St. Andrews University for feuding with the powers-that-be, so he's now a curmudgeonly recluse who works alone. But he's still considered a brilliant mind. And he told me that Lowell's skills in the laboratory bordered on supernatural."

If that was true, then Lowell had deliberately lied. "Are you positive?"

"Aye. Julian Lowell was a veritable wizard when it came to analyzing arcane elements and understanding their potential. I believe he created a new formula for a lucifer match during his time there, which allowed for a flame to be struck under damp conditions."

"Ah. Wrong Lowell," said Wrexford, feeling himself relax. "Our fellow is Declan Lowell, the Marquess of Carnsworth's younger son."

Henning gave a grunt. "Nay, McLachlan's Lowell certainly didn't sound like an aristocrat. My friend said he was a strange fellow, with an intensity about his work that bordered on frightening."

"And ours is known for his polished charm and easy manner."

"Which leaves you still stumbling around in the dark about your Golden One," observed Henning grimly. He sat on one of the stools and took out his pipe. "D'you mind if I blow a cloud, Mrs. Sloane? It helps me cogitate."

She nodded absently.

A spark flared, and a silvery plume of smoke curled up, only to be quickly swallowed by the gloom.

A taunt from the cosmos? Wrexford watched another puff rise. However faint, the murderer had left a trail.

They just had to see it.

Charlotte couldn't shake off the niggling sensation that a telling clue was hovering just beyond the outer edges of her consciousness. *Special books, intricate images, strange phrases*—they all seemed to be tangling together, trying to tell her something.

Uno. With a sinuous whisper, the Latin word for *one* slowly uncoiled from the amorphous jumble.

She exhaled a harried sigh. Yes, *one* thing seemed certain—her life was tumbling to hell in a handbasket.

The sound drew a swift glance from Wrexford. He, too, looked unsettled. Shadows hung from his dark lashes, accentuating the deep-set hollows under his eyes.

Unable to sit still, Charlotte rose and began to gather up the sketches lying on her desk and shuffle them into an orderly pile.

"I've asked my friend Sheffield to help with checking what other members of the Institution are fair-haired," said the earl to the surgeon.

"You have no other clue as to the identity of 'Golden One'?" pressed Henning.

"It may be spitting into the wind, but unless you have any better ideas . . ."

Their voices blurred to a low hum as Charlotte suddenly set the papers aside and fumbled in the desk's top compartment for the hidden key. A quick twist unlocked the bottom drawer.

With the men still deep in discussion, she took out the top book and hurriedly thumbed through the sections. *Canaday.* Yes, there was the baron's entry at the top of the page, but she ran her finger down the other entries. *Canterfield, Cappell, Carberry . . .*

Carnsworth.

Charlotte stared at the crest and for several long, painful moments found her lungs refused to draw a breath. Swallowing hard, she made herself read over the entry for the Marquess of Carnsworth twice before looking up.

"Declan Hervey Julian Lowell," she announced loudly.

Wrexford turned. "I beg your pardon?"

No doubt he thought she had lost her mind.

Charlotte held up the book. "According to *Debrett's Peerage*, the Marquess of Carnsworth's third son is named Declan Hervey Julian Lowell."

Henning coughed on a mouthful of smoke.

"But that's not all," she added, trying to keep her voice steady. "You need to look at this."

The earl crouched down by the desk as she put the volume down and turned it to face him. Henning crowded close behind him.

"Ye god," muttered Wrexford after careful scrutiny. "At times, I'm tempted to think you have the gift of black magic, Mrs. Sloane. How the devil did you think of that?"

"It's not magic, sir. I'm merely following the scientific principle of empirical observation," explained Charlotte. "I spent some time studying Canaday's crest, and as you see, this one is on the facing page. It attracted me because it's rather unusual, and when you mentioned the Golden One, it triggered a connection." She made a face. "Though it took me a while to figure out what it was."

"I'm not sure I understand what you mean,"

said the surgeon, squinting at the page. "What am I missing?"

Wrexford tapped a finger to the ornate colored crest of the Lowell family. "Look more closely at the quartered shield." Two sections held a scarlet lion rampant. And two held a large golden numeral one. "Now, let me read you the motto in the fancy scroll—*Ab uno disce omnes*."

"From One, Learn All," translated Charlotte.

"Ye god," said Henning, echoing the earl. "I could have stared at that until Doomsday and not seen it."

"I respond to visual images," she said simply. "I suppose you can say that art gives me a different perception of the world."

"And a brilliant one at that," observed the surgeon. "Kudos to you, lassie." He looked to the earl and raised his bushy brows. "It seems to me Mrs. Sloane has found your murderer."

"Lowell is guilty of something," said Wrexford slowly. "I'm just not quite sure of what."

Puff, puff. A scrim of smoke now hazed the room. "You have the incriminating scrap from Drummond's laboratory, and it clearly warns that Golden One is concocting some dangerous chemical substance for a nefarious purpose," pointed out Henning. "Alchemy terms are mentioned, and you know that Holworthy got alchemy books from his cousin, was spotted within the Institution, and then was murdered.

And on top of that, I told you about the recent thefts of mercury from a number of apothecaries. The superintendent of the Institution would have intimate knowledge of all the stocks of chemicals throughout London."

Wrexham pursed his lips.

"Ergo," finished Henning, "it seems a logical deduction that Lowell is the villain."

"I doubt Griffin will agree," countered the earl. "Logical though it may sound to us, it's still mostly conjecture—and even more telling is the fact that we haven't a shred of evidence to show what he's supposedly concocting or how it is to be used."

"Show him the charred fragments," said the surgeon.

"The charred fragments that *I* stole from the laboratory?" The earl slowly curled a sardonic smile. "Do you really think the Runner is going to be inclined to take my word for it that I didn't try to burn them in the first place?"

"I have to agree with His Lordship," cut in Charlotte. "You see, the question of guilt is not as clear-cut as we might wish, Mr. Henning. We've discovered another element to the mystery of the murders, and as of yet have not worked out how it fits in. It, too, may involve alchemy."

"Alchemy rears its ugly head in yet another guise?" quipped Henning. "Well, well. We've certainly got a potent brew of unknown ingredients coming to a boil." He flicked a bit of ash from his cuff. "Which threaten to transmute Wrexford from a Tulip of the *ton* to a rotting corpse."

"How edifying that my situation serves as a source of amusement to my friends," said the earl dryly.

The surgeon shrugged. "One must laugh at the vagaries of Life, laddie." He blew out a perfect smoke ring and watched it float up to the rafters. "Now, tell me about the other problem."

Charlotte looked to the earl, suddenly feeling too weary to explain. She was like a fly caught in a spider's web, with the delicate filaments inexorably wrapping round and round, their deceptive strength squeezing and squeezing . . .

As Wrexford began to tell his friend about the suspected art forgeries and their connection to her husband's death, she braced her elbows on the desk and pressed her palms to her eyes. Beneath her heat-prickled skin, her blood felt feverish.

It was I who dared spark the fire, she reminded herself. And fire was an elemental force in alchemy. She had known the ingredients were dangerous—The Ancients were powerful men—and yet she had gone ahead with her print. If Lowell, the son of a marquess, was allied with them, there was no telling what they would do to retaliate.

And the most likely target was Wrexford. Once a noose was around his neck, the murders would quickly be forgotten.

A touch to her shoulder drew her out of her chilling thoughts. "You're pale as a cod's underbelly, Mrs. Sloane. Take a drink of brandy," counseled Henning.

"I don't have any brandy," answered Charlotte, feeling the absurd urge to laugh.

"Ah, but I do." Taking her hands, he wrapped them around a flask. "Drink," he commanded.

She did, and somehow the alchemy of fire mixed with fire was surprisingly comforting.

"Now, assuming you don't mean to sit meekly and wait for the noose to loop around your neck," said Henning to the earl, "what the devil are you going to do next?"

Wrexford seemed to retreat into himself. All the chiseled planes and angles of his face became as emotionless as granite. Charlotte was tempted to take up her sketchpad and try to capture the supreme sense of self-command. But she felt too spent to reach for paper and pencil. Far more appealing was the thought of taking refuge in her upstairs bedroom and seeking blissful oblivion in sleep.

But then, bad dreams might be even worse than her own wakeful imagination.

The earl finally responded to Henning's question.

"As to that, I've an idea. It's time for the hunter to become the hunted."

CHAPTER 19

It was nearly midnight, but the shadows flitting through the dimly lit room couldn't quite hide Tyler's disgruntled expression. "Are you sure I shouldn't come with you?"

"Quite." Wrexford eased the thin steel probe in a touch farther and delicately pressed it up, and then down. "There, you see?" The lock had released with a satisfying *snick*. "That's three times in a row."

He removed the blindfold. "Your tutelage over the past hour has knocked the rust off my skills. I'll have no trouble opening the door."

"Yes, but creating a diversion is key to getting you inside the building without being seen," argued his valet. "Do you really think it wise to entrust the task to a pair of unfledged urchins?"

The earl had weighed the risks and decided there was no danger in asking Raven and Hawk to make enough of a disturbance outside the Royal Institution to draw the ire of the night guard. The plan was for them to lead the man on a merry chase before disappearing into the night, and he had every confidence that they were far too quick and agile to be in any peril.

"Those unfledged urchins responded with exactly the same question when I mentioned that

I was considering using you," replied Wrexford dryly. "Along with a number of very rude observations on the abilities of a Mayfair man-milliner."

Tyler looked bemused by the insult. "Me? A man-milliner?" The term was a bawdy disparagement of a fellow's manhood.

"Their words, not mine. But they do have a point. They've lived all their lives on the streets. Raising holy hell with watchmen and shopkeepers is second nature to them. A few well-flung stones rattling against entrance lanterns and the guard won't hesitate to leave his post to box their ears."

He wrapped the set of picklocks in a piece of chamois and slid the roll into his boot. Unless his wits were turned arse over teakettle, they were finally in a position to take the initiative away from their adversary. Let it be *his* turn to react to unexpected attacks. The plan, which he and Tyler had worked out in meticulous detail over the last few hours, was to break into Lowell's basement laboratory and look for proof that darker passions lay beneath the gossamer tales of collecting butterflies.

"Don't sulk," he ordered, slanting a sidelong look at his valet's face. "We can't take a chance of you being spotted anywhere near the building. I'll be exceedingly careful, but Lowell is a clever dastard. There can't be any connection to me if he notices the place has been searched."

"What if the brats are caught?" asked his valet, who was still looking unhappy at ceding his place in the action. "Or don't show up?"

"They won't let us down," assured Wrexford. The boys had greeted the request with undisguised enthusiasm. What Charlotte's reaction would be if she knew of it was a moot point. Like the knives, it was decided this midnight foray was to be a secret between men.

He rose from his crouch by the door and entered his workroom, followed by a still-scowling Tyler. "Your task is just as important. Read over Edward Howard's lecture on the early alchemists that Henning gave me. Then I need you to search through the library shelves and gather everything you can on his work with mercury."

"I shall have it all bookmarked and a summary written waiting for your return." A long-suffering sigh punctuated the reply. "*If* you return."

"Thank you for the vote of confidence." Wrexford checked his pocket watch. "Time to be off."

"Let us hope the urchins also carry gold timepieces," muttered Tyler under his breath.

"Don't be sarcastic."

"It must have rubbed off on me from you," huffed his valet.

"The church bells ring the hour," pointed out the earl as he slipped on a black coat and knitted cap. "And those who live on the street are attuned to the natural cycle of the day. I've tested the boys, and they're more accurate than my fancy Breguet ticker."

Tyler surrendered his pique with a resigned sigh. "You have the special lantern?" Clever fellow that he was, the valet had designed a pocket-sized metal apparatus with a glass lens that focused candlelight into a narrow but powerful beam. Useful in illuminating experiments, it would also prove an asset in more clandestine activities.

Wrexford patted his coat pocket in answer, and then opened the window overlooking his back garden.

"Godspeed, milord." The whisper was quickly lost in the ruffling night breeze.

Unable to sleep, Charlotte pulled on her wrapper and padded down the stairs, intent on brewing a cup of chamomile tea. She paused halfway down and cocked an ear.

The whisper of rustling blankets and low-pitched voices rose up from the gloom. She tiptoed down several more treads and stopped to listen again.

A boot scuffed against the planked floor.

"Shhhh, you're gonna wake her," hissed Raven. "Sorry."

It was unusual for the boys to be going out at this hour. They either hared off after supper or settled in by the stove for the night. Of late, they had been loath to leave her alone.

Puzzled, she abandoned any pretense of stealth and hurried down to the main room.

Raven spun around, the dappling of moonlight from the window catching the spasm of guilt that flitted across his face.

Charlotte feigned a yawn. "I couldn't sleep. And it seems neither could you. Will you join me in some tea? There's sugar in the pantry so we can sweeten it." Wrexford had left another purse that morning and she had splurged on a treat for the boys.

"Naw," said Raven, evading her gaze. "Me 'n' Hawk just feel like a breath of fresh air, that's all."

Suspicions roused, Charlotte turned to his younger brother. "What are the two of you up to?"

"N-Nuffink!"

Her senses were now on full alert. Hawk only said "nuffink" when he was nervous about something.

"*Nothing,*" she corrected softly.

Hawk hung his head. "Sorry."

"I hope 'nothing' truly means you have no mischief in mind." Charlotte ran a hand over the thick nighttime braid of her hair, wishing she dared to gather them in her arms. "I worry about you," she said honestly. "If you run afoul of the authorities, I haven't the connections or the money to secure your freedom." Boys of their age were routinely transported to the Antipodes for stealing an apple or a loaf of bread.

"We've no mischief planned, m'lady," said Raven. "I swear it."

The boy was an excellent liar, but she had dealt with far more jaded scoundrels.

"I'm glad to hear it." Another false yawn. "Lud, my eyes now feel heavy again. I think I shall forego tea and return to bed." Hugging her arms to her chest, she started back up the steps. "Please take care."

"Aye, we will!" they chorused.

Weasels. Wrexford's teasing moniker popped to mind. They were, she knew, sneaking out on some adventure—and one of which she would definitely not approve.

I'm not their mother or legal guardian, she reminded herself. They were free to do as they pleased.

As soon as she turned the corner of the landing, Charlotte took the treads two at a time, moving swiftly and silently to her bedchamber. Crouching down at the window, she watched the street below and waited. Several moments passed, and then two small shapes slipped out into the shadows, their stealthy steps heading west.

Charlotte dressed in a flash, grateful that breeches and boots were so much easier to don than the cursed layers of feminine frills, and

337

hurried out into the night. A thin haze of mist dulled the starlight, and puffs of pale vapor skittered through the darkened streets. The boys were no longer visible, but thank God, she was familiar with their favorite routes to the heart of Mayfair.

Be damned with legalities. If danger lay ahead, she wasn't about to let them face it alone.

The sky was fast darkening with clouds. Hat pulled low on her brow, Charlotte wove her way through the maze of alleyways and side streets, avoiding the occasional tavern and ginhole where trouble might gather. It was near the markets at Covent Garden that she spotted the boys up ahead. They were moving at a cautious pace and taking care to blend into the surroundings. But she knew what to look for. The hunch of their shoulders, the angle of their heads, the rhythm of their gait—she knew every nuance by heart.

As they cut up Coventry Street and crept into Piccadilly Street, she slowly but surely shortened the distance between them. The boys were skilled, but they made one cardinal mistake.

Charlotte ducked into a gap between the buildings and held herself very still as she checked the way behind her.

No sign of movement or sound of footsteps. She took up the chase again, just in time to see the boys take shelter in a passageway by the corner of Albermarle Street.

The nape of her neck began to prickle.

I have an idea. Wrexford's eyes had taken on a dangerous glint earlier in the day, just before he had rushed off. If what she suspected was true, she would save the Crown the bother of an execution and hang him herself!

She, too, took cover and made a quick assessment of the situation. A glance showed the boys were still in hiding. Guessing that the Royal Institution building was their ultimate destination, Charlotte considered her options. Darting up Old Bond Street, which lay directly to her right, would allow her to circle around to the other end of Albermarle Street and find a vantage point from which to observe what trouble was brewing.

Damn the earl. It was one thing to risk his own neck . . .

Slipping out from her hiding place, she followed the line of darkness cast by the buildings, anger giving impetus to her steps.

In a matter of minutes, the massive fluted columns of the Institution rose out of the gloom, the pale stone taking on a pearlescent glow as the moon broke free of the clouds. Finding a recessed set of stairs, she took up position just as a nearby church bell struck a single ring.

Charlotte tensed.

The sound seemed to reverberate through the air for an eternity.

Nothing.

A chill licked down her spine. She shifted uncertainly, trying to swallow her fear. Had her instincts been wrong? As if taunting her doubts, the shadows came cruelly alive, flitting and rippling under her confused gaze.

But suddenly a distinct shape materialized at the corner of the building. A silhouette of a man, stark black against the dark-on-dark charcoal swirling. It was gone in an instant, hidden by the unyielding stone—

Thwack!

A rock ricocheted off one of the pristine pillars, then several more.

Charlotte bit back a cry as the boys ran closer and flung another fusillade at the stately entrance.

The main door flung open. "Oy!" A beefy guard lumbered out, waving a cudgel. "Be off with you or I'll call for the authorities!"

Raven shouted an obscenity as he reared back and launched a missile that hit the man square in the chest.

Enraged, the guard stumbled down the steps, bellowing for help from the night watchman who patrolled the local streets.

The boys backed off, just slowly enough to invite a chase.

Run! Charlotte kept the warning bottled up as she knew what they were doing. Though she didn't see the earl slip into the building, she was sure he was already inside.

Raven must have sensed it too—or more likely, Wrexford, with the focus of his scientific precision, had spelled out exactly how long the diversion should last. No matter how angry with him she was at the moment, she didn't believe he would expose them to foolhardy risk.

Sure enough, after tossing a few more insults at the guard, the boys broke into a run and were gone in the blink of an eye.

Charlotte had seen enough. She slipped away from her hiding place. But instead of retracing her steps east, she turned and headed west.

Forty . . . forty-one . . . forty-two . . . Moving noiselessly across the wide entrance hall, Wrexford entered the stairwell and descended to the basement well ahead of schedule.

"Well done, weasels," he murmured as he paused to pull the picklocks from his boot. Less than a minute had now passed since the first stone had been thrown. The boys should be flying for home.

Assuming Raven obeyed his orders to the letter. The guard, he knew, couldn't outrace a slug. But unexpected complications could happen . . .

The earl forced such worries from his head. The boy was bright and understood that the streets were always teeming with unexpected dangers.

Easing the basement door open, he hurried down the pitch-black corridor, navigating by touch rather than sight. Lowell's laboratory was the last one on the left, the entrance hidden behind a jog in the wall. He felt around for the keyhole, and after exploring the opening chose two of his thinnest probes.

Practice had been a wise precaution. The supervisor had installed a complicated German puzzle lock. A difficult challenge.

Snick. But not impossible.

After closing the door behind him and rebolting it, he lit his tiny lantern, courtesy of Lowell's ingenious invention. Tyler had only recently received a supply from Scotland of the highly reliable lucifer matches. The irony was amusing, but only for an instant. If what he suspected was true, the brilliant chemist's talents had been turned to far darker pursuits.

He turned and shadows spooked to life, their crypt-like leers a taunting reminder that death was taking perverse pleasure in following his every move. Angling the beam of light to the near corner of the laboratory, Wrexford began a methodical search of the space.

After a half hour of peering and poking into every nook and cranny, he sat down at the desk and steepled his fingers. A prayer to the Almighty? Divine intervention was unlikely to save a sinner such as himself. He would have to rely on his own wits.

Ah, but I like conundrums.

He tap-tapped his fingertips together. The place was spotless. Too spotless. The display cases of exotic butterflies, prominently arranged on the work counters according to color, had nary a speck of dust on the glass. As to any chemical components, only a rudimentary assortment of glass beakers and metal crucibles was in the storage cabinets, and the spirit lamp's gleaming brass spoke of its never having been used.

Leaning back, Wrexford closed his eyes and inhaled deeply. And yet a faint whiff of acid tinged the air.

The laboratory itself may not have been used for clandestine activities, but some chemical compound had recently been stored here. So far, Lowell had outwitted them all, but however diabolically clever, no man was perfect. There had to be a clue as to what it was.

He just had to find it.

Taking up the lantern, the earl returned to his original starting point and began again, this time looking more carefully for any signs of hidden compartments or places of concealment. The work was tedious, and his candle was soon burned down to a stub. He stopped to slide in a replacement, gauging that he had perhaps an hour left before the city streets began to stir.

The desk and storage drawers yielded no secrets, save for a few love notes from an amorous Lady Clothilde, written in French. He moved on to the cabinets. But after a meticulous examination, he was forced to concede defeat. *Damnation.* He had to be missing something. Logic dictated that Charlotte's discovery was too compelling to be wrong.

Lowell was no more an innocent aficionado of *Lepidoptera* than the Man in the Moon was made of Stilton cheese . . .

A glint of iridescent blue caught in the lantern light. Wrexford blinked to clear his vision—and then slowly walked over to the fancy wood display cases. In each one of the four, the butterflies were pinned on a board covered in pristine white felt, with tiny labels neatly placed beneath each specimen. Crouching down, he studied the height of the ornately carved oak before carefully unfastening the brass latches on the first case and lifting the lid.

Using his pocketknife, Wrexford carefully worked the board free of its base and lifted it out. Beneath was naught but empty space. The lantern flickered, warning that little light was left. And the precious seconds were ticking away. He quickly replaced the board and relocked the case, then blew out his breath and forced himself to think.

Blues, reds, browns, yellows—his gaze skimmed over the cases. Lowell had chosen to display his collection by color rather than size or wing shape . . .

Yellows. He looked more closely at the specimens, noting that they ranged from pale buttery hues to deeper shades of gold.

"Oh, you clever devil," muttered Wrexford as he slid the tip of his blade around the board and eased it up and out. But once again, the lantern beam revealed that the space was empty.

He stared in disbelief, refusing to accept what his eyes were telling him. Thinking of Charlotte's urging to trust one's instincts, he set the lantern down and ran his fingers over the fine-grained wooden bottom. Grit rubbed against his skin, and almost immediately he felt a burning sensation. Something had been stored here, and recently. There was still a bit of moisture in the substance.

Retrieving the light, he angled the beam around the perimeter of the box.

He would have missed it if he hadn't been so stubbornly certain his reasoning was right. Lodged upright in the V created by the rear left corner block was a tiny glass vial, no more than an inch high and half the width of a pencil. Wrexford freed it with his knife tip and rolled it to the center of the space.

Its top was sealed with thick black wax, and beneath the covering a pale granular powder gleamed within the glass.

He took out his handkerchief and swathed the delicate vial in a roll of silk before tucking it inside his shirt.

Keeping rein on his impatience, the earl took the time to replace the specimen board and recheck that no sign of his search was evident. His gut feeling was that Lowell wouldn't be returning here—whatever malevolent plan he was brewing, it was likely nearing completion.

Which meant that time in which to stop him was ticking away . . .

Wrexford blew out the candle and hurried to the door.

CHAPTER 20

Finding a small foothold in the brick, Charlotte scrambled to the top of the garden wall and dropped down on a patch of soft grass bordering a graveled path. A breeze ruffled through the well-tended ornamental plantings, stirring a swirl of mist fragrant with roses and the piney tang of yew.

The scent of money, she thought, taking an extra moment to fill her lungs with its sweet, clean perfume. Outside of bastions of privilege like Berkeley Square, the London air was always edged with far less salubrious smells. But the rich, they lived in their own world, swathed in luxury.

And their own insular arrogance. Which was, Charlotte reminded herself, why she was here.

Rising, she dusted the dirt from the knees of her breeches and followed the path to the stone terrace at the rear of the mansion. Even though it was illuminated in nothing but the muted moonlight, its classical lines and elegant simplicity were striking. Pale Portland stone cornices and moldings faced the deeper-hued blocks of limestone, giving the tall building an airy, graceful feel despite its solid bulk and steeply pitched slate roof.

A light shone through the dark draperies of the high mullioned double windows at the left corner. One of them was cracked open to the night air. She hesitated, but with her blood up, anger won out over prudence.

A man raised his head from the eyepiece of a large brass apparatus as her boots tapped down upon the polished wood floor. "And who," he asked calmly, "might you be?"

"Where's Wrexford?" she demanded. Was he a servant? His clothing said no. He was dressed casually, with his coat off and linen sleeves rolled up. A distinct brownish stain occupied the spot on his shirt where a cravat should have been.

"Out," he replied. His face was too thin and bony to be considered handsome, but there was something arresting about the sharpness of his hazel eyes.

"So I suspected." Charlotte moved to the large pear wood desk and took a seat in the very comfortable-looking chair. "I'll wait."

He seemed amused by the statement. "Would you care for some warm milk and biscuits while you do so? I imagine it's way past your bedtime, lad."

She was quite sure his basilisk stare had not failed to discern her sex. Had he learned from the earl that sardonic humor tended to intimidate people? Well, he was wasting his breath. In her current state of mind, nothing short of bodily force was going to remove her from the premises.

There were a number of open books piled atop each other on the desktop. Others, she noted, were spread out over the work counters. Ignoring his question, Charlotte picked up one of them and began to read.

That wiped the insouciant smile off his lips. "Put that down," he said rather sharply. "It's a rare edition and *very* difficult to come by."

A Scottish accent. Which explained his pale complexion and ginger-colored hair.

Without looking up, she turned to the next page.

A curse—at least, she suspected it was one. Everything said in Gaelic sounded a little rough around the edges. He rose abruptly. "I really must insist."

"Very well," answered Charlotte calmly. "You may bring me the biscuits. But I would prefer brandy over the warm milk."

His jaw tightened. He was, she observed, no doubt trying to decide whether gentlemanly scruples allowed him to toss her out on her ear. Or perhaps his uncertainty centered around the small pistol she had seen him ease out of the workbench drawer the moment she had dropped into the room.

Whatever the moral dilemma, it was interrupted by Wrexford's hurried entrance.

He appeared agitated. "Tyler—"

Be damned if the book was rare. Before he could say more, Charlotte smacked it down on the desk with a ferocious *thump* and shot to her feet. "You, sir, are an unmitigated arse."

The earl stopped short.

"How dare you!" she continued. "I swear, if I had a piece of rope right now, I'd hang you myself."

He had the grace to look a little abashed. "They were in no danger."

On hearing his curt reply, all her pent-up fears came bubbling up. "Has God suddenly given you the powers of Almighty omniscience to go along with your lordly arrogance? Or is it simply what the devil does it matter if two homeless brats get shipped off to the penal colonies half a world away! There are hundreds—nay thousands—of such worthless weasels roaming the streets of London." To her dismay, Charlotte felt tears well up, but quickly blinked them back. "Of course they wouldn't be missed."

His face expressionless, Wrexford fixed his stare not on her but rather on some spot on the far wall.

Detachment, she thought bitterly, was a great gift to have when faced with inconvenient truths.

Tyler didn't move. The only sound was the sinuous whisper of the heavy silk draperies as they stirred in a gust of air.

"I'm sorry," he said softly. "You are right. It was wrong of me to involve the boys without first discussing it with you."

She blinked again.

"But rest assured, I would never have allowed them to come to any grief."

The unexpected apology drained away the rush of righteous anger, leaving her feeling naught but hurt and exhausted. Charlotte sat down again and folded her hands in her lap. There was an ink smudge on her calloused thumb, an all too visceral reminder that in both action and thought, her behavior was beyond the pale of Polite Society decorum.

A black mark. She contemplated the thought, then decided to see it instead as a badge of honor. A pattern card of propriety had no more substance than the pasteboard on which it was printed.

Let the beau monde consider her disgraceful for having passions.

As to what the earl was thinking of her . . .

It didn't matter.

Charlotte made herself look up and pretend to possess more strength than she felt. "I hope that the risk proved worth it." Strangely enough, her voice sounded strong and steady.

"It did," answered the earl with equal calmness. "Indeed, we may soon know the truth about at least part of the mystery."

Without further ado, he gestured at the ginger-haired man. "Tyler!" Turning to her, he added, "By the by, this is Tyler. A mediocre valet but an excellent laboratory assistant."

Tyler inclined a courteous nod.

"Allow me to introduce . . ." Wrexford hesitated.

"A. J. Quill," said Charlotte. Seeing as the valet was privy to the other secrets, it seemed silly to keep this one.

If Tyler was surprised by the announcement, he hid it well. "What a pleasure to meet you," he murmured. "I am a great fan of your work."

"Never mind that." The earl had already moved to the central worktable, and with great care he took a wad of silk from inside his coat and placed it down as if he were handling the most fragile of eggs. "I need two of our thinnest glass squares, and be quick about it."

Tyler hurriedly prepared the items and carried them over. "Milord, I have been reading about Howard and his experiments while you were out—"

"Hand me a scalpel," said Wrexford, as he unwrapped a tiny glass vial and examined its top. "A sharp one."

The surgical tool was promptly handed over. "The top has been double sealed with wax. Which likely means—"

The blade slipped as a chunk of the wax suddenly broke off, causing the earl to momentarily juggle the vial, spilling some of the contents.

Moving with lightning quickness, Tyler grabbed the earl, and in the same violent movement hustled him away as the grains fell to the floor.

Charlotte cringed, expecting the worst.

Nothing happened.

"What the devil!" exclaimed Wrexford

"My apologies, sir. After what I had read, I expected the substance to be extremely volatile. And extremely unstable." Tyler stared balefully at the sample. "Apparently I was wrong."

"Unstable in what way?" asked Wrexford, looking curiously at the spill.

"It should have exploded at the slightest impact." The valet looked a little disappointed. "Land's research was on—"

Before Tyler could finish, the earl dropped a polished marble paperweight atop the grains— and was nearly knocked on his arse by the force of the thunderous *bang*.

"Hmm. That's very odd," said Tyler, squinting at the charred oak flooring as the shower of sparks and smoke subsided.

"Milord! Your trousers are on fire!" cried Charlotte.

Tyler quickly smothered the flames with a rag.

"Have you suffered an injury, sir?" she asked.

"Only to my vanity. I take pride in always being faultlessly attired."

Sarcasm—blatant sarcasm. Lately his attitude had softened, so this sharpness clearly showed he was as unhappy with her as she was with him.

Wrexford looked down at the badly singed wool and then at the vial, which was still clasped between his fingers. "Odd, indeed," he mused, his full attention shifting back to the chemicals. "That had far more force than ordinary gunpowder."

"Quite a bit more," agreed Tyler.

"We had better take a closer look at Lowell's hellfire invention. I wonder . . ."

"Allow me, sir, just in case." The valet held up a small pair of tongs padded in chamois. Taking hold of the glass, he carefully tipped out a small measure of the powder onto one of the pieces of glass, and ever so carefully covered it with the other, then stoppered the vial with a tiny piece of cork. "The microscope is ready to be calibrated, milord," he said as he placed the remaining sample upright in a metal tube rack and then handed the slides to the earl.

"How does looking at the powder tell you anything meaningful?" Charlotte couldn't hold back her curiosity. Even magnified, the grains would be . . . simply grains, and the substance looked to be colorless.

It was Tyler who answered. "Lord Wrexford is one of the most expert chemists in London. His skills lie in analyzing the structural nuances of different compounds. In fact, he's identified a number of new elements. For example, he isolated sodium from molten sodium hydroxide— though he's allowed Davy and Faraday to take the public professional credit." He paused. "I suppose he worries that were it widely known that he possesses a serious scientific mind, it might ruin his reputation."

Charlotte hadn't realized the full measure of his expertise. She had been under the impression that it was merely an odd hobby.

"Hell's teeth, do be quiet! Your chin wagging is an infernal distraction." Wrexford slid the sample beneath a complicated array of brass tubes.

Charlotte guessed they contained some sort of high-powered lens. Fascinated, she edged her chair closer to watch the procedure.

"That's close enough, Mrs. Sloane," counseled the earl without looking up. "Just in case there's an accident, the flying shards of glass and metal could be dangerous."

"It appears to require a strong percussive force to set it off. And yet . . ." Tyler made a series of adjustments to the tiny mirrors that amplified the light. "And yet, it seems to have the same properties of Land's discovery . . ." His voice trailed off again.

Wrexford took charge of the controls and leaned into the eyepiece. "Which was?"

His valet drew a deep breath. "Mercury fulminate."

A spin of the gears brought the chemical sample into focus. Wrexford was momentarily mesmerized by the sight. Under the high-powered magnification, its crystal structure had a striking abstract beauty. That such tiny elemental particles could combine in so many infinitely complex ways was still a source of never-ending fascination to him. Science was full of wonders.

And terrors, if Drummond was to be believed.

"Explain to me why you thought that," he said, bringing his thoughts back to the problem at hand. His valet was a meticulous researcher and rarely jumped to wrong conclusions.

"Based on Drummond's accusation and the recent thefts of mercury, it's a logical deduction. Land discovered the compound twelve years ago, and wrote extensively about its properties." Tyler picked up one of the open books that were stacked along the work counter. "He presented a paper to the Royal Society called 'On a New Fulminating Mercury,' which was subsequently published in the Society's journal."

"*Philosophical Transactions* is a very well-known scientific publication," interjected Wrexford for Charlotte's benefit.

"At the time, there was great debate on how such a powerful substance might be used in practical applications," explained Tyler. "The thing is, if it's mercury fulminate, interest in it quickly died out because of its extremely unstable volatility."

His interest in chemistry was in other areas, however. Wrexford vaguely recalled reading about it. "One possible use was in mine excavation, wasn't it?"

"Correct." Tyler's expression tightened. "But what sparked an even greater interest was whether it could be used to revolutionize the way weapons fire bullets."

Charlotte's brows pinched together in puzzlement. "How could that be possible?"

"As we just saw, it's a more powerful explosive than gunpowder. A number of inventors discussed the possibility of making a chemical primer encased in a copper cap to replace the traditional firing mechanisms," replied Tyler. "The caplock system would make a weapon quicker to load, and be far more effective than gunpowder in damp weather."

He reached for one of the other books stacked on the counter. "In fact, a Scottish clergyman by the name of Alexander Forsyth invented just such a cap in 1807. But it was deemed impractical because mercury fulminate was considered too unstable—and too dangerous."

She still looked mystified.

Tyler's explanation sparked something in Wrexford's memory. He took up a pencil and piece of paper from the worktable and drew a quick sketch. "Yes, yes—now I recall the concept. Pistols and muskets could easily be redesigned, eliminating the flint, frizzen, and flashpan. Boring out the flash hole would allow the insertion of a small cylinder with a tiny nipple at one end. A cap would be inserted into the cylinder, like so."

He added a few details to the diagram. "Pulling the trigger would release the hammer, which would strike the cap holding the mercury fulminate. The nipple would pierce the cap, igniting the chemical—and bang, the bullet and powder charge in the barrel would fire."

"It would no longer be necessary to use fiddle with a powder horn to load the flashpan," added Tyler. "One would simply insert a cap, saving precious seconds during the heat of battle."

"Mother of God," she whispered as the import of the invention dawned on her. "Anyone who possessed such a weapon would have an unbeatable military advantage against any adversary, wouldn't they?"

"Precisely," said Wrexford grimly.

"Yes, but as I said, tests showed mercury fulminate was too unstable to be reliable. It tended to explode unexpectedly, so any plans for practical use died," pointed out the valet.

"That was back at the dawn of the century," murmured Wrexford. "Since then, we've made great strides in science. There are new discoveries being made all the time."

He drummed his fingertips together and shot a sidelong look at the glass vial. But as he studied the crystals, something didn't look quite right.

"Have you a list of all the elements that make up mercury fulminate?"

"Yes," answered Tyler.

"Read them to me."

"Mercury, acqua fortis . . ."

The earl made a few adjustments to the lenses as Tyler rattled off more chemicals, enlarging the specimen's magnification. "No sulfur?"

"Not according to Land's recipe."

Wrexford was positive that this compound contained the mineral. But several of the other ingredients were puzzling. "Come have a look," he said to Tyler. "Any idea what the diamond-clear granules might be? Or that pulverized greenish powder."

The valet took his time in studying the material. "I haven't a clue," he admitted.

Several ideas came to mind. Highly unusual ones. But science was all about tossing aside preconceived notions. "Prepare some acids for testing." Wrexford picked up the glass vial and grimaced. There was precious little with which to work. They would have to be precise.

And lucky.

"I'm convinced your surmise is right and that the basic compound is mercury fulminate. But it's been altered."

"Y-You think . . ." Charlotte didn't finish her question. She didn't have to.

"Do I think that Lowell has discovered the

secret to making the explosive more stable?" he said. "Yes, I think that's a reasonable conjecture, based on what we just witnessed. But conjectures are worthless. We need to prove it, and that will take time."

"Something of which we have little to spare," mused Charlotte. "If that sample proves he's succeeded in making a new explosive, he must be ready to put whatever plans he has for it in motion."

Wrexford was thinking much the same thing.

"I'm so sorry." Contrition shaded Charlotte's voice. "My satirical print likely made him bolt, just when you might have caught him at work on his devil's brew."

"I think not, Mrs. Sloane," answered the earl. "Lowell was too cunning for that. My search showed that he didn't use his laboratory at the Institution for brewing up his experiments. It's too small a space, and chemical smells would have attracted unwanted attention from the other members. Based on Drummond's claims of people prowling through the corridors, my guess is he used the room for collecting chemicals and research materials, like old books and manuscripts on chemistry, that he stole from other laboratories. As to the real work, I would guess he has another laboratory somewhere in the city."

The ring of clinking glass and metal punctuated

the opening and closing of the cabinet doors as Tyler moved with methodical quickness to prepare the various solutions of acid. Charlotte took up a pencil from the desk and rolled it nervously between her palms.

"Is there anything I can do to help?" she asked.

"This will probably take hours. I suggest you return home," he replied. "I'm sure you wish to check on the lads—but don't ring too fierce a peal over their heads. I'm to blame for their transgression, so if punishment is to be meted out, I should be the one to receive it."

Her gaze held his for a long moment. "I shall," she said softly, "think of a suitable one."

An interesting response. Her mood seemed as changeable as quicksilver. But before he could explore the matter, the sound of footsteps—running footsteps—reverberated through the corridor.

Griffin? Springing to his feet, the earl lunged for the door, intent on barring entry to the Runner.

A fist thumped against the paneled oak. "Hurry, Wrex! There's not a moment to lose!"

Wrexford slid the bolt back and admitted Sheffield.

"I've just learned that Canaday has fled the country. And Stoughton is panicking as well." His friend paused to catch his breath. "Apparently Quill's pen has pricked at a vulnerable spot, for his latest drawing has unleashed holy hell."

"What's happening?" demanded Wrexford.

"As you asked, I've been keeping an eye on St. Aubin, and a message was just delivered to him while he was playing at the gaming tables of the Scarlet Cockerel. Stoughton has summoned him to a meeting at the clubhouse of The Ancients, and if we hurry, we can catch them at it."

CHAPTER 21

"Tyler!" barked the earl.

The valet was already opening a drawer of one of the storage chests. Charlotte watched him lift out a large brass-banded ebony box and set it on the counter.

"They were cleaned just yesterday, milord." Tyler offered Wrexford a pair of long-barreled dueling pistols.

He took them and handed one to Sheffield.

"And you may also pass me that pocket pistol you hid in your waistcoat, Mr. Tyler," demanded Charlotte.

"Who's this raggle-taggle bantling?" asked the earl's friend, darting a curious glance at her. "If you are asking for charity, lad, hare off to the kitchen. You look like you need a slice of beef-steak and bread, not a weapon."

She snapped her fingers impatiently. "Mr. Tyler, we have no time for shilly-shallying."

The valet looked to Wrexford, whose expression boded no good.

Seeing the earl was about to speak, she added, "And don't you *dare* tell me I'm not permitted to come along unless you wish to be wearing your guts for garters."

"Holy hell," Sheffield angled a look beneath the brim of her floppy cap. His gaze then slowly slid down over her baggy jacket and loose moleskin pants.

Perhaps they were not quite loose enough, for he cleared his throat with a cough. "It's a *woman*."

"How *very* astute of you, sir," she snapped, in no mood to deal with the usual horrified huffs on how females should know their proper place. "Let us hope you are also smart enough to stubble any insulting platitudes about women being the weaker sex."

Tyler swallowed a laugh. "I see that her tongue is as sharp as her quill."

"Give her the weapon," said Wrexford tightly.

"Wrex, I really don't think that's a wise idea," murmured his friend.

"Nor do I," answered the earl. "You are welcome to try reason, but I'll not waste my breath. She is an unholy force of Nature unto herself."

Sheffield stared at her warily, as if she had suddenly sprouted horns and cloven hooves.

"We ought not waste time either." She shoved the pistol into her pocket. "You said we must hurry."

"I should come with you, milord," said Tyler. "This could turn ugly."

"No, I need you to stay here and run an analysis on the explosive," replied Wrexford, and gave a terse explanation of what he wanted done.

"Damnation, Wrex," muttered his friend. "We can't put a female in danger. It's . . . ungentlemanly."

"Calm your conscience, Mr. Sheffield. As you can see, I'm no lady."

"How do you know who I am—"

"Because she's A. J. Quill, Sheff," snapped Wrexford. "Which ought to explain a great deal."

Sheffield's brows shot up in surprise, but he kept silent.

Charlotte was already at the open window. She had made it her business to know exactly where The Ancients had their lair. "I suggest we go out this way, milord. I know a shortcut through the alleyways that will bring us to the clubhouse quicker than any hackney."

"Do lead on, m'lady," he said with exaggerated politeness.

He hadn't used that moniker in ages— which proved he was no more happy with her than she was with him. *Trust*. Whatever fragile one had developed between them, God only knew whether tonight had shattered it beyond repair.

The breeze rippled through the draperies as she swung a leg over the sill. Silvered by the moonlight, the mist-swirled garden had an enchanted aura to it. A sense of peace and calm that no devil or demon could penetrate. But beyond the high walls, the looming stretch of midnight blackness warned that no spell, however sublime, could promise to keep evil at bay.

"This way," whispered Charlotte pointing to one of the footpaths once the earl and his friend had dropped down to the damp grass beside her. "Stay close to me. It's easy to get lost in the maze of passageways."

Her thoughts were quickly caught up in the coming confrontation. Was there redemption in revenge? Catharsis through tragedy? That her enemies were members of The Ancients had a certain twisted irony. The Greeks and Romans explored the conflicting complexities of human nature in their myths and drama.

There were few happy endings. Even victory rarely came without a price.

Slipping, sliding through the rutted mud, Charlotte quickened her steps. The darkness squeezed tighter around her, splintered boards and jagged brick clawing at her coat.

The chorus of inner voices grew louder, chanting Anthony's anguished cries.

The gods punished hubris. They did not like mortals who challenged the order of the universe.

As she well knew.

But what more could they do to her? They had already exacted their pound of flesh.

Charlotte skidded to a stop, lungs burning, heart pounding with the force to burst through bone and skin. She blinked, willing the haze to clear from her head.

"We're here," she whispered, inching closer to the opening of the passageway. Directly across the deserted cobbled street was an elegant Italianate town house. No light peeked out through the windows. Like its neighbors, it appeared to be deep in peaceful slumber.

Wrexford drew close—so close she could hear the hammering of his heart. Gripping her shoulders, he gave her a swift shake. "This is far more than personal now. I must have your promise that from here on, you will obey my orders. A misstep and many people may die."

The voice of cold, calculated reason. He was right, of course.

Charlotte nodded, her throat too tight for words.

He hesitated, and though the gloom hid his eyes, she could feel his gaze searching her face for a lie.

Her lips moved, silently mouthing her pledge.

Seemingly satisfied, the earl turned to survey the surroundings for a moment. "We'll approach from the rear and find the tradesmen's entrance. Follow me."

The lock yielded with no resistance to the earl's metal probe, allowing them to slip into a darkened foyer. Easing the pistol from his pocket, Wrexford noiselessly drew back the hammer.

Sheffield did the same. Despite his reputation as an indolent fribble, his friend always showed his hidden steel when trouble threatened. As for Charlotte . . .

She was shrouded in shadows. He could only guess at the emotions roiling inside her. But it was too late to question his decision.

Spotting the servant stairway, Wrexford eased the door open and then led the way up to the main floor.

The front of the house was pitch dark, but a glance to the rear showed a weak pool of light seeping out beneath a set of double doors at the end of the carpeted corridor. Within moments he had them in position, Sheffield on one side of the fluted moldings, he and Charlotte on the other.

Had she drawn her weapon? Her hands were fisted, making it impossible to tell.

Pressing a palm to one of the dark wood portals, he tested whether the latch was engaged. It swung open a touch, and the muffled voice within became clearer.

"I tell you, I won't swing for your stupidity!" It was Stoughton's voice, wound tighter than a watch spring. "Our plan for the art forgeries was ingenious—and promised to be highly profitable with no risk! I knew nothing of your other endeavor."

Wrexford ventured a peek into the room. Stoughton was leaning heavily on one of the leather armchairs, his face looking leached of all color in the oily lamplight. In front of him St. Aubin was standing by the unlit marble hearth, hands clasped behind his back.

"Come, there is no need to panic," said St. Aubin.

"No need to panic?" repeated Stoughton shakily. "Bloody hell, there have been two grisly murders, and now that devil-cursed artist is pointing his infernal pen at us! And once he starts poking around, no secrets ever seem to stay safe."

"I tell you, there's nothing to tie us to Holworthy's murder. All I did was steal a few moldy old books from the cathedral at Canterbury for him, that's all."

"Bloody hell—*why!*"

St. Aubin's expression twisted to a sneer. "Because through my older brother I could gain access to a private archive, and was paid very well to do so."

"Well enough to ruin a far more lucrative plan?" retorted Stoughton. "Damnation, everything was going so smoothly. But then you and Canaday had to get greedy and spook Sloane."

"The fellow was mentally unstable. It wasn't our fault he cracked and fell to pieces."

Wrexford felt Charlotte's body tense, but she remained still as a statue.

"If it ever comes to light—"

"It won't," said St. Aubin. He moved to the sideboard, his lanky body casting an elongated shadow over the decanters, and poured a glass of brandy. "Here, calm your nerves," he soothed, offering Stoughton the drink.

Uttering an oath, Stoughton lashed out an arm, knocking the glass away. It flew through the air and hit the hearth, exploding into a shower of crystalline shards. "How can I be calm when that damnable Wrexford is asking too many questions, and is getting too close to the truth. He put the fear of God into Canaday. What if he comes for me next? I tell you again, I won't be blamed for whatever you and Holworthy were scheming."

St. Aubin stepped back and watched the rivulets of amber liquid meander down the polished stone. The angle gave the earl a clear view of the man's hand slowly dipping into his coat pocket.

Charlotte saw it too. "Wrexford!" she whispered.

He nodded. The miscreants were welcome to savage each other later. Right now, it was imperative to keep them both alive.

Catching Sheffield's eye, he indicated that he wanted to take their quarry by surprise. His friend signaled his understanding. Weapons raised, they banged open the doors and stepped into the room. Like a wraith-like shadow, Charlotte followed right on their heels.

"As you see, I *have* come," announced Wrexford.

Stoughton spun around, his face spasming in shock. Emitting a low groan, he sagged back against the chair.

The earl shifted his aim to St. Aubin. "Drop whatever weapon you have hidden in your pocket."

St. Aubin hesitated.

The rasp of metal against metal sounded as Sheffield drew back the hammer of his pistol. "*Now.*"

Bullies, observed Wrexford, were quick to lose all their bluster when the odds were not heavily stacked in their favor. Another furtive glance, and then with an ugly smile of surrender, St. Aubin drew a double-barreled pocket pistol from his coat and let it fall to the carpet.

"Now both of you step over to the sofa and take a seat," commanded Wrexford. "I am looking for answers and am tired of finding only lies."

Charlotte had often wondered what emotions she would experience if she ever encountered her husband's tormentors. *Rage? Hate?* Her fingers tightened around the weapon in her pocket, its smooth steel blessedly cool against her flushed skin. *The uncontrollable urge to take a life for a life?*

She expected fire, but felt only ice. A strange alchemy. Perhaps time tampered with the elemental chemistry of revenge. In watching the two men take a wary perch on the sofa, she was suddenly, viscerally aware of only one sentiment—

"The pair of you have two choices," announced Wrexford, wrenching her out of her own thoughts. "You may either tell us all about your smarmy schemes now, or you have us march you to Bow Street and let the magistrates squeeze it out of you."

"And if we do tell you," countered St. Aubin, "what do we get in return?"

"That depends on what your information is worth to us," answered the earl coolly. "You had best hope it's of considerable value."

The reply sparked a feral glint in St. Aubin's eyes, as he quickly tried to gauge how to manipulate the situation to his own advantage. Stoughton, however, was on the verge of panic.

She had always sensed he was the less clever of the pair. St. Aubin had taken care to hover in the background, allowing his partner in crime to do the actual filthy work.

"W-Wrexford, you must believe me," stammered Stoughton. "I had nothing to do with any murders." He wet his lips. "We came up with a plan involving the copying of a few paintings—a harmless one that hurt no one."

Charlotte shifted her stance, willing the pulsing rush of boiling blood to recede.

Whether or not Wrexford heard the whisper-soft brush of her boots, his shoulders gave a menacing twitch. "I doubt Anthony Sloane would agree with that."

Stoughton's features went slack with fear. "H-How did—"

"Keep your gob shut," snarled St. Aubin. To Wrexford he said, "What have you heard?"

The earl laughed.

"Sloane readily agreed to be part of it," blurted out Stoughton. "We all were going to get what we wanted. It wasn't our fault that he became unbalanced."

"What was he going to get for his efforts?" asked the earl. "And what were you?"

"Don't be a fool, Stoughton," St. Aubin said through his teeth. "They know nothing—they can't."

"Canaday was more forthcoming than you," said Wrexford. "I want to know the details of the art forgeries. And then we'll discuss the matter of Holworthy and stolen books."

For an instant, St. Aubin's mouth pinched in uncertainty, but he quickly recovered his equilibrium. "If you want information from us, you will have to buy it at a fair price."

Fair. The word was an obscenity coming from St. Aubin's foul mouth.

"Which is?" queried Wrexford.

"We tell you what we know, and in return, you agree that we need not face the authorities. As Stoughton said, we know nothing about any murders. The art forgeries harmed no one. Sloane's demise was because of his own weakness. He was a deranged dreamer whose wits were addled by laudanum."

"No, they were deranged by the lies and false promises you fed him," said the earl softly. "And I wonder what other poisons?"

Stoughton flinched. His brow was beaded in sweat. "I had nothing to do with—"

St. Aubin grabbed hold of his arm, causing him to fall silent. Wrenching him closer, he whispered something, and then Stoughton, biting his lip, sunk back against the cushions.

"Speculate all you like, Wrexford," said St. Aubin, looking up at the earl with a smug smile. "The spineless slug is in the grave, and not a soul mourns his passing. As for you, you've naught but wild guesses to present to Bow Street."

Charlotte drew a shaky breath. He was right.

"So, if you wish for information—though God knows why you think it will help you evade the gallows—you'll have to agree to our terms."

"I think not."

To Charlotte's surprise, he shifted again and

cast a sidelong look at her. The wavering light caught the narrowing of his eyes. A wink of smoke-dark green seemed to flash a warning.

Her finger found the crescent curve of the trigger. Would that her nerves would match its steel.

"You see, Sloane is not unmourned. He has a son," went on Wrexford.

"*No!* That can't be!"

It took all of Charlotte's self-control to mask her own shock.

Stoughton looked at her as if he were seeing a ghost. "S-Sloane had no son. I spent time with him and his wife in Italy, so I am sure of it."

"An indiscretion, from before he was married, but no less kin."

St. Aubin was looking at her, too, but his was a reptilian stare. The cold, opaque flatness of his eyes reminded her of a snake. No remorse within that primitive, predatory brain, merely an instinct to eat.

Keeping the brim of her hat angled downward, Charlotte forced her eyes elsewhere. The muted pattern of the Turkey carpet, the graceful gilt-edged legs of the escritoire, the exquisite fragments of classical sculpture on the fluted marble pediments—beautiful but soulless within the confines of this god-benighted mausoleum to greed and power run amok.

A draft stirred the unlit chandelier overhead, setting the crystal baubles to a brittle clinking against each other. Like the rattle of long-dead bones.

The sound stirred a faint echo of Anthony's agonies. Whatever the earl had in mind, she would try to play her part.

Wrexford's voice rose again to silence her own inner whispers. "Here's what I think, lad. One should never bargain with blackguards. Draw your pistol and shove it up against the skull of one of these miserable muckworms. Start with Stoughton."

A wordless cry of pure, primal fear.

"We'll give him to the count of three to start talking or go ahead and spatter his brains over the bust of Aristotle."

"I've a better idea." Keeping his pistol aimed at St. Aubin's heart, Sheffield edged around the fancy furniture to pick up the double-barreled pistol from the carpet. "Use this one. It will save the bother of reloading. And the authorities will simply assume that they came to blows over some personal matter." A flash of teeth—not meant to be a smile. "Not a soul will mourn their passing."

"You won't—you can't!" blustered St. Aubin.

In answer, Sheffield moved and handed the weapon to her. "Have at it, lad. I rather hope they keep their jaws locked."

Charlotte thumbed back one of the hammers. The click sounded unnaturally loud in the dead silence. No doubt it was evil of her, but she felt a spurt of savage satisfaction as she shoved the short metal snout up against Stoughton's temple.

His eyes were closed, and his body was trembling uncontrollably.

"*One,*" intoned Wrexford.

"They're bluffing!" cried St. Aubin.

"Two."

"Wait! Please!" Tears were now streaming down Stoughton's ashen face. A pitiable sight, though Charlotte could muster no compassion. "I'll tell you everything!"

"Go on," ordered the earl. "But if I scent a whiff of a lie, I shall counsel the lad to be done with listening."

The story was quick to spew out. "It was by mere chance that I encountered Sloane in Rome," began Stoughton. "I was accompanying a friend on the Grand Tour—"

"You mean leeching off a friend, to escape creditors here in England," cut in Sheffield. "Yes, I heard the story from Milton."

"Bloody hell, you know how it is, being a second son with no blunt to cut a decent dash here in Town."

"No more interruptions, Sheff," counseled Wrexford. To Stoughton he added, "We care only for the facts, not your whinging."

"Before I left England, Canaday and I were commiserating on how hard it was to keep from sinking into debt—The River Tick has a strong current and is damnable deep. And so much of a man's wealth is entailed in the estate," continued Stoughton. "Canaday was especially upset about the moldering paintings hanging on his walls. They would bring a fortune if he were free to sell them. We talked about the need to be . . . creative in ways to fill one's coffers."

Or criminal, thought Charlotte.

"I saw right away from his copies of Italian masterpieces that Sloane possessed a remarkable artistic talent—and it soon became clear that he yearned to return to England and win recognition for his own original art. So I had an idea."

He paused to clear his throat with a raspy cough. "Brandy—I need some brandy."

Sheffield wordlessly fetched a glass of spirits.

Stoughton gulped down a swallow and then resumed his story. "It seemed to me that we could both help each other. So I offered to pay his way home. His wife presented a problem as she was a cold, calculating termagant. Try as I might, I couldn't get her to warm to the idea, though a woman of her low birth should have been flattered by any attention from a gentleman. But Sloane finally prevailed."

Another thirsty gulp. The glass was now empty. "Once he arrived back in England, I introduced Sloane to Canaday and"—a nervous glance at St. Aubin—"and other gentlemen who might be useful to him."

Or, rather, to gentlemen who would use him for their own purposes, thought Charlotte. Anthony, at heart an innocent, could not see guile in others.

"So far I've heard nothing that might serve as a bargaining chip for your life, worthless though it is," said Wrexford.

The warning spurred Stoughton on. "We had the connection to introduce Sloane to people who might help him gain admittance to the Royal Academy."

But you didn't.

"In return, all we asked was for him to copy some of Canaday's Old Masters paintings—no hardship to him, as he did it as an artistic exercise to keep his skills sharp. St. Aubin and I had friends on the Continent through whom we discreetly brokered the sale of the baron's paintings to several collectors in the German principalities. The copies were inserted into the original ornate frames, and Canaday kept the real paintings and shared his profits with the two of us."

"Sloane received no money for his labors?" interjected Wrexford.

Stoughton blotted his brow with his sleeve. "H-He received our patronage, which he felt was more v-valuable than a p-price for his paintings. It was all a very agreeable arrangement until—"

A feral growl from St. Aubin made him pause.

379

"U-Until he fell ill," finished Stoughton lamely.

"You're diddling us with half-truths," exclaimed the earl in disgust.

"The English courts have no call to charge us with a crime," began Stoughton.

"Be damned with playing cat and mouse. Pull the trigger, lad."

CHAPTER 22

Had he miscalculated? For an instant, Wrexford feared that Charlotte was going to obey his order. Her eyes were hidden by the crescent sweep of her hat, but a terrible grimness had hardened the curves of her mouth.

Her finger tightened, a barely perceptible twitch of pale flesh on gunmetal grey.

"*No!*" screamed Stoughton. "That's God's own truth about the art copies, I swear it. But yes, there's more concerning Sloane's death and I was just about to tell you about it." With a swindler's instinct for self-preservation, he sought to distance himself from his partner in crime. "It was all St. Aubin's fault! He and Canaday went too far!"

The earl held his breath. Charlotte had every reason to act the avenging angel, but he sensed she would deeply regret it.

St. Aubin lunged at his companion, but Sheffield caught his collar and held him back.

"Hold off, lad," murmured Wrexford.

She slowly eased back the pistol from Stoughton's temple. Its pressure had left a red *O* imprinted on his skin.

"You had better pray that this time you are convincing," added Wrexford.

"Sloane used one of the back rooms of the clubhouse to make his first copy, but after that, Canaday decided it was too risky to continue working here. He arranged for a place somewhere in the stews. That was when Sloane suddenly took a turn for the worse."

"Where?" demanded Wrexford.

"I don't know!" Stoughton edged to his end of the sofa. "But St. Aubin does. I know that he and Holworthy were involved in a scheme to steal books from Cambridge University." A triumphant glitter flashed in his eyes as he looked at his companion. "And I overheard the reverend demand that Canaday share the space with him as he, too, needed a private place in which to work."

"Lies!" insisted St. Aubin, but the arrogance was fast leaching out of his voice. "The sniveling rat is just trying to save his own skin."

"Canaday tried to say no." Stoughton was speaking in a rush. "But Holworthy had discovered what the baron was doing with his paintings and threatened to expose it."

That explained a good deal, thought Wrexford. And yet . . .

"What sort of work did Holworthy need to do?"

"He didn't say, though he spouted some habble-gabble about how Canaday would be sorry he had turned down the chance to discover the secret to immortality. It involved some sort of religious nonsense—he was babbling about philosophy and stones," responded Stoughton. "Ask St. Aubin! He was up to his neck in whatever intrigue the reverend was up to."

God Almighty, has the last piece of the puzzle finally fallen into place?

"Yet more lies!" St. Aubin's face blazed scarlet in anger, but beneath the color an ashen tinge was creeping along the ridge of his cheekbones. His voice was now brittle as broken glass.

"I think Stoughton is telling the truth this time." Wrexford gestured with his own weapon at St. Aubin. "What say you, Sheff? You look tired of holding the bastard. Shall we just have the lad blow his brains out and be done with it? We know all we need to know."

"You've got it all wrong," insisted St. Aubin. "I didn't steal the books for Holworthy. I'll tell you who it was, but in return, you must promise—word of a gentleman—that you'll release me unharmed."

"Very well, you have my word." Wrexford slowly smiled. "But we both know that despite our gilded pedigrees, neither of us are gentlemen, so my word isn't worth a vial of piss."

St. Aubin sucked in a shallow breath. The pulse point at his throat was racing erratically.

"Still, if I were you, I would take the gamble that I keep my pledge. After all, what do you have to lose? Stay silent and the lad gets to scratch his itchy finger for sure."

St. Aubin slanted a furtive look at Charlotte, who had stepped back into the yawing shadows cast by the table lamp. Tangled in the tentacles of dark and light, her silhouette had an otherworldy menace to it. And then all of his bluster leaked out in a ragged exhale.

"Lowell," he whispered. "I stole the books for Declan Lowell. He knew I could get access through my brother to a special library archive at Cambridge."

"Which college?" asked Wrexford, though he was sure he knew the answer.

"Trinity," answered St. Aubin, confirming the surmise.

An institution whose illustrious alumni included Sir Isaac Newton.

"But I can't tell you for what purpose," he hurriedly added. "Lowell gave me two titles and paid me very well. I didn't ask why."

"What titles?" demanded Wrexford.

"A manuscript by Newton and a chemistry manual by someone with an unpronounceable name."

"Eirenaeus Philalethes?" suggested the earl.

"Yes—that sounds right."

"I think you're lying about not knowing what he was working on," said Wrexford flatly. "And without that piece of the puzzle your information is worthless to me."

"I'm not!" St. Aubin was beginning to sweat.

"Yes, Lowell and I were friends, but he was becoming increasingly obsessive and . . . well, I knew of his penchant for violence. It's a great secret, but as a student, he caused the death of a fellow student in one of his laboratory experiments. The scandal was covered up by his family—and Lowell left the country for a year for it to blow over."

He swallowed hard. "Somehow Holworthy learned about his skills and hired Lowell for some sort of bizarre alchemy experiment to transmute the soul! But I swear to God that's all I know. Whatever he was actually working on was knowledge I didn't care to have."

That Wrexford could well believe. Men like St. Aubin had a finely honed sense of self-preservation.

He looked to Charlotte. "I think we've learned all that we came here for." And perhaps more. He now had an inkling of why Anthony Sloane had died. "Shall I keep my word? Or do you wish to extract your pound of flesh?"

A hesitation, so slight that if he hadn't come to know her subtle signs, he might have missed it. And then, in answer, she slid St. Aubin's weapon into her pocket.

Stoughton slumped back against the cushions with a groan of relief.

St. Aubin lost no time in rising, but the earl moved to block his path to the doorway. "Not so fast. I promised you could leave unharmed. I said nothing about going away unpunished."

"What the devil do you mean?"

"Listen carefully. I am about to explain," replied Wrexford. "You and Stoughton will step outside, flag down a hackney, and have it take you to Blackwell."

"B-Blackwell?" stammered Stoughton.

"The East India dockyard," clarified the earl. "Where you will take passage on the first ship sailing east to India."

"Travel half a world away to a godforsaken, primitive country full of pestilence and heathen savages?" said St. Aubin. He chuffed an uncertain laugh. "Why on earth would we do that?"

"Because, if you are still on English soil by noon tomorrow, I will hunt you down for the vermin you are, and see that you hang along with Lowell, who will soon be arrested for the murders of Holworthy and Drummond. There's now enough evidence to prove you were accomplices to those crimes, as well as the sordid business of Sloane's death and the art forgeries."

"You're bluffing," rasped St. Aubin.

True. But he doubted the fellow had the nerve to call him out on it. "Then let us put our cards down on the table and see who holds the winning hand."

Stoughton staggered to his feet. "I've no friends,

no connections in India," he said in a piteous whine. "What will I do?"

"You'll find a way to survive. Which is more than can be said if you choose to stay here," replied Wrexford. "For if the courts don't sentence you to death, I'll take it upon myself to mete out justice."

"For God's sake, show some mercy!"

"I'm showing you more than was shown to Anthony Sloane." He flicked his pistol. "I suggest you get out of my sight before I change my mind."

As Stoughton stumbled for the door, the earl turned to St. Aubin. "The clock is ticking. Or do you really fancy your chances at beating me at this game?"

Their gazes locked for a long moment, hatred darkening the other man's irises to pure black. But St. Aubin's bravado had already proved to be an empty shell. After spitting out a venomous oath, he let his eyes slide away.

"I didn't think so."

Fists clenched in impotent fury, St. Aubin stalked off after his coconspirator, trailed by Sheffield's parting jeer. "As you see, a cowardly cur never plays unless he's sure he knows how to cheat the odds."

The heavy oak portals fell closed, muffling the doleful tread of retreating footsteps.

"I would be willing to wager that one of them

murders the other before their ship rounds the Cape of Good Hope," added Sheffield with a hint of ghoulish glee.

"For once you might actually win some money," quipped Wrexford, hoping humor might lessen the tension in the room. Charlotte had shifted even farther into the coal-dark shadows. *Withdrawing into herself?* Her shape was nearly lost in the amorphous shades of grey.

"Mrs. Sloane," he called softly. "My apologies for improvising. It was, I realize, waltzing along a razor's edge—"

"No need for an apology on improvising, Lord Wrexford. It is a dance I do daily," she replied. "You've proved extremely adept at it tonight." A tiny pause. "Especially for a man of science, who values precision above all else."

There were meanings within meanings entangled in the short statement. He was too tired to try to unknot them.

"As you've pointed out, at times intuition must overrule intellect."

"So it must," she said blandly. The lamp was burning low. A sudden last flare painted her upturned face in a reddish glow, and then with a hiss and spark the flame went out, leaving them in the dark.

"We ought to be going." Her disembodied voice floated through the gloom.

There was nothing more for them here, agreed

Wrexford. He turned and silently led the way back the way they had come.

"Mrs. Sloane, we ought to escort you home," began Sheffield as they filed through the narrow opening into the back alleyway. But as he turned, there was only a shiver of mist-shrouded shadows behind him.

"Damnation, she ought not be out on the streets alone—"

"Let her go, Sheff." A fitful breeze tugged at Wrexford's words, swirling them into the other night sounds. "It's not for us to say what she can and cannot do."

Her steps guided more by instinct than any conscious effort, Charlotte made her way through the labyrinth of byways back to the fringes of St. Giles. Strangely enough, a search of all her most vulnerable places found only a dull numbness. She had imagined that retribution would feel better than that.

Choices, choices. Could one truly choose to unwind the grip of guilt, of sorrow, and put them in the past? Or was it ruled by its own elaborate alchemy, an indefinable mix and measure of ingredients that defied mortal longings?

Wrexford would have an opinion. A sardonic one, no doubt.

Ah, but Wrexford was yet another complicated alchemy. At the moment Charlotte had not yet decided how she felt about his actions. Presumptuous, yes, but he had, through sheer force of will, helped reach a point of resolution and redemption.

She should feel gratitude, not resentment.

The sensation of relief was also sharp, but in a way she didn't expect. Not that any of her emotions were making sense.

The streets had turned narrower and muddier, the sweetness of Mayfair giving way to the less salubrious scents of St. Giles. Darkness pinched in from all angles, the crooked buildings and overhanging roofs crowding out the weak starlight. But as she reached a fork in the way, Charlotte felt a small frisson tickle over her shoulders, as if the weight of past mistakes might be shifting. Perhaps—just perhaps—it was possible to shed old burdens, to forge new paths.

Hope, however, was a two-edged sword, a dangerous weapon in careless hands. Those who chose to wield it must always be on guard.

Dawn was softening the night sky by the time she arrived at her door and let herself in.

Raven was curled up by the stove, a blanket snugged around his shoulders. But by how quickly he sat up as she relocked the door, it was clear he hadn't been sleeping.

"The streets are dangerous at night, m'lady," he chided. "You shouldn't be scarpering around alone."

"That's rather the pot calling the kettle black," replied Charlotte.

"Aye, we wuz out," chimed in Hawk. "That's because . . ." He looked to his brother.

"That's because Billy Black Hat has a new set of ivories," said Raven without hesitation. "And he was keen to teach us te play hazard."

"Actually, it's because Lord Wrexford asked you to create a disturbance at the Royal Institution," she countered, deciding to dispel with any shilly-shallying around the events of the night.

He ducked his head. "Sorry. I know it's wrong te tell a clanker, but we were sworn to secrecy. And a gentleman must always keep his word, right?"

Like most things in life, honor wasn't always black and white.

"We will discuss the fine points of morality at another time," she answered. "Be that as it may, in this instance it was more the earl's fault than yours so you are forgiven."

Both boys looked relieved.

"However, I ask that you don't lie to me in the future. It's important for us to be able to trust in each other."

Looking pensive, Raven nodded.

His brother responded with fiercer enthusiasm. "I won't! May I be struck dead and roasted on a spit in hell if I do."

"A very noble gesture." She smiled. "But I

don't require such an extreme sacrifice. I simply ask that you do your best to be a man of honor."

"Besides, you wouldn't be more'n a mouthful fer the Devil," quipped his brother. "He wouldn't squibble his time cookin' you over the coals."

"Speaking of meals," interjected Charlotte. "I'm sure you are famished after all your activities. What say we have a treat of fresh-baked bread, butter, and some gammon for breakfast."

Their faces lit up.

"And eggs?" asked Hawk hopefully.

"And eggs." She fetched some coins from the purse in her desk and handed them over.

"No stopping to play hazard," she murmured.

Raven grinned. "Billy *does* have a new pair of dice an' he *did* ask us te come learn the game. So it was only a half lie, m'lady."

Dear Lord, what a frightful little Sophist he was becoming.

"Run along," she shot back. "Before I decide you only deserve a *half* portion of breakfast for your cheekiness."

The lads scampered off, and though Charlotte was weary to the bone, she knew that sleep would be slow to come. Instead she took a seat at her desk and set a fresh sheet of paper atop the blotter.

Her fingers instinctively sought the pen. However hopelessly tangled her personal emotions became in thought or words, her commentary on Society's inequalities and injustices seemed to flow with a crisp clarity in her art. Bold strokes of ink, confident colors—through line and paint she had the ability to cut to the heart of an issue. It was, she knew, a flaw, a fundamental contradiction in character.

How could she be both weak and strong?

Even Wrexford, with his relentless logic, would likely have no answer to the conundrum. He would find that bedeviling, while in contrast, she did not expect to have rational answers for everything.

Which no doubt explained the drawing that was taking place as she was trying to parse the conflicting sides of her nature.

Charlotte stared at the outlines of the sketch with a rueful smile. She was angry with Wrexford, and yet her sense of justice demanded that she use her influence with the public to raise the question of his innocence. Hints about the Runner's judgment, and his incompetence in missing telltale clues, would play very well to the vast majority of people who mistrusted the authorities.

Perhaps he didn't need her help.

A quick flurry of lines and cross-hatching and she leaned back, satisfied with the composition. All that was left to do was paint in the color highlights and write a provocative caption.

Once the lads were finished with their breakfast, she would send them off to the print shop with the finished drawing.

"So that means the mystery is solved concerning the art forgeries and their connection to Holworthy's murder?" asked Tyler. The earl had just finished giving a terse account of the confrontation and was pouring himself a glass of Scottish malt.

"Yes." After an appreciative sip, Wrexford held the dark amber spirits up to the light. "You know, the ancient Gaelic name for this is *uisge beatha*, which means spirit of life. Wise men, your fellow Scots. And brilliant alchemists." He pursed his lips. "Here Holworthy was obsessively chasing after the philosopher's stone and its transcendent power to raise the soul to a higher plane when all he had to do was uncork a bottle of whisky."

"In all fairness, I should point out that the Irish claim it was they who first brewed the magical elixir," murmured the valet. "Be that as it may, you are digressing from the matter at hand. I assume you will be heading to Bow Street shortly to present the proof of your innocence and Lowell's guilt. Shall I pack up the vial of the remaining chemical sample in cotton wool and a sturdy box?"

"Proof?" Wrexford finished the rest of his whisky in one smooth swallow. "What we have is a fanciful story, based on scraps of evidence that a clever villain could easily have manufactured. As for corroboration, there is only the word of reprobate swindlers—assuming they haven't already fled the country—who would sell their virgin sisters to the brothel in order to save their own skins."

He shrugged out of his coat and rolled up his shirtsleeves. "Griffin, while a thoroughly annoying fellow for his lack of imagination, has been meticulous in assessing the physical evidence. His conclusion is logical."

"But the library mark that Mrs. Sloane found in Holworthy's hand," protested Tyler. "And the footprint she saw in the church."

"Unfortunately, those things had disappeared from the scene of the crime by the time Griffin got there," pointed out the earl. "I doubt he is going to take her word for it."

"Surely you don't intend to do nothing?"

"Come, you know what an indolent fellow I am." Wrexford took down several books from the shelves above the work counter. "But in this case, no. It greatly offends what few moral sensibilities I possess that Lowell has perverted science to serve his own nefarious plan. So I feel obliged to stop him."

"How, if I might ask?" said Tyler as he watched the earl take a seat at the microscope.

Preoccupied with his own thoughts, Wrexford

didn't take any heed of the question. "Have you had any luck in identifying the elements in Lowell's chemical compound?"

"All but two. The list is there beside the reflector. It's the clear crystals and the greenish substance that are proving devilishly elusive."

Wrexford read over the paper. "Bring over a selection of acids. I wish to run a few more tests. An idea occurred to me when I thought more about Forsyth and the problem he had with his original percussion cap . . ." He twirled the instrument's dials, increasing the magnification of the sample.

Tyler assembled the bottles, along with a selection of empty glass vials. "You still haven't answered my question as to how you intend to stop Lowell." He set the tray down on the worktable. "Forgive me for pointing it out, but it seems there are more pressing things to be doing at this moment. Why are you spending time analyzing the compound?"

"Because I am curious." The earl squinted into the lens and adjusted the reflectors. Charlotte would likely also say it was because he was trusting his intuition. "Move the lamp a bit to the left."

The polished metal caught the light and angled a brighter beam onto the slide.

"And knowing the exact science behind his creation may help in understanding exactly what he is up to."

Tyler made a skeptical face.

"It also may help pinpoint the location of Lowell's secret laboratory. That's the key to ending this—if we can lead Griffin to where he is working, the evidence will speak for itself."

The earl leaned back. "Put a bit of the remaining sample in one of the testing vials and add one drop of spirits of salt."

They both watched intently as the liquid fell onto the powder.

"Nothing," murmured Tyler after a long moment.

"Excellent."

"You are pleased?"

"Exceedingly," answered Wrexford. "Attach the adapter to the lens and I shall show you why."

The procedure increased the microscope's power of magnification. The earl refocused on the sample and gestured for Tyler to take a look.

"What does the greenish powder look like to you?"

The valet hesitated. "If I didn't know better, I'd say it was ground glass."

"Sometimes the most obvious answer is the correct one," answered Wrexford. "I suddenly remembered reading an obscure text by Newton on the properties of glass, and how it could serve as a stabilizing substance." He contemplated the sample in the vial. "I think we can safely speculate that Lowell has come up with a formula for an improved mercury fulminate that may be used in practical applications." A pause. "Such as weaponry."

Tyler let out a low whistle.

"One other thing—that particular shade of green is typical of wine bottles from the Rhine Valley near Mainz." He thought for a moment. "Perhaps you're right—identifying the last ingredient can wait. Right now, I want you to start checking on whether there are any warehouses here in London that are used by German importers from that region."

"Yes, milord!"

"While you are engaged in that task, I will pay a visit to Mrs. Sloane," went on Wrexford, "and see if she can remember any details from her husband's last days that might indicate where he was working." Fatigue gave way to a rising sense of anticipation. "I think we're closing in on the bloody devil."

CHAPTER 23

"Given the events of the past evening, isn't it rather early for you to be up and about, Lord Wrexford?"

"I could ask the same of you, Mrs. Sloane," he replied dryly. When she didn't move from blocking the doorway, he added, "Might I come in? Or am I persona non grata for corrupting the tender morals of children?"

Heaving an inward sigh, Charlotte stepped back into the foyer and gestured for him to enter. It was ungracious to feel angry with him. She would never have learned the truth about Anthony without his resolve and resourcefulness.

But perhaps that was part of her mixed emotions. She didn't like feeling beholden to anyone.

"I thought aristocrats never rose until well after noon," she murmured as he followed her into the main room.

"By now you should know I rarely do what is expected of me. A flaw, I know, but there you have it."

She relented and allowed a faint smile. "I neglected to thank you for your efforts. You were impressively intimidating, sir. Had I been facing your fearsome phiz, I would have been quaking in my boots."

"Bollocks," quipped Wrexford. "You have never been the least intimidated by me. It's very lowering." He looked around. "Where are the weasels? Sleeping the blissful sleep of Innocents?"

She strangled a laugh. "You really must stop calling them that. They are no worse than other lads their age."

"No other lads their age would dare stab me in the leg, or cosh me on the head with a bottle." He was smiling. "But I admit, they are clever little beasts."

"As for where they are," Charlotte explained, "I've sent them out on an errand." She decided not to mention the new drawing they were taking to Fores's print shop. No reason to provoke an argument.

Wrexford stopped and sniffed the air. "But not before they had an excellent breakfast. Eggs and gammon, by the scent of it." His gaze strayed to the half-finished loaf on the table and held there. "Lucky lads. I, on the other hand, left my house without so much as a crust of bread."

"Surely you have a cook at your beck and call."

"Alas, unlike me he keeps lordly hours. But then, there is no rest for the wicked."

Impossible man. Charlotte wasn't yet sure whether he took anything seriously.

But she did owe him a debt of thanks.

"Sit. I assume you have something you wish to

discuss, so we might as well talk while you eat." Charlotte moved to the stove and set a frying pan on the hob. The familiar ritual of cooking would help ease the awkwardness of finishing her thanks. It would be easier to leave the words unsaid, but she prided herself on not shirking from unpleasant truths.

At least she could do it with her back turned to him. "I still do not condone your having enlisted Raven and Hawk in such a dangerous plan without first consulting me." *Crack, crack*—two eggs plopped onto the cast iron, setting off a satisfying sizzle in the grease from the frying gammon. "But your actions, however unorthodox, served to cut through the knot of unanswered questions regarding both your conundrum and mine. I . . . am grateful for your help in learning the truth."

She added several slices of bread to the pan. "And for the meting out a degree of justice for what was done to Anthony. Revenge may be an ugly sentiment, but it gives me a measure of satisfaction to know his tormentors have not gone unpunished."

The eggs bubbled and turned brown around the edges. Charlotte slid them onto a plate, along with the crisped meat and bread. "My husband was naive, and perhaps not as strong as he should have been. But that isn't a crime that deserves the penalty of death."

Wrexford accepted his breakfast without comment and dug in with gusto. She busied herself making tea, unsure whether to feel relieved or piqued at his silence.

Words or no, Charlotte was acutely aware of his presence in the room. The dappling of early morning light, the creak of a chair, the cozy click of cutlery—there hadn't been a man sharing the mundane moments of everyday life here since Anthony died. *The same, and yet so different.* There was a devil-may-care grace to Wrexford. He was comfortable with who he was, and that confidence radiated from every pore.

Was it disloyal to notice? Repressing a guilty twinge, she poured boiling water over the tea leaves. It was merely a dispassionate observation. As A. J. Quill, she had learned to look at the world around her with unflinching honesty.

"Do you take sugar?" Steam curled up from the spout as she placed the pot on the table.

"No." He looked up. "I am not a man who requires any sweetness."

An oblique message? Charlotte noted a fleeting glimmer in his eyes but it was gone too quickly for her to read.

The earl went back to soaking up the remaining yolk of his eggs with a bit of bread. And yet he must have sensed her indecision, for a moment later he added, "We've both helped each other, Mrs. Sloane. The ledger is balanced—you need not be distressed by thoughts that you owe me a debt of gratitude."

"I . . ." She took up a cloth and wiped away some errant crumbs.

"Now that we've settled accounts, we have more important things to discuss." Cutting off any further talk of personal matters, he quickly explained about identifying the ground green glass in Lowell's compound.

"Will you take all this to the Runner? The evidence now seems overwhelming as to who is responsible for the murders."

He shook his head. "I don't wish to take the chance that Griffin will interpret things differently. Time is of the essence. It's imperative for us to locate the secret laboratory, not only to catch Lowell in the act, but also to prevent him from accomplishing his ultimate objective. To that end, I have Tyler searching for any information on German wine warehouses."

He set down his fork and propped his elbows on the table. "I need you to think very carefully, Mrs. Sloane. Is there anything you remember about your husband that would give us a clue as to where he was working?"

The question caused her chest to clench. She had been so concerned with Anthony's mental state that it had never occurred to her to wonder about anything else. She had, until last night's revelation, simply assumed he had been telling the truth about spending his time away from home at the clubhouse of The Ancients.

Now who is the naïve fool?

Charlotte mutely shook her head.

"Come, you have a rare gift for noticing the small details," he pressed. "You've seen something. You just have to remember it."

She forced herself to think back on those terrible days. But her brain refused to focus. The only image in her mind's eye was a spinning, swirling blur of shapes and colors.

Her stomach lurched, and she felt the sour taste of bile rise in her throat.

"Mrs. Sloane." Henning's rough-cut burr penetrated the front door, saving Charlotte from her failure. "We need to talk."

She hurried to allow the surgeon entrance.

Sheffield was with him, his look of grim concern lightening somewhat on spotting the earl. "Thank God you're here. Tyler sent me to warn you," he said in a rush. "You can't return home. Griffin is waiting there—with a warrant for your arrest."

"Bloody hell," swore Wrexford. "Just when the pieces of this infernal puzzle have finally come together." Frowning in thought, he asked, "Did Griffin give a reason? I doubt he would have dared make the move without some new piece of evidence."

"He said he has an incriminating letter,"

404

answered Sheffield. "One addressed to the Institution's board of governors in which Drummond says he overheard you admitting that you had lured Holworthy to the church in order to silence his attacks on you. It seems that Lowell found it behind the work counter when he was supervising the carpentry repairs to the fire damage."

"Diabolically clever of him," muttered Wrexford. "He just needs to keep Griffin occupied until he's made his final move."

"Any idea what that might be, laddie?" asked Henning.

"No," he conceded.

Sheffield cleared his throat. "As to that, I've been thinking—an admittedly rare occurrence, I know—and an idea came to mind."

Wrexford shifted impatiently. "Go on."

"Well, there was a lecturer of logic at Oxford who used to repeat an old Latin adage when trying to solve a certain type of conundrum: *Cui bono*.

"Who benefits?" murmured Charlotte.

The earl stopped his fidgeting.

"Yes, precisely, Mrs. Sloane," agreed Sheffield, giving her a quick, curious look before going on. "So I asked myself the same question in regard to a percussion cap for firing weapons, and the obvious answer is the military."

Well reasoned, Kit, thought Wrexford. He had always assumed that Sheffield slept through all the droning of their dons.

"The thing is, if Lowell had been working on it for our government, there might have been great secrecy—indeed, I've heard rumors that Humphry Davy nearly lost an eye experimenting with explosives for our war effort at a special laboratory in Tunbridge—but no need for murder and skullduggery."

"The rumors are correct," interjected Wrexford. He had been privy to the private details. "Davy was mixing chlorine and ammonium nitrate, based on a formula given to him by Andre Ampere. It was for the Royal Engineers to use in blowing up the siege fortifications of cities on the Peninsula. But it proved far too dangerous to handle."

"My point is, if Lowell isn't working for our side, might he be working for the French?" said Sheffield. "The Little Corsican would likely pay an emperor's ransom for anything that might help turn the war back in his favor," explained Sheffield. "Look, it's not always easy being a younger son in an aristocratic family. One often resents the power, prestige, and money that goes to the heir simply by virtue of a quirk of birth. What better way to avenge the unfairness of it all than to strike at the system? Revolutionary France rewards ability, not the degree of blueness in one's blood."

A prolonged silence followed. Henning and Charlotte looked to the earl, waiting for a reaction.

"Right. It's likely a foolish conjecture," said Sheffield, lifting his shoulders in apology.

"No, it's likely a brilliant one, Kit," replied Wrexford, giving himself a mental kick as he recalled the billets doux written in French that he had seen in Lowell's desk drawer. They had appeared to be love notes making assignations for a clandestine liaison. But they could very well have disguised a more sinister meaning. "The one thing missing is motive, and you've hit on a compelling one."

"Be that as it may," pointed out the surgeon, "if we can't find Lowell, all our fancy conjectures are worth no more than a pile of horse dung."

"Lowell is clever but he's not infallible. He will have left a telltale clue. We just have to find it." The earl fixed his gaze on Charlotte. "I'm thinking about what it could be. As is Mrs. Sloane."

Charlotte had quietly seated herself at her desk during Sheffield's explanation. She now had pen in hand and was sketching random doodles on a sheet of paper.

Perhaps, Wrexford mused, she was trying to draw divine inspiration from the familiar feel of the sharpened quill. The alchemists of old had understood an elemental truth about human nature. Symbols and talismans possessed a mystical power.

"Any ideas yet?"

She didn't look up.

"Think harder. We haven't much time."

Henning uttered a low oath. "Don't badger the lassie. I'm sure she is doing the best she can."

"Aye," agreed Sheffield.

"That's not good enough! She must do better," began the earl, but the faint jiggling of the door latch caused them all to fall silent.

A hand signal from Wrexford sent his two friends to flank the inner doorway. Grabbing his pistol from his coat pocket, he moved swiftly into the entrance foyer.

Out of the corner of his eye, he saw Charlotte flinch at the *click* of the hammer cocking. It was followed a moment later by a faint scrape of metal as he eased the bolt open.

Every muscle tensed, Wrexford waited for a moment, ear pressed to the blackened oak.

More scrabbling at the outside latch, iron rasping against iron.

Wrenching the door open, he pivoted, aiming in that instant of surprise to strike the intruder with the butt of his weapon.

"Hell's teeth," swore Wrexford, dropping to his knees just in time to catch Raven as he stumbled over the threshold.

CHAPTER 24

The boy's clothes were torn, his face bloodied.

"I tried . . . I tried . . ."

Repressing a cry, Charlotte dropped down beside Wrexford and tried to push him aside so she could reach for Raven.

Evading her grasp, he rose and carried the boy into the main room.

With a brusque swipe, Henning cleared a section of the table, scattering papers and several plates, which shattered on the floor. Sheffield hurriedly stripped off his coat and cushioned the rough planking.

"I . . . I . . ." Raven tried to speak but he appeared dizzy, disoriented.

"Hush, lad," said the surgeon, taking charge as Wrexford gently lay the boy down on the makeshift blanket. "Just lie still."

Charlotte had lingered at the open door to look up and down the street. She turned, her face rigid with dread. Wrexford could guess why.

"H-How badly is he injured?" she whispered.

Henning didn't answer right away. His callused hands worked with surprising gentleness as he removed Raven's jacket and shirt, then carefully examined his head and neck.

The boy's pale, scrawny body looked so small

and vulnerable against the dark wool. And what of his younger brother? Wrexford felt his jaw clench.

"Hmmph." Henning leaned down to listen to the boy's chest, then made a quick check of his limbs. "Aside from a nasty lump on the back of his head, the lad seems to have suffered no real injury. He's woozy, but he'll sleep it off."

Charlotte expelled a sigh of relief, but a look of agony remained etched on her face. "I'll take him upstairs and put him to bed."

"Let me help." As Wrexford picked up the boy's jacket from the floor, a folded piece of paper fell out. It was addressed to A. J. Quill in an elegant copperplate script. For an instant he was tempted to conceal it. But no—he knew she deserved better and wordlessly handed it over.

Her fingers were cold as ice.

She hesitated. He could almost feel the air shiver as fear tried to break her will.

Paper crackled. The wax wafer snapped.

The dastard, he noted, had chosen a blood-red color.

Charlotte read over its contents and looked up. "He has Hawk," she announced in a toneless voice. "He'll release him if I inform the Runner that Lord Wrexford has been bribing me to withhold evidence that proves he's the murderer."

As she paused to brush an errant curl of hair from her cheek, the earl took the note from her.

"Our adversary gives Quill until nightfall to decide whether the boy lives or dies," he said. "And goes on to provide the location of the weapon he used to murder Drummond."

"Clever," conceded Henning. "Who better to convince Griffin that you're guilty than the artist who's known to have eyes and ears in every corner of London."

"Mrs. Sloane," began Wrexford.

"If you are going to explain that Lowell is going to kill Hawk whether I betray you to Griffin or not, I'll save you the effort," snapped Charlotte. "I'm not naïve."

"He intends to do just that," agreed the earl calmly. "But I intend to stop him."

"Lowell is not as clever as we are," added Sheffield with a show of bravado. However, he looked uncertain of how to go on.

Wrexford felt all eyes slide to him. He looked over at Raven, whose thin face was fast purpling with bruises, and thought of the boy's younger brother being used as a pawn in this devilish game.

"Kit is right," he said slowly. "Lowell is not as clever as we are."

The burst of emotion had left Charlotte feeling utterly drained. She stood numbly as the earl barked out a series of orders.

"Kit, return to my town house and find a way to have Tyler give you the remaining sample of Lowell's explosive without Griffin knowing about it. Have him make up a package of these chemicals too." He grabbed a pencil and paper from Charlotte's desk and scribbled a list.

She couldn't seem to make her limbs move. A sense of helplessness had taken hold of her. Even the mere act of breathing was difficult.

"The Runner may try to have someone follow you," Wrexford added. "So it would be best if you meet up with Henning, who's more experienced in how to lose someone in the stews." To Henning, he added, "Rendezvous with Kit in Bloomsbury Square. Use the maze of alleyways around the Foundlings Hospital to shake off any surveillance, then bring the chemicals here as quickly as possible."

"What for?" asked the surgeon.

"They might come in handy," replied Wrexford. "It's always wise to meet an enemy armed with equal firepower. And in this case, surprise may add an advantage."

"What about me?" demanded Sheffield. "I'll be damned if I let you fight this battle without me."

The earl hesitated. "Go to White's after you leave Henning and wait for an hour, then slip out one of the back entrances you use to avoid creditors. Make your way back here carefully— but I swear, I'll cut off your bollocks if Bow Street shows up right behind you to disrupt our plans."

"How are you—" began Sheffield.

"*Go!*" commanded the earl.

As his two friends hurried off, he turned to Charlotte. "Mrs. Sloane."

His sharp tone snapped whatever force was holding her in thrall. She started for Raven, but he caught her arm, none too gently. "Things will likely get worse. You can't afford to surrender to fear."

The momentary pain set a welcome frisson of angry heat pulsing through her blood. Better fire than ice. "I don't frighten easily, Lord Wrexford." Would to God that remained true. "And I've never shied away from a fight."

"Good." He released her. "Ready the bed. I'll carry the lad upstairs."

Once Raven was settled under the covers, Charlotte drew a chair to the bedside and took hold of the boy's hand. He had lapsed into a fitful doze, his breathing shallow but regular.

"Don't fret. He'll be fine." To her surprise, the earl took a seat on the edge of the thin mattress and stretched out his legs. "Lads his age are shockingly resilient. Bumps and bruises are a badge of honor. Blood or a broken limb is even better."

"You speak from experience?"

"Unlike Athena, I did not step fully formed and wearing a set of battle armor from Zeus's forehead," he replied dryly.

Charlotte smoothed a tangle of matted hair

from Raven's brow. How was it that the lads and dirt were such kindred souls? She tried to keep them tidy.

She tried to keep them safe.

Wrexford was looking around the small room, and for a moment she was embarrassed that he was privy to the humble state of her most intimate space. A simple dressing table, a battered chest of drawers, a rag rug, rather the worse for wear. But she quickly pushed aside such thoughts. There was no place for pride between them. All that mattered was Hawk.

"How are we going to find Lowell's lair?" she asked softly.

His gaze swung back to her. "By thinking very carefully about the tiny clues that will lead us to his door." He shifted slightly, the wool of his trousers whispering over the thick-spun cotton bedcovering. "You are very good at details, Mrs. Sloane. You notice things other people miss."

A burble of panic rose in her throat. "Yes, I am good but I am not infallible, sir! Do you think I haven't been wracking my brain for an answer to your question? I've tried, and I can't recall anything that might hint at where Anthony had been working."

His expression remained unruffled, which helped calm her own nerves. "Perhaps you are thinking *too* hard. Let's start with some basics. Was there mud on his boots?"

"Yes, but that was not unusual." She made a face. "It's impossible to avoid it in this neighborhood. Just look at your own."

He contemplated his feet for several moments. "What color mud? Was it black, brown, red, clay?"

Charlotte saw his point, which only made her feel more miserable. "I . . . I can't remember."

"Yes, you can. Think harder, Mrs. Sloane."

"You have to understand, I was distracted by Anthony's suffering in a way that is hard to define. I was not looking at him in the same way as I do at other people."

"I see." Wrexford looked thoughtful. "You mean to say love painted him in a unique hue?"

"I didn't . . ." God Almighty, how to answer? She was not about to bare her soul to him. "It's not that simple."

He gave a wry laugh. "It is a universally acknowledged truth that Love is never simple. Nor easy."

Glib phrases, which glided smoothly from his tongue. And yet she couldn't help but wonder if he spoke from experience.

Raven stirred, drawing her attention, but his eyes remained closed. She started to turn back to the earl when a sudden flash of memory froze her in place.

"Red," she whispered. "The mud had a distinct reddish cast to it, and was flecked with bits of broken brick."

Wrexford edged forward on the bed. "A warehouse area." He thought for a moment. "I wonder what sort of goods would be familiar to Canaday? He had an expertise in geology and the history of mining in Cornwall."

"Tin," said Charlotte. "Cornwall is known for tin."

"Which is used to produce pewter," he mused.

"Blossom Lane off White Lion Yard is an area that caters to cheap kitchenware and tavern supplies," offered Charlotte.

"It is a start. When Henning returns, he and I shall pay a visit—"

"N-Not B-Blossom Lane, m'lady."

Charlotte nearly wept in relief at hearing the boy's voice.

"Farther south, in Artillery Lane," croaked Raven as he struggled to sit up. "T-That's where Mr. Sloane went."

Wrexford helped him settle against the pillows. "Are you sure, lad?"

"Aye." Raven shot a guilty look at Charlotte. "I . . . I couldn't help being curious. He was going out more and more, so . . . ."

"So you followed him," said Wrexford.

The boy nodded. "It weren't hard. He never bothered te keep a rum eye on his surroundings, even though I kept telling him te be more watchful."

As did I, thought Charlotte.

"It seemed an argy-bargy sort of place for him te be visiting, so I sneaked in after him. There was a big room and lots of paints and rolls of canvas. Mr. Sloane worked in there."

Raven paused and swallowed hard. "But there was also a dark stairwell past the workrooms, and I heard voices comin' up from the cellar. So I scarpered down te have a look, but the door was closed, and I didn't like the stink. It smelled like something right nasty was burning."

"What else?" pressed Wrexford.

Charlotte, too, felt the boy was holding something back. "We won't be angry, sweeting. We just need to know."

Remorse shadowed his face but he nodded. "I went back the next night—just te see what was down there. I shimmied through a back window on the main floor, but the cellar door had a big, fancy lock and I didn't want to diddle with it."

He ducked his head in contrition. "I know I shudda told you, but Mr. Sloane was acting so spooked. I-I didn't think it were right to tattle on him. Then, after he died, I didn't want te upset you. It just seemed better te let the dead rest."

"It's all right," assured Charlotte. "I understand."

Raven didn't appear reassured. "I'm sorry."

"You made the right choice, lad," said Wrexford softly. "You did no harm in keeping things to yourself at the time. But it's very important you tell us everything you remember about the place now."

"It may help rescue Hawk," added Charlotte.

The boy's eyes widened, betraying both hope and dread. "You think the scurvy bastard who nabbed Hawk is holding him there?"

"There is a good chance of it," said the earl. "Think very carefully, Weasel. Can you tell me exactly where I can find the building?"

"We," she corrected. "Where *we* can find the building."

"Right, *we.*" Raven sat up a little straighter. "Ain't no way I'm gonna be left behind."

"Don't say *ain't,*" murmured Charlotte, even though grammar was the least of her worries.

Raven played deaf to her chiding. "I can lead you straight there blindfolded, sir. I know the stews better'n the back of my own hand."

Charlotte did not care to speculate on what substance had left the greasy smear on his upturned knuckles. "You need to stay here and rest."

A string of oaths followed.

"Let the lad come," said Wrexford.

Sighing, Charlotte surrendered without further argument. Short of locking Raven in Newgate Prison, she knew there was no way to keep him from the fray.

The boy began to stammer his thanks, but the earl silenced him with a brusque wave. "Stubble the sentimental claptrap, Weasel. We need to draw up a plan of attack."

He shot her a look that promised she wasn't going to like what was coming next. "It's clear that Lowell has spies everywhere, so we are going to have to be very careful in how we make a preliminary reconnaissance of the area around the warehouse. I think there's only one course of action that has a chance of going undetected."

She uttered one of Raven's highly unladylike oaths under her breath.

If Wrexford heard her, he pretended not to. "Can you muster a band of your fellow street urchins, lad? You must choose only those who are clever and resourceful. Hawk's life may depend on it."

Raven's thin face screwed in thought. "Skinny, One-Eyed Harry, and Alice the Eel Girl," he said slowly. "And Pudge and Sally Roundheels. They won't let us down."

"Good," replied the earl. "We need to gather them as quickly as possible. But don't have them come here," said Wrexford. "Pick an out-of-the-way spot where they are well hidden from the street."

The boy nodded in understanding. "Skinny will help."

"Then let us go find him." Wrexford rose and turned to her as Raven scrambled out of bed and hurried down the stairs to find his shirt and jacket. "I know you don't approve. But guttersnipes have sharp eyes and draw little attention. And for us, the element of surprise is crucial. Lowell cannot have any inkling that we are coming." He didn't have to explain why.

It would have been hypocritical to argue. Children were a key part of her own information-gathering network. They were far more observant than people thought.

He took her silence for the pragmatism it was. "The urchins will be able to spot whether Lowell has any sentinels posted," he explained. "They'll also be able to give us an accurate description of all the building's windows and doors. That Raven has seen the interior is an important advantage."

"Raven," she repeated. "You actually know his name."

"A lucky guess," he murmured. "The choice of scavengers is limited."

And the ways to mask emotions were infinite, as she well knew.

"For God's sake, he's just a boy. He's not as tough as he appears. You should try to be more . . ." Charlotte fumbled for the right word and then quickly gave up. "You should try to be more sensitive to his fears and longings."

Wrexford responded with a cold shrug. "We can all stand around wringing our hands and sniveling with sentiment, or we can try to save his brother.

Which would you prefer, Mrs. Sloane? We can't do both."

She itched to slap him for being right.

"You ought to snatch a few hours of sleep," he advised. "It will take some time for the urchins to come back with their reports. And I wish to wait for dusk to provide some measure of cover for the final confrontation."

Sleep? Exhaustion was not nearly as terrifying as the prospect of dreams.

Raven called to the earl, impatient to be off. "What do you think our chances are, sir?" she whispered.

"Come, Mrs. Sloane, at heart you are as much a clear-eyed cynic as I am." Wrexford patted at his coat, and on finding the pouch of bullets quickly shifted it from one pocket to another. "You know damnably well what the answer is."

CHAPTER 25

Early evening was giving way to dusk.

"When do you think the first urchin will return?" Sheffield had salvaged a broken crate from the adjoining alley and was sitting with his shoulders slouched against the soot-dark wall in the narrow cul-de-sac.

"When she finishes with the task she's been given," growled Wrexford. Charlotte and Henning had found perches on a low stone ledge. He had chosen to stand, though the muck slowly seeping through a gash in his boot was making him reconsider his options.

"Alice is a great gun," piped up Raven, who had found foot-holds in the crumbling mortar of the corner building and climbed high enough to peer into the street. He had been angry at the earl's refusal to let him be part of the surveillance, but had grudgingly accepted the explanation that Lowell or his spies might recognize him. "She ain't gonna muck up."

All of the urchins had been impressive, mused the earl. Their ragged clothes and rough language hadn't disguised the glint of sharp intelligence in their eyes. They had listened carefully and asked savvy questions. If the plan failed, it would not be because of any mistake on their part.

"They've been told to go in at different intervals, and by different routes so as not to raise suspicion," added Wrexford in further explanation to his friend.

He turned and took several steps. Had he failed to think of something? The thought was gnawing at him. One slip on his part and a young boy would pay for it with his life.

Whinging at the unfairness of life had always struck him as a self-indulgent exercise. Now, however, he was tempted to hurl a litany of curses at the gods. Punish a man for his hubris, but do not strike at him obliquely through an innocent child.

"You're squelching," said Sheffield, making a pained face. The sucking sound of his boots sinking in the foul-smelling mud was not a pleasant one.

"And you're stinking," he shot back. Sheffield was dressed in grubby, ill-fitting clothes that reeked of garlic.

"Beggars can't be choosy," replied his friend airily. "I thought it was quite a stroke of genius that I thought to return to Mrs. Sloane's house by way of Petticoat Lane." The outdoor used clothing market was one of the largest in London. "You ought to be grateful that I thought to purchase you a suitable set of togs. Your Mayfair finery would have stuck out like a squealing pig in this neighborhood."

"Next time, kindly check the footwear for knife holes."

"Point taken," replied Sheffield. "By the by, you owe me two pounds, tuppence for the rags."

"That's bloody highway robbery," muttered the earl.

An evil grin. "That's only fitting, seeing as the previous owner of your coat was hanged at Tyburn last Saturday for robbing a Royal Mail coach on Houndslow Heath."

Henning let out a snort of laughter.

Charlotte attempted a smile, but the lines of worry at the corners of her mouth quickly pinched it off. She appeared distracted.

Wrexford gave himself a mental kick for stating the obvious. He couldn't begin to plumb the depth of her feelings at this moment. Unlike him, she had the capacity to care—more passionately than was good for her. For him, this was mere logic. The supreme satisfaction of taking on an intellectual challenge and seeing that no untidy elements marred the elegance of his solution. He still did not know for sure the motive behind the murders, and that bothered him.

And yet, that did not quite explain why he felt jumpy as a cat on a hot griddle.

"I see Alice," announced Raven, and dropped down to the ground.

"*Amat victoria curam*," Wrexford murmured. *Victory loves preparation.*

Charlotte looked up sharply. Her lips moved—a silent prayer?

He stepped closer, just in time to catch the last of her whisper before it was tugged away by the breeze.

". . . and let us hope you are correct, sir."

Dusk was fast leaching the light from the sky. Angled shadows stretched over the alleyway as one by one the urchins darted in to report on what they had seen. Wrexford pressed and prodded until he was satisfied that he had extracted every last detail from them.

"You've done very well," he said, taking out his purse and shaking out five gold guineas into his palm. "For your efforts," he added, extending his hand to the grubby figures gathered around him.

One of the urchins—Skinny, he guessed, by the painfully thin silhouette cast by the sinking sun—stared at the unspeakable riches for barely a moment before shaking his head. "Don't need no reward. Hawk be a friend, and friends take care o' each udder."

The other four urchins nodded solemnly.

Honor appeared in the oddest of guises. "It's not a reward," he said softly. "It's a token of our gratitude."

"Grati-what?" whispered the girl who smelled of fish.

"He's saying thank you, Alice," explained Raven. "Take the blunt—he's rich."

"Oiy, well in that case . . ."

Five hands shot out and snagged the coins. Like fireflies flitting through the gloaming, they scampered away, trailing tiny flashes of gold in their wake.

"So, laddie . . ." Henning rose and removed the unlit pipe from his mouth. He had kept quiet, perhaps sensing his usual sarcasm would only rub raw on Charlotte's already tender nerves. Instead of tossing out verbal barbs, he had busied himself with unwrapping the vials of chemicals sent by Tyler. They were now neatly arranged in the small box, which he held out for inspection.

"I assume you have a plan of how to fight fire with fire."

"These may prove useful." Wrexford pocketed several of the vials. "But I am counting on stealth and surprise rather than flash and bang to win the day."

"Subtlety is not usually your strong point," murmured Sheffield. "But of late, you are proving surprisingly capable of the unexpected."

Charlotte said nothing, which had him worried. However well she hid her innermost feelings, she had never shied away from expressing her opinions or observation. He had grown used to her sharp-tongued intelligence, her badgering, her challenging his every move. This unnatural silence was unnerving.

"Let us hope our plan will be completely

unexpected by Lowell. I think his cleverness will play into our hands. He has every reason to be confident that his hiding place is safe from discovery, and that hubris may prove to be his Achilles heel."

Moving to one of the few remaining spots of faint light, Wrexford crouched down and sketched a rough map in the mud with a stick. "I intend to enter here, at the back window of the storage room used for the art materials." Skinny had noted that because of the spiked iron fence around the coal chute door that particular window was unbarred. The gate lock would not be a problem.

"From there I can make a methodical check of the other upper rooms, though I doubt I shall find Hawk there. Lowell will likely be holding him somewhere in the cellars, close to the laboratory."

"Lucifer toiling away to create misery and mayhem in his private hell," muttered Henning.

"My aim is to free the lad, and get him safely out of the building. Then I will confront Lowell," went on the earl. "Henning, you will take up position at the west end of Artillery Lane, while Sheff, you will stand here, at the east end." Based on what the urchins had observed, he was confident that Lowell had no sentries posted around his lair. "If Lowell escapes from me and tries to flee, your job is to stop him." He looked up. "I take it you didn't come unarmed?"

Two grunts confirmed the surmise.

"And me?" Charlotte's voice finally stirred the air.

Her place was a far more ticklish choice. He knew she—and Raven—would never accept a spot safely away from any danger. But too close and he worried they might ignore his orders and plunge in to help.

And that could prove a fatal mistake.

He glanced at the map for an instant before making his decision. "Here," he said, pointing to the building directly across the street from Lowell's secret laboratory. A narrow cart path ran along its right side, and Alice the Eel Girl had noticed a recessed stairwell leading down to the coal hatch. It was a good hiding place and had the added advantage of being far enough away that reason might have enough time to overcome impulse.

"I want you and the weasel here," he said.

Charlotte studied the sketch. "And our job is?"

"To wait for me to bring Hawk to you," answered the earl decisively.

Raven met the assertion with a stony-faced acceptance that belied his age. "S'all right. You don't have te pretend. I know Hawk's going to die. I just want you to kill the bastard who snatched him."

"We'll get him back," repeated the earl.

"You can't promise that." Raven wiped his nose with his sleeve. The fabric came away rusty with dried blood. "Bad things happen all the time. M'lady's husband died, your brother died. Now Hawk's gonna die, too." He sniffed. "It's just how it be."

"The reaper doesn't always win," said Wrexford.

"Yeah? Who's gonna beat him to a bloody pulp? You?"

"Yes, lad. Me." In that instant, Wrexford had never believed anything so strongly. *I will get him back.* For all the brothers who had perished.

The force of it took him aback. God curse it, had he become a sniveling sentimentalist?

Raven was watching him intently, with eyes too old and too wary for a boy.

Curling a light fist, he brushed a quick cuff to the upturned chin before turning away. What did it matter if one more entry was added to the litany of his faults? Both the Devil and St. Peter had likely long since lost count.

Charlotte wasn't sure whether she wanted to laugh or weep. The sardonic Earl of Wrexford— an irascible cynic, renowned for his hair-trigger temper and utter disdain for sentiment—was seeking to comfort a ragged little imp from the stews?

Perception, she reminded herself, rarely aligned with reality. In her experience, no one was either all bad or all good.

All of us are all simply human.

"Mrs. Sloane?" Shadows tangled with the strands of black hair curling, making his face as shapeless as his rag market hat. "No protest? No demand to charge in where angels fear to tread?"

Charlotte wished she could see his expression. There was an undertone to his question that she couldn't quite identify. "I know you think me ruled by impulse rather than logic—"

"Intuition, not impulse," he corrected. "Which I've learned to respect. If you have an objection, I am willing to listen."

"And I, sir, have learned to respect the way you use reason to attack a problem. Even with all the information we've gathered, there are many unknown variables within Lowell's hideaway. It would be foolhardy of me to demand to accompany you. Worrying about me making a misstep would be a dangerous distraction."

"A wise decision," said Henning. "But then, I expected no less of you."

She glanced up at the sky. The purples and pinks of dusk were darkening. Lowell's ultimatum was fast approaching. "Shouldn't we be going?"

Wrexford took Henning and Sheffield aside. A quick exchange, too low for her to hear, and then his two friends slipped away into the gloom. "We will follow shortly," he said. "By a different route, to err on the side of caution."

She nodded. A fluttering rose in her chest, a

steel within velvet sensation of butterflies beating their wings against her ribs. The curse of a febrile imagination, she thought. In her mind's eye, they all were colored in garish shades of gold.

Wrexford was calmly contemplating some faraway spot on the wall. Charlotte sought to draw strength from his unruffled attitude. For him, life was like science. It had a certain ruthless logic to it. One could control only so many variables of an experiment; then one simply had to step back and let the physics of the universe take its course.

Detachment disengaged from emotion.

It was a trait she seemed to be lacking.

Head bowed, Raven shuffled his feet. She moved closer to him and set a hand on his shoulder, sensing any further show of emotion might embarrass him. He flinched at first, but then allowed his scrawny body to slump against hers. The warmth of him was comforting.

Time seemed mired in molasses. The minutes slid by with a viscous slowness. The fluttering was now a drumming against her tautly drawn nerves.

Bang. Bang. Bang.

At long last, the earl turned. "Let's be off."

They moved in single file, three wraiths threading their way through the shifting shadows. Charlotte led the way, with Wrexford guarding the rear. He moved lightly, his steps sure and silent over the uneven ground. She could feel the thrum of a stalking predator's flexing muscle in the night air. Repressing a shiver, she quickened her pace.

They were still several streets away from their destination when the earl drew them deep into a gap between two buildings. He pitched his voice low, the terse whisper nearly swallowed by the creak of a rusty sign swinging in the breeze.

"I'm counting on you to keep your position, no matter what you might see or hear."

"I understand, sir," answered Charlotte. She felt she owed him that.

"What if there's an explosion?" demanded Raven. They hadn't told the boy about Lowell's chemical compound, but she wasn't surprised that he had caught wind of it.

Crouching down, Wrexford leaned in nose to nose with him. "You don't move."

Charlotte didn't hear a response. She wondered if the earl remembered just how defiantly stubborn boys could be.

Wrexford seemed, however, to have taken that into consideration. He held out his hand, the upturned palm a flicker of pale silver in the mizzling moonlight. "Give me your pledge of honor that you'll do as I say."

Raven hesitated, then slowly sealed the promise with a touch of his own hand.

"Excellent. I should have disliked hanging you

by your toes from that butcher's sign overhead. But I would have done so."

Charlotte didn't doubt it.

Raven grinned. "I wudda found a way te wriggle free."

"I think not, Weasel. But we shall leave testing each other's mettle for another time." He rose, and Charlotte felt the brush of his clothing against hers as he edged toward the opening. "I'll leave you two here, Mrs. Sloane, and will count on you using your good sense to take your appointed place."

He was gone before she had a chance to wish him good luck.

Perhaps that was for the best.

"Come," she murmured to Raven. "Let us hurry."

The knife blade found the brass catch. A slight jiggle released it, allowing the window casing to ease open.

Wrexford held himself still, listening for any sounds from inside before pulling himself up to the ledge and slipping inside. The long room was still cluttered with art supplies. Perhaps Canaday and his coconspirators had harbored illusions of reviving their swindles. The trouble was, men of artistic genius were far rarer than those who counted greed and an utter lack of morality as their primary talents.

Like had found like, he thought, as he quickly searched the space for any sign of Hawk. Lowell's evil had proved even more powerful than that of The Ancients. His clever manipulations had destroyed their schemes.

As I shall destroy his.

The central corridor was unlit. Feeling his way along the rough, plastered wall, Wrexford cursed the fact that Sheffield had convinced him to trade his supple, well-fitting boots for the Petticoat Lane pair. The loose leather and frayed stitching around the thick sole was making it hard to move quietly. He slowed a half step, hoping the deference to disguise wouldn't turn out to be a grave miscalculation.

There were two other rooms abutting the art storage area. A quick look in each showed them to be empty. The large space across the corridor was also devoid of furnishings, save for a few old writing desks and a three-legged chair sitting forlornly in the dusting of light allowed in by the barred windows.

Wrexford had expected no less. The basement and cellars were Lowell's lair, and when vermin were being hunted, they always went to ground.

He drew the door closed and headed for the stairwell leading down to the bowels of the building. As he approached the double doors, he paused to slip his knife back into his boot and readjust the weight of the pistol in his pocket. His coat, a plain-cut garment thankfully unembellished by the shoulder capes and fancy lapels favored by a gentleman, buttoned up snugly to the throat, hiding the white of his linen. The hat he dropped as an unnecessary encumbrance.

Drawing a measured breath, he pressed an ear to one of the portals and listened for sounds of activity behind the age-dark oak.

Nothing, save for an oppressive silence.

Was the boy still alive? A pawn was often played for just one move, then carelessly sacrificed in order to move the game along. Wrexford forced himself to forget such thoughts. Distractions were dangerous.

The latch yielded to the pressure of his palm, allowing him to slip into the stairwell. An odor of acid, sour and slightly metallic, hung heavy in the damp air. He could feel that the stairs were made of stone. How many there were was impossible to make out. The darkness was as viscous as India ink. Placing a guiding hand on the rock and mortar wall, he started downward, step by tentative step.

He counted twelve treads before coming to a small landing. There the stairs reversed direction and continued to descend.

A thin line of light was visible below. The fumes were growing stronger. Raven had said the laboratory was at the base of the stairs, and as

Wrexford came closer, the faint glow from under the door showed a fancy lock fabricated from steel and brass, just as the boy had described.

Pulling his pistol from his pocket, he noiselessly drew back the hammer and continued on to within a pace of the door.

There were rustling sounds from the other side, punctuated by the muted click of glassware. But no voices.

Which meant it was damnably impossible to know whether Hawk was being held prisoner there or in some other part of the basement.

Reluctantly turning away, Wrexford began to retrace his steps, exploring along the wall for another access into the basement. Just before reaching the landing he found a small horizontal door, barely wide enough and tall enough for a man to shimmy through. The hinges swung smoothly in response to a testing tug. A hint of light danced deep within the narrow crawlspace. After a tiny hesitation, he once again pocketed the pistol and slipped inside.

Inching along over splintered floorboards that clawed at his clothing, the earl gingerly traversed a short, tight passageway that opened up to a catwalk of exposed wooden beams. A sconce holding a single candle hung on the wall below him, casting just enough fluttery light for him to make out the bare bones of his surroundings. From his vantage point, he saw it was a long drop down to the floor, where scattered stacks of large crates indicated that this, too, was another storage area, one where heavy goods were kept. Just ahead, a heavy iron pulley was bolted to one of the beams, a heavy rope and hook still dangling down into the murky shadows.

Wrexford slithered out onto the narrow rough-cut timber, intent on reaching the rope, when suddenly a loud clang echoed off the walls of the cavernous space. He froze as a second door was thrown open and a beam of skittery light cut through the gloom. Footsteps sounded and a figure appeared. The slim silhouette, the well-tailored clothes, the artfully tousled curls— Lowell was instantly identifiable as he crossed to a tall column of crates near the far wall.

The earl held his breath, willing the man not to look upward.

After setting his lantern down, Lowell turned the wick up. A flame hissed to life, throwing a circle of weak illumination over the planked floor. His movements were not quite as casually elegant as his attire. They betrayed a taut nervousness as he clumsily adjusted the angle of the light.

The beam wavered, and then picked out a chair. Hawk was tied to it, the high slatted back and coiling of rope making him look pitifully small.

Wrexford felt a surge of outrage.

The boy's face was purpled with bruises and one eye was nearly swollen shut.

"It's almost dark. You had better pray that Mrs. Sloane turns the Earl of Wrexford over to the authorities. Else you are going to die."

Hawk stared at him in defiant silence.

The earl mouthed a silent curse. He couldn't reach for his weapon without risking that Lowell would spot him.

"Actually, you're going to die whatever she does."

Hawk had the temerity to laugh. "Ye daft bastard—ye think she ain't smart enough te know that? She won't squibble on His Nibs. He'll come find ye, and I won't be the only one wiv the Devil's pitchfork poking up my arse."

His face mottling with fury, Lowell cocked a fist and hit the boy with a hard punch that landed flush on the jaw.

Hawk's head snapped back and blood spurted from his lip. It took a moment for him to shake off the shock, and then . . .

Wrexford watched as Hawk inhaled deeply through his nose and then spit out a broken tooth with an audible *whoosh*. The tiny missile shot through the air with pinpoint accuracy and hit his tormentor smack in the eye.

Bloody hell—the little imp possessed more backbone than most men.

Lowell cried out in pain and slapped out another blow. "I swear, I shall beat you until you scream for mercy."

"Hit as hard as ye like. Ye ain't never gonna make me cry."

Lowell gave a nasty laugh. "You worthless little piece of gutter scum. Much as I'd enjoy killing you now, I'd rather wait and make that she-bitch watch me cut your throat while she begs for your life. Oh, you'll cry then—in fact, you'll squeal like a stuck pig for I'll take care to do it slowly."

Hawk blinked as the man taunted him with a series of high-pitched snorting sounds.

"Enjoy your last night alive, brat," finished Lowell, finally tiring of tormenting the boy. Taking up the lantern, he turned on his heel and stalked off.

Wrexford waited until the door clanged shut, then quickly wriggled his way to the rope and pulley.

CHAPTER 26

Charlotte tried to keep her mind occupied as she sat hunched in the lee of the outside stairwell, refusing to let herself stare at the building across the street. Fog was starting to ghost through the streets, quicksilver puffs of vapor riding a chill breeze that seemed to bite to the bone. Hugging her arms to her chest, she made herself think about how she would draw Lowell in his laboratory. The imagery offered some sensational elements—a deadly explosive, a demented genius whose family ranked as one of the leaders of the aristocracy.

The public would lap it up.

Yes, on paper it was oh so titillating, an artistic and intellectual challenge to use her skill with word and image to fan emotions. But as flesh-and-blood reality, the terror was all too palpable. All too personal. She could taste its bile at the back of her throat, she could feel its icy fingers squeezing the breath from her lungs . . .

Raven shifted. He was slumped against her shoulder, and while she wanted to believe he was dozing, she could sense that his body was coiled tighter than an overwound watch spring.

Tick, tick. It felt like they had been there for hours. Surely it wouldn't hurt to sneak a quick glance.

"Any sign of them?" The boy was instantly alert.

"No." All sorts of hideous reasons sprang to mind. The curse of a colorful imagination. She looked away from the dark shape looming up from the mist and drew him a little closer. "We must be patient."

Grasping both lengths of the rope, Wrexford slowly lowered himself down from the beams. He dared not call out a warning for Hawk to stay silent, but no sound came from the shadowed chair. Thinking of the brutal beating he had just witnessed, he feared the boy might be unconscious—or worse.

However, as he darted between the crates, a small voice quickly put his worries to rest.

"Cor, that was a wery neat trick, m'lord— just like a spider spinnin' down from its web!" Hawk's one good eye was widened in admiration. "It wuz awfully brave of ye te try it."

The boy thought him brave? *God Almighty.*

"Not as brave as taking a punch to the mouth from a bastard four times your size." The earl took a brief moment to gently blot the blood from the boy's face.

"It didn't hurt wery much," lisped Hawk. "The sweetmeat vendor at C'vent Garden hits much harder wid his fives. The thrashing he gave me when I filched some sugarplums wuz a lot worse."

"Shhh, don't try to talk, lad. I'll have you free

441

in a tick." Wrexford reached for the knife in his boot.

Bloody hell.

He stared at the hopelessly knotted tangle of rope around the boy and cursed himself for a clumsy fool. The blade must have fallen out in the crawlspace.

Hawk was staring, too. "I fink we need a knife."

Or an avenging angel with a grand sword to smite through the bonds.

"Aye, lad, but I was damnable gudgeon and dropped mine—"

"I got the one ye gave me." The boy flashed a lopsided smile. "I did what ye told me and hid it wery carefully in my boot."

A quick tug, a quick shake, and the stag-handled knife plopped into his palm. Exhaling a pent-up breath, Wrexford cut through the rope. "Well done, lad. Can you stand?"

Hawk rose, and though a little unsteady on his feet, he managed to stay upright. Wrexford took a moment to chafe the blood back into the boy's limbs as he considered his next step. The basement's layout presented a dilemma. Getting the boy to safety meant it couldn't be done without taking the chance that Lowell would escape with his devilish concoction.

A ripple of air stirred through the space. The candle flame quivered, and the overhead pulley rattled.

Or could it?

It was risky. Damnably risky.

He swept the boy up in his arms. "What say you, Weasel? Can you be strong and brave for just a little while longer?"

Hawk grinned, showing the gap in his teeth. "Oiy."

"Good lad." Wrexford hurried to the dangling rope and lading hook. Grabbing the curved piece of iron, he cut a small slash in Hawk's breeches and worked it through the fabric. "Listen carefully. I'll pull you up to the rafters. Crawl across the center beam and you'll find a passage-way. It will bring you to a set of stairs . . ." He quickly explained how to exit the building. "Mrs. Sloane and your brother are waiting directly across the street in a stairwell. I want you to fly like a falcon, and don't stop for anything until you're in m'lady's arms. Can you do that?"

"Oiy."

There was no time for second guessing. "Then up you go."

Mist swirled in the sunken stairwell. Charlotte was so stiff from the chill dampness that it hurt to wriggle her toes. Stifling a yawn, Raven flexed his shoulders and crawled up to the top step for a peek at the surroundings.

"Trouble," he grumbled. "His Nibs must have run into trouble, else he'd be here by now."

"Patience," counseled Charlotte, though she, too, was aching to know what was happening inside the building.

"Maybe I ought te have a look around."

"Absolutely not." She understood the urge, but Wrexford had trusted them to keep their word. A promise. Like mist, it had no corporeal substance. Try to grab hold of it, and *poof*—one's fingers caught nothing but a faint tickling sensation against the skin. And yet she felt it a bond of honor that ought not be broken.

"Come down from there," she added. "We ought not risk being spotted."

"No, wait—I think I see something," said Raven

"Don't gammon me," warned Charlotte.

"There, between the buildings. Someone's moving!"

She joined him on the top step. But her eyes seemed intent on playing tricks. The shadows all started to sway in time to the rapid-fire beating of her heart.

Charlotte tried to draw a steadying breath.

"There!" repeated Raven and rose to his knees.

She grabbed hold of his coat to hold him back.

At that instant, a small figure burst out from the muddled darkness of the passageway, legs pumping, arms flailing as if a bat from hell was snapping at his coattails. Charlotte heard a voice rise above the thudding footsteps. And then she, too, was scrambling out to the edge of the street.

"M'lady, m'lady!"

Catching hold of Hawk, she gathered him in a crushing hug, tears mingling with an inarticulate bubbling of joy as she pulled him and his brother back into the shelter of the stairwell.

"Thank God," she murmured, brushing back his tangled hair to press a kiss to his brow.

Raven fixed Hawk with a critical squint that couldn't quite hide his smile. "You look disgusting."

"I lost a toof," announced Hawk proudly. "But that bastard who snatched me is gonna look much worse. Lord Wrexford was spitting fire and threatening te chop off his bollocks."

Charlotte shrugged out of her coat and wrapped it around Hawk. The sight of the boy's bruised face and injured eye had her hoping the earl would carry out his threat. What sort of man was monster enough to torture children?

A very dangerous one. And Wrexford was now facing off against him, mano a mano.

She darted a glance at the darkened building, then pulled both boys close and offered up a silent prayer.

Wrexford pushed the chair and severed rope deeper into the shadows and paused to reprime his weapon. Anger was still boiling through his blood. Judging that surprise was enough of an advantage, he decided to dispense with any elaborate subterfuge and simply walk straight into the devil's den.

He rather hoped Lowell would put up a fight. The man had a number of sins for which to atone.

Pistol at the ready, Wrexford set his shoulder to the iron-banded door of the storage area and pushed it open. The second door loomed ahead, bracketed by wall sconces that cast flickers of dark and light over the wood and metal. He crossed quickly through the short passageway and took hold of the latch.

With a well-oiled *snick,* a pistol hammer cocked.

Not his own.

He turned slowly.

"Tsk, tsk, Lord Wrexford. As a man of science, you should know enough about mathematics to understand that a complex equation always has a number of variables. You should have considered that there would be more than one entry and exit point to my laboratory." Hinges creaked. "Kindly drop your weapon."

Lowell sounded smug, and with good reason. Wrexford had let anger get the better of him, and had rushed ahead without thinking. He mustn't let it happen again.

"The thought had occurred to me," he replied, calmly obeying the order. "I did take into account the main one by the stairs and this one. It was apparently a mistake to assume there weren't three."

"You've made a number of mistakes." Lowell stepped out from the narrow door set within a recessed archway and came closer. The snout of the pistol was aimed at his forehead.

Improvise. He could hear Charlotte's recent comment echoing in his head.

"Oh, come, give me some credit. I added up a great many complex sums correctly."

"True." Lowell expelled a mournful sigh. "Which is why you must die. A pity. You, of all the members of the Royal Institution, possess a modicum of creative thinking."

"High praise, indeed," said Wrexford dryly. Keep the man talking—the boy needed more time to make his way to safety.

"Humor me before putting a period to my existence," he went on. "I've figured out most of your plan, but several pieces of the puzzle still elude me. What drew you and Holworthy together in the first place? I've deduced that his interests lay in alchemy, while yours are decidedly more practical."

"Far more practical," agreed Lowell. "Holworthy was seeking eternal life." A curt laugh. "While I merely wish to enjoy my allotted time here on earth as a very wealthy man."

"The philosopher's stone," murmured the earl.

"Correct. The right reverend was obsessed with the idea that the medieval alchemists had discovered the secret of immortality. He had contrived to steal a number of very rare books and manuscripts on the subject from church and university archives."

"Including works by Newton, Boyle, and Philalethes," he interjected.

"Yes, hidden among all the claptrap he had collected was some priceless knowledge—that is to say, priceless scientific knowledge. The men you mentioned possessed brilliant minds, and had made discoveries that I sensed would help me reach my own goal."

"How did you learn about Holworthy's endeavor?" prodded Wrexford.

"One night, when I was making the rounds of the Institution laboratories—my position as superintendent made it easy to steal the chemicals I needed for my own experiments—I overheard a clandestine meeting between Holworthy and Canaday. The reverend asked for his help in concocting the philosopher's stone, claiming he had priceless manuscripts from which a man of science could decipher the formula."

Drummond had been right, thought Wrexford. At night, the Institution's corridors had been slithering with serpents intent on no good. Unfortunately, he himself had been one of them.

"The baron refused, calling it nonsense,"

continued Lowell. "But as it happens, I was searching for rare books that related to my own research. So I approached Holworthy—masked, as I couldn't afford to have him know my real identity. Unfortunately, he noticed my signet ring."

"Golden One," said the earl. "So you had to kill him."

"As soon as he brought me the book I needed, he had outlived his usefulness."

"I assume you met with him several times in Canaday's laboratory. And at some point you realized Drummond had overheard one of your conversations."

Lowell smiled. "I knew Drummond had a large amount of mercury, and I happened to see his notes when I entered his laboratory to steal it. He was a filthy sneak, and had also overheard me meeting with an agent from Paris." A smirk pulled at Lowell's lips. "In which we discussed *my* life-altering chemical compound."

"An enhanced version of mercury fulminate," said Wrexford. "I assume they offered you a king's ransom for the formula."

"They did," answered Lowell. "I will soon be rich beyond my wildest dreams. Let that be a lesson to England and its unfair inheritance system, which gives all the prestige and money to eldest sons, leaving the others to scavenge for pennies and a scrap of respect."

Hubris and greed. Was there a more volatile combination?

"You're a man of intelligence," added Lowell. "Surely you agree that a man ought to be rewarded for his talents, not simply an accident of birth."

Put that way, it sounded so reasonable. But then, Lucifer was known for his seductively smooth tongue.

"Even when such talents include slitting throats and beating children?" he replied.

"Advances in science often demand great sacrifice."

As long as it is the blood of others, thought Wrexford. "We could parse the fine points of morality until Doomsday."

"Unfortunately, I've no time for that, thanks to you and that gadfly Quill." Lowell gave a curt flick of his weapon. "Enough chin wagging. I admit, it was ungentlemanly of me to strike the brat. I lost my temper, but it was A. J. Quill's fault. She's even more cynical than I thought. And by sacrificing the gutter scum to keep her pen pointed at me, she's forcing me to move more quickly than I had wanted."

"I'm still curious about one thing. Quill's husband—the artist working here—why kill him?"

"Simple. He was here often enough that he might have seen me slipping into the laboratory.

450

And I suspected he had been snooping around in the cellars. I couldn't take a chance of him gabbling about it."

"How did you poison him?"

"Another easy answer. There are a number of hidden passageways in this building. I set up a small burner by a ventilation shaft in his workroom and sent a steady stream of mercury fumes into the space. It quickly addled his wits." Lowell smiled. "For good measure, I switched oil of vitriol for the turpentine he used to clean his brushes. The burns spooked him from coming back."

"Clever," murmured Wrexford. "But you didn't anticipate that his wife would prove an even greater danger, did you?"

A huff of annoyance slipped from his lips. "The two of you have caused a great deal of trouble by upsetting the timing of my plans. But her ink will soon run dry. As for the brat, he's no use to me anymore, and since I have to kill you, I may as well do away with both of you at the same time. She'll be next."

"Just one last question," said the earl, dutifully turning to march back to the storage area, satisfied that he had gained the boy enough time to be out of harm's reach. "How did you know I was here?"

"Physics, my dear Wrexford! Newton was, among other things, a serious student of light,"

451

said Lowell, looking extremely amused at his own cleverness. "I saw the reflection of you overhead in the metal casing of my lantern." They passed through the two doors. "Oh, and in case you are wondering how I know the imp of Satan is still tied to the chair, I spotted a knife that had fallen atop a stack of burlap sacks. It had to be yours, as it wasn't there this morning."

He laughed again. "You were not half bad at solving intellectual conundrums, but as a knight in shining armor, you've proved to be a bumbling fool."

"So it would seem," affirmed the earl.

Lowell's mirth proved short-lived. A vicious oath rent the air as he looked into the alcove and spotted the empty chair.

"How—" he began.

Wrexford turned to face him. *"Poof!* It was alchemy, my dear Golden One, not physics. Newton was, among other things, a religious fanatic who spent much of his time dabbling in the occult!" He knew he was playing with fire. Lowell's trigger hand was now quivering with fury, but he hoped to use the man's overweening pride and nervous anger against him.

"I used an ancient unraveling incantation," he said, goading his captor to lose his temper. "And a black magic levitation spell."

Lowell clenched his free hand in a fist and swung at the earl's head.

Wrexford was ready. Ducking away, he grabbed the man's wrist and twisted hard.

Lowell screamed in pain.

In the same movement, he slammed his knee into Lowell's thigh, buckling the man's leg. "It's far easier to attack a helpless child, isn't it?" The pistol fell to the floor and skittered off into the gloom.

Wrenching his hand free, Lowell stumbled back a step.

"I may be a bumbling fool, but you don't really think I was stupid enough to come here alone, do you? Now that the lad is free, the authorities will be moving in." Artistic license, but no doubt Charlotte would approve. He snapped open Hawk's pocketknife. "The game is over, Golden One."

A hesitation, and a hand waved in surrender. The distraction was only for an instant, but at the same time Lowell spun around and raced for the still-open door.

Wrexford was right on his heels, but the other man was too quick. He lost ground in the short corridor, just enough that Lowell reached the laboratory first and managed to slam the portal shut in his face.

He heard the key turn in the lock.

Damnation. The building was riddled with passageways, and many of the old warehouses in this part of Town were interconnected by way of the cellars. If Golden One managed to slip away and reach the subterranean labyrinth, he and his deadly formula might very well escape to France.

Spotting his pistol on the floor, he grabbed it up. Pulling the vial of Lowell's chemical from his inner pocket he wrenched off the top and sprinkled some of the powder between the latch and the molding. He then stepped back, took close aim at the door, and, turning away to shield his face, pulled the trigger.

The wood exploded in a welter of flying splinters, one of them cutting a gash across his temple. A kick loosened the bolt. Another, and then another. On the fourth, the door sprang free. The earl burst in, just in time to see Lowell stuff some papers and a metal flask into his pocket and dart into a side alcove.

He shoved aside a work cart on wheels, sending a rack of glass vials crashing to the floor. Broken glass crunched under his boots as he sprinted after his quarry.

Thank God for the thick soles.

In the alcove was a half-open paneled door, revealing a narrow circular iron staircase that led up into darkness. Hearing rapid-fire steps above him, Wrexford plunged in, taking the treads two at a time. Up, up, up he went, feet pounding at a dizzying pace. He heard another door open and shut. The stairs made one more turn and ended abruptly on a small landing.

Sensing he was catching up, the earl lowered his shoulder and barreled through the wood paneling at a run.

Lowell was only a dozen strides ahead of him, and looked to be limping. He looked back, and seeing that the distance between them was narrowing, he suddenly cut to his right and disappeared behind a billowing sheet of canvas.

"Damn," muttered Wrexford, taking a moment to assess his surroundings. The chase had brought them to the top floor of the warehouse, a cavernous space that stretched the full length of the building. It was crammed with aisle upon aisle of old mining supplies—the detritus of Canaday's failed business venture? In this row, racks of ghostly pale tarps fluttered in a gust of air let in through a broken windowpane.

He slowed his steps and shifted his weight to the balls of his feet.

Flap, flap, flap. He didn't need the whispered warnings to stay alert.

At the next gap, he turned to make his way to a less cluttered vantage point. Halfway along the line, the rasp of metal on metal sounded for just an instant. Wrexford ducked, just as a pickaxe tore through the canvas, smashing the wooden frame overhead. Spinning sideways, he pushed through the tangle and lunged for Lowell. He caught the chemist's wrist but Lowell twisted and hammered a hard blow to his hand.

His fingers slipped and Golden One darted away.

"Give it up!" shouted the earl, kicking aside the wreckage. "I'm not going to let you get away."

Silence. And then the faint creak of the flooring betrayed a stealthy step, moving for the far side of the room. Lowell knew the layout of the building by heart and must have an escape route in mind.

Ducking low, Wrexford used a row of nail barrels as cover to cut ahead to another aisle. A flicker of moonlight showed Lowell lifting a trapdoor in the floor.

Snakes were by their very nature drawn to dark holes.

Shooting to his feet, he hurdled the barrels and sprinted for the opening, only to have the hatch fall shut while he was still several strides away. Be damned with Lowell's serpentine tricks. Fatigue gave way to a grim resolve to play the mongoose.

Wrexford wrenched it open and grabbed hold of the iron ladder. He heard the scrabbling of a slip and a curse float up from the void. Golden One's endurance was flagging. Fear quickly sucked away bluster and bravado, leaving only the bare bones of what a man was made of.

Glancing down, the earl saw a faint square of hazy light below his feet.

A thump signaled that Lowell had dropped down through the opening. Wrexford gritted his teeth and let go of the rung. *One . . . two . . .* at three heartbeats his feet hit the floor and he threw himself into a defensive roll, just as Lowell heaved an open bottle of turpentine at his face. It shattered on the floor, the caustic liquid spraying harmlessly over the planking.

Wrexford realized he was back in the art storage room. Crawling quickly around the paint cans, he rose to block the door just as Lowell rounded a jumble of easels.

"There's no escape, Golden One."

Lowell drew in a ragged gulp of air and retreated a step. He had grabbed an artist's pen-knife and for several moments they moved warily, mirroring each other's movements through the slanting shadows of the storage shelves. The only sound was the scuff of leather sliding over wood.

Or was that a whisper of panic seeping into Lowell's breathing?

Wrexford made no move to attack, letting fear weaken the other man's resolve. He merely made sure that Lowell couldn't bolt for the door. But was Golden One heading for the windows? Unlikely, as he didn't know the gate was unlocked. Or was there another hatchway?

The answer came crashing down an instant later. In a last grasp at escaping, Lowell grabbed a bookshelf and tipped it over to block the way between them. Spinning around he raced for the far corner of the room, where, sure enough, another trapdoor was inset into the floor.

The laboratory. The roundabout dance had been all about circling back to the laboratory. From there, Lowell would have a carefully mapped out route for eluding pursuit.

Ah, but the best-laid plans of mice and men . . . Having spent time in Scotland, Lowell ought to be familiar with the poet Robert Burns and his wry observation of chance and luck.

The earl reached the hatchway just as Lowell half stepped, half slid down the first rungs of the ladder. He peered into the gloom, watching the man miss a handhold and nearly lose his balance. The ladder passed through an opening in the ceiling below, and beyond that he could see the flicker of the laboratory's lamps.

"Golden One," he called, "your dream has turned to lead. I'll chase you to the very pits of hell to keep you from getting away."

Lowell looked up, a wild light in his eyes. He tried to hurry his descent, but his foot slipped and he lost his grip.

A plummeting scream was followed by a thud as he hit the metallic counter of his worktable. There was an instant of utter calm and then a horrific *boom!* ripped through the silence. Flames erupted, sending up a cloud of black smoke.

"*Qui gladio ferit, gladio perit,*" murmured Wrexford as he stared down into the hellfire conflagration. The flask in Lowell's coat must have contained a large sample of the mercury fulminate—which was stable unless hit with a sharp impact.

"If you live by the sword, you must be prepared to die by the sword."

A blast of heat forced him back from the opening, and with a crackling bang, another explosion sounded within the bowels of the building. The fire was rapidly spreading through Lowell's arsenal of chemicals. The laboratory would soon be a raging inferno.

Perhaps the scientific laws of the universe were governed by an elegant symmetry after all. Unfathomable as of yet to mortal man.

But that, mused Wrexford, was infinitely intriguing to one who was curious about how the world worked.

As for how the human mind worked . . .

Another searing flash, bringing with it an upswirl of a whirling dervish of gold sparks that singed his skin. A reminder that time was an elemental force in science.

This particular experiment had run its course.

Drawing his coat up over his nose, Wrexford fought his way through the billowing smoke. Heat scalded through his boots. The fire below was already crackling against the floorboards. The aged wood would soon burst into flames.

Turning to get his bearings, he tripped over a roll of canvas. Close by, a tin of paint varnish ruptured, spattering him with burning-hot liquid.

Choking down a cough, he scrambled to his feet, intent on reaching the open window. But a sudden wall of fire shot up to block his way, fueled by the oil paints and solvents.

The smoke was getting thicker and heavy with noxious fumes. He spun around and plunged blindly through the swirling clouds in search of the door.

CHAPTER 27

Henning grabbed Charlotte's arm to hold her back. "You promised you wouldn't interfere, lassie."

"The building just exploded into flames!" she shot back. "So I daresay that means the earl is either dead or in need of assistance in escaping the fire. I think that good reason to amend the original agreement."

"The code of honor governing promises is rather rigid—it doesn't bend to individual interpretation."

"To the Devil with gentlemanly strictures!" responded Charlotte. She shielded her eyes to the flare of blindingly bright light that exploded through one of the windows. "In case you hadn't noticed, I tend to make my own rules. Wrexford may chastise me for it if he wishes, but it would be like the pot calling the kettle black."

Expelling a bemused grunt, he let his hand fall away. "I'll come with you. I'm not very good at obeying orders either."

"No! I need you to stay here with the lads." She darted a glance back at the stairwell, where Hawk had fallen asleep in his brother's arms. The noise of the fire had not yet roused them, but she feared they would both fly into danger as soon as they awoke.

"Please," she added.

Henning hesitated. "Auch, you're putting me on the horns of a hellish decision—"

Charlotte darted away, making the choice for him. The earl had risked his life for one of her dear little weasels. She wasn't going to leave him to fend for himself when all hell was erupting within the warehouse. Her racing steps cut through the thin skirling of smoke in the passageway between the buildings. Hawk had described his escape route, but as she rounded the corner, she saw that a blaze of flames made the window impossible to enter.

Unwilling to accept defeat, she retraced her steps and headed for the front door, hoping against hope to find it unlocked.

Damnation! The latch, already hot to the touch, wouldn't budge. In frustration, she slammed her shoulder against the paneled oak—and felt it give a little. Heat was buckling the molding. Charlotte hit it again and heard a crack. Stepping back, she threw herself forward at a dead run.

The bolt popped free.

"Wrexford!" she screamed, as she stumbled into the fiery maelstrom. All sense of sound and space was distorted. The whoosh and crackling seemed to swallow her words.

Was that an answer? Or merely wishful thinking?

Wincing from the heat slapping at her cheeks, Charlotte called again.

This time the voice sounded more real.

Drawing a sooty breath, she moved into the corridor and saw a flare of red-gold flames licking out from a room on the right. She rushed for the half-cracked door and kicked it all the way open. A blast of heat drove her back, but hunching low, she called again.

"Wrexford!"

A dark shape materialized within the swirls of pewter smoke.

Charlotte stumbled forward and grabbed the earl's coat. Her eyes were stinging, her throat was burning. Holding on for dear life, she yanked as hard as she could.

Both of them fell into the corridor. Scrabbling up, she hauled him to his knees. "Move!" she cried into his ear. "We have to move!"

Somehow, she managed to get him upright and stumbling for the exit.

"What in blazes are you doing here?" he croaked.

"Gathering all the details for my next drawing, what else?" she replied, dodging a piece of falling plaster. "You know what a stickler I am for accuracy."

Wrexford turned his head, the firelight igniting a flash of blue in his eyes. "You're incorrigible," he muttered. But the stern line of his mouth gave way to a quicksilver smile.

She smiled back at him. "By now that shouldn't astonish you."

"You never . . ." He ducked away from more crumbling plaster. "You never cease to surprise me, Mrs. Sloane."

Charlotte wasn't sure how to interpret the reply. Quite likely it meant nothing—the earl was facile with clever quips. Instead of responding, she reached up and touched his temple. Her fingers came away smeared with blood. "You're hurt."

He winced. "It's just a scratch. The lad—"

"Is safe and sound, thanks to you." She hurried him through the doorway and out into the street, where they both stood for several moments, drawing in deep gulps of air.

"Where's Lowell?" she asked, reaching out to bat away the glowing red sparks clinging to his coat sleeve.

Wrexford coughed to clear his lungs. But before he could answer, a shout from the head of the street drew his attention.

Sheffield started running toward them. Right at his heels was the Bow Street Runner, and behind him was another group of a half dozen men.

"Bloody hell," muttered the earl as his friend skidded to a halt.

"Sorry, Wrex." Sheffield gave a grimace of apology. "Allow me to explain." He glanced back at Griffin and lifted his shoulders. "Alas, but with all the mental stimulation of late, my brainbox seems to have decided to be more active. You may choose to ring a peal over my head, but I took the liberty of giving Alice the Eel Girl a message for Bow Street before she darted off. I thought it made sense for Griffin to be here to take part in Lowell's capture, and to witness for himself the man's perfidy."

"Thinking is not your strength, Kit," muttered Wrexford.

Charlotte thought that rather harsh. The earl's friend struck her as a very clever fellow. However, Sheffield did not look the least offended.

"But thank you. I may have to revise my opinion," added the earl—which only confirmed to her that the bond between men could take peculiar forms.

However, at this moment the confrontation between Wrexford and the Runner was the only one that mattered. She shifted deeper into the shadows, intent on remaining inconspicuous.

Griffin eyed the burning building and signaled to one of his cohorts, who had come to a halt a short distance away. "Alert the fire brigade, Putney. The rest of you, block the street and keep onlookers away."

The Runner then turned to the earl. "Where's Lowell?" he demanded, echoing her own question.

"I would be happy to turn him over to the authorities, but alas, he's already frying in hell," answered Wrexford. "Which, by the by, saves the government the expense of a trial and the length of rope for the gibbet." He curled a mocking smile. "You will just have to take my word about his guilt. Or are you still intent on arresting me? It would be a mistake—you'd only end up looking like a fool."

Griffin narrowed his eyes. Charlotte expected a war of words to erupt, if not outright fisticuffs, given the accounts she had heard of the previous meetings.

But the Runner looked more unhappy than outraged. "I had already come to the same conclusion. *If* you had deigned to return to your residence this morning, milord, instead of taking justice into your own hands, we could have talked." A baleful blink as another window shattered from the raging flames. "And avoided setting London ablaze."

"Forgive my skepticism concerning your intentions," replied Wrexford tartly. "Trust hasn't exactly been thick on the ground between us."

Sheffield fixed the Runner with a curious look. "What changed your mind about Wrexford's guilt?"

"The accusatory letter Lowell gave me didn't look quite right. I had a sample of Drummond's handwriting, and in making a careful comparison between the two, I became convinced it was a forgery," replied Griffin. "Its discovery also seemed a little too convenient. So I began to do some digging into Mr. Lowell's background and discovered that he had told me a bald-faced lie when he said he had no interest in science. It seems he was involved in a deadly laboratory accident while a student, which his family covered up. He then spent a year in Scotland studying advanced chemistry. Which certainly shed a whole new light on Holworthy's murder."

"Going on facts rather than conjecture?" Wrexford arched a brow. "Have a care, Griffin. I might come to think of you as a man ruled by reason, not blind prejudice."

"I am more of a cart horse than one of your fancy racing stallions, milord," responded the Runner. "I plod along slowly, but I keep my ears and eyes open, perhaps more than you think." He shrugged his beefy shoulders. "Yes, I pushed you hard, to see if you would buckle. But I was also meticulous in following up every other possible clue. And they led me to the conclusion that Lowell might be involved in the murders—though I couldn't figure out the how and why. That is what I wished to discuss with you this morning. But . . ."

The two men locked gazes. The silence held for several heartbeats and then Wrexford expelled a wry sigh.

"But I daresay you would have carted me off to Bedlam had I tried to explain the whole story." He ran a hand through his wind-snarled hair. "Most of it is best left buried with Lowell beneath the rubble. Let us just say that all's well that ends well."

"That's assuming we don't burn down half of London." Griffin blew out his cheeks. "Mother of God, what sort of explosion ignited that fierce of a blaze?"

"We'll likely never know," murmured Wrexford.

Charlotte ventured a quick glance back at the building. She had been so preoccupied with Wrexford she hadn't yet taken a moment to commit the details of the scene to memory.

The movement must have caught his eye, for Griffin suddenly seemed to take notice of her. "Who's the brat?"

"A Good Samaritan," answered the earl without hesitation. "Luckily for me, the lad just happened to be passing by and came to my aid."

The Runner fixed her with a flinty stare.

Charlotte quickly dropped her head. Her informants were all of the opinion that he was a hard man to fool. She had no intention of putting his abilities to the test.

"Lucky, indeed," said Griffin slowly. He seemed to hesitate, but then turned his attention back to the earl. "I'm not sure what Lowell was involved in here, but I'm sure the government will want to explain his crimes as simply as possible. God only knows what lurid speculation A. J. Quill will provoke if he gets wind that Holworthy's murder might be tied to some . . . explosive secret. It could stir panic throughout the city."

"I suggest you simply tell the newspapers that

Lowell and Holworthy fell out over money," said the earl. "And that Drummond overheard the truth, forcing Lowell to do away with him, too. It's close enough to the truth that it will stand up to scrutiny."

"That could very well work," mused Griffin. "My men can all be trusted to be discreet." He glared at Charlotte. "And you, Master . . ."

"Smith," she rasped.

"A word out of you to anyone about this night, and you'll be answering to Bow Street for it."

"Me?" Charlotte let out a low bark of laughter. "And just who would I be telling? The Prince Regent when he invites me te take tea wiv him?"

The Runner huffed a grunt, but seemed satisfied that she was no threat. "Be off with you, then." He turned back to the earl. "You and Mr. Sheffield ought to disappear as well, milord. The less chance of that infernal artist's spies seeing you here, the better." A pause. "And if you'll excuse me, I had best go organize things for the arrival of the fire brigade. But be advised that I shall be paying you a visit tomorrow to clear up some of the details of this case."

"I thought it best for us to stay out of sight until the Runner toddled off." Henning stepped out of the stairwell, holding both boys firmly by the scruff of their collars. "No easy feat with these—"

"Weasels," said Wrexford.

They stopped squirming. The surgeon had smeared some greenish ointment on their bruised faces, making them look even more feral than usual. And then Hawk flashed a lopsided gap-toothed grin, and to his surprise, the earl felt a laugh well up in his throat.

"I did just what ye told me," said Hawk. "I scarpered like the devil had his pitchfork pricking at my arse."

"Don't say arse," chided his brother. "It isn't gentlemanly."

Wrexford saw Charlotte bite back a smile.

Henning released his hold, allowing Raven to shuffle forward. The boy looked up. He appeared to be struggling for something to say. Unlike his younger brother, words did not come easily to him.

Swallowing hard, he simply held out his hand.

Wrexford solemnly shook it.

A loud *boom!* punctuated the moment, as another window exploded in a brilliant shower of gold sparks and shards. Hawk chuffed an admiring gasp as tongues of fire rose up to dance against the somber silhouettes of the surrounding buildings.

Wrexford saw that Charlotte, too, was staring at the inferno, her profile limned in a reddish light. "I shall, of course, temper my caption, but this will likely outsell all the other prints in this scandal," she murmured. "I may be able to ask Fores to raise my fees." A cynical smile flickered on her lips. "At least for another week or two, until it's time for a new peccadillo or murder to take its place."

Murder. They had all come perilously close to death.

"Henning, take the weasels back to the house. Mrs. Sloane and I will go by a different route."

"I'm not in need of an escort, sir," she murmured.

"Nonetheless, I'm coming with you. Gentlemanly scruples, you see."

"I'm too tired to argue." She waited for the others to move out of earshot before adding, "You don't have any gentlemanly scruples—or you've told me so yourself several times."

"On occasion I lie."

Charlotte let out a low snort. Or perhaps it was a laugh. The crackling of the fire made it impossible to tell. Turning, she beckoned him to follow. "This way. I know the area better than you do."

Wrexford fell in step beside her. They walked on in silence, the tendrils of smoke and the crackling booms growing fainter as the darkness of the stews closed around them. It wasn't until Charlotte led the way into a narrow alleyway that she spoke again.

"Thank you for everything, milord, especially saving Hawk—at no small risk to your own life. I . . . I am in your debt."

"And you saved my life, at no small risk to

your own. So the debt is of equal measure," he replied. "Though I'd rather think that friendship does not require one to keep a ledger."

She slanted an inscrutable look at him. "*Are* we friends, Wrexford?"

"That's not a question I can answer for you, Mrs. Sloane. Ask me a scientific query, and I could give you facts and measurements. But as to feelings . . ." He shrugged. "That's your bailiwick."

"I think you underestimate yourself, sir."

A sharp turn forced them closer. The earl was aware of her shoulder touching his. "Perhaps we both have things to learn about our hidden facets."

A brief scudding of moonlight caught the flicker of a smile touch her lips. "A frightening thought."

Despite being dressed as an urchin, she looked a little vulnerable, reminding him that the path she had chosen in life was not an easy one.

"Be that as it may," she added slowly, "my answer is yes—I should like to think of us as friends."

The answer pleased him more than he expected. He walked on for a few strides mulling it over.

"Then speaking as a friend, perhaps you should consider . . ." And then suddenly the words died in his throat. What right had he to ask that she give up her passion? Were someone to suggest he walk away from his scientific interests, he would tell them to go to the devil.

"You aren't going to suggest I abandon my pen, are you?"

"Would you listen?" Wrexford gave a grudging smile. "In truth, I can't imagine you without it. You keep Society honest. A needle in their highborn bums keeps them from becoming too arrogantly complacent." His smile widened. "The truth is, I look forward to seeing who you skewer next."

Charlotte bit back a laugh as she ducked under a rotting timber. "As long as it's not you?"

The earl followed and quickened his steps to catch up. "Oh, come, you've seen for yourself that my life isn't nearly as exciting as everyone seems to imagine. For the most part, Tyler and I potter away in my workroom."

She was suddenly aware of how much she would miss his cynical, self-mocking humor. Gentlemen who could laugh at themselves were rarer than hen's teeth.

Shoving aside the thought, she asked, "What do you intend to do with Lowell's formula?"

"Like its creator, it went up in smoke." He hesitated. "We haven't yet figured out all the ingredients." Another slight pause. "And perhaps my scientific talents, such as they are, could be put to more positive endeavors."

Charlotte nodded. "There is great wisdom in that idea, milord."

"Then perhaps you will allow me to offer another one." Wrexford hesitated, appearing to choose his words carefully. "It seems to me that you should consider moving to a different part of the city. The miscreants have all been dealt with, but too many people may have been privy to their sniffing around for your secret."

Her insides clenched. She was not unaware of the possible dangers, but hearing the words said aloud gave them sudden weight.

"Given the bargain we made concerning this case, you can now afford a better neighborhood," he went on. "One with a school for the lads."

So many choices to be made. But at the moment, she felt too exhausted to think past putting one foot in front of the other.

"I . . . I can't contemplate the future right now," said Charlotte softly. "I need some time to decide on the right course."

"That's quite understandable." In Latin he added, "*Vita non est vivere sed valere vita est.*"

Life is more than merely staying alive.

Charlotte chuffed a laugh. "True."

"You understand Latin, Mrs. Sloane—quite well, I might add," murmured Wrexford. "You have a set of Shakespeare and the Greek tragedies on your work desk, so I can't help but wonder about them . . ."

As they emerged from the alley onto a wider lane, he looked up at the sky. The clouds had blown off, leaving a black velvet expanse dotted with a myriad points of winking light. "We've unraveled some complex conundrums tonight, and yet there is still an unsolved mystery here."

"Perhaps not all mysteries are meant to be solved, sir." She, too, glanced upward. "We all have secrets. Ones that are best kept to ourselves."

"So you have said," he replied. "Just as you have also said that no secret, however private, is ever safe."

As they came to the head of her street, Charlotte stopped abruptly and held out her hand.

"Good-bye, Lord Wrexford."

"That sounds awfully final, Mrs. Sloane."

"We move in different circles, sir," she pointed out. "Ones that are far from overlapping."

His fingers clasped around hers, and for a long moment they stood joined together, palm pressed to palm, as the chill breeze tugged at their clothing.

Then she slowly disengaged her hand and turned away.

"And yet," murmured Wrexford as she started to walk off, "large as London is, the circles occupy a finite space."

Charlotte paused, then hesitated for a heartbeat before darting one last look over her shoulder.

She felt, rather than saw, the cynical amusement softening the chiseled planes of his face.

"So logic and the laws of chance," he added, "dictate that our paths will likely cross again."

AUTHOR'S NOTE

For me, Regency England is a fabulously interesting time and place. Not only was it a world aswirl in silks, seduction and the intrigue of the Napoleonic Wars, but society as a whole was undergoing momentous changes. Radical new ideas were clashing with the conventional thinking of the past, and as a result, people were challenging and changing their fundamental view of the world. Politics, social reform, literature, art, music, science—all were in a state of upheaval. Indeed, many historians consider the era the birth of the modern world.

While the plot twists in this book are purely fiction, I've tried to ground the science in the story and the ambiance of historical London and its different strata of society in actual fact.

With that in mind, here are a few historical notes:

Sir Isaac Newton really did spend much of his scientific time on alchemy. So, too, did many of the luminaries of seventeenth-century science. While much of their work may seem crazy to us in the present day, their experiments were often thoughtfully done with what for the day were quite rigorous methods. Absent an atomic theory, they just didn't know the impossibility of transforming one element into another through chemistry, no matter how carefully the experiment was performed.

The Royal Institution (which is still going strong in its impressive building on Albemarle Street in London) was one of the leaders in scientific research during the Regency. Men like Humphry Davy, its charismatic head, were treated like rock stars. London's high society did in fact flock to attend the lectures, and scientific innovations were followed avidly by the public.

I've taken a little artistic license with the chemical secret in the book. It's a very real invention, however I've shifted the timeframe of its discovery. Perhaps a brilliant scientist could well have figured out its formula a number of years before it actually happened.

And lastly, satirical cartoonists were the paparazzi of the day. Their work was wildly popular with both high and low society (in the days before photography, the prints were the sole source of images that poked fun at the rich and famous.) While Charlotte Sloane is fictional, artists like Thomas Rowlandson, James Gillray, William Hogarth and the Cruikshanks (George and Isaac) were celebrities in their own right.

For those interested in reading more about science in Age of Romanticism, I highly recommend *The Age of Wonder* by Richard Holmes, a wonderfully engaging overview written for a general audience. For those interested in the era as a whole, *The Birth of the Modern* by Paul Johnson is an impressively detailed history of the world in the early 1800s.

—Andrea Penrose

Center Point Large Print
600 Brooks Road / PO Box 1
Thorndike, ME 04986-0001 USA

(207) 568-3717

US & Canada:
1 800 929-9108
www.centerpointlargeprint.com